WINTER'S CHILDREN

Leah Fleming was born in Lancashire to Scottish parents, and is married with three sons and a daughter and six grandchildren. She writes from an old farmhouse in the Yorkshire Dales and an olive grove in Crete.

Find out more about Leah at www.leahfleming.co.uk and visit www.BookArmy.co.uk for exclusive updates.

By the same author:

Remembrance Day
Mothers and Daughters
Orphans of War
The War Widows
The Girl From World's End

LEAH FLEMING

Winter's Children

AVON

This novel is entirely a work of fiction.
The names, characters and incidents portrayed in it are
the work of the author's imagination. Any resemblance to
actual persons, living or dead, events or localities is
entirely coincidental.

AVON

A division of HarperCollins*Publishers*
77–85 Fulham Palace Road,
London W6 8JB

www.harpercollins.co.uk

A Paperback Original 2010

6

A catalogue record for this book is
available from the British Library

ISBN-13: 978-1-84756-104-6

Set in Minion by Palimpsest Book Production Limited,
Falkirk, Stirlingshire

Printed and bound in Great Britain by
Clays Ltd, St Ives plc

Mixed Sources
Product group from well-managed
forests and other controlled sources
www.fsc.org Cert no. SW-COC-001806
© 1996 Forest Stewardship Council

FSC is a non-profit international organisation established
to promote the responsible management of the world's forests.
Products carrying the FSC label are independently certified
to assure consumers that they come from forests that are managed
to meet the social, economic and ecological needs
of present and future generations.

Find out more about HarperCollins and the environment at
www.harpercollins.co.uk/green

Author's Note

In May 2001 I was witness to how foot-and-mouth disease closed our local farms and footpaths for over a year. Farmers had to reassess their livelihoods, rethink their strategies for survival and come to terms with the loss of pedigree livestock built up over generations. All the incidents apart from the above are entirely fictitious but I hope I have captured the spirit of the Dales community during this terrible time. I have watched with admiration how nearly ten years on, they have risen to the challenge.

Turner, the artist did visit the Yorkshire Dales in the summer of 1816. For further reading on this I recommend: *In Turner's Footsteps: Through the hills and dales of Northern England*. By David Hill. John Murray 1984.

Not being in any way psychic, I have relied on the many sightings and anecdotes of others who believe that energy both positive and negative leaves a residue in buildings and landscapes. For further reading I recommend: *Cutting the ties that bind*. Phillis Krystal. Element Books 1989.

Most of the recipes I've used are tried and trusted family favourites. Of the many books I read while researching, I'd like to make special mention of: *Traditional Food East and West of the Pennines*. Edited by O. Anne Wilson. Sutton Publishers 1991.

I'd like to thank the Wiggin family for showing this Scots

lass how Christmas is done and recommend *Memoirs of a Maverick* by the late Maurice Wiggin (Quality Book Club 1968).

I would also like to thank our village school, now sadly closed, for providing such great Christmas memories and the carollers of Langcliffe who know how to keep up local traditions.

I'd like to say a huge thanks to all the team at Avon for their support and enthusiasm for this story, especially Caroline Ridding and Kate Bradley. Their attention to detail has raised my own writing awareness and confidence.

Finally I'd like to imagine my reader enjoying this Christmas tale curled up by the fireside supping mulled wine with Sting's album: *If on a winter's night . . .* in the background. His music certainly helped me along.

Leah Fleming.

For all the Wiggins, past, present and future who
love this season.

Christmas Eve

Sutton Coldfield, December 2000

When the doorbell rang on Christmas Eve, at first Kay and the Partridge family were too busy wrapping up last-minute presents to answer it.

'Tim's forgotten his key again,' Kay shouted to her mother-in-law. 'Trust him to be home late!' Since their house had been sold, they were living with Tim's parents until the move to London in the New Year. 'Evie, go and open the door for Daddy!' she yelled to their small daughter, who was as high as a kite on chocolate decorations that had been destined for the Christmas tree. Kay hoped Tim had stopped off at the garden centre to pick one up. He'd promised to dress it with Evie a week ago but the firm had wanted him to go north to secure a deal in Newcastle.

'Is that you, darling? You're *so* . . . late!' she yelled down the stairs. There was no response so she trundled down to hear his excuses. Evie was standing at the foot of the stairs looking puzzled.

'A policeman's come, and a lady one, they want to speak to you,' she said smiling. 'Has Daddy been naughty?'

Kay looked beyond her child to the open door and her knees began to buckle. The expression on the two faces said it all . . .

At the Eve of All Souls

She glides through Wintergill House, drifting between the walls and closed-up passageways. No floorboards creak, no plasterwork flakes as she brushes past, only a tinge of the scent of lavender betrays her presence. The once mistress of the hearth lists where she wills. She knows every nook and cranny, every dust bowl and rat run, loose boards and lost tokens, cats' bones crumbling in the roof spaces.

Hepzibah Snowden patrols her kingdom as she did in her own time, keys clanking on her leather girdle, a tallow candle in the pewter hold, still checking that the servants are abed and Master Nathaniel, lord of her nights, is snoring by the fire. She knows her dust is blown into every crevice of the old house, circled by the four winds of heaven. The autumn mists rise from the valley but Hepzibah has no eyes for the outdoors. Her spirit imbues its benign presence only within the confines of these stone walls.

November is the month of the dead. The barometer falls and daylight shortens its path across the sky. She knows the year is beginning its slow dance of death when the leaves curl and rust and sap sink to the roots.

The air is stale, silence reigns. The house is empty of joy. These tenants, an old woman and her son, ignore the patches of damp, the peeling plasterwork, loose slates on the dairy roof. It is a cold, empty and barren hearth. No servants warm their master's bedpans with hot ashes. No wife warms the master's buttocks. No horse's muck steams in the cobbled yard. She hears no shepherd's cough or stable boy's whistle. They have made another dwelling of the barn.

It saddens her heart to see all Nathaniel's toil fall into disrepair. The Lord in His wisdom hath rained down such a plague upon these pastures of late. Now not a living beast bellows from the byre; not a sheep bleats across the meadows. The Lord hath shown no mercy to Godless Yorkshire. All was lost to the summer slaughter in the killing fields below. Now is only silence and tears.

Hepzibah peers out from the window into the dusk. There is another out there she fears. Watching. Waiting. Her erstwhile cousin patrols around the walls, ever searching. The restless spirit who hovers between two worlds. The tortured soul who roams the fells with fire burning in her eye sockets. Blanche is out there in the gathering darkness, waiting to sneak through any open door, seeking what can never be found

Hepzibah shakes her head, safe in the knowledge that this fortress is ringed against this troubled spirit by circles of rowan and elder, by lanterns of light no human eye can see, by sturdy prayer and her own constant vigilance. For she is appointed guardian of this hearth. It is both her pride and penance to stay on within this place.

Each year the two of them must play out this ancient drama with dimmer lights and ever-fading resolve; an endless game of cat and mouse for nearly four hundred years. When, O Lord, will Blanche Norton's spirit be at peace? Who will help me guide her home?

Soon the yule fires will burn and the seasons will turn towards the light. Hepzibah senses her own powers must fade in a Christmas house without the brightness of a child.

Wintergill House needs new life or it will crumble. It is time now to open her heart for guidance and cast her prayer net far and wide.

Wintergill waits for the coming of another winter's child.

Yet with such a coming there is always danger, Hepzibah sighs. For if her prayers are granted she must summon her most cunning ploys to protect such an innocent from Cousin Blanche's consuming fire.

Lord have mercy on Wintergill.

Yorkshire, November 2001

Mincemeat

1 lb Bramley apples
1 lb mixed dried fruit (currants, seedless raisins, sultanas, dates)
8 oz chopped mixed peel
1 lb finely chopped suet of choice
1 lb demerara sugar
grated rind and juice of 2 lemons
2 oz chopped nuts, almonds (optional)
1 tsp ground spices (ginger, nutmeg, cinnamon)
4 tbsp whisky, rum or brandy (optional)

Chop the apples, add the lemon rind and juice, and mix with the dried fruits together in a bowl. Add the peel, nuts, spices, suet and sugar.

Stir in alcohol and leave at room temperature covered with a cloth overnight. Restir the mixture. Heat in a low oven for an hour.

Pack into clean, dry jars, cover with wax discs and Cellophane or pretty cloth circles and store in a cool dark place.

Makes about six 1 lb jars.

Sutton Coldfield, October 2001

'There's a Place for Us.' Kay stood transfixed in the supermarket aisle lost in the *West Side Story* tune in her head until her mother-in-law nudged her with a basket. 'Oh, there you are, Kay . . . chop chop! You'll be late for Evie at the school gate again.' Eunice was hovering over her. 'They've got a special offer on Christmas cake ingredients . . .'

'Christmas already?' Kay felt the panic rising. It was only October, not yet half term. Her head was spinning at the thought of the coming season. She looked at her watch and knew they must dash. Evie got upset if there was no one waiting for her. After the checkout she pushed her trolley into the car park with a sigh as she looked around the familiar tarmac where a flurry of women were bustling shopping into their boots. Eunice was loitering by the car door with that impatient look on her face.

I don't want to be here any more, Kay thought. Ever since Tim's accident she'd been living in a daze of indecision knowing this wasn't the place for them any more. Then there was that summer painting exhibition in Lichfield Cathedral that still haunted her.

It was just one of Terry Logan's Yorkshire landscapes: sheep grazing in snow by a stone wall, taking her straight back to Granny Norton's cottage in the Dales where she'd spent the long summer holidays. Oh, for open space, grey-green hills and daydreaming by the beck . . . Suddenly she felt such a rush of nostalgia for her childhood. If only she could snuggle back into that dream, back to the old farmhouse set like a doll's house high on a hill; a house with windows on fire, catching the low evening sun as it drifted across the snow; a sunset of pink, orange and violet torching the panes of glass, a winter house amongst the hills.

She sat in the car with tired eyes averted from the halogen town lights. Always the same haunting dream calling her, tapping into her deepest yearnings. Why was it always the same stone house set above a valley? What did it mean? Was there somewhere waiting for them?

For nine months they had camped out with her in-laws and she could face it no longer. Since the terrible events in America only weeks ago, nothing felt safe in the world. Eunice was protecting them both like lost children . . . doing her best to keep them close by and Kay had gone along with it for Evie's sake.

Now with a certainty she'd not felt for months, she knew it was time to move on and away.

'I need hills around me,' she whispered with a sigh.

'What was that?' Eunice Partridge edged closer.

'Nothing,' Kay replied. 'Just thinking aloud.'

The phone was ringing in the hall of Wintergill House Farm. Let it ring, thought Lenora Snowden as she threw another log in the wood-burner. She was in no mood for a chat, or making mincemeat. What was the point? Christmas preparations were supposed to wrap up the fag end of the year in some festive package. Who could wrap up this terrible season in anything but sackcloth and ashes, she sniffed as she banged the basket of Bramleys on the chopping board.

She inspected the dried fruit, the apples and suet shreds, the box of spices, the cheap whisky, without enthusiasm.

Why was she tiring her legs standing on the stone flags in the old still room, now reclaimed as her private kitchen, little more than a cubbyhole, she sighed, choking back the tears.

Things had to go on. The WI needed jars of preserves for their Christmas stall. She always gave to the village school bazaar and the party for the old folks. Though her world had collapsed around her there were still others worse off than herself. She could make a pie for Karen and her boys, who were burying their dad this afternoon.

'Damn and blast it!' she muttered, chopping with vigour, as if to release all the tension of the past few months. The dale had never seen such a back end – storms, floods, snow keeping them stuck in for days. Then had come the distant threat of foot-and-mouth, and they'd made a desperate attempt to disinfect and stay protected, all to no avail.

The newly converted barn, which had taken the last of their capital, lay unlet for the whole summer season as the footpaths were closed and the moors cut off. The tourists stayed away dutifully but the bank still required monthly payments on their borrowings. All their diversification plans came to naught.

Chop, chop! She nearly sliced off her thumb in anger. Just when it was all over, just when they thought they'd escaped, when the lambs were gambolling across the fields, a phone call from their neighbours blew Wintergill's hopes apart.

'Nora! We're being taken out! I'm sorry but they'll be taking you out too . . .'

Foot-and-mouth had arrived silently across the tops weeks before. The Wintergill sheep were doomed as part of a contiguous cull, but both the cattle and sheep were already infected.

Her eyes were watering recalling those anxious hours.

Waiting for the auctioneer to value their stock, a circus of army and vets trampled over their fields. Their death wagons parked up waiting to remove the carcasses, sinister slaughter-men in white suits sweltering in the sun. All she could do was make cups of tea and hide indoors, but the pop of the bolt guns would stay with her for ever, and she was glad her husband, Tom, wasn't alive to see the destruction of his life's work.

Nik, her only son, stayed at his post, grim-faced. No amount of compensation would make up for the loss of his prize-winning tups and ewes. They were his life's work. Now there were green fields but no livestock, proven sacks of feed and nothing to give it to. She was sick of the silence. The heart had gone out of both of them after that day. The bombing of the Twin Towers and all that suffering only added to their gloom that autumn.

Nora sighed, knowing it was easier to hark back to happier times when the making of mincemeat heralded the annual run-up to Christmas: choosing the cards, the gathering for the pig kill. All the old rituals of farm life were going fast. How could they carry on after this? Nik was finished but he did not grasp that there was no future for him now. What was the point, she had argued, and he had stormed off to his part of the house, not wanting to listen to common sense or reason.

So why am I here at my post, chopping apples and grinding spices: cinnamon, ginger root, nutmeg? she mused, wiping her eyes. In her heart she knew she was drawn back instinctively to something ancient and female, soothed by the ritualistic comfort of a seasonal task.

Tosh and bollocks, she sneered, surprised by such sentimental humbug. I'm here because I've nothing better to do on this drab morning.

Life must go on and the cooking would take her mind

10

off the funeral this afternoon of a young man who could not face the future without hope.

Since he lost his stock Nik was like a knotless thread, poring over Defra reports on his computer, filling gaps in walls, sorting out his compensation bumf and waiting for the all clear to restock his farm. Six months living on a knife edge of loneliness and despair, and now Jim, his friend, taking his own life just when the worst was over. It didn't make any sense. It was so unfair on his wife and kiddies, but who said life was fair?

You get what you get and stomach it as best you can, she mused, grabbing her coat and plonking her beret on her head, glancing in the mirror with disgust. You look about ninety, old girl, she sighed, watching the creases and lines wrinkle up her weatherbeaten face. Her country bloom was lost years ago. The mirror had never held much comfort. Her face was too sculpted and her chin too pointed, her tired blue eyes were more like ice than cornflowers, and there were telltale shadows under them from sleepless nights.

All she yearned for now was a quiet hearth and a peaceful retirement. Surely the compensation package would release them now from this hard living. I've served my sentence on these harsh northern uplands, battered by winds and wild weather, she argued to herself, bruised by a lifetime of disappointments. Only the turning of the seasons brought life and renewal each year but now time was out of joint. There was no seedtime and harvest, no crop of lambs, no rewards for all their labours, only death and destruction and a tempting cheque. Lenora Snowden could see no future for Wintergill House Farm. It was time to take the money and run.

The phone rang again and the unexpected news she learned sent her scurrying out to the far fields to find Nik.

He would be out somewhere avoiding her. It was some good news at last. Perhaps this was the turning point they needed: a sign of hope.

In the far field by the copse Nikolas Snowden was hacking off the branches of a felled ash with a ferocity that satisfied the rage inside him. He knew a chain saw would tackle the job in no time but this was the day for an axe. The physical effort to pit his strength against the ancient trunk was just the challenge he needed to take his mind off this afternoon's funeral.

He should be beginning to feel a little calmer; quarantine would soon be over and he had been planning his restocking, preparing the fields to restart the cycle with lamb ewes. But his heart was leaden and he felt sick.

He paused to wipe the sweat from his furrowed brow, staring out across the green to the valley below, to the patchwork of grey stone walls rising as far as the eye could see and not a white dot among them. The rooks were cawing down in the churchyard, the curlews had long gone, a flock of redwings were grazing in the distance in the field where his best-in-show tups should have been preparing to service his flock. His eyes filled with tears when he thought of them. They were not just rams, they were old mates, tough proud stock.

How trustingly they had followed his shaken bag of feed nuts as he led them down to their deaths. His ewes were edgy amongst strangers and sheltered their lambs at their side. He had stood with the slaughtermen to the very end, trying to calm their panic on that terrible afternoon when the world was watching the Cup Final indoors, unaware of his terrible betrayal. Like lambs to the bloody slaughter indeed.

It was all in a day's job for the slaughtermen, but the young vet, new to the job, had the decency to blanch as she grabbed each lamb with her needle. He could hear the bleating panic of his ewes crying, the panic rising as some made a dash for it in vain. And gradually as his flock was destroyed, there was only the silence of a summer's afternoon, the blaring of the wagon driver's radio, trying to catch the latest score.

He could see that heap, all he had worked for, piled up lifeless and he'd broken down, unashamed of his grief at such a loss. It was unspeakable the way the diggers scooped up their bodies like woolly rags but he'd seen it through to the end. They were his flock. He had seen each calf born and he must watch them die. It felt like mass murder.

They lambed late in the Dales to avoid the harsh winter and wet spring. It made no odds. How could he have unwittingly nurtured such a disease in his flock? No amount of compensation would ever drive that terrible scene from his mind, or the fact that Bruce Stickley was on the phone minutes after the cull to bid for the valuation of them for compensation.

Nik raised the axe and swung down. It was tempting to give up. The house was a millstone around his neck. His mother was weary. What was the point in all his research, the advice being dished out right, left and centre to the small farmer? 'Try this, buy that'. Everyone knew there was money in the Dalesmen's pockets and Nik was wary.

Wintergill had cost him dear; his first youthful marriage had foundered because his town-bred wife, Mandy, couldn't stomach the loneliness or the harsh winters. Yet he was tied to the place by myriad invisible threads. He was damn near forty-two! Was it too late for life outside the dale? Perhaps he could retrain or retire – and do what?

For God's sake, this is the only life you've ever known, he cried. How do you go on with nobody to follow? Even Jim had taken flight and topped himself, and he had two sons. He had made his own decision. He did not want his children to suffer the burden of being farmer's sons. It was a terrible solution.

Nik was no longer certain about anything as he looked once more to the beautiful scene before him: how the farm stuck out on a high promontory overlooking the valley and the river snaking through the autumn woods down below; the trees turning into russet and amber and the wind sending storm clouds racing across the darkened sky. The first snows were on their way.

He felt a familiar tingling in the back of his neck. He was not alone.

She was watching him.

Even if he whipped round suddenly he would not see her face, whoever she was, this ancient phantom who wandered over his fields and hid in his copse. There was no comfort in her presence, no benign aura in her haunting. She flitted from lane to wood and moor. Only once had he ever seen her face, years ago, by the Celtic wall when he was young.

'Bugger off, you old hag!' he yelled, and swung his axe again in fury.

To be reduced to bagging logs for sale, fixing gaps and repairing machinery – it was no life for a farmer, but it kept his muscles firm and his thighs stretched. He had seen too many of his mates turn to fat in the last few months when reality had kicked in. The bar of the Spread Eagle was a tempting crutch to lean on to sup away sorrows. If he lost his fitness, he would lose what little pride he had left.

Not even his mother knew he could sense stuff with his third eye. It was usually reserved for the female Snowdens to inherit. 'The eye that sees all and says nowt' was how his father had once described it. It was not a manly thing to feel spirits up yer backside so he kept quiet about this unwanted gift. If only it had warned him of the danger to his stock.

A movement caught his eye and Nik looked up to see his mother waving from across the gate, calling him inside. What did she want now? He dropped his axe, stretched his back and made for the house. He could do with a coffee and a pipe.

'What's it now, Mother? If it's another rep . . . put them off again!' Nik yelled, bending under the lintel of the back kitchen scullery door, unpeeling his waterproofs and muddy boots. His mother was standing in his kitchen with a mug of coffee. She usually kept to the front portion of the old house, looking south onto the garden – he kept to the rear with ready access to the courtyard and outbuildings. He looked at his watch and supposed it was time to set aside farm chores in favour of a scrub and polish, ready for the funeral.

His mother was looking flustered, already dressed in a navy two-piece wool jersey suit. 'Would you believe it! That was Stickley's. They've got us a winter let for six months . . . someone from the Midlands saw the house on their website and booked it up on the spot. They're on their way. Fancy, a winter let out of the blue after all this time.' She made her way to the ironing board, which always sagged under a mound of creased washing.

'Honestly, Nik,' she said, looking around. 'If you think I've got time to do this load . . . Get your skates on and shift yourself . . . I hope there's a decent shirt among this pile. I'm not having you turned out like a crumpled rag, not with half the county coming to see Jim off. Can you bring me in some logs before you shower?'

Nik grunted, banging his boot across the stone-flagged floor, sending the house dog, Muffin, a collie cross, scurrying for cover under the table.

'Who on earth would want to come up here in this weather? I thought we'd told them to hold back on lets. It's been empty all summer. It'll need a good airing.'

'Don't look a gift horse, Nik. Be thankful for small mercies after the season we've not had. Shift yerself and fill the log basket, turn on the water for me. They'll not be here until late, and I've got Annual Parish Survey meeting tonight so you can let them in when they arrive.' She paused, looking at him. 'And no scowling. Be civil.'

Nik was watching his mother glancing around his living room with dismay at the unwashed pots in the sink, the grubby tea towels and the cluttered table, but she buttoned her lip. This was his half of the house and how he organised his affairs was none of her business. Washing up and clearing away was women's work, he muttered, and he'd no mind to change his old ways. Ever since Mandy left him years ago, this back-to-back living suited them both. The hall door was their own Berlin Wall, dividing north from south, mother from son, chalk from cheese, Mozart from Bach.

Nik could see she was itching to clear up his mess and put the room back to times past when you could lick your porridge from her shining floor, but there was no time for arguments if they were to sort out the Side House and make the service on time. Damn the estate agents for conjuring up this holiday let out of thin air! Perhaps Bruce Stickley had a conscience after all and was trying to make up for that insensitive intrusion.

'We spend a fortune doing up that barn and now you grumble because it gets let out. After the summer we've had, we should thank the Good Lord that we still have this asset left,' she added.

'Yes, and look what it cost us!' Nik thought of the antiques they'd had to sell to fund the project. 'I don't like townies cluttering up the place, leaving gates open and asking silly questions.' He did not want any post mortems with strangers, their pitying glances when they realised what had happened. He had good reason to hate what the summer had done to farmers. Was he not burying one of them that very afternoon?

'Bruce Stickley gave good advice when he suggested we went for a top-of-the-range conversion: double glazing, central heating. We'll be getting top whack for the let. It has a view second to none down the valley. There's no pleasing you, son,' Nora snapped. 'It's the only decent investment we've got left apart from the house. If we decide to sell up—'

He did not want to hear another word about selling up. 'Stickley's not having the house. Over my dead body! I know what he's really after; soft-soaping you with a good letting, for once. He's got his eyes on Wintergill for himself, always has had . . . He'll slap planning permission on every bloody barn, shed, nook and cranny, strip the assets and keep the real prize for himself. I know his little tricks.'

Nora knew he was right. 'Bruce has a point, you know,' she replied. 'This place is too big for the two of us. We rattle round like dried peas in a drum. What do we need twenty rooms for? It's not as if—' She stopped abruptly. 'You know what I mean.'

'Stop that, Mother. Wintergill House has been in this family for generations and I see no reason to change. Snowdens have made a good living from this land. Peaks and troughs, ups and downs, this is just a bad patch but we'll survive,' he argued, standing his ground.

'Do you really think so in this climate, son? Be reasonable. I'm getting too old . . . I'm the wrong end of seventy and you're not getting any younger . . . Who's going to follow us then?' She paused for breath, sensing this was not the time for recriminations. There were no other Snowdens left to inherit . . . 'Rationalisation is the word on everyone's tongue,' she continued. 'It makes common sense to take the money and run. We've got choices now. You haven't decided on spending anything yet.'

'That money stays in the bank for restocking and I don't intend to restock until I'm sure where I'm going,' Nik argued. 'I'm not listening to your doom and gloom; I'm off for a quick bath.'

'What about the logs?' she shouted up.

'Later, there's plenty of time,' he replied, bounding up the stairs, peeling off his clothes as he went in search of his dark best suit, peering at his outline in the tallboy mirror. He paused to examine his torso: not in bad shape at all, broad shoulders, not much of a beer belly when he stood sideways, strong haunches, muscular legs from years of rugby, and a decent set of tackle in fine working order but underused lately.

He would still make a good tup! If only he had sired a son to pass on the name and the heritage. How could Mother begin to understand how he felt about this house, the farm and its land? The love of it was bred in his bone. Damn it, this was the only thing he had left to love!

Nik dipped his head in the lukewarm water to rinse off the shampoo. If only there was a son to follow him, but he'd left it a bit late now. *Oh, Mandy! I thought you were the one* . . . He'd met her at a Young Farmers' ball in Harrogate. She was a hairdresser out for fun, dancing on fire with gorgeous black hair and a figure to match. It was lust at first sight. She'd been dazzled by the size of the farm, enchanted by the James Herriot setting for a while until the reality of this life dawned. They married in haste, too young and love blind to the fact that their worlds were too far apart to make a lasting relationship work.

Nik shut his eyes to block out the image of her in the barn with her legs coiled round Danny Pighills' waist as he pumped himself into her. If his gun had been handy he'd have shot them both like vermin. He'd torn them apart and given Danny such a beating. He wasn't proud of himself but he was drunk, shamed and humiliated. She'd left that night and returned only for her clothes under armed guard. It was all around the district that Nik Snowden couldn't keep his wife. He was deeply hurt by her rejection of all he held dear. The bitterness he'd felt then had eased to a dull ache of regret. He had not heard from her in years.

Now he was resigned to the single life – once bitten and all that . . . Occasionally there was a fling with one of the pub crowd but nothing serious. He was never in a sound enough financial position until now to take on another partner, and he was wary. Women were not to be trusted. The world around had changed since his youth, when farmers' wives knew their place. Now they ganged up together and argued their corner, demanding equal shares in the business and working outside the farmstead just to keep their kids clothed and heeled. In his heart he knew that such women deserved respect but if the truth were told, the confidence of some of those brass-faced lasses scared the pants off him!

Now Jim Grimoldby's sudden death had shaken his faith in his own judgement. There he had sat, on the same bar stool at the Spread Eagle with his old school mate for years, moaning on about Defra and all the EU regulations, working out plans for their compensation, laughing at Jim's terrible jokes, playing darts, the occasional game of rugby, while Jim was going through hell.

You never knew what was going on in someone else's head. That space between the ears is always a lonely place, he thought. Was it just depression at the sight of his sheep culled, too much to drink, or was it utter weariness with the whole damned shooting match that made his friend walk onto the moor with his shotgun and blow his head off? What sort of friend had he been not to recognise such despair? There'd been enough leaflets and confidential phone numbers to ring for counselling but Dalesmen are proud and stubborn – shy of talking to strangers, however well-meaning.

Brian Saddleworth had had a stroke when his stock was taken out, and was selling up. Poor Nigel Danby was in the last stages of lung cancer and in no fit state to carry on. It had been a bad year for the dale farmers on top of foot-and-mouth. So he must stomach this coming intrusion and think about the monthly rental cheque. If his father could see the state things had got to . . . Tom Snowden once refused even to consider bed and breakfast as a small side-line. Now every farm had a sign at the lane end. That was, until the blanket closure of every footpath, and the walkers all but disappeared.

When he thought how they had slummed it over the years in this cold barn of a house with its winding oak staircase, dark panelling, mullioned windows and ancient furniture. It didn't seem right to sell off their heirlooms to help fund a project that would have their guests living in a luxury his own mother had never enjoyed.

Old Joss Snowden, Nik's great-great-grandfather, would be turning in his grave if he knew what he had done. If truth were told, he'd been dipping into the family silver for years, oak settles here, a piece of silver there, topping up his losses. It couldn't have gone on for much longer. Now there was money coming out of his ears and Stickley was suggesting they sell the place, lock, stock, to some London magnate for a shooting lodge, though even the grouse here were thin on the ground in this grim weather. Who would want to take on this albatross?

Sandringham it wasn't – more like Wuthering Heights on a bad day – but he loved every wooden nail of it. It was his castle and his domain, his kingdom. There'd been a dwelling here since before recorded history. He was always digging up shards of Roman pottery, Celtic pin brooches, clay pipes and medieval tiles and coins. Nik had quite a collection stashed away somewhere.

The rear of the house went back to the fifteenth century, with its arching roof timbers. Nathaniel Snowden had added to the house in the seventeenth century: sturdy rubble-filled walls and square neat windows befitting the Puritan gentleman. Then his grandson Samuel restored the fortunes of Wintergill with the purchase of enclosed land, rebuilding the house looking south down towards Pendle Hill and the River Ribble. He had sired sixteen children, ten sons to expand his fortunes across the globe.

Then came George and his son, Joss, and his son, Jacob, the teetotal Methodist whose festive spirit was the talk of the dale, who prospered when Victoria was Queen. All of them had built on the strengths of their forebears, all were famous for their hospitality and open house. Grandpa Jo lost three sons with the Yorkshire Light Infantry and Tom, Nik's own father, had ploughed a straight furrow for the war effort in the forties, seeing some of Wintergill's most prosperous years.

How could he now be the one to finish them off?

Nora couldn't settle while Nik was in the bath. She opened up the Side House, put on the heating and brought the linen down from her own airing cupboard. There would be time after the funeral to buy some bread, milk and flowers for the welcome basket. It was such a long time since the last let that she was nervous.

Now she was sifting through her glove box to find a

leather pair big enough to hide her gnarled fingers. No one wore hat and gloves much to church, but she believed a woman was undressed without them. She sat at the dressing table stool, staring at her hands.

What a sturdy pair of friends these had been over the years, grasping the hind legs of newly delivered calves, planting vegetables, pickling fruit, plucking feathers, grabbing sheep, soothing sick beasts and children, grasping reins, steering wheels, holding the hands of the dying and whipping up the best sponge cakes in the district.

Now they were gnarled and horny, coarsened by wind and rain, with mottled liver spots, as wrinkled as cooked apple skins. They were long and square with over an octave span: more a man's hand than a woman's. No amount of elderflower and lanolin ointment would alter that.

Her dad's only compliment on her marriage to Tom Snowden over fifty years ago was to look at her hands with pride. 'You'll earn your keep with those spades,' he said. By then any dreams of further education and foreign travel as far from Scar Top as possible were blighted by war and the sense of duty that sent her scurrying back home to do her bit. There was never choice in the matter when Ben Frost, her dad, gave his orders.

As a child she had lived off the moor, boarding in school houses in the town to attend the local girls' grammar school, matriculating with honours with a place at university a certainty. Then war broke out and it was all ploughs to the furrow, trying to grow arable crops on wet, sodden hilltops. There was no time for regrets when there was a nation to feed.

Where was that nation in the last few years when their produce was bottom of the heap of imported meat? When fleeces lay rolled in the shed and lambs were not worth the slaughter – and as for the poor pig farmers . . . If only supermarket shoppers would buy British then this terrible disease might not have happened.

Once upon a time it was one sheep, one lamb, one acre but the temptation to intensify had taken over. There was little humanity in farming – not a local abattoir left in the district but a plethora of regulations and directives. Now nature had had the last word. Suddenly her hands started to twitch again as she fingered a silk scarf from the bottom drawer.

Every Christmas for forty years, one new scarf was added to her collection from Tom. He was not one for lavish presents or romantic gestures. They weren't bred like that in the Dales, but what he bought was always quality and long lasting so she picked out a navy and lilac stripe, not too flashy for a funeral. No one bothered much with full mourning but it was right to make the effort. The old-fashioned symbols were long gone: mourning veils to hide your tears, black armbands, funeral cards and mourning wreaths on the door, curtains closed in respect and hats off as the cortège passed. She would wear a hat out of respect and make sure that her son was decently dressed for the occasion.

There was a time when Nik was one of the smartest, handsomest young men in the dale, with his rugged good looks. He reminded her so much of Tom in his prime; the man who stopped her heart with one of his grins and his blue, blue eyes. If Nik's shoulders were stooped now it was for good reason. Worry was weighing them down. He was fighting a lost cause and she feared trying to hold back the hungry tide. This afternoon he must shoulder his friend's coffin to an early grave.

Jim's suicide brought the pain of the collapse of their industry right to their doorstep. There was anger and confusion. If the vicar doled out any platitudes in his service, she would lynch him personally. She was not on familiar terms with their new vicar, being more a Mother Earth than God the Father believer, but she would attend high days and holy days as neighbours must, to honour the dead and their living. Solidarity was the word they bandied about but actions spoke much louder.

They would bounce down from the tops to the church by the gill, with its stream coursing down the rocks that gave their village its name, and park Land Rovers and pickups where they could. There would be tea and sandwiches in the Spread Eagle, and the women would crack and gossip until it was time for evening milking and farm chores, but there were gaps now to fill in the farm routine. She powdered her red cheeks mapped with red veins. She had not missed doing her own farm chores one iota.

How she longed for a cottage down by the village beck, centrally heated, draught free, with lamps lit in the dusk and a good fire. She would soon get her energy back if she had only a small house to heat and clean instead of this barn. Lately she had found herself dosing off in the afternoons over her reading, breathless at the slightest exertion, but now was not the time to moan about her health when there was a young man in his forties, leaving a wife and children to bury him.

The service was mercifully short. She had to admit there was dignity in the old Prayer Book proceedings. It carried the distraught family through the ordeal. Even non-believers could take refuge in its language. Nik stood grim-faced, supporting the widow as the mourners stepped out into the autumn wind and rain towards the burial plot.

She did not want to see the look of incomprehension on Karen's face as she gripped her sons in anoraks. The farm hand had found Jim in the field with a note thoughtfully pinned to his jacket in a plastic freezer bag. He was a proud man. He wanted to free his children from the curse of being farmer's sons. This was his only way out, but what a legacy for his poor kids. The mourners gathered awkwardly just as the clouds parted and the sun glinted for a second, bathing the stone walls in a soft pink light.

It was more an afternoon for a ramble across the moor, if only the footpaths were open, than the burial of a young man gone mad with fear of failure. Nora stood silently for the final part of the ceremony, knowing a little of the grief Karen Grimoldby must be feeling. Time was not a great healer. It just took the edge off some of the pain so that you could breathe and carry on. The pain would never go away.

She was not one for small talk. Women had to be brick walls when it came to their children, appearing tough and hard. Family was what mattered most, she believed. If you indulged your unhappiness then it would linger longer. Feelings were best kept under control.

There would be time later to take Karen a plate pie and a tin of flapjack for the twins. When the sympathy letters were answered and the funeral expenses paid in the months to come – when winter held them in its iron fist – that would be the time to bob in and encourage the girl. That was when the chill of grief took its hold on a woman. Karen would be selling up and moving away, and another farm would be broken into lots to be bought as a holiday cottage for some blessed offcomers.

She turned towards the corner of St Oswald's that would always be her own. All that was once precious to her was buried there. There were just two simple headstones with Latin inscriptions.

'*Nos habebit humus.*' Earth will hold us.

'*Mea filia pulchra.*' My beautiful daughter. Latin was such a dignified language to hide one's grief in. She didn't want the world to read her sorrow. It was enough that Father and child were together under the maple, *Acer pseudoplatanus* 'Brilliantissimum', that fired each spring.

Farmers were used to death and the cruelty of nature, she mused. The hooded crows pecked out the eyes of newborn lambs if the ewe did not birth quickly enough. Foxes tore the heads off them for fun. Nature separated the weakest and picked them off, but this contagion levelled all in its path. Only the fit would survive the rigours of this coming winter.

Tom had a decent span, Shirley did not. She never talked about it much. What good would it do? There was no point in weeping and wailing and falling apart when there was another child and a farm to run. Sorrows were best kept in the family under lock and key. That's why offcomers often called Dales folk cold, unfeeling, a subhuman species, impervious to suffering, but Jim's death and foot-and-mouth showed otherwise. Underneath the weatherbeaten faces assembled on this bleak afternoon were the same fears and sorrows. Farmers had their own ways of dealing with them. Some took to religion or drink. She was the worst of all when it came to bottling things up.

'Sad business is this, Mrs Snowden,' whispered Bruce Stickley in her ear, looking every inch the successful country land agent in his navy Crombie coat and knife-edged trousers. She never trusted a man who had time to put his trousers in such a shape. But she nodded quickly and looked away.

Bruce Stickley was quick to strike up conversation these days. 'It makes you think what'll be happening next, doesn't it?' he continued. 'Soon there won't be any farms to manage, if this climate continues. You'll be the last farm left in the dale.'

Nora shrugged in reply.

'Don't look so worried,' he continued, oblivious to her disinterest. 'You've got one of the most sought-after properties in the Dales with those three magic ingredients.' He grinned.

'Go on, surprise me,' she quipped sharply.

'Location . . . location, location,' he replied. 'There's nothing to beat a south aspect, a hilltop view and a splendid array of ancient buildings to create interest in a sale. You'd get a tidy packet for all of it, even in the condition it's in. If ever you think of selling I hope I'd be your first port of call.'

If she'd been a man she'd have socked him in the bollocks just to wipe that smug expression off his greasy face: odious little man with his slicked-back hair and hooded eyes. He thought he was the bee's knees, but he was nothing but a blowfly feeding off a carcass. 'This is hardly the time or place,' she sniffed haughtily, piercing him with her icy stare.

'Of course . . . but I just wanted you to know,' Stickley countered with about as much sensitivity as a wolf on heat.

'What gives you the idea we'll be selling up?' she snapped back.

'With Nik having no one to take over, and the change in your circumstances,' he answered, not so sure of his ground now.

'So?'

'I know how it is for hill farmers now. I saw Nik at the diversification lecture. Have you thought about developing the other barns?'

'What we decide to do is none of your damned business, young man,' she snapped. 'Like father, like son, so I see. I knew your father. He always drew a hard bargain, always on the lookout for something cheap or run down. You've done well out of other people's sorrows over the years . . . We're

27

here to honour a poor man who couldn't take any more bad luck, not to do deals over his corpse. Show some respect!' She turned her back on the estate agent and made for the open grave to throw her handful of soil into the hole. She did not want Bruce Stickley to see that his words had hit home.

So the news was out that they were hovering on the brink of a decision like so many here today. You need only be seen going into the estate agent's office on market day for nosy parkers to put two and two together to make five. Nik was right: Bruce had an eye on their house for himself. Well, tough, she'd rather sell it at a loss than allow him the deeds.

Northbound

It was raining in Bradford when the travellers slipped off the M62, and sleeting on the road to Skipton, but the intrepid driver ploughed on northwards along the A65. The snow was settling on the pavements in Settle as they made their way cautiously upwards where the snowflakes floated as thick as goose feathers onto the windscreen.

Trying not to panic, thankful that gritters were already ahead clearing a path, Kay Partridge continued to climb upwards over clanking cattle grids in the dusky light.

'Are we nearly there?' said Evie, her daughter, with thumb in mouth, eyeing the snow with fascination.

'Last lap, muppet,' she answered, not daring to stop in case they slithered to a halt and found themselves stranded halfway up the hill. The Freelander was stuffed to the gills with bedding, toys, books, the contents of her mother-in-law's freezer, radio, video, plastic bags full of clothes. There was plenty of ballast.

Within days of deciding to rent a cottage in the half-term break, everything slotted together so neatly that surely this impulsive decision was meant to be?

She plumped for Wintergill House the minute she saw its details on the screen. Perhaps it was the name that caught her attention. It was as close to her dream home as she could find, and she wanted a place for winter. Wintergill looked old, remote and on a hillside. The details were just right. There were three bedrooms and it was part of the old estate, now a working farm. Kay also ran off loads of bumf about the district, just to be sure. It wasn't far from Bankwell and Gran's old place, although no one would remember her now. Even the village school had its own website. It was familiar territory, and even if she'd not been back for years, she felt a lightening of her spirit to be back in Yorkshire.

Now they were in another world and the wheels scrunched on pristine snow. It was all very exciting but scary. November was a little early for a blizzard, surely? Soon the lights of Wintergill would shine out like beacons guiding them forward. The weather could close them in for weeks and she wouldn't care.

'We've made it,' she sighed, turning to her daughter, but the child had snuggled back under the blanket and gone back to sleep. It was time to stop the car, light up a ciggie and draw a deep breath, blowing the smoke out of the window, ashamed at her weakness but it gave her time to savour the moment. Was this real or was she dreaming? Would she wake up back in Sutton Coldfield, with her mother-in-law bending her ear?

Poor Eunice! She'd swept into Kay's bedroom without knocking, waving tickets in her hand. 'I've got front seats in the dress circle on Boxing Day . . . won't that be fun?'

'That's very kind of you but I'm afraid we'll not be here for Christmas this year,' Kay whispered. 'I've booked a country cottage away from it all.'

'Without telling us first?' Eunice snapped. 'For how long? I suppose I can exchange them for January.'

'We'll be leaving after half term . . . it's a six-month winter let,' Kay said, not wanting to see the horror on Eunice's face.

30

'You can't be serious . . . just packing up and leaving us on a whim,' screamed Eunice. 'It's nearly Christmas . . . What about Evie's schooling? You can't just bundle her off like a parcel into the middle of nowhere. Whatever has got into you? After all we've done. I think you should speak to your counsellor.'

'I've had it up to here with grief counselling,' Kay answered. 'I've been sensible, not done anything in a rush. I've been ricocheting off the walls like a pinball. You've both been more than kind, and we do appreciate all your advice, but it's nearly a year since Tim died and I can't go sponging off you both for ever, living in your house. We have to move on, Eunice. I have to pick up my career again.'

'Nonsense. This is all part of the upset. Poor little Evie, doesn't she have a say in all this? She's so looking forward to Christmas. She's settled in the school now with a trip to the panto arranged. Daddy and I are going to give her a special treat. I know we can't make it up to her for not having her own daddy here.' Eunice Partridge's eyes were brimful of tears and Kay felt a monster for spoiling all her plans.

'No one can bring Tim back. It's going to be an awful Christmas for you too, remembering last year and the upset, as you call it. So I've decided to do something different. I did wonder about a holiday in Africa, a safari, or Morocco where there's no Christmas to remind us . . .' she suggested.

'You can't take a child from her Christmas.' Eunice was horrified.

'Christmas is not compulsory, you know. Lots of people escape from it. But then I got a better idea. We can take a country let for a few months and I've found something on the internet in Yorkshire.' She paused, knowing Eunice would not understand.

'Yorkshire! It's miles away!' Eunice spat out the words as if they were rancid.

'Why not? It was good enough for my mother to be brought up in. The Dales are beautiful. It's quiet and safe, with friendly people. They've been through a bad time. I want to show some solidarity with my kinfolk,' Kay replied, deciding not to tell them the real reason or the dream that had given her comfort and the courage to make this move.

For months the grief of Tim's sudden death in that motorway crash on Christmas Eve had lain upon her like a hard frost, nailing down her resolve, leaving her unable to make the slightest decision. Cocooned by his parents, cosseted from reality by their smothering kindness, she had let them organise their lives to suit their own need of Evie. She could hardly breathe for their kindness and fussing. Now was the time to break free or go under before that first anniversary came round.

'It's cold and wet up there, and they've had foot-and-mouth.' Eunice sniffed. 'You should be going up there in summer, not in the middle of winter. What about Evie's schooling?' Eunice was not going to give up easily.

'They do have schools up there too. It's not exactly Antarctica.' It was hard to be polite but Kay bit her lip and tried to breathe deeply.

Eunice decided to call in the troops, shouting to her husband, who was cowering in the conservatory under a newspaper. 'Dennis! Come and hear this. You'll never believe what Kay is dreaming up for Christmas. How will we manage without Evie? She's so like Tim, with those grey eyes, his nose.' The floodgates were opening again but Kay had her arguments well rehearsed.

'I'm sorry but she's not Tim. She's not a substitute for your son. She has to get over his death in her own way. Pretending he's not dead doesn't help either.' It was out in the open at last, the resentment that had been building up for weeks.

'What do you mean?' Eunice screeched, going pink in the face.

'You talk about him as if he is still alive, suspended in midair somewhere, waiting to descend when he's finished his business trip. Evie thinks he'll come home for Christmas. She wrote a letter to Santa asking him to send her daddy back. I don't want her deceived.' Kay paused. 'I should have said something ages ago. I know you mean well—'

'How can you be so cruel? We've been trying to protect her. She's too young to understand about death. It will give her nightmares. She's only seven.'

'You're never too young to learn that death is part of life, that sometimes terrible things can happen. Every time I try to tell her about Tim's accident, she covers her ears and says he's gone away to make more pennies. We mustn't turn him into some plaster saint or pretend he's just in some other place.' Kay paused, seeing the look of pain on Eunice's face, but the truth had to be spoken.

'We're only doing what we think best for Evie,' Eunice muttered uncomprehending.

'Of course, I know ... we all miss him but he was so driven sometimes ... I wonder if it was worth it,' came the weary reply.

'You wanted for nothing, my girl. He gave you both a good life. He died for his family.' Eunice's eyes flashed with accusation as she spoke.

'If only he hadn't tried to squeeze too much into his frantic schedule. He was belting down the motorway in bad weather, late as usual for his next meeting, when he should have been spending time with us. He died as he lived – in the fast lane. It's so unfair, and I just don't want to be here ... on Christmas Eve. Can't you understand?' Kay argued.

33

'I have to go now before we get sucked into everything.'
There was nothing more to say.

'You've grown so hard these past few months. I might have known you'd something up your sleeve. I hope you're not filling Evie up with bitterness.' The gloves were off now.

'Someone has to be there for Evie. I gave up my career gladly to bring her up but I'll not stand by and let you fill her up with the notion Tim is not dead. How many times have we moved to further his career? How many uprootings and refurnishings were there to organise? Have you forgotten that all our furniture is still in storage and that we were in the middle of a move when he died? Or that he wanted us to move over Christmas so as not to miss that sales conference in Frankfurt? I've been stranded with you ever since, rootless, paralysed by shock and inertia. He worked so hard – too hard – and what appreciation did he get from that bloody company? Hardly any of his work colleagues turned up for his funeral. They just threw money at us to salve their consciences . . . I need never work again . . . Don't you think I'd love nothing more than for him to walk through that door? But I've seen his body . . . I can't bear to go through that day again in this very same place . . . I'm sorry.'

'What was it all for, Eunice, tell me? One day he was there and then he's not, and I'm left neither one thing nor the other. I'm not single, I'm not divorced but I am a widow with a child.' All the bitterness was pouring out in a torrent. She looked at Eunice's crestfallen face but she couldn't back down now.

Kay reached out her hand in a gesture of conciliation and whispered, 'One minute life was hunkydory, waiting for the Christmas jamboree to begin, cake in the tin, pudding on the shelf, turkey in the pantry, Evie jumping up and down waiting for Father Christmas, and then the balloon was burst in our faces and we were left to wipe our tears, smile to protect Evie, trying to pretend Tim was delayed. We've been doing that ever since. It has to be different this year, for all our sakes.'

She looked up to see Eunice nodding in silence. Dennis was standing by the door and he put his hands on Kay's shoulder.

'The girl's got a point, Mother. Evie needs something to look forward to. We've got our memories and she's got her mum. They have to do what's best for them. I don't know how you've coped all this time, Kay.' Dennis Partridge was not one for long speeches and Kay felt mean to have upset them both.

'What'll we do, Dennis?' Eunice looked up shaking her head.

'We've got each other and a chance to visit your friend in Bath, who's been begging us for years to come and stay. It's time we moved on too. They'll come and see us when they're settled, won't you?' Dennis pleaded.

'Of course, and you can come and visit us in the New Year,' Kay said, relieved that her decision was out in the open. There was no turning back from this strange impulse to get the hell out of Sutton in time for Christmas, to find somewhere to hide from the festivities, where no one knew her as 'that woman who lost her hubby on Christmas Eve'.

They were lucky. There was insurance money enough for choices and treats and distractions. Now she was going to follow that dream. That was enough for now.

Kay stubbed out her cigarette, peering into the darkness. She was taking a ridiculous gamble in renting a house she had never seen, but it felt right. Wintergill sounded so solid and the perfect spot to hide for a few months until she rethought their future. It would be a bolt hole. The darkness of the season would shield them from view. No one knew their business here. Few would remember her mother, who left home when she was a student. If only her parents were still alive but, as an only child, she'd no family of her own for support.

The move would give her time to sort Evie's understanding of why Daddy could never be on her Christmas list.

She wound down the window further and sniffed the air. The snow had turned back to rain, dowsing her face with stinging droplets. It was time to make her way down the track. Time to test out her fantasy and the four-wheel drive.

Nik was soaking in the bath when he heard the doorbell ring in the hall and Muffin barking wildly. There was no expecting his mother to answer it for him for she was down in Wintergill, not due back until she had caught up with all the doings down the dale.

The keys for the Partridges were waiting on the hall table. The couple were late, very late and Nik had hoped with all the rain Yorkshire had been having lately they might have called off their holiday. The barometer was looking grim. Townies were soft when it came to bad weather. He tried to ignore the ringing but it carried on. Nik grabbed a towel and sloshed his way downstairs, leaving a trail of drips on the dark oak.

'Yes?' he answered gruffly.

'This is Wintergill House?' said a woman, shivering in the doorway, trying not to stare at his shrunken towel.

'Yes.' He tried to look casual.

'I'm sorry we're so late but we got held up. I've come for the key. Sorry to disturb you.'

'No problem,' he replied, muttering oaths and curses to himself. 'Come inside while I change.' He left a trail of drips up the stairs when he left her standing in the hall examining the old prints and the black oak panelling. Damn and blast, he'd have to get dressed and sort them out. Why couldn't they have arrived at a civilised hour? This was just the sort of nuisance holiday lets invited. His quiet evening in was spoiled now. He searched for his keys in the clutter on the table.

Time was when they could leave everything unlocked on the farm – doors, tractors, pickups. Now it was getting like Fort Knox. Only last month some spark took a length of coping stones from the tops of their boundary walls; hundreds of them, to be sold for a fiver a time on some car-boot sale miles away, no questions asked. The quad bike had to be locked in the barn or it would go walkabout.

Nik pulled on his jeans and sweater, his ragged Barbour and old flat cap out of habit. Muffin jumped in on the act, thinking they were going out into the fields in the back of the pickup. The moon was rising now in the dark sky. The storm had abated as he guided the Land Rover towards the Side House. There was only a woman and a child in the car. Where was the couple Mother was expecting? She would not be well pleased at a child in tow.

The courtyard was in complete darkness, only the working dogs barking at the arrival of strangers. He took them down the track to Side House Barn and brought out the keys from his pocket. It was usually Mother's job showing lets around the house, pointing out switches and timers and points. He just about knew about the fuse box and the fuel store. This was women's work.

'The storage heaters are on. The place is warm and aired. Mrs Snowden will see to the rest in the morning. She's left a welcome basket on the table so help yourself,' he answered, standing in the darkness, not thinking of anything else to say. Be damned if he was going to make a fuss.

'Thank you,' nodded the redhead in a bobble hat. 'Say thank you, Geneva.'

The child surveyed her surroundings suspiciously. 'Is this it?' Evie was half asleep. 'It's dark. I don't like—'

'That'll do, Evie. She's so tired. I thought we'd be staying in Wintergill House itself,' ventured the woman.

He could feel their disappointment and shrugged his shoulders, towering over the two strangers. 'Oh, not another one . . . You can thank Bruce Stickley's website for any misinformation given to you. He puts our house on the website and describes the cottage but omits to say they're separate. You can have him for trade descriptions but this is what's on offer. It's all brand new. I'll leave you both to it then, Mrs Partridge.'

He backed off towards the courtyard and his own back door with relief. He'd done his good deed for the day and now it was time for a whisky and some Bach.

Kay was in no mood for arguments when Evie started whingeing, sniffing the stale farmyard aromas of disinfectant, old manure and mud in the sharp air.

'I don't like this place, it smells.'

'We're here now. Let's unpack what we need for tonight and have some cocoa. It's late and we're both tired. We'll take stock in the morning.' Kay was trying to keep the disappointment out of her own voice when she looked at the barn conversion. It smelled of pine and fresh paint, of emptiness and newly lined curtains, hardwood windows and a Radoxy smell of artificial cleansers.

Their accommodation was pristine, neat, perfectly appointed but soulless: neutral with sea grass carpeting, ubiquitous pine furnishings, very nineteen eighties décor. The kitchen was spotless, well fitted with basic utilitarian units. What had she been expecting? A clutter of dark oak, stone-flagged floors, ancient beams and a large inglenook fireplace. This was not how her granny had lived in their Bankwell cottage.

This house could be lifted up and transported to any suburb. Even the pictures on the walls were tasteful prints, discreet old maps and villagey scenes. Suddenly Kay felt tears welling up. They were exiles in a foreign land at the mercy of strangers. The man could not have been more gruff and begrudging. Perhaps his wife would be more helpful. Her heart was sinking with weariness. *What have I done, uprooting us into this soulless place?*

She poured the cocoa for her exhausted child, made up her bed with the plastic mattress cover. Since all the upheaval Evie was unreliable at night. Kay rooted in the box for her daughter's toadstool lamps and Beanie Babies. They would need no rocking tonight.

Then she poured a generous dollop of rum into her cup of cocoa from the booze box. There was no going back now. They were stuck up a track in a house on top of a hill. She was following that strange dream for better or worse, but why did things always seem worse in the dark?

Next morning Kay woke with a start, staring up at a beamed ceiling. The silence was unnerving: no town noises; brakes screeching, doors slamming, radio blaring or police sirens in the distance. Both of them had slept in late, and she pushed back the curtain to see the garden enveloped in a misty rain swirling like smoke. She could make out the white outline of Wintergill House itself, but no more.

She lay back again, making lists in her head. If they were going to make this their home then it needed customising a little: a throw over the tweed sofa, some gaudy coloured cushions, posters on the walls to cover the anaemic paintwork. They would find the nearest market town and find a few items to cheer up the place.

The two of them ate breakfast slowly at the breakfast bar, slices of toast and boiled eggs from the welcome basket. Evie retired to the sofa to watch children's TV, surrounded by her latest Beanies, sucking her thumb while Kay inspected the barn conversion with closer interest. Why was the conversion so suburban in design? Where were the galleried upstairs and exposed rafters she'd seen in *Country Living* magazine? Even the great barn doors were walled in with stone, disguised rather than enhanced, ruining the spirit of the place, well crafted though it all was.

It was only when Kay put her head out of the door that she realised that the wind was whipping up the rain across the garden like smoke from a bonfire. She had forgotten how damp it was in Yorkshire. They were going to need some serious weather gear, Wellingtons and waterproofs. Their anoraks would hardly keep this onslaught from soaking them to the skin.

This was not exactly the picture of rural bliss Kay had in mind for an autumn arrival; no newspaper through the letterbox or pint on the doorstep, no bus passing on the way to market. How would she survive without her *Guardian*? There was so much she was going to have to find out from Mrs Snowden and she must thank her for the welcome pack. In the rush to offload her larder she had brought only frozen packets wrapped in newspaper. What if they were cut off by snow? Kay started to make a survival list of provisions for their store cupboard just in case they were stranded. She felt like a pioneer in the Arctic.

Once all their clothes were unpacked, they looked too flashy for country living. Evie's books and toys would have to go in the spare room somehow. Kay was just slamming the door shut when a hooded apparition in a battered mackintosh, looking for all the world like the famous Hannah Hauxwell in a blizzard, came battling across the path carrying a tray covered with a cloth.

'Glad to have caught you, Mrs Partridge. Sorry I wasn't in last night but I hope you're settling in. Not much of a weekend, I'm afraid, the forecast is dire . . . very unseasonal for the time of year,' said a rosy-cheeked woman peering out from under the hood. 'I've brought you some of my baking just in case you're short. It's just some parkin.'

'Come in, come in, Mrs Snowden,' ushered Kay with her hands full of videos. 'We were going to come and thank you for the milk and eggs and bread.'

'You're welcome, lass. It takes a brave soul to land themselves up here for the back end of the year. You're our first visitor this season. As you can imagine we've not exactly been the most popular of venues this summer,' replied the older woman. Her voice was soft and low, an educated voice with only a hint of a Yorkshire accent.

'Do thank your husband for coming out to rescue us last night,' answered Kay, and watched the woman's face burst into a smile out of which came a deep throaty laugh.

'Just wait until I tell Nikolas. I know it's been a rough year but my son hasn't aged that much, I hope. It was my son who let you in,' she replied.

'I'm so sorry!' Kay muttered. 'It was dark, I was tired, I wasn't really looking at him properly. Oh dear!' The old lady laughed. At the sound of chatter Evie came to the kitchen still in her pyjamas, her fair hair straggling over her face. 'This is my daughter, Geneva. Say thank you to Mrs Snowden, who gave us our breakfast and a tray of parkin for our tea.'

'What's parkin?' Evie looked at the flat brown squares with suspicion.

41

The smile on Mrs Snowden's face faded as she beheld the child.

'I thought it was just your husband and yourself, Mrs Partridge, the two of you?' she stammered, eyeing the girl with surprise.

'We've got our wires crossed, I'm afraid. No, there's just Evie and me, just the two of us now, come to have some peace and quiet for a while,' Kay replied, not wanting to go into details.

'So she'll be off to Wintergill School then? The bus collects them at the end of the lane.'

'We've not decided yet . . . I might teach her at home for a while until we go back to the Midlands. It's a bit of an experiment, isn't it, Evie?' Kay turned to her daughter but she just shrugged her shoulders.

'It's a good village school, one of the best. Pat Bannerman runs a tight ship. Both mine went there when they were little . . .' Then the woman stopped abruptly. 'I'm not sure this is the right place for a kiddie.'

'I'm sure it will be. She's no trouble and we need a break from routine so I'm not sure I want to settle her into another school.' Kay looked up as Evie disappeared back to the television. 'We do need to gear ourselves up for this weather though. Where's the best place to go?'

'How old is she?' asked the woman in a far away voice.

'Nearly eight. She's tall for her age but quite young in other ways.' Kay was curious as to why Mrs Snowden wanted to know about Evie.

'She'll happen find it lonely up on these tops. There aren't many children left on the farms. They're all bussed to school. Do watch out for her – farms are not playgrounds. I don't usually encourage families here. I thought you were a couple or I'd have said. We couldn't take the responsibility if anything . . . not that there's much farm work happening

42

yet,' said the woman whose eyes were darting to the little girl as she was talking.

'Don't you worry, Evie is a sensible child, used to dodging traffic. I'll make sure she knows her country code. And thank you for the cakes. Baking is not something I've done for ages,' she confided. Eunice had kept the pantry full of cakes and pies but her own appetite had still not returned.

'It's a way of life up here, or was, but now the young 'uns seem to like shop-bought stuff. You never know what's in it, do you? I'd better leave you to settle in. Is everything to your satisfaction? Anything else you'd like to know?' Mrs Snowden made for the door.

'I'd like to know more about your old house. I thought we'd be staying in part of it. I can see it's got a history,' Kay replied. There was no use in hiding her interest.

'It's got so many bits, added on and knocked off, you'll have to ask my son about all that. It's his interest. It's been in my husband's family since Queen Elizabeth's day. Ask Nik to give you the tour, if you don't mind the mess. We live back to back, so to speak. It suits us that way.' Mrs Snowden smiled and, despite her forthright manner and stern visage, Kay liked the look of the woman. She must have been a beauty in her day with such high cheekbones and fine piercing blue eyes.

'And your husband? Does he still farm?' Kay asked.

'Lord, no! Not unless he's ploughing St Peter's fields. He passed on years ago, before all this bother with the farming industry. He was a Maggie's man and thought the good times would last for ever.'

'I'm sorry. I can see the fields are empty. It must have been a terrible year up here,' Kay nodded with sympathy hoping she hadn't upset the widow.

'Aye, lass, one I never thought I'd see in my lifetime. Tom had a good innings. I was younger than him and times were easier then. You could educate your children off the moor. He worked hard for his family – you can't ask for more. I'm glad he wasn't here to see his stock culled. Are you on your own by choice?' Mrs Snowden paused, waiting for an answer.

'My husband died suddenly last Christmas in a car accident. It's not been easy.' She always found it hard to spit out those words but it was better to be open. She wanted no misunderstandings.

The older woman looked her straight in the eye and something unspoken passed between them. 'I'm sorry . . . You won't be wanting much of a Christmas then, I reckon.'

'That's about the sum of it,' she sighed. 'But Evie is too young to understand this.'

'I hope you don't mind plain speaking,' Mrs Snowden whispered. 'Put her in the school. She'll get a good Christmas there. Then you can step back and let it all wash over you. It might help. I hope you have a good stay though. A change is as good as a rest, but you never get over what you've been through.' The farmer's wife paused. 'Get yourself down to Skipton market on the High Street. You'll find your winter togs there at half the price. The weather here is unpredictable. Still, you know what they say about Yorkshire climate: it's nine months winter and three months bad weather,' Mrs Snowden laughed.

'My granny Norton used to say that. She lived in Bankwell. It used to rain for England in my school holidays,' Kay offered.

'A Norton, indeed! Then we're practically relatives, if that's the case. There's been plenty of them in this family way back . . . Should I know her?'

'She was Betty Norton, married to Sam. My mother was Susan . . . she went to the High School at Settle.'

'I'd be long gone by then . . . Fancy, it's a small world. Was she in the WI?'

'I expect so. She died many years ago though. Mum sold the cottage.'

'Something small in Bankwell would suit me fine but that's another story . . . I must shift myself. Just wait until I tell Nik you thought I was his wife!' Mrs Snowden edged out of the room but not without pointing to Evie. 'Mind that child and get her into school.' She waddled back to the big house still etched in the mist shaking her head.

'So what shall we do today, muppet?' Kay perched on the edge of the sofa.

'Get a video and a takeaway pizza,' came the reply.

'Dream on. This is the country so let's go out for a walk and get an airing. I want to see the old house. There's so much to explore. Let's blow the cobwebs away and collect autumn bits for our windowledge. Come on, boots and anorak, it'll do us good,' Kay said briskly, trying to sound more positive than she felt. There was no harm in telling the old lady the bare bones of her circumstances but she hoped they would not be pestered. Perhaps the village school was not a bad idea.

Mistress Hepzibah watches over the tray bakes cooling on the kitchen table. The dog in the corner has his eye on the pepper cakes but dare not move for fear of her. It is the season for soul cakes but these are but a poor effort. Holy day cakes begin the little Lent at Martinmas, a time of prayer and fasting. Hepzibah sniffs for the scent of honey and milk, tokens of heaven and earth, for pepper, allspice and almonds. Where were her bakestone and griddle pan gone? The young know nothing of sacred culinary arts. How can the poor be fed and the sufferings of the dead be alleviated by such tokens?

She peeps from the window unseen as a dancing child skips across the courtyard like a puffed-up sunflower with tansy hose, jumping into a puddle. Oh, Mother, take heed! Hepzibah senses movement in the spinney that borders Wintergill Farm.

If only Cousin Blanche would but listen to reason and not come a-calling, but a child will draw her hither like a lodestone. There will be no peace. Blanche is so careless with other people's children. This season is ripe for mischief when darkness overcomes the light. Rise up, Wintergill, and keep watch. Danger is coming. Our prayer has been granted with the coming of a child but this time we must finish the business or be damned.

Why alone doth this season bring only sorrow to my heart? How can such a season of goodwill bring forth hatred and despair? It all begins again.

Hepzibah Snowden, 1653

Her Soul Cakes

8 oz of honey
2 oz of butter
12 oz of ground oatmeal with a little milk to soften
ginger, allspice and ground peppercorn

Melt the butter with the honey until soft and add all
the rest of the ingredients. Shape to form a thick ring.

Soften the griddlestone or pan with butter, bake on
one side very slowly for about an hour. The honey
must not burn.

Butter the griddle or pan again. Cut into smaller
pieces, turn and cook for 15 minutes until dry.

Better left for a few days to ripen.

'Hurry up or we'll be late and the parson will give us one of his stares.' Hepzibah chivvied her servant girls to cover their heads and find their cloaks. It was always a rush on the Lord's Day to get them down the fell to St Oswald's in Wintergill. Nathaniel was struggling with his boots, not wanting to waste time when there were a hundred jobs to be doing, even on the Sabbath. The new incumbent was a stickler for attendance and would send his spies to see if the Snowdens were still abed or neglecting their spiritual health. Parson Bentley was not a man for compromise. He was a staunch supporter of Cromwell's army and the Puritan ways.

Hepzibah clucked over her charges like a mother hen with a brood. No one went without clean linen collars and cuffs, warm boots and thick cloaks in her household, master or servants. The spinning wheel clacked by the hearth and the knitting sticks were never idle. In keeping with the times there was no fancy lacework round their necks, and sadly no baby cloths to sew, much to her despair. She must learn to wait on the Lord's will but it was not for the want of trying to bring a bairn into the world, she blushed as she scurried down the hill.

It was freezing in the stone church, and the household sat huddled together. Hepzibah could see this parson wanted to stamp his authority on this motley congregation of papist miscreants and former Royalists as he strode up into the three-tiered pulpit, his face purple with zeal. The Snowdens were sitting in their appointed pew, their feet numb with the chill. The bareness of the stone walls, stripped of any offending artefacts, could offer no distractions from the coming storm. Nathaniel, her husband, was already half dosing and she could hear his stomach rumbling for its next meal.

'The word of the Lord came to me like fire in my bosom. Now we approach the Advent season of fasting and penance, it has come to my knowledge that there be those in our midst who still practise heathen festivals with fire burnings, feasts and are already making preparations for yuletide.

'Let it be known that for some years now the practice of Christmas-keeping has been outlawed by the government of this realm. It is an abomination of Scriptural truth. The birth of Our Lord is a solemn occasion of prayer and fasting but I hear that there are those among you who make it an occasion of sinful profanity, licentious liberty as make it more Satan's mass than a service of penitence.'

There was a shuffle and stir among the pews and heads bent to spare blushes, recalling past gambling parties, mummery shows and drunken revels. Hepzibah listened intently. Bentley was going hammer and tongs this morning.

'You might well hide your shame, you wantons, who dance and sing on a holy Sabbath; who play cards and spend this holy day in drunkenness and debauchery. The eye of the Lord seeth all, brethren! He is not mocked! It is written in the Book of Judgement that Mistress Palmer did consort with others in lewd and wanton apparel, flaunting her body in such cavortings as to fetch the constable. Did not Scholar Knowles be found in the bed of one Bess Fordall, having handfasted together like man and wife, making mockery of holy wedlock as Lord of Misrule? Some of you dishonour Our Lord more in the twelve days of Christmas than the whole twelve months besides.' He paused to deliver his cannon balls of spit.

'Be ye no more a Christmas keeper. Shame not His sufferings with your disobedience. For some years now it hath been the universal custom to omit the observation of this festal season in favour of prayer and fasting. Let it be just another working day in this district and nothing more, or else be punished. However lax hath been the overseeing of this season in times past, you have before you one that hath great zeal to uphold the law. The season is condemned and those who disobey shall be stripped and cast into outer darkness where no light perpetual shall shine on them!

'I speak plain. Let your feast be as Lent, plain, meatless and meagre. Let no green boughs from the hedgerows be brought into your hall with no pagan berries. Let not your children hanker after sweetmeats and trinkets, singing and carolling. Dress them in soberness and humility. Our Lord is meat and drink enough to those who love Him. He will reward your abstinence. Hear and inwardly digest the word of the Lord on pain of your soul's salvation. Amen.'

Since the parson's arrival at Michaelmas, Hepzibah had never heard him so fired up; his spittle was shooting from his lips like a fountain. She looked across the pew to where her cousin, Blanche Norton, sat, her pale face looking ahead, white as ice set against her widow's weeds, flaunting yet another lace collar for all to see, her ringlets dripping out of her fancy cap. Her only child, Anona, sat quietly unheeding the warnings in her own drift of thought.

Blanche's hair turned white almost overnight on hearing news that her husband, Kit, was slain with the Royalists at Marston Moor in 1644. There were those in

51

the congregation only too glad to reap a bitter harvest on her of fines, robbing her of stock and chattels for taking up the Royalist cause and not attending church services each Sunday. This late war had sliced the district into two camps. Nathaniel neither turned right nor left but paid his dues when asked, steering a careful course in the middle, causing none offence. He said he only awaited the judgement of the Lord, who in His wisdom came down hard on the King. Her cousin's delinquency brought her in the path of the constables and she was made to pay dearly for her husband's treachery with the loss of land.

We are strange relations, she thought; I being little and dark and she being tall and fair. Considered still comely of face, with lands still worthy of ploughing, the widow had many callers to woo her but she preferred to run her household as if Kit were still in residence. They were but distant cousins in truth. Since Hepzibah's own father took the plainer path of worship and Blanche married into a once popish household, they had seldom met until her widowhood.

Nathaniel Snowden of Wintergill was considered a good enough catch for a plain daughter. Marriage suited them both well. But for the want of an heir she was well satisfied with her stone house on the hill. It was a great sadness that her babes did not thrive above a few breaths of air.

This parson's edicts were mightily strict for a country district where folks did things in the old ways and paid little heed to the pulpit. He would have his spies in the two constables, Robert Stickley and Thomas Carr. If there was some profit to be made from spilling oats of information Stickley was your man. They were both doing well from this change in governance.

Hepzibah had no great quarrel with the idea of banning Christmas. It was a great expense and distraction to their servants who expected roast beef, mutton pies and plum porridge. She thought the season but a ploy to swell the coffers of all the costermongers in the town. Servants wanted play days, dances and fiddling. Everyone knew that dancing was devil's mischief for more lasses got with child at Christmas than ever fell in Lent.

Let the candle-makers and grocers, spice merchants and pedlars feel the draught. All the money she saved could be spent wisely on a fine tup or breeding mare. There were still the pigs to be killed and the hog's head to turn into brawn and pies.

Her work was never done. Christmas-keeping was an old popish practice after all, and now that Cromwell reigned in London it was time to call a halt to frivolity. She was a sober matron now, not a flibbertigibbet of seventeen, but she must admit her feet would tap when she heard a jig.

Nathaniel would have his own thoughts on such matters. If he saw fit to give alms and tokens of thanks to his cowmen, stable boys, shepherds and yard boys, strengthen their brew or let the house servants go for a day to visit with their kin folk, that was his affair. She would heed the parson's words for her own purposes.

'What think you of our parson's words, this Advent morn, Blanche?' she said as they were walking primly down the aisle, her head held high in her broad-brimmed black hat.

Blanche followed grim-faced, clutching the child's hand. 'He talks through his arse, this sobersides!' she whispered. 'Does he not know that Christmastide is a season of joy, not mourning? There's little enough to cheer us in a dark dreary winter of snow and ice, when the lanterns are lit all day and the fires give off little heat. 'Tis the time when folk need a bit of singing and dancing to look forward to. I will not heed his words one whit.'

Blanche ignored the parson at the door and swept out

like the grand lady she once was. It did not go unnoticed. 'Nonie shall have a new gown and we shall call in our neighbours and make merry,' Blanche said loudly. 'I owe it to my late husband to keep a good Christmas. Why, in the old days we drank the cellar dry and ate haunches of venison and beef with fruit pies and all manner of exotics. Now I can little afford to feast but I will sell my last trinket to give my little one her wish. She shall not go without just because some preacher with a sourdough face tells me so. We live in sorrow because Kit can be no longer at our side to protect us. Have we not suffered enough for our troubles?' Blanche stopped in her tracks to see if he was listening.

'When I sit and look around this plain church with its bare walls, I see only treachery and self-seeking. Was it not Brother Stickley who knocked on my door and demanded four cows as a penance for our allegiance to His late Majesty? Did not our fine Constable Carr take three pounds from my coffers before my poor Kit was cold in his grave? Were we not passed from pillar to post, hurled from our home to make way for Cromwell's army to ravage our granary and steal our horses? I am sick of all these ordinances that rob us of any joy in our brief sojourn on earth. If Parson Bentley's bosom swells with fire then so doth mine for the opposite reasoning, and I shall tell him so.'

Hepzibah had never seen Blanche so animated and careless in her talk. 'Have a care, Blanche. It does not augur well to anger him. There are those who wish to profit from your distress. Give them no occasion to denounce you,' she warned.

You are my true friend, Sister, and mean well enough. I can take care of this myself but if aught untoward should happen to me, I trust that your hearth would always be open to my child. Shield her from their envy. I do not always hold with your beliefs, nor you with mine. I come here because I must. I can no longer afford to stay away and pay the fines but your heart is ever warm towards us. Nonie is all that keeps me in this vale of tears,' said Blanche, grabbing Hepzibah's cloak.

'Then think on, dear coz, give no occasion of offence to this parson. Of course Anona is welcome any time to visit. You have fought bravely to keep your lands and chattels. Don't throw them away in one act of defiance. We are kin and who harms you shall have us to answer to, is that not so, Nate?' she answered, hoping her husband would back her up, but he was striding ahead out of earshot.

'This parson is but a bag of wind,' laughed Blanche, tossing her curls. 'He likes the sound of his own voice. I care not who hears me!'

'Shush! I fear for your stubbornness but each must behave according to his conscience and Scripture. Where does it say in the Holy Writ that we should worship on Christ's birthday?' she argued.

'I care not for the printed word. It has no flesh or blood,' Blanche was arguing. 'I will not desert the old path just because some black crow caws that I should tread only his highway.' Blanche lifted the child onto a waiting cart and set off away from the church at a pace.

Hepzibah found herself shivering in the cold sunlight, hearing the rooks in the churchyard screeching. Blanche was too proud for her own good. Surely she would not tempt providence by gainsaying a man of the cloth.

Stone Walling

Evie ran through the farmyard splashing in the puddles and the tethered sheepdog, Fly, barked. It was black and white with pale blue eyes, jumping up excitedly as she passed. She would play hide-and-seek from her mother, who was slipping and slithering on the cobbles. There was a line of trees and wood where the leaves were fluttering down like golden snow. Then she saw a rabbit dart from the stone wall ahead of her and she chased it. She would hide from Mummy in the wood and jump out.

This was her playground now, fields and fields of it to explore. This was her fairy wood, just like the story she was reading where people lived in the tops of trees and there were lands you could visit. It was going to be magic. There were so many things at her feet to collect: feathers, stones, pine cones and fallen nuts. She could hear birds rustling in the leaves, drawing her deeper into the peppery darkness. She found some toadstools almost in a ring, jumping into the middle to make a wish. It was the enchanted wood and she expected to see houses in the trees but she looked up into the bare branches with disappointment for there was not even one door in the trunk, just a startled squirrel which darted quickly from her gaze.

For a second Evie felt a stab of fear, suddenly aware that someone was watching her, and she spun round to catch a glimpse of a poor lady with long white hair, dressed in a ragged cloak, who stared like a princess lost in a wood. Evie made to talk to her. How strange to see a white candyfloss mist floating through the trees, and there was a smoky perfume in the air.

Evie blinked and looked again but there was no one there, just the smell of a bonfire. She walked on tiptoe, trying to see where the lady was walking through the thicket. It was getting darker and colder, and suddenly her fear returned. It was time to walk backwards until she got her bearings but even so, she came out of the copse not where she went in. It was scary and exciting at the same time.

There was nothing Nik Snowden liked more than an afternoon's walling, plugged into Bach and a pipe full of rich tobacco. His tape was playing the Double Violin Concerto, followed by a Mendelssohn Octet, guaranteed to set him up for the day. There was something satisfying in repairing a gap in the wall; eye and hand working together in a harmony of skill, knowing which stone to place where or facing a stone with a chisel to fit a space exactly. It was like making your own jigsaw puzzle.

A good wall was built to last. There were two on his land dated to Celtic times with high stones built in top-heavy fashion. This repair would see him out if he built it up well. It was always a sign of a good farm if there were few gaps in the stonewall boundaries. In the days before the cull he could count up to forty gaps in some stretches on the moors alone, and with grants for walling there was no excuse for slackness. Many of his friends had lost heart and made do, could not afford the expense of a decent stonewaller, but he was determined to put his walls in good nick even if his fields were a mess.

He had been taught by a champion waller. His father, Tom,

was one of the best. Whenever there was a row with his wife he would always come out to mend a gap. It soothed his spirits and gave him time to think. It was better than any stress management course, alone on the moors with the wind.

Then he saw the girl from Side House sitting on a piece of bulging stone wall that was far from safe.

'Get off the wall, it's dangerous!' he ordered, but she sat with her arms folded.

'Why?' she answered him back.

'Because I say so.' He looked up at the sharp little face and piercing eyes staring at him, unused to such cheek from a kid like her. 'I don't want my wall flattened and your mother on my heels for letting you bash your head. Just get off my wall this minute.'

'You can't make me, Mr Grumpy,' came her riposte.

'Yes I can. If a wall breaks and sheep get out, I'll send you both back south on the next train, Little Miss Rude.' He was trying not to chuckle. Mr Grumpy just about summed him up these days, but he kept a straight face.

'You've missed a bit . . . There's a hole in the wall down there.' She pointed to a small gap through the wall.

'That hole is for the sheep to go from one field to another, clever clogs. We call it a cripple hole and you should be in school,' he snapped, carrying on with his work, ignoring the madam in the orange tights and Puffa anorak.

'What are you doing now?' she said, pointing as she leaped down.

He could not help but notice she was a funny kid, typical only child, nosy and solitary, old for her years. He should know, he had been almost one himself. Why was she not in school? Kids today seemed to have no respect for their elders.

All he wanted now was a bit of peace and quiet to see his way through next month's decisions. The fact they had to take in strangers to make ends meet was no comfort. Now he couldn't even wall in peace with those eyes on him.

'Where have all your sheep gone?' the girl asked, pointing out the obvious.

'I'm waiting for some new ones,' he answered carefully.

'Did all yours get killed?' she asked nonchalantly.

It was his turn to go pink. He nodded, then he saw with relief that her mother was storming down the field, her red-gold hair flying. They were a pair, those two, like peas off a pod.

'Where've you been, Evie? I've been looking for you every-where!' shouted the Partridge woman.

'I was only exploring and I found nuts and leaves and feathers, and a white lady walking through the trees,' the kid replied.

'Oh, yes, where did you see her then?' he quipped, watching the mother's lips smile though her eyes weren't.

'She waved to me but I couldn't catch up with her and she disappeared right through the trees like magic,' Evie replied.

'What do you feed this kid on, magic mushrooms?' Nik couldn't help laughing and the mother blushed.

'Geneva has a vivid imagination. Only children often do . . .'

Seeing she was rattled, he tried to explain. 'We do get hippies wandering up the slopes on the magic mushroom trail,' he offered, well aware that his waxed coat smelled to high heaven and he must look like a tramp himself in his mucky clothes. 'Just get her off these walls. This is not a play-ground. I've told her if the wall breaks and my new sheep get out, she'll be for it. The new stock won't be familiar with these fields and will wander away.' The woman did have the dignity to blush as she pulled her kid down in one fell swoop.

'I did see a lady playing hide-and-seek,' the brat argued, pointing to the far copse.

'Never mind about that, do as Mr Snowden says,' Evie's mother bristled.

'Will we see lambing time?'

Nik could see that Evie was a persistent kid so he shook his head. 'Not this year, you won't, and you'll be gone before the season starts again.' What a relief, he thought.

'Can we stay until the next lambing then?' asked the girl, tugging at her mother's sweater.

'I'm not sure . . . Perhaps we can come back for a weekend another time and see them then,' came the mother's diplomatic answer. 'Come on, muppet, let's not bother Mr Snowden any more than we have to.' She grabbed Evie's hand. 'Don't sneak off like that again. You must always tell me where you're going.'

'But I did see a lady in the wood; she was just like Cinderella gathering sticks. I did, I did!' Evie pleaded in vain.

'If you say so,' came the weary reply.

Nik watched as the woman gave him a look and a sigh, not believing a word. They were an odd pair and he wondered just what was driving them so far north with only each other for company. Perhaps they were running away from someone or something. If so, they'd picked a strange hiding place. There was nothing in Wintergill that wasn't ferreted out by gossips. Dalesmen were secretive about themselves but curious about offcomers, and his mother would be quietly gleaning information to fill in the gaps, he smiled to himself.

So the kid sees the White Lady too, he mused, lighting his pipe and turning back to his task, switching on his Walkman and losing himself in music. He could have said something to explain who she was but he'd stayed dumb, not wanting to admit to seeing something odd himself now and again. That was none of their business.

He needed no third eye nor any reminders that there would

be no lambs, no new life in his fields. The thought of waiting another year to tup his ewes did not bear thinking about.

Suddenly his canned music was grating on the ear and his back ached. Enough of pretending he was busy, he decided, and made for the back door.

He paused, staring over the empty fields again. How many generations was it going to take for his new stock to be hefted to these hills; to know where to graze safely out on the moor, read the weather signs and learn the best walls to shelter underneath out of the snow? He didn't want kids roaming around, he wanted stock and a proper income. When would life ever return to normal?

Will this journey never end? Blanche sighs, for she has travelled down the weary paths of time, over fell and fountain for so many years; a trick of the light, a shadow on the wall. She shimmers in the darkness, seen only in the glint in the eye of a barking dog, which whiffs her scent, growls in the air and sinks its teeth into nothingness.

Only the eye of the innocent may catch a glimpse of a trapped spirit lost between worlds. Cousin Hepzibah will sense her coming and her purpose, but she knows nowt of the world, confined within that cursed house.

Hepzibah is powerless against this annual visitation like some drab nag tethered to a farm's stable, while she, Blanche, is free to roam like a wild white horse of the hill at a gallop, ever searching in winter's light. But now her powers are waning.

I am weary of this everlasting search. Only a child's heart sees my faerie triangles in the woods, my silver toys by the waterfall. I sense a maid is close by even now . . . I do not know myself any more. Lord have mercy. Give me back what is rightfully mine and I will be content. Jesu, Maria, Libera Me.

Farmhouse

On their way back to the Side House, Kay and Evie took a detour to inspect the front of the old house from a vantage point in the higher field. It was a strange house of two halves, a Janus of a house with two faces, one painted white with sandstone lintels, three storeys high with six mullioned windows on each level, three on either side of the main door. There were eighteen windows catching every inch of sunlight like a bright smiling face looking down over the river valley.

To the rear, the house slumped low at the back, facing north with narrow slits of window eyes in rough stone, the side that took the brunt of the weather.

There was no birdsong in the winter air. The hawthorn berries were splattered on the grass like blood clots, leaves were cartwheeling across the walled garden, smoke billowed from the tall chimney stack and Kay was bursting to see the inside. She would have to find some excuse to knock on the door.

Just before darkness closed over them, she tapped on the back door clutching a bottle of red wine as a peace offering to Mr Grumpy, hoping he would offer them a tour. The collie barked as his master opened the door and ushered them in with a nod, surprised by the bottle, thinking they'd come to the wrong entrance.

'What's this in aid of?' He looked down at the label with interest.

'Just a peace offering from Evie for jumping on your walls . . . Your mother said you might show us around inside. I hope you don't mind,' Kay smiled.

'Mother's round the front . . . but you can go through if you shut your eyes to my mess.' The farmer ushered them quickly round the table. The kitchen smelled like a farmyard: cow muck, wet dog, damp washing and stale tobacco with a tincture of burned toast and bacon. The breakfast table was littered with *Farmers Weekly*, junk mail, invoices, a loaf in its wrapper and a milk bottle, a pile of unwashed plates and mugs in the sink; a busy man's domain. On the rack above the cooking range hung overalls and log-cabin shirts. Kay scuttled past trying not to be nosy, feeling every inch the intruder, tripping over a sack of dog biscuits and a tin bowl of water. Evie made for the dog cowering under the table from her enthusiasm, sniffing her outstretched hand with interest.

After a few minutes of small talk, Kay wished she hadn't angled for this visit but she was determined to see the inside for herself. They stepped through a black oak door into a corridor and then into a large hall with stone-flagged floor covered with a ragged kilim rug on which sat a huge mahogany table. On the side was a large inglenook fireplace. The table seemed to form a barrier between the two halves of the downstairs. There was a huge dresser full of pewter plates and resting there a telephone, unopened post and a stuffed curlew in a glass dome. She glanced at an old bill dated 1753 framed on the wall, and a salmon encased in its cabinet. The walls were lined with sepia photographs and larger portraits up the stairs. There was a smoky musty smell of dampness as their shoes echoed on the stone flags.

In a side room Kay glimpsed a den of books, CDs, a sound system, a battered old sofa and a marble surround to the fireplace, a once formal room turned into the farmer's den. The key to this man was music, she mused. The other doors were firmly shut.

They mounted the staircase slowly, looking at the portraits with eyes following them up to the first floor, which opened into a formal sitting room, frozen in aspic, unused and chilly, with some fine Georgian furniture, and miniatures on the walls. This could be a pretty drawing room if the fire was lit and the curtains drawn back, for it faced south, with a magnificent view.

'Do you ever use this room?' she asked. 'It's gracious and well proportioned.'

'Every blue moon when we had guests, but not now. It's just one more place to heat. One of my ancestors built it for his wife. The rest are bedrooms on this floor.' He marched them up to the next floor, opening piles of rooms full of junk, antique brass bedsteads and washstands. There was a spinning wheel that caught Evie's eye but as she touched the wheel a shower of dust fluttered into the air and made them sneeze.

'As you can see, there's not much to Wintergill,' said their guide briskly, dismissing his home as if he were an estate agent.

'Oh, but there is. Every one of these rooms could tell a story – and the view!' Kay enthused, admiring the spacious bedrooms. 'There must have been wealth here to build such a place.'

'Sheep made many a fortune until now,' Nik replied, shrugging his shoulders. 'It's said Cromwell spent a night here on a table surrounded by guards during the Civil War. The Snowdens were for Parliament for a while but somehow they ended up right even after the Restoration of the King. They were Dissenters – puritans – and paid fines for worshipping at a chapel not the church,' he added, sensing her interest. 'I guess these stone walls could tell the history of Yorkshire, good times and bad. If I had more time, there's a pile of old papers needing sorted out, deeds, wills and suchlike.'

'How exciting,' Kay smiled. 'If you need any help with Latin . . .'

'Thanks, but even farmers like me did Latin at school,' he quipped, and she blushed, hoping he didn't think she was patronising him. For a few seconds she could see the enthusiasm bursting out of his grim face. His eyes were blue – not cold ice blue, more the colour of Delft plates. Had the Norsemen left their mark in these hills and dales? she mused, looking at his tall outline, long legs and suntanned skin with interest. Then the warmth of the moment was gone and the grimness returned.

Nik was anxious to get rid of these intruders. The woman was getting too close to what was dearest to his heart. He could sense her fascination with this ancient house or why should she give up a good claret to make this tour? He didn't normally show people around or let them in through the back door to see the muddle he lived in. What he felt about Wintergill was private. Sometimes he felt it wasn't just a house, it was a living, breathing being with a character all of its own.

Wintergill had its own heart and soul. It belonged to no one generation, no one time.

He was convinced it was his duty to keep the lifeblood flowing even if it was just keeping the roof sound and the walls intact. If he gave up farming, took his compensation, perhaps he could bring it back to full repair. That was about it. He could rent out the land for grazing and develop the farm buildings, but for what? Without stock Wintergill would no longer be a living entity, but who would take on the burden of its repair when he was gone?

* * *

65

Evie had never been in such a rambling house, with passage-ways you could ride a bike along, and all those grand faces looking down at her from the walls. There were ladies in funny hats and old men with moustaches and funny collars. There were photos of children on horseback, sitting stiffly in white frilly dresses and floppy hats just like in *The Railway Children*. There were lines of ladies in sticky-out skirts, who were scowling at her.

The house smelled of smoke, not of soap like the Side House, and as she climbed the stairs she could sniff sweet lavender wafting up the stairs so she turned round. There was a lady, staring ahead, in black skirts all bunched up and her hair hidden under a cap. She was carrying a bunch of pointed feathers tied up like a brush.

Evie paused to point out the lady. 'Who's that down there?' she asked, pulling her mother's sleeve.

Mummy turned and leaned over the banister rail. 'Who's where?'

Evie looked but the lady had disappeared. 'There was a lady watching us,' she whispered.

'It must be Mrs Snowden, she told us to pop in for coffee.'

'No, it wasn't her. It was a lady with feathers,' she insisted, so Mummy felt her forehead.

'If you say so, muppet. Nobody's there now. Does this place have ghosts?' she asked Mr Grumpy. He was waiting at the top of the stairs.

'Hundreds, but I've never seen one in here. Have you spotted someone?' he asked, looking over her head.

'I'm not in the least bit psychic . . . only wish I were,' Mummy said.

'I did see a lady at the bottom of the stairs, I did,' Evie protested. Why would no one believe her?

'There's a fair few of them up these stairs giving you the eye,' Mr Grumpy laughed. 'Their eyes follow you from every angle . . . Old Jacob there, my great-grandfather, he could tell you a few tales, and that's his wife . . . they say she was a witch.' He pointed to a lady with black eyes and poky bonnet.

Evie was indignant. That wasn't the lady with the feather brush. She spun round to see if she was there again. The upstairs was disappointing. There were no rocking horses or toys, no secret hidy-holes. It was dark and sneezy, and she was hungry.

'Can I go and find Mrs Snowden now?' she asked. 'I'll carry the basket back, if you like . . .'

'Your mother did invite us to call . . .' Mummy was being very polite to Mr Grumpy.

'Downstairs, turn left down the corridor to the door at the end. She has her own kitchen,' he replied, and Evie shot down the stairs two at a time.

She was glad they slept in the Side House and not up those creepy stairs, miles from the living room. The Side House was bright and cosy, and she could hear Mummy down the stairs. Suddenly she smelled the lavender again and stopped. The woman in the black skirt was walking ahead, ignoring her, walking straight through the wall as if it wasn't there. Evie blinked. This was a strange house, and if she told Mummy what she had just seen no one would believe that either.

Then she remembered the story Mummy was reading to her of the Brontë children, who made secret little drawings and stories. This was going to be her very own secret to put in her drawing book. She would write in tiny words and pictures, copying what Emily, Charlotte and Anne were doing. She was going to be a spy in Wintergill and find out if there were any more smelly ladies walking into walls.

'What are you doing?' Evie was watching Mrs Snowden chopping carrots and apples into a bowl on her kitchen table.

'I've been making Christmas puddings with carrots and

apples, raisins, currants and nuts, all mixed up together,' she said, pointing to a baking bowl full of a gloopy mixture. On the table were a line of pots waiting to be filled. 'Now I've got to steam them for hours,' she added.

Evie could smell spices and toffee apples. It looked yummy.

'You can stir it up for me, if you like, and we can pack it into these tiny bowls. Here's a spoon, and let me wrap the tea towel round your waist or we'll get all your clothes sticky.' There were bowls waiting to be filled, all different sizes.

'Why do you make so much?' Evie asked.

'To sell on the Women's Institute stall and to give to my friends. Home-made puddings are always favourites. This is my very own recipe. Have a taste,' said Mrs Snowden, finding a teaspoon and dipping it in the goo. Evie sipped it cautiously. It was sweet and spicy, but something rubbery was sticking to the roof of her mouth so she wasn't sure.

'When they're steamed properly, you can take one home for your mum. Then you can help me make some mince pie mixture,' said Mrs Snowden. 'It has to soak for a while yet so all the flavours settle down.'

'I like your kitchen.' Evie stared at the shelves full of jars, the bunches of dried herbs and the cauldron bubbling on the stove. It was a witchy kitchen. 'But why do you have two kitchens here?' she asked, knowing Mr Grumpy had his own big stove.

'This was once the dairy room, but it suits me fine. I can do all my baking and read a book at the same time. My son has the big one. It's handy for the yard and all his mucky clothes. I expect you've noticed farmers get very muddy. Come and fill the pound pots,' she said, not looking at her but offering her another spoon.

'We don't do pounds and ounces. We do grams and kilos,' Evie announced proudly as she shovelled the gloopy mixture into the bowl.

'Well, I'm too old for all that newfangled stuff. My scales

are imperial, not metric. Does your mummy do any baking?' the old lady asked. Evie wasn't sure how to answer. She was a bit frightening, like a stern teacher.

'We cook pasta and rice and noodles and stir-fries,' she answered.

'No, I mean real baking: cakes and pies, scones and biscuits.'

Evie shook her head. 'We buy all our stuff from Sainsbury's. Mummy says sweet things are bad for my teeth. I'm only allowed pudding on Saturdays, so we have fruit yoghurts and fromage frais.'

'I'm sure it's all very healthy, but there's nothing like a bit of home baking to warm your ribs on a cold day.' The lady paused and gave her a smile. 'When I was a little girl, we used to buy the flour in sacks, and a tub of treacle and sugar too. We stored eggs for winter and churned our own butter and milk. There was nothing my mother didn't make on a Thursday. That was baking day, and I used to run home from school just for the smell coming through the kitchen door; bread, floury barm cakes, oven-bottom loaves, scones, tarts and pastries. You get very hungry on a farm.

'It was a sight to behold, and if we were having company then there were even more to put away in tins until Sunday. Sometimes we'd be snowed in for weeks so we had to have plenty in the larder to tide us over. Who bakes your Christmas cake?' The old lady was plopping round circles of paper and lids onto the bowls.

'We buy a small one, because Daddy doesn't eat cake. Nanny says he's away on business and he can't live with us now.' Evie remembered she wasn't supposed to talk about Daddy. 'I only eat the icing but Mummy likes the marzipan.'

'I shall have to show you how to bake a cake then.' The cooking lady nodded. 'I don't suppose you have cooking lessons yet.'

Evie shook her head. 'I can put topping on a pizza base.'

They carried on filling the bowls and she wondered what Mummy was doing.

'Mrs Snowden...' she paused uncertain whether to continue, 'who's the lady on the stairs?'

'In the painting? That's Jacob's wife, Tom's grandfather ... Now she was a real baker and very proud of her kitchen. I've got one of her old recipe books. Would you like to see it?' She wiped her fingers on her apron and pulled an old leather-bound book from a cupboard. The notebook was full of spidery brown writing. 'Look, this is Agnes Snowden's ginger parkin, and I still make it to that recipe – I brought you some the other day – and her Christmas pudding is the mixture I'm using now. She was supposed to be a bit of a fortune-teller and a tartar to her servants.'

Mrs Snowden was sniffing. Nanny Partridge never sniffed like that when she was talking.

'She looks like butter wouldn't melt in her mouth but it's said she ruled this place with a rod of iron.'

'Why does she live on the stairs?'

'I don't understand ... no, just in the portrait on the wall. What stairs, Evie?' she asked, curious.

'I saw a kind lady at the bottom of the stairs with a big white collar round her neck and a long black skirt. She looked very busy.' Evie watched as the old lady brought down her spoon.

'When did you see her?'

Evie pointed to the back of the house. 'I think I saw her looking out of the window this morning but she was there when we went to see Mr Grumpy ... your farmer ... and he showed us round the house. I saw her again coming to you and she walked right through the wall. But no one will believe me,' Evie added. 'Is she a nice ghost? She had a bunch of feathers in her hand.'

'I think she must be, but I've never seen her. It sounds

70

like Mistress Snowden. I heard tell that she's never left the old place. My little girl used to see her sometimes . . . They say old houses gather spirits like dust. She must love this place to hang on for hundreds of years with her goose-feather duster. My mother used to have one of them too. They got right into the corners . . . We never wasted any-thing in the olden days . . . not like today. Goose feathers made pillows and eiderdowns.'

Evie was relieved that someone else had seen her.

'Where's your little girl?' Evie was busy licking the bowl.

'Gone to live with Jesus and the angels, like your daddy,' Mrs Snowden sighed, looking out of the window and shaking her head. 'She was only lent to us for a season . . . too good for this world.'

'My daddy's gone away to work but he'll come back for Christmas. I've asked Santa and he can do magic. Have you ever seen an angel?' Evie asked.

'Not as I can rightly think of, Evie. I don't believe in angels with wings flapping. I think they come in other disguises to trip us up.' Mrs Snowden was shaking her head again and Evie noticed she had a stray whisker on her chin.

'I saw a white lady in your wood with silver hair. Do you think she is an angel too? She waved to me,' she added, but the old lady wasn't listening, just scowling.

'It's about time you went to school, young lady. You'll like it at Wintergill. I'm sure they dress up as angels for the Christmas play. You'll make lots of friends in the village, not imaginary ones. I think your mother reads you too many fairy stories,' Mrs Snowden replied. 'And don't go wandering off on your own in the wood. I don't want you messing up Nik's hard work. This isn't a play park. It's not for kiddies, do you hear?'

Evie made her grumpy face. She didn't want to think about school.

'If you stay here I'll show you how to make angel cakes with wings. They have to be as light as feathers, and you can make the butter cream,' said Mrs Snowden looking at her watch. 'I thought your mother might be coming for coffee. You go and rescue her from my son's witterings and I'll put the kettle on. You can tell Mistress Snowden to go and haunt him!'

When Evie had gone Nora sat down suddenly drained. That poor bairn was old before her time. Angels and ghosts indeed! Oh, to be a child again when her own world was full of such dreams. For all she was a town-bred kid, sophisticated beyond her years, there was something reassuring about her daydreams, but Nora was uneasy about a child around the place.

How strange she could see old Hepzibah with such clarity, as Shirley did all those years ago. Nora felt the old ache in her heart. It was coming to that season when Shirley was always uppermost in her mind. She didn't want another girl in the house to remind her of what she had lost, especially a little girl of the same age.

Nik was a good lad in many ways but he was no substitute for Shirley . . . What a dreadful thing to admit to yourself, she thought. He'd never replaced her firstborn in her heart and he'd always been Tom's favourite.

This child was different, reddy fair like her mother, bright-eyed, sharp-faced, and it was hard to ignore her. They shouldn't have let a barn to a family with a child. It had so many secret memories, that barn at the end of the yard. Changing its name, reshaping it would never change what had gone on there all those years ago. No point in going back over it, old girl.

Everyone who mattered then was long gone and she must think only of better times: Shirley riding Bess, her plaits

72

hanging under her riding hat, her plump thighs, black wellies and gaberdine school mac. Now she was frozen for ever in black and white photographs. You never get over the death of a child, not ever. Nothing could compensate for her loss, not even Nik. He was always shielded from the truth of those post-war years, the tragedy was never mentioned in his hearing. No one spoke to children in those days about such events. You got on with life and made no show of grief. And no amount of flowers laid around her grave would bring her back to them. Now, she chose to live at the front of the house away from the back yard memories. It was the only way. She was glad she had no pious belief to fight this lifelong bitterness.

Yet stone by stone she'd built a wall between herself and her son. She feared to love what might be snatched away. Life was no longer safe. The worst had happened and it could happen again. Nik was always Tom's ally against her. Two couples living in one house was never easy and warring factions made everyone jumpy. Nik's wife had sensed these tensions and rivalries, and she herself had done nothing to help the girl cope with this new life. No wonder Mandy left them to get on with it all. She'd seen Nik's pain and done nothing to soothe it, knowing better than anyone the loss of hopes and dreams. If only she could make a bridge between them, but it was too late now.

She wondered if Evie could also see Shirley playing in the Far Meadow, throwing her ball against the west wall, chasing the chickens? It would be such a comfort to know her daughter's spirit was roaming free in the fresh air, not cooped up in a little box in Wintergill churchyard.

Nora slumped down, her heart beating wildly. This won't do! She blew her nose and wiped her eyes. Thinking only made things worse.

Anona Norton, 1653

Hepzibah's Brawn

Half a pig's head, cleaned out
Water and vinegar, salt and pepper
Chopped onion
A bunch of herbs: sage, bay leaves, marjoram, 12 peppercorns, 4 cloves
Teaspoon of allspice, mace, parsley

Soak head in water and vinegar for an hour. Re-soak in clean salted water for another half-hour.

Put in fresh cold water, cover and bring to the boil. Simmer, skim well.

Change water again, add all the seasonings and simmer until tender. Lift from the pan and cut off all meat into diced pieces.

Strain the liquor, boil until reduced by half and to a jelly when cold.

Add the meat and season to taste. Pour into moulds and chill. Turn out and garnish.

Recipe for a Dish of Frumenty

Take the crushed grains of new season's wheat still in the husk with equal parts of milk and water and soak overnight in a stone bowl.

Cook slowly with some sugar in oven until the frumenty be as thick as jelly.

Flavour as pleases you with cinnamon, nutmeg or honey. Dried fruits may be added.

To be served on Christmas Eve, piping hot with cream or top of milk.

'Where are those dozy wenches?' Hepzibah muttered, seeing a maid running through the yard with no cap on. There were strangers tramping everywhere and the noise of the stuck pig rang in her ears. She scurried with her feather brush from her busyness in the little parlour that was her pride and joy. 'Why did the girl vanish like morning mist when there was so much to be done?' The screams were ringing in her ears, echoing from the yard where the men were at the kill. She scuttled through her chores, flicking over her ark chest and carved bedposts, her fine table and stool, and the wall-hung rack of her best pewter plates. Only Blanche had more finery than she, and much of that was disappearing fast from Bankwell House.

The pig had been lured, stuck in the throat, and even now its blood dripped into the pail. Soon she must heat the water for the scalding of its skin to scrape off the bristles. So much to do: larder to be scrubbed ready for salting down the joints before the Advent fast, the hog's head to be set boiling in the cauldron for broth and brawn. It was a pity to waste even the trotters; they would be shared out among the helpers, for they would not keep for long.

Hepzibah was in no mood for celebration for a flood of monthly blood had woken her with such bellyache, and hopes of a summer bairn were dashed again. She was still fretting about Blanche's boldness in church against the parson and wondered if she should bring them both under her watchful eye over this Christmastide.

She hurried back through the kitchen to chivvy up the butchery. She had great plans for their modest dwelling. Already she'd made a private parlour and a hearth for her spinning. Nathaniel bred fine sheep for market. She must keep on pestering him for a proper upstairs befitting their standing, a carved oak staircase and private chambers. The thatched roof at the back of the house was in need of repair. Sturdy stone slates would look better but Nate grumbled that it hath seen his father and grandfather through terrible winters, it could wait one more. But what was the point of fancifying their quarters if there was no heir?

She must visit the healing goodwife down in the village who sold her berry-leaf tea and prayers to the Virgin for a blessing. She hesitated many a night over that one, for it was a popish practice to make supplications in that direction. *Why am I barren and Blanche is not?* Hepzi paused. Perhaps if she gave alms to the poor, prayed three times a day, curtailed any frivolity of dress, the Lord would be merciful. Obedience and vigilance in worship might bend His ear in her direction too.

There must be no Christmas in this house, however much Nate complained, and perhaps there might be another way to secure His holy favour too . . . Oh, where was that dozy wench?

Two days later Hepzibah and her maid wrapped the brawn in its pot with a muslin cloth. Their hands were raw with rubbing saltpetre into the hams but the pig was cured, hanging safe for the winter. She had prepared the brawn especially for the parson as a goodwill offering behind Nate's back. He was on Blanche's side when it came to sermons.

'Mark my words, if that old skinflint doesn't come and prod us in the belly to see if we've eaten a Christmas pie,' he sneered. 'What does he need with our sustenance when he's already as puffed up with air as a pig's bladder?'

Hepzi took no notice, for she knew the holy man lived frugally in his cottage by the churchyard. It was her duty to share the Lord's providence as a token of respect. Parson Bentley kept no servants and welcomed them to his hearth with a grey gaunt face, looking as if he were half starved, his eyes sunk deep in their sockets burning with such zeal. His house was more like a monk's cell than a kitchen, and smelled of neglect. The rushes on the floor were stale and in need of refreshment. It lacked a woman about the place to soften the edges of its bareness and sweep out the cobwebs, brightening the shelf with trinkets rather than books. There was a bare table in need of a scrub, a stool and hard bench, nothing more but the scriptures set in a plain box.

Hepzibah presented the wrapped gift with a hesitant smile but he jumped back in alarm when he opened the wrapper.

'I hope this be not some yuletide offering, Mistress Snowden. I cannot accept any such thing,' he rasped.

'No, no. It's time for the pig kill, yuletide or no. There is more than enough for our needs, being as yet a small household. You have taught us many a time to share God's blessings, and Nathaniel and I would deem it an honour to offer this gift for your enjoyment,' she replied.

'Enjoyment? Nay, lass,' said Bentley. 'Rich food in the belly excites the carnal urges that disobey the higher mind. There must be no pleasures of the flesh while I am God's shepherd in your midst. Pleasure leads only to gluttony and lust.'

'Sadly then I must take it home with me. I would not want to lead you into temptation. It was well meaning but

I fear I have done wrong,' she said, making to withdraw the parcel, but the parson stayed her hand.

'Be not hasty, mistress. I'm sure the Lord in His wisdom prompted you to such a gesture of mercy. I see it was offered in honesty of spirit, which is more than can be said of some of your kin.' The parson snatched the parcel and ushered her to the bench while the maid stood in the shadows. 'I heard your cousin Norton disclaiming the word of the Lord, Sunday last. She comes weekly in my sight with her haughty manner and brings up the child in the dress of popery and idolatry. Is that not so?' He was questioning her, his eyes burning into hers.

'My sister in Christ hath had many troubles of late, sir. She is a widow, unused to straitened circumstances. She finds it hard to hold silence in her opinions,' she answered with a frankness that surprised her heart.

'Opinions, indeed! What doth a widow woman need with opinions?' Bentley spat out his words. 'It is forbidden in scripture for women to speak in worship. How dare she cast doubt on the Holy Writ? Is she or is she not a Christmas keeper: that is the question here?'

Her face flushed even though the fire at the hearth was meagre. All of Blanche's conversation had been overheard, the walls of any church had ears eager to pass on mischief, the righteous spies who were only too willing to see another Norton brought down low.

'You know, in times past the Nortons kept a great house with many celebrations but all that is long gone since the Commonwealth now rules,' Hepzibah said. It was the best she could muster in Blanche's defence.

'I am pleased to hear it but what of worship? Does she intend to defy me and hold a Christ's Mass in the chapel?'

The parson asked such direct questions that she was too flummoxed to proceed without untruths.

How would the Lord answer her longings if she spoke lies to His minister?

'I'm not sure, sir, but she does not visit us often,' she lied. 'We do not meddle in each other's affairs. She attends church as is prescribed, that I do know.'

'But I fear such a wayward spirit within her. Was she not of the Royalist cause? I fear for her everlasting soul. A little chastening in that direction would be to her eternal interest,' he smiled, and his breath smelled of rancid milk for his teeth were but few.

What did he mean, 'a little chastening'? Did he mean to punish Blanche? A shiver of fear went through her.

'If you would like me to speak to her myself . . .' she offered.

'No, but you must be my eyes and ears. The Lord will come unannounced in the night. We must prepare daily for the Judgement. I have my own plans for Mistress Norton. If ever a soul was in dire need of a humbling . . .'

His words trailed away as Hepzibah rose, feeling faint and nauseous by the stench of smoke and stale body odour, and the knowledge that this man would pursue her cousin further.

I must warn her and soon, she thought, warn her to be vigilant against his spies. There was a crazed hungry look in his eyes, which frightened her. She wished she had not brought meat to his door and stirred up his wrath against her cousin.

Next morning they woke to a blanket of snow: December snow that would stick, blocking all tracks, but she took heart from this as a good sign that at least the drifting would keep Parson Bentley at his hearth. He would not find it easy to go snooping. This gave her spirit some consolation.

Blanche was still her own flesh, and there was the

child to consider too. She resolved to send a servant to Bankwell, to the hall down by the river, to warn her cousin not to provoke the parson into some idiocy this Christmastide. Better still, the two of them must come up to the farmhouse where no harm would befall them both. He would not dare to call on them unannounced, not with the stains of her fresh brawn on his jacket. That night it snowed hard again, blocking them fast in with drifts. The message to Blanche would have to wait. No one would be going anywhere now.

Anona Norton peered out of the mullioned window with excitement as the snow lay like a thick coverlet along the lawns and paths of Bankwell House in the winter of 1653. She wanted to run around and dance, roll over and make snowballs, leaving her footprints like deer tracks, but Mama wouldn't let her play outside for fear of catching a chill and wearing out her boots. Why did they have to live shut away in this cold house with meagre fires when it was much more fun to go out of doors?

The snow covered the ruins at the side of the house with its whiteness. Everything looked mysterious, like the dust-sheets hiding the furniture in the great parlour, which lay cold and empty all year round where she would gallop on her hobby horse, looking up at poor Papa on the wall 'who art in Heaven'; the papa who died even before she was born.

She knew about the bad man, Cromwell, whose army foraged over the district and sacked their store barns of all good provisions so that ivy was growing over the ruined walls and there was little monies for repairs. She knew that Mama had a hidden box of treasure to pay for the fines so they didn't have to go to Wintergill church every week.

Bankwell House stood tall in its park but everything was overgrown. It was close by the river crossing and sheltered from the northern snows but it could not withstand this new parson and his snooping spies. There was a chill wind of change in the air when he arrived. They were not allowed to use their own little chapel except in secret, and Mama said that the soldiers had stripped it bare to use as their stable. Anona thought that was nice for the horses but they left a fearful mess. Once they had gone it was put back again as best they could with windows boarded up, for the stained glass was smashed beyond repair. Here some of the villagers gathered for worship for no one could stop old Father Michael from coming over the river from his hiding hole to say Mass.

She liked the old priest, who was bent over like an arch, but he never came without some comfits in his pocket, a sweetmeat or two and nuts.

Soon it would be yuletide, and Mama promised it would be a special time, with fresh rushes strewn on the floor, proper candles and evergreens brought into the little parlour to cheer them up: holly and yew, mistletoe from the apple orchards and fresh rosemary from the little herb bed.

Since Sunday last Mama was sharp and crotchety with everyone and withdrew into her chamber to cry quietly, but Nonie knew if she pushed back the bed drapes and crept inside to hug her, she would soon sigh and feel better.

Sometimes she wished she had a real father like Uncle Nate, who was round and jolly, and laughed a lot. Aunt Hepzi was plain dressed and strict, but kind enough, so different from Mama in every way.

'Are you sad because we can't hold a Christ's Mass?' she asked once, puzzled by the parson's angry words. If only Father Michael were the priest, but Mama said she must never tell anyone about his visits.

'A little, child, but we will keep the holy feast days. It is our duty, whatever that black crow says,' Mama said. 'How else are we to give our tenants something to warm their bellies with for a few days? It is what your father did, and I will carry on even though it gets harder each year to find the extras. I cannot bear to think his cause and all who loved it died for nothing,' Mama sighed, but Nonie did not understand.

She was glad that Christmas would be going ahead. 'Can I help make frumenty, with the new wheat?' she added.

'In a while. Don't pester now, Meg has enough to do. Yule is no yule without a dish of the finest wheat and cream brose.' Mama turned over on the bed. 'Be patient! I will rest and say my prayers for I don't trust that black crow o' Wintergill. His heart is hardened to our cause.'

For the next few days there was treason in the kitchen, a bustle of forbidden activities as Meg stirred up the plum porridge and the wheat was soaked for the frumenty, the cream lying thick in its bowl on the slate shelve. Nonie was set to sweeping out the stale rushes in the parlour and dusting the pewter, for the silver plates were long gone, but the last of their glasses were rubbed to a sparkle. When her jobs were all done she was allowed to roll out shapes with pastry dough. Mama laid out their best gowns with the lace-ruffed collars and cuffs, and lengthened the hem of Nonie's skirt, for she was growing fast.

Then on Christmas Eve she was allowed to go out at last with the yard boys to collect holly and greens to decorate the parlour and the chapel. It was bad luck to gather greens before that day, and boys dragged in a fine log for the fire, one that had been saved secretly in the coppice to see them through the twelve festive days.

Christmas morning dawned dry and clear, and Nonie sat at the window waiting for visitors to appear. They would break fast after the service. In the distance she could make out the shape of old Father Michael coming at first light with boots lined with sacks and wadding. Each year he grew smaller and smaller, bending like a little gnome. She hoped he had got something in his pocket.

The little chapel was dark and chilly, but once the candles were lit and the secret cross and chalice came out of their hidy-hole, she knew Christmas had really come. Out of his pocket the priest brought some carved figures and made a little crib with straw for all to worship. The door was wide open, waiting for the faithful from the village: old men, widows, children of the dale who were huddling against the cold in old cloaks, plodding through the snowy fields from all directions.

'Why are there so few this year?' she whispered. There were but a dozen folk standing.

'Fret not. The servants, prentices and scholars are forced to attend to their work and head counted to make sure they're not out carolling or mumming,' Mama replied, and Nonie felt sad that it must be a work day not a holy day, thinking about Uncle Nate out with his sheep and Aunt Hepzi at her wash tub.

The service was well underway when suddenly there was a thunderous rap at the door and in stormed the constables with two men-at-arms, who pushed aside those standing at the back, making their way forward to the altar.

Nonie noticed that Father Michael continued as if they were not present, reciting his office, but her heart nearly stopped when she recognised the intruders as ordinary neighbours. Mama was staring at the constables and Nonie held on tight to her hand.

The men stood abashed for a moment, not sure how to proceed. Thomas Carr had the decency to remove his hat but Robert Stickley stood with his rod, his arms hovering over Father Michael as if to strike him, and she was very afraid.

'For Mercy's sake, let him finish the Communion!' Mama shouted in such a deep voice, her eyes blazing. 'How dare you interrupt God's work?' Nonie found herself pushed forward and kneeling to receive the blessing. Stickley made to stay them but Thomas Carr, to her relief, allowed them all to continue.

One by one the few who remained kneeled before Father Michael with trembling knees; many had already fled from the door, back over the fields, fearing a fine. How can this be happening on Christ's holy day? There was only one person behind this and even a child could guess who that was.

They were bundled out of the chapel with Father Michael, back to the house where Parson Bentley was already sitting in Mama's parlour on her very own tapestry chair, his head held up in triumph.

'How dare you enter my house without a bidding?' Mama shouted as Nonie hid behind the back of her cloak.

'Your goose is cooked this time, mistress. I smell roasting flesh on the spit, and have seen with my own eyes the very dish of frumenty, full of the indulgence of your gluttony. No doubt if I search further I will find plum porridge pots and mulled ale. Why do you receive what is but a popish Mass in English from this priest? Why think you that you alone may act in this disobedience above what is lawful to others, pray answer me?' The raven spread his black winged cloak and seemed to Nonie like the very devil himself.

'I do as my conscience requires of me. This is Christ's holy nativity. It must be honoured,' Mama replied in a soft voice, but Nonie could feel her body shaking, drawing in deep breaths of chill air.

'And I say you are deceived. You flaunt yourself at your peril, mistress. You pray for the King, no doubt? For Charles Stuart to return over the water?'

'We pray for all Christian kings and rulers and govern-ors at this tide.' Mama looked so fierce.

'Aye, for papists and traitors too,' the parson replied, and his eyes flashed like flint sparks at both of them.

'Are we not one under God's eye?' Mama was arguing, trying to stand firm against his threatening presence.

'Do not blaspheme, woman! Who gives a woman leave to hold an opinion on such matters? You will accompany the constables from this place at once. You are charged with delinquency and will appear before the Justice to answer for your disobedience. I will not be overruled by a woman, whether she be of rank or no.' He wiped his forehead. 'I did warn your sister in Christ to check your tongue and arrogance but she hath not seen fit to follow my instructions. I will make an example of you before this congregation.' The parson summoned his two lackeys and pointed to the door.

'But what of my child? Who will bide with her while I am gone?' Mama grabbed Nonie tight and she felt a stab of fear in her chest.

'She goes with you. She attended the service. It is never too early for children to learn the wages of defiance. The priest must come too to explain his treasonous acts,' said the parson savouring their discomfort. 'You are a disgrace to your calling, old man.' He shoved the priest out of the way.

Father Michael touched Mama's arm for support. 'Let the little maid go to her aunt, I beg you, in the name of all that is holy.' Then he turned to the constables. 'Do as you are bid but there are those who'll look favourably upon us, I pray. Send word to Wintergill. They will vouchsafe for our good conduct.'

He pressed Nonie close to his cloak and whispered in her ear, 'You must dress warmly for the journey and take provisions, for I fear more snow in these leaden skies.' Then he turned back to the parson. 'Let the child go, for pity's sake.'

Parson Bentley was in no mood for leniency. 'You will all walk like prisoners. The Justice will decide what to do with miscreants. You, priest, are a disgrace to your cloth. Have you no shame in perilling souls?' Nonie cowered as the raven turned on the holy man with disdain.

''Tis you, sir,' answered Father Michael bravely, 'who shames our calling with the coldness of your charity. It is many miles to walk to the Justice's lodgings in this bleak weather, a long walk for a child and a widow. In the name of our Lord and His Virgin Mother, be merciful. We must all answer at the Day of Judgement.'

'Silence, priest. This be my parish and I decide how best to humble the proud. The mother must be taught a lesson in humility and the child be shown that all yuletide celebrations are forbidden by law. This lesson she will never forget.' His lips curled into a tight line. Nonie peered out from behind her mother, not understanding the man's words. Her blue eyes filled with tears.

The black crow man looked long and hard at her as if fighting some inner weakness within himself. 'I will show mercy on the maid, but she must first walk five miles for her penance.'

Father Michael turned back, holding his hand up in protest. 'Shame on you. Be wary, man of the cloth, that you do not wander too far from the path . . . I see a cold end for you if you proceed with this business.'

The crow man laughed in his face. 'I take no heed of your devil's words.'

Mother wrapped them warm against the weather but it started to snow again an hour into their journey. Even the thick wrapped cloaks were no match for the swirling storm.

At first Anona set out gaily, thinking this some game, but as the storm blew them in all directions at once, she began to cry out with cold and whimpered under the shelter of her mother's cloak. They took refuge in a barn close to an inn where there was the noise of merriment and ale drinking. Then they were housed as common criminals and she cried for her warm mattress and feather quilt.

'We must make do with straw, tonight. Tomorrow will be a better day,' Mama promised hopefully. 'I will give the guard our fine lace collars to buy us some food. You will soon be on your way homewards to Aunt Hepzi.'

Father Michael looked weary and ill, but slept fitfully by their side, guarding them from rude enquiries and jeers.

Anona sunk into the folds of her cloak, not understanding why the black crow was so angered by a goose roasting. Her hems were sodden with melted snow and there was a stench of dung and hay. Mama tried to shame the constables who escorted them from Bankwell House into helping them. How could they sleep easy knowing how in times past Papa had helped their families? Mama was kind to old Will Carr and kept him in his cottage long after he could not do a day's work.

Thomas Carr kept glancing in their direction.

Nonie watched as Mama fingered the gold ring on her finger, set with seed pearls, the only ring she had left in her jewel box. It was always kept on her left hand. Then she beckoned to Carr in the darkness and held out the ring. 'Miss Anona must go no further on the morrow, five mile or no,' Mama whispered. 'She's but eight years old and feels such hunger and cold. By all that is holy, Thomas Carr, please take her back to my cousin at Wintergill. The ring is yours for your trouble. Do what you must to secure her release, I beg you. It is all I have of value but if you do my bidding I will reward you tenfold.'

He moved forward and nodded and she could see that he was sore tempted by the offer and his own discomfort. "Tis less than four miles back over the moor towards Settle and beyond on the high road. Miss Anona must be safe housed at Wintergill with my kin.' Mama was pleading now, sniffing her daughter's golden curls that frizzed up in the damp air.

'I don't like it here, Mama,' she wept.

'I know, but think about that first yuletide when the Holy Mother laid her baby in a manger for there was no room for them at the inn. Here we are in a stable just like them and you smell like a new-born calf, not of our hearth and home or fresh rosemary water. Father Michael will take care of us,' Mama cried.

That was no comfort, for he was old and sick, but Nonie thought of Jesus in the stable and tried to take heart. They were close enough to the night brazier to glean some warmth for chapped hands and feet. It would be a long night and she was so tired as she lay now strangely at peace with the world in her mother's lap.

'Hold on to hope, little one. When Aunt Hepzi hears what has become of us, she'll noise abroad what this parson has done. Surely the Justice will be lenient, especially if he is in sympathy with the King's lost cause. There are many such hidden in these northern hills. We will not be harmed.'

She watched the goose feathers of snow settling over carts and rooftops, across the courtyard where the sound of a fiddle rent the chill air. How quickly the white covered their muddy tracks. She could not believe that they were come into this sorry state. Surely it was all some terrible nightmare and she would wake up with the curtains of her four-poster bed tightly drawn against the draughts?

Thomas shook them both at first light. 'Mistress Norton, I've found someone who travels northwards with a cart.

He says that they will relay your daughter but only to the inn at the crossroads by the marketplace. She must make her own way from there to Wintergill. It is the best I can do, but no word of this to anyone and I shall say she has slipped away in the night.' The man turned from her in shame, speaking softly. 'I thought that this was but a prank to shock you, mistress, not to lead us all abroad on fearful business in such fierce weather.'

'Thank you, Thomas, I shall not forget your mercy. Wake up, little one, wake . . .' Mama roused her daughter into life. 'Now listen to Mama . . . you will go back with the carter to Settle and make your way to the wise woman's house down the passageway into Kirkgate. Tell Goody Preston, the seamstress, what has happened and ask her to send word to Wintergill. Lodge with her until Mistress Snowden sends for you and wait for me there. Do you hear what I say? Do not venture out on your own. Tell the goodwife I shall pay her for all your care when I return.'

'I don't want to go, Mama,' Nonie cried, suddenly wide awake, shaking her head. 'Don't send me away. I want to stay with you,' she pleaded burying her face in her mother's cloak, but Mama pushed her away roughly.

'I don't understand,' she said, looking at her mother with such sadness. 'Why must I go?'

'Because it is a long journey and I know not where it might end,' came the reply. 'It is I who must answer for my actions and be punished, not you. Be good for Cousin Snowden and do her bidding. I shall return for you as soon as I can. Fare thee well, my treasure . . . Go quickly and God speed.'

'No, Mama, I'll not go!' She clung ever tighter to her skirts but Mama unpeeled her hands and shoved her towards the constable.

'We must not wake the others. Shoo . . . do as your mama

bids. You are all I have left in the world and all that I have of Kit. You must be preserved from the chill and ice on your chest. Be brave like your father in Heaven.' Mama was waving her away as if she didn't care, and her heart was beating like hailstones on glass.

News of Blanche Norton's arrest was carried on the wind of whispers and half-truths through the snowdrifts and over the moor to Hepzi's hearth. Her heart sank at the report.

'How could he take such cruel action? What is to be done?' she cried to Nate, who sucked on his pipe and shook his head.

'It doesn't do to thwart such a man as Bentley. Your cousin has gone too far and stirred his wrath.'

'They say he overturned all the pottage pots and stripped the spit of its roast, turning out all their servants into the snow. Now the village will go hungry. Who else will feed the poor at this time?'

'We'll do what we can but this blasted snow holds us fast in. It's not fit to throw a rat out of the barn in this storm.'

'And my cousin and her child are set adrift in such a wilderness. Lord have mercy, I cannot bear such a thought! I must go to their aid . . . If only I could've warned her in time. I must go now.'

'You will do no such thing. Are you cracked in t'head? They will find shelter until the storm abates. Fret not, the constables will want to preserve their own skins.'

Yuletide passed uneventfully; just a normal Sabbath followed by winter working. There were no unwelcome visitations from the parson because Nathaniel made sure that his farmhands were well fed. Any fiddling and gaming was held well out of earshot of their mistress who, true to her word, passed the holy day in fasting and prayer, feeling guilty that her intention to warn Blanche had been interrupted by snow and busyness. She had been too lax in her duty to her cousin and her child. A farm boy could have gone down to Bankwell on snow shoes, happen. There were no excuses other than the bad weather. Now she couldn't sleep for worrying.

Never for one moment did she think that this parson would carry out his threats in such bad storms. She prayed for her cousin. What if she refused to pay a fine or was sent to prison? Hepzi's thoughts were racing now. 'Have you no word of them yet? This be all my doing. I ought to have sent word and warned her that the parson was intent of making an example of her,' she said, twisting the wool between her fingers, but her spinning thread kept snapping.

'Blanche is her own worst enemy. How many times have you told me such? Fret not . . . 'tis but a storm in a puddle!' Nathaniel stretched out his leather boots to warm his toes by the embers.

The weather continued foul and fierce, with driving snow, sleet and the lashing of gales and rain, which turned the sodden tracks into quagmires. They sent a boy on snow shoes down to Bankwell House to see if the Nortons had returned, but there was little fresh news.

Rumour said they were all sent to York gaol on foot and had perished in a snowstorm. Then it was said they were released and were safe, staying with the Justice, who once was for the Royalist cause.

Then one evening Thomas Carr arrived, cap in hand under cover of darkness to tell his sad tale.

'The old priest died on the journey,' he stuttered. 'He was buried where he perished with no decent offices. Mistress Norton was fined full whack and returns to pick up her child from you.'

'What child?' Hepzi asked, puzzled that he was sent ahead as messenger. A constable was usually above such a menial task, being held high in the district.

'The Norton child was sent back to lodge with Goodwife Preston down the Kirkgate in Settle and to be brought here to you. Is that not so?' He was looking at her as if she knew all of this scheme.

She held up her hands in horror at his words. 'I know naught of this. No one in this past week would venture forth into these hills with a bairn. Nonie is best where she be with the goodwife.' She wiped her brow with relief. ''Tis a consolation to know that leniency has been granted to my kinswoman by the Justice—' She cut off her words. It was never wise to say more than was necessary to a constable.

'You were right, husband. It was but a storm in a puddle.' Yet why did her heart shake with unease?

Nathaniel turned to their visitor. ''Tis pity that it be Christmas or we'd be offering you the wassail bowl, a slice of spice cake and a dish of frumenty for your trouble, but alas, parson's rules must be obeyed, aye?' He winked and guided him out of sight for a jug of warm ale.

'You speak true enough, more's the pity,' answered the constable. 'This be now a meagre season with no brightness to cheer the dark nights. Where's the harm in a bit of Christmas cheer?'

Nathaniel tapped his arm in agreement. 'Our mouths are sealed, Brother Carr. We all know from whence this new Lent doth come . . . from that sobersides in our pulpit. This business with our sister Norton is so petty as to be mean of spirit. What think you?'

'We have had none worse these past few years. The old priest was a kind enough soul. He did not deserve to die by the roadside like a dog. It hath troubled me much,' sighed Tom Carr, looking shamed by his part in the action.

'What of Constable Stickley, is he of the same mind as you?' Hepzi asked softly.

'Robert Stickley serves only one master and that is himself,' Carr replied. 'Will you collect the child or wait for Mistress Norton to do so on her return? She cannot be far behind now.'

'We will send for them straightway and I shall prepare a room for them to rest here awhile after such a bothersome experience,' she nodded, relieved that her worrying was needless.

All's well that ends well, she mused. Blanche had been spared. There was no harm done. Nate was right: she was a fusspot indeed.

She gave no thought to the matter as she spun the wool for the winter weaving, churning the butter, layering dirty linen, cuffs and collars in the buck tub until the following morning, when there was a great rapping at the main door and a voice crying in the wind.

'Hepzibah Snowden! Let me in!'

The kitchen girl went to the door as she was taught, but Blanche Norton stormed in, white of face with cheeks afire, her white hair streaming wildly behind her, her cap awry. 'Where is she? My Nonie . . . Mama has come for her!' she cried around the stairs.

'Where's who? Calm yourself, Cousin.' Hepzi was caught with flour on her face, in her working skirt and mud on the stone flags.

'You have Nonie here with you?' screamed Blanche, breathless with her long uphill walk from Settle.

Hepzi shook her head. 'No, I'm told she bides still with the goodwife in Kirkgate. She's not here. We thought you both abiding there,' she replied, but her heart was thumping. Something was amiss.

'Word was sent for you to collect her. Did you not go?' Blanche insisted, her hands rubbing on her face.

'No, I did not know until but yesterday what had befallen

any of you,' she answered, breathless with fear. 'I thought she was with Mistress Preston.'

Blanche sat on the stairs in a half-fainting swoon, crying and rocking with grief.

'The goodwife knows naught of my baby's arrival and did not clap eyes on her once. Oh, what is happening?' Blanche's composure was breaking down.

Such was her alarm at these ill tidings that Hepzi sent for Nate. He would know what to do and vouchsafe for her actions. 'Truly, Sister, as God is my witness. I knew naught of my part in your plans. Nonie must surely be biding with someone else in the town,' she pleaded, hoping it was so.

'But she was told to bide with Goody Preston, the seamstress, and not to leave the lodgings until you came for her and you did not come?' Blanche was screaming like an animal in pain. 'She must have set out for Wintergill on her own. Oh, tell me this is but some mad dream and I will wake up. Where is Nonie? Why did you not go looking for her?'

Hepzi tried to explain. 'How could I go if I didn't know this was my task? The snow was so bad, no one came to tell me. Don't blame me.'

Nathaniel came and, sensing the trouble, sat down on the steps beside the distraught woman. 'Calm yourself, tell me exactly how this all came about. You sent her back with Thomas Carr then?' he asked, pushing a glass of warm spiced beer in her hand but she pushed it away.

'Thomas came with us partway. It was he who helped me put her on a cart. Nonie cried to stay by my side but it was for the best that we got her back safely, was it not? Did I do right? Oh, tell me,' Blanche wept.

'What was the carter's name, pray?' Nate continued his questioning, trying his best to direct her thoughts.

'I know not,' Blanche confessed. 'But we paid him to

96

return my bairn to the marketplace where it is but a short hop down the street to Goody Preston's dwelling. She has been there many a time before.'

'So you don't know his name. Who vouchsafed for him?' Nate continued, looking up with alarm at his wife as she shuddered that Blanche had given over her child to a stranger.

'Thomas the constable made the arrangement. I gave him my bride ring. It was all I had of value to secure safe passage for my child.' The widow looked so woeful, rocking back and forth in her distress.

'Did this carter say in what direction he was heading? What was his load?' Hepzi patted her cousin's cold fingers, trying to bring some warmth into Blanche's frozen body.

'He was heading for Settle to cross the river and onwards, I expect. Did I do wrong?' Blanche pleaded.

'Was he worthy of trust, this stranger? What did he look like?' Hepzi asked gently, but Blanche shook her head.

'Like any such journeyman in the darkness, wrapped in sacks, but his cart was covered. I trusted his word. He promised to drop her by the inn at the crossroads. She was to make her way to Mistress Preston and then to you. Thomas Carr knew of him. You must have known I would send her here.'

Blanche was looking up with such childlike surprise that her cousin felt a fear in the pit of her stomach.

'But I knew naught,' she insisted. 'That's what I told the constable. There's been much snow and floods. Perhaps she lodges at the inn or some kind soul has taken her in and she waits by a warm hearth. Do not despair.' Her words sounded hollow.

'I should have kept her by my side. Where shall I look for her?' Blanche began to stir from her strange lethargy.

'We will send for the constables and the watchmen,'

Nathaniel butted in to reassure her. 'They will go from house to house in the town and make enquiries. Anona is a sensible maid. She would not walk out in the wild weather. Whatever made you send her from your side?'

'I thought only of her safekeeping. I feared that we might be sent to York and she could not walk sixty miles. I thought I was doing the best for her. Surely I have not caused her more harm?' Blanche was weeping, tears filling her eyes.

'I'm sure not . . .' Hepzi lied. It was days since the child was sent away. Even one day was a long time to be homeless and without shelter. What if . . . Her thoughts were racing ahead with terrible possibilities. 'We must talk to Thomas Carr at once. He will know who the carter was. There will be a search party and we will get down on our knees this minute and pray for her return.'

Blanche paced the flagstones all night and the next morn refused to break fast with them, preferring to be out on horseback with Thomas Carr, who rode disconsolate by her side, blaming himself for the child's disappearance.

Hepzi polished and swept and prayed. Keeping busy was the only cure for this dreadful foreboding. If only they had known that Nonie was coming. Blanche's spur-of-the-moment decision might bring such a dreadful result. If only it had not snowed. If only she had warned her cousin in time. If only this holy parson was not so diligent in his righteousness.

'We cannot sit here and do nothing,' she cried when the thaw began and paths were clear enough to tramp down to Bankwell.

'Now don't go upsetting things,' warned Nate.

'How can you say such when a child is lost because of Parson Bentley? Are you feeble-hearted in this matter? If this were our own child . . . I must go to Blanche.'

Hepzi made her way down to Bankwell House, slithering

along the wood path by the packhorse bridge. Her cousin was pacing the cold rooms distraught.

'There's no news. How could you all conspire against me like this? If only you'd warned me . . . I am fire and ice,' Blanche cried. 'My heart is frozen but my mind is afire with the injustice. 'Tis time to turn tigress and grab by the throat all those who have wronged my cub. I will kill that wicked man!' she screamed, crossing herself in fear at her own murderous words. 'Cousin, I cannot cease from this travail until I find my child. Why is it taking so long?'

'Whisht, Sister, and calm down,' Hepzi answered. 'Let the men go looking, stay awhile by the fireside.'

She tried to comfort her but Blanche shook her head. 'It's all right for you to talk. You haven't lost a child. What do you care? I cannot rest. I will go back to Settle one more time and see if there is news.'

'Not in this storm, I beg you,' her cousin pleaded, but the distraught woman was already through the door. 'Get away from me. This is all your fault.' Hepzibah stared into the snow, sick with fear. Another storm was on the way.

It was cold sitting on the cart, watching the black pony stumbling over the snow. Anona was cold and wet and her tummy was rumbling with hunger. How did she come to be here? She sat quietly hoping that the smelly man wouldn't pinch her with his bony fingers again. If I am very quiet perhaps he will forget I'm here, she thought. How she wished she was with Mama. The old man on the cart kept staring at her so she pulled away from him as far as she could.

It was a narrow lane and the snow was falling. She couldn't see far in the mist. The man on the cart beside her was dressed in sacks with rough leather and fingerless gloves, and his legs were wrapped like bandages. His face was covered with spots like potholes on the track. When he grinned he had only one tooth, and she didn't like those bulging eyes.

Her clothes were heavy with wetness and her cloak gave no comfort. Round her middle her stomacher was stiff like a board, cutting her in two. Covered up as she was, her hair in a tight cap over her ears, she was still cold as ice and her fingers were frozen.

They were clip-clopping along the track but it was getting harder to see ahead, and the steaming old nag stumbled again and snorted. Wet snow was covering their tracks behind them, and she sensed danger. Why was she here alone in the dark with this stranger? We are lost, she thought, and there was menace in the old man's greasy smile. Edging away from him, from the stench of dung, her belly was churning and fear was creeping up her body, freezing her legs and her hands into wood.

On and on they trundled but in the half-light it was getting harder to fathom out where they were heading. She did not know this road. She had never left Bankwell but to go visiting with Mama in Settle and Wintergill.

Then they came to a steep slope and the poor horse slipped, lurching Anona into the ribs of the stranger, who cackled and tried to hug her tight. The nag gathered himself with fright and started to pull harder and harder, skating over the ice, slithering faster and faster, rocking them from side to side down the hill. The old man tried to 'who-oah' the creature, to lash it with his whip, cursing with strange words she couldn't understand.

Clinging for dear life on to the side of the old wooden cart, jolted by the motion, she felt sick. Her throat screamed out with terror at this spinning-top ride, 'Mama! Mama!

Save us!' But there was no one there to help them as the horse shot round the bend into the stone dyke and the cart tipped on its side on top of the man, who screamed in mortal agony.

Anona was flung into the air. It was the carter who took the weight of the wooden wheels on his back. Barrels scattered and rolled like cannons. She landed in the soft snow unharmed, but her head was spinning.

'I want Mama, I want my mama!' she cried into the dawn light. The snow had stopped and she looked down at the man with horror.

'I can't lift the wheel,' she cried out, but no one came. The man looked at her with empty staring eyes and said not another word.

The nag lay on its side, helpless, and she wept icy tears for the poor animal's leg was all twisted. She watched the wheels of the cart turning as if in some daydream. She had to find help. Wrapping the wet cloak around her body, she felt the squelch of dampness in her leather boots, her skirts dragged her down. Was it better to go back up the hill and follow the track home to Mama or to go on while she could?

Perhaps if she kept on walking Mama would be waiting, but she didn't know the way home and tears rolled down her nose. Her heart was beating in her ears and her lips were stinging with cold. If only I can find something I recognise, but these stone walls all looked alike in the snow, she whimpered, knowing she was utterly lost and there was no one there to help her find her way home. Keep on walking, she told herself, be brave like Papa, but it was so cold and windy and her legs were getting tired. She could no longer feel them, or her toes.

The track was getting fainter and narrower and the drifts loomed like mountains. She felt so tired and sleepy. Sitting down to rest for a while to gather her strength, she felt her eyes closing.

It would be daylight soon.

The house was filthy, in need of a good scrub, what with the comings and goings, the wet clothes and the foddering of stock in the bad weather. No news of Anona was good news surely, thought Hepzi, waiting until Nate returned empty-handed once more with a report that the constable could find no trace of the child.

Who shall tell Blanche? she thought. There was no comfort, no consolation and the burden of pain grew each day.

Blanche would take little food or drink. All that was precious to her was now lost. Her mind was tormented; like a fierce creature, sniffing at the slightest scent of news, darting hither and thither like a dog with fleas, hearing sounds no longer there: the tinkling laughter of Nonie at play, singing rhymes and ditties, lullabies, her footsteps echoing down the passageway. She was weary of travelling in circles, spiralling down the hours of each day, aching for the scent of her child.

There were strange apparitions before her eyes, voices echoing around her head. 'She is dead,' one minute; 'Nay, she lives,' the next, icicles of doubt shattering inside her head like shards of broken glass.

There must be no let-up in the search, she decided. I will not abide in this house again until Nonie comes home.

Nonie woke on a straw mattress with the smell of hot gruel under her nose.

'Take this, child, and this'll warm yer bones,' said a gruff voice.

'Where am I?' she asked, looking round at the little hut that smelled of sheep wool and warm dog.

'Shepherd Ackroyd is my name, and the one as found you half dead on the moor. 'Twere lucky I were out wi't dog checking them ewes, when I come across these footprints by the high wall. I were in a gnat's breath of missing you. I thought it were a deer stuck fast at first, and then I saw yon bit of your cloak poking out from a drift. The Lord showed His mercy on thee, lass, for I reckon another few hours and you'd have been for kingdom come. You've slept a whole day and night, so sit up and sup thy broth and tell me thy tale.'

She tried to sit up but the beams were spinning around, and her hand was shaking as she tried to swallow from the bowl. She was lying by the fire wrapped in sheepskins, and her clothes were drying on the hook. There were pots and pans and a smell of salve and grease.

The man was young, with red cheeks, wrapped in a leather jerkin and sheepskin. He sat on a stool listening to her story about the church and Father Michael, the black crow and the march in the snow, the cart turning over. It was all jumbled up in her head but he smiled with interest and she carried on.

'Bankwell is many a mile down from here, lass. I reckon you was going in the wrong direction altogether. 'Twere lucky you stopped when you did. The old wall is high and gave shelter. It has saved many o' my ewes. You never would have made it across the moor on thy own. Where were you heading?' he asked, and she told him about Goodwife Preston and Aunt Hepzi Snowden at Wintergill.

'A've heard of them, right enough. Happen that's the closest place to be dropping you. Yer mam'll be fair worrit when she gets back, poor woman, and all because of a little yuletide feasting, you say,' he sighed, sucking on his pipe, staring into the firelight.

'If it's clear on the morrow,' he continued, 'we can head across wi' dog. I knows a shortcut to Wintergill that'll save a deal of bog-trotting, but first you must rest and eat up until thee is stuffed with broth and oatcakes. You need some rib-sticking stuff in that little belly. Yer nowt but skin and bone,' he laughed, picking up a wooden pipe and playing out a tune.

'We can have a bit of a yule song now, if you like, to while away the time, and if you sup up, I'll happen teach you how to play one yerself,' he promised.

She lay back, warm and safe and full of excitement. Tomorrow she was going home.

'Praise the Lord! I can't believe you're restored to us . . . You fair give us a fright, young lass,' smiled Hepzi with relief at the sight of Anona safe and well.

They had given up hope of any good news when Shepherd Ackroyd turned up with this lost sheep. She sat him down and thanked him, filling him up with pie and sending him on his way with enough cheese and meat to see him through the next few weeks, such was their gratitude.

The child was too exhausted to walk back down to Bankwell, the sky was full of feathers, and Blanche would get the good news as soon as Nate came back from his search. Hepzi could not believe that Nonie had appeared out of nowhere.

'The Lord hath tempered the wind to the shorn lamb, indeed! Let's get some colour back in those cheeks, get you out of them rags and into summat warm. We don't want your mother seeing you like a frozen statue, do we?' She knew she was fussing but her heart was full of joy and relief. 'All's well that ends well, I say,' she smiled, turning to the bairn, but she was curled by the hearth already fast asleep.

This yuletide had been a topsy-turvy ride, she reckoned,

looking out at the blackness. Suddenly she wished everyone was safe under one roof where she could gather them in, feed them and let them all face the coming storm together.

Then she thought of the old parson's death. That was something Blanche would have to tell the child herself. As she barred the door and shutters against the weather, the wind was howling around the stone walls and the draughts blew the rushes across the floor. She would have to face the storm and bring in extra peat from the store, but the force now was so great that she daren't open the door.

Suddenly she felt a fear, alone with a child with a gale ripping at the roof and the trees and snow on the wind. This was not fair. This was not the welcome home she was planning. Nate would have the sense to take shelter in a field barn. Blanche was safe in Bankwell House. Things could be worse, but not much. The wind was whipping the snow into drifts that would cover the back door to the yard. The servants were down in the village and Nate in the fields. The animals would be trapped; the cow and calf, the chickens, the dog. There was nothing she could do, and as for the sheep on the moor, they would probably be buried for days, ripping off their own wool for something to chew. The Lord gives and the Lord takes, she sighed, not understanding the wisdom of the Almighty in sending such a trial on top of all the others.

She could hear the screaming gale and the ice scratching to come inside, whirling familiar shapes into monstrous mountains, into some strange frozen land.

She prayed for the poor shepherd on his way back to his lookout hut, frozen by some wall, and Blanche pacing the floor of her cold house. Keep busy, she said to herself, stuff the wadding under the door and around the shutters. The stone walls are thick. The Lord will protect us. The roof was her fear, the weak bit that had not been repaired. These are not the walls of Jericho, she told herself stoutly. They will stand.

Anona was snoring in her sleep and Hepzi smiled at the innocence of a child who can sleep through this battering and menace, but they must stay warm and dry and well fed. She was on her own now and this was a test of courage and resolve. She would not be found wanting. Blanche must have her bairn restored hale and hearty. That was her duty and Hepzibah Snowden was no shirker.

Blanche could not sleep, treading the stone flags in her agony, watching and waiting for news. She could not idly stand by and let others do the searching. If her child was biding in some refuge then she must be found. It was time to cross the river bridge and make her way first up by the waterfall at Gunnerside Foss and on to Wintergill. That was the safest route in this terrible wind. She would seek company with Hepzibah until there was more news. She could not stay one minute in this empty house. She would not return until she had Nonie by her side once more. She must keep searching.

The leaden clouds did not threaten her in the north-western sky, nor the wind whipping her skirts and cloak around her. She was wrapped in her warmest fur wrap and her feet were leather-bound in servant's boots. She held a sturdy staff to steady her. She needed to be doing something and her cousin might have more news to give her.

There was a track of prints across the icy footbridge, and she strode out at first with purpose, climbing upwards towards the narrow gill that would shelter her from the worst of the weather, leading her up to the foss where Nonie liked to pick primroses and violets in the spring. Come the warmer weather they would rise early and make a votive offering into the water, listen to its bubbling and sit awhile. That was what they would do when they were together again, and the thought gave Blanche courage as the storm rose to greet her.

As she drew closer up the side of the gill she sensed danger, for the water was frozen as it fell and the sides were a sheet of ice sculpted into strange shapes. It was too slippery now even to stand, and she must move further into the woods and the heavy branches of snow; a darkness of whirling snow, as the higher she climbed the worse it was getting.

Soon all was a whirling whiteness, particles of snow scratched her eyelids, stinging her cheeks like whips. She was blinded, breathless, imprisoned by the weight of it on her cloak, but she was not giving up in the confusion of this white world.

There was now no sun or sky, nothing but the faint outline of trees, nothing to guide her but her heart's desire and determination. 'Jesu, Maria, keep me safe,' she cried out.

Then out of the whiteness she stumbled onto something hard and long: the corner end of a high stone wall, and she knew she must have reached the edge of Gunnerside, close to where Nathaniel's land began. Here was the old boundary stone with the strange carvings made by ancient people. She knew where she was.

She was so weary that all she could do was creep slowly, feeling with her stick for the edge of the precious wall. She fingered it with frozen mittens, her arms ached with the effort, and the snow swirled over her ever faster, like a blanket suffocating in its brightness.

Only the lamp burning in her heart forced her ever onwards for she sensed that Nonie was nearby, guiding her onwards. 'I'm coming, little one, I'm coming,' she whispered. As Nonie had suffered so must she, for her foolishness in sending the child with a stranger. It was all her fault, her pride and disobedience, but she would not give in to weakness. There was no going backwards now. 'I'm coming, Nonie. Mama is coming, wait for me!'

Snow came hard on the wind, blinding her from everything, so she kneeled by the wall with clenched fists and hid from its fury like a lost sheep sheltering for cover. I'm coming, she sighed.

Anona woke with a start, suddenly wide awake. 'Mama is coming. I saw her. She's not far away,' she said, but Aunt Hepzibah shook her head.

'Nay, not in this blizzard, lass. Only a mad woman would leave the hearth in such a storm. She is thinking of you,' she answered, but Nonie knew she was coming.

'Shall we open the door for her and put a lantern out to guide her?' she insisted, for she had seen her mama smiling and calling out to her.

'Are you moonstruck? We cannot shift the door for the pile of snow covering us over. 'Tis that what keeps us warm and safe. Come away and we'll keep the fire going. It'll pass soon and then we can find your mother and give her the joy of seeing you in the flesh.'

They scooped up the snow that piled up under the window shutter, clean snow ready to be melted over the dwindling fire. All the fuel was gone but they burned the dried rushes and straw, anything they could find to keep the hearth warm and the air from chilling into icicles.

At first it was fun helping Aunt Hepzi make broth, lying by the hearth, until they had to burn the flock mattresses, for the fire was greedy. But the cold crept ever closer and they wore all the clothes they could find to keep warm. Then Aunt Hepzi's mouth went in a straight line and Nonie was afraid when the stool was put on the fire to burn.

''Twere a pity we had no yule log to burn,' said her aunt

108

with a sigh, 'but we were that obedient to the parson. Wait till I get me hands on him, man o' the cloth or no. This is all his doing. A proper Christmas yule log would have tided us through the whole twelve days, storm or no. It would still be burning and keeping us warm. We must pray to the Lord to deliver us from temptation for I am sore tempted to dance and sing a carol or two to warm my feet and arms.'

Nonie jumped up and tried to pull up her aunt, who was quite pretty when she smiled.

'I know a jig . . . I can do a jig.' Anona hummed a tune.

'Whisht, do you want to bring the wrath of God upon our heads? We must not weaken, but a holy dance with a bit of arm-waving might be deemed an offering of right-eousness, I suppose.' Her aunt rose and shook herself, but their clothes were frozen and stuck out, and there was smoke coming from her breath as they moved.

'You've got dragon's breath,' Anona laughed.

''Tis the zeal of the Lord, Anona, that's all. He shall warm us with His glory. We'll sweep the room, melt more water and throw what we can to feed the fire. When our work is done happen we'll sing a few psalms to warm our breath and spin a little wool,' Aunt Hepzi said. But Anona shook her head. 'But, Aunt, all the wool has gone on the fire,' she reminded the woman.

'Ah, well, happen a dance or two will have to do in its stead.'

I can go no more, Nonie. My eyelids close with the ice but one more footstep, one more aching finger towards the light, one more breath and I can see the lantern in the snow. The sky lifts for I can see stars in the night sky and the moon will rise soon to torch my path. This ancient wall has been my rock, my refuge and my strength. It brings me ever closer. I am so tired, Nonie, but I cannot give in to weakness now . . .

*　　*　　*

Hepzi could feel the stillness outside. The wind had stopped its shouting and there was rain now pitter-pattering on the shutters. It was the rain she feared most after snow and a quick thaw, with all the weight of snow on top of them, but she said nothing to frighten the bairn.

They must not open the door yet, though the child in her fervour was convinced that her mother was close at hand. Much as she herself wanted to see to the creatures frozen and starving in the barn, she knew that the straw and dung would keep them warm and they could peck at the snow. Suddenly she felt so utterly alone, with only common sense and an instinct for danger to guide her.

The snow would insulate them for a time, and with its melting would come rescue. There was water enough to drink and a larder of food, safe provisions that this 'wise virgin', as the Bible story advised, had laid up against such harshness, but it was the blasted roof that worried her. She did not trust the sodden timbers.

'Keep close to the hearth, child, and no more talk of opening doors.' The fire was out and she must think of burning her best ark and box and chair. They supped the elderberry fruit cordial and looked at each other in horror as a huge creaking groan filled the room. 'Into the chimney breast, child,' Hepzibah screamed, grabbing her precious charge. After blizzard and blast, no rotten beam was going to get them if she could help it.

The inglenook, with its stone arch and hollowed fire hole, the little oven, the fancy decoration of carved figures, leaves and suns around its border, must save them now. Now was the test of its craftsmanship as the rafters crumbled in front of them, crashing down snow and wetness, dust choking them, but there was sooty air coming down from the chimney.

'Lord have mercy on us, miserable sinners, our very refuge

and trust in times of trouble. Sing, Anona, sing praise to God who reigns above, the Lord of all creation,' Aunt Hepzi whispered, holding her hand tightly, thinking this test was not how it was meant to be, but she could do no more now but pray. 'Lord, if we survive this deluge I will see to it that Christ's birthday will be for ever honoured in this house in the old way, with merriment and feasting, and the parson can go hang. 'Twas he that hath stirred up Thy wrath by his wilful neglect of goodwill and charity! Have mercy on us . . .'

From the parish records: 12th January 1654
A great drift of snow fell on Wintergill Farm demolishing all but the chimney.

Mistriss Blanche Norton, reliq. of the late Mr Christopher Norton, esq. was found close by the thatch, snow dead.

Hepzibah, Wife of the house, and female were hidden in the chimney and saved.

They buried Blanche's frozen body when the thaw came. It took pickaxes to cut the sod in the churchyard. She was but thirty years in the world. Anona stood speechless for many months, unable to talk of these terrible things, so Hepzi kept her close by while Nate and his men rebuilt the roof that had so nearly killed them. Nonie's presence brought a strange joy to the household and the Lord blessed Hepzi with a quiverful of sons: Samuel, Jacob, Reuben, Silas and Thomas. The farm rang with their noisy doings. Yet she knew they were but dust in the eyes of the Lord, blossoming and flourishing like leaves on the tree.

Then the second King Charles took back his father's throne and ruled the land, and all was as it was before the Commonwealth. Those who had prospered under Cromwell felt the chill wind of change. The candles once hidden decorated the altar of St Oswald's. Christmas was proclaimed as a holy day of feasting. The country folk were glad to welcome the mummers and dancing troupes once more.

Hepzibah could never return to the steepled church, and joined in fellowship with a band of Seekers after Enlightenment who worshipped in barns and houses. She preferred a simpler pathway to eternal truths. Nate was raised up for his fairness and honour and made a constable, despite his wife's new religion. They prospered and Nonie alongside them. It was a joy to teach her spinning and fine threadwork along with a little lettering so she might keep a good household. She was always one for animals and hounds and anything with four legs. She would run after her brothers as if she were a boy for a time until she grew into such a comely maid it was thought only seemly to send her to her uncle Norton near York to be a lady, not a farm girl.

It grieved Hepzi's heart to let her go but she was only a borrowed child. How she prayed that Blanche might know her Nonie was safe in the world and rest in the quiet earth, but there were troublesome tales of maids lost on the hills. It was in the first winter of her demise that Seth, the shepherd who rescued Nonie, was betrothed to a young widow with a little maid. She was out in the fields with him when a stray beast came from a cave and savaged their hound. The girl leaped between them and was bitten so savagely for her kindness that she fell into a fever that no apothecary could heal. She screamed like a beast caught in a poacher's gin. It was a mercy when the Lord took her spirit unto Himself. There was no sighting of the hound ever again and it set Hepzi to wondering if Blanche's fury was in the bite on that poor lass. Only a mother knows how to tear out the heart of another.

It was an ungodly thought to carry within, but much as

it was grieving her heart, there were other accidents and sightings, and Hepzi felt sending Nonie away was right and proper, for once Nonie was removed to a higher plane she would never return.

Anona was in her sixteenth summer when the King was restored. There had been much pestilence but none had trespassed over the high fells to Wintergill. The Snowdens gave her refuge and had prospered. There was a fine slate roof on the stone house and a new stone hearth with a broad inglenook to replace the one that had saved their lives all those years ago.

She was kept busy stitching linen for the baby sons who appeared every year, wearing poor Aunt Hepzi to skin and bone. Now she was to leave the house to serve in her Uncle Bevis's household near York.

'You're a Norton and must be trained up as such so you can marry well as your mama would have wished,' smiled Aunt Hepzi. 'But I shall miss you.'

None of them had ever forgotten the night in the snow or the finding of that poor frozen body so near to rescue, and they wept many a night that they had been parted by that cruel priest. He had left the district in disgrace and now King Charles would appoint one of his own for the village church.

Sometimes Nonie thought she could hear her mama's voice calling out to her and she would spin round, hoping to catch a glimpse of her, but there was nothing, just the crying wind on the fells howling a gale.

As the coach rattled over the muddy tracks, carrying her away from Wintergill, she turned to wave to her dear kin, knowing she might never see them again, and her heart was sinking with fear at what lay ahead. Her hands were coarse and her accent thick but she would not have swapped the Snowdens for any other folk. They were the closest link she had to Mama and to her past.

They were well on the road east when the wind blew the coach and the snowflakes began to flutter. Nonie wrapped her thick cloak around herself, glad of her muff and thick petticoats. There was a manservant and maid sent to bring her safe to her uncle's hall and she was glad of their company when the horses halted, stopped by someone standing in the road.

She peered out of the carriage, seeing a man waving a stick, and feared the worst – a footpad or highwayman set out to rob them. All she had of value was the ring Thomas Carr had given back to her, her mother's bride ring, the one that had saved her from the long walk. She'd fingered it lovingly and he had had the grace to blush as he returned it.

'It were a bad job that night,' he'd muttered, and she'd nodded, knowing what it cost him to admit such a mistake. 'They say her spirit roams abroad for justice . . .'

'I have heard nowt of that,' she snapped, not wanting to learn of such tales. Over the years there had been sightings and goings-on blamed on a wild mountain spirit calling in the wind but she had seen nothing. Now she would make a new life for herself away from such sad memories . . .

'What's the trouble?' she shouted to the coachman.

'Only some old bogtrotter stuck on the moor, wanting a lift to Ripon,' came the reply.

Nonie peered closely at the bent man in tattered rags, stooping, his cheeks sunken with age, waving wildly at them. Then she saw those staring eyes – eyes she would have recognised anywhere in the land. 'Drive on!' she shouted.

'But, miss, there's a storm brewing. The poor soul is but skin and bone and harmless . . . a wandering preacher no less . . .'

She paused for a second. 'I know you . . . Parson Bentley . . . Do you know who I am?'

He stared up at her, shaking his head, a pitiable sight, and for a second her heart softened at the sight of such a broken spirit. 'I'll not treat you as you once treated me and my mother, but if you are to ride with us I first must hear sorrow and regret from your lips that you sent my dear mother and this child out in the snow on Christmas Day. God forgives all sinners who repent . . .'

He stared up again with a flash of recognition in his eyes but his words were shrill. 'I did the Lord's will to a proud lady. I would do it again . . . Vanity, thy name is Woman!' he screeched.

'Drive on!' Anona yelled. 'There is nothing more to say.'

The parson stepped aside, waving his stick into the wind. Months later his body was found on the fell, a bundle of rags, bones picked clean of flesh by the carrion crows.

Vengeance is mine, saith the Lord. I will repay.

Village School

Evie could not believe this was a real school. There was only one big room divided up into work stations and a small room for the infants. There were no PE hall or dinner tables, and they had to put their desks together when the dinner lady arrived. The piano, computers, sinks, library and music shelf were all in the same room too.

She was given a drawer with her name on and a hook in the cloakroom for her anorak. Everyone was staring when she came through the door but then they just got on with what they were doing. The walls of Wintergill Village School were plastered with paintings. There were mobiles hanging from the ceilings and a big red carpet on the floor so the juniors wore slippers. Millicent and Arthur, who were twins, were given badges to be her helpers, showing her where everything was, and her Friend for the Day was Karly, who showed her the playing field, the wildlife garden, and the hopscotch path. There was a pets' corner and herb garden, a fishpond, which was fenced off, and a football pitch where the rough boys played, who called her Posh and Ginger Spice. They threw conkers at her but Karly chased them off and let her join their game in the quiet corner.

Mrs Bannerman was very kind and asked her to read out loud and do some sums. She then took her by the hand

and introduced her to thirty pairs of eyes that made Evie go all hot and fidgety.

'Geneva has come to stay in the village for a few months. She's never lived in the country before but her great-granny once lived in Bankwell,' said Mrs Bannerman. 'She had over two hundred children in her last school so this school will seem very strange. I want you to give her a special Wintergill welcome and be helpful.'

Then she was given a desk drawer on a table with Meg, Sam, Josh, and Thomas, who walked with two silver sticks.

It was all very strange and she wanted to go home but there was so much to stare at and listen to that the hours raced by until it was home time. The little bus carried them back up the hill to the end of the farm track where Mummy was waiting with her car.

This was her third school and they were all different. Sometimes Evie wondered why they couldn't just stay in Sutton Coldfield with Granny. She had cried on that first morning when Mummy left for the car park. What if she didn't come back? Who would pick her up if the car broke down or she was ill? Since Daddy went away she felt very sad inside. If Mummy disappeared who would look after her? Sometimes everything went fuzzy at the edges and she couldn't see properly, but she cried inside so as not to upset Mummy.

She phoned Granny Partridge when she could, just to make sure they were still safe, and told her about the big house and the Lavender Lady, and how they were going to do Christmas in far-off lands at school.

An Indian lady in a long silk dress visited the school and told them about Diwali and the festival of little lights. They painted pictures and made decorations, lit candles and baked some special biscuits. That was great. She liked candles and torches and lights as night-time was scary.

She always had her toadstool lamp on when she went to bed and kept the landing light on all night just in case she had to get up to wee. Sometimes she forgot and there were wet sheets. Then they started another star chart with gold stars for dry nights and if she managed a line of stars she got to choose a video or a book as a reward.

Why did darkness have to come? She would lie awake watching the shadowy lights flicker across the ceiling, the strange shapes dancing on her curtains. Sometimes they looked like bears and tigers waiting to pounce on her bed. Other times they were just pussycats and rabbits.

Every time they moved house there were new creaking stairs and noises outside to scare her. What if bad men were going to come in and rob them? Now Daddy was away, who would stop them getting in?

The Side House was creepy in a different way. There was only the owl hooting and the wind howling, rattling the doors, and then it went quiet and she could hear herself breathing. Sometimes the dog in its kennel woofed and she wondered what he could see in the darkness. Perhaps the Lavender Lady, who could walk through walls, would pop out of the wallpaper and walk all over her.

Mummy gave her tapes to listen to and a little album full of photographs of Daddy when he was young to keep by her bed. If only he would come back and live with them again. Then she would feel safer. She could hardly recall his face or hear his voice on the telephone, but she had a shelf of pretty dolls in costume, one for every visit he made, and tomorrow she would bring the Indian doll to school and the sari he gave her, for the Diwali shelf. Then she remembered they were all packed up in cases somewhere out of reach.

How would Daddy know how to find them when Christmas came? Mummy said he was never coming back but she didn't believe her. He always helped her choose a Christmas tree. They would find the biggest and the best and strap it to the roof of the car. Last Christmas he had forgotten to come and everyone had cried. Granny had a pop-up tree with purple balls. It was not the same but this year she could see Christmas trees everywhere in the wood. She was sure he would not forget to come this year and then they could all go back to Glenwood Close to live. That was the last house she remembered. Then she could go back to her old school. This would have to do for now.

Evie felt a tap on her shoulder and she woke up with her face on the hard desk.

'Wake up, Evie,' whispered Mrs Bannerman gently into her ear. 'Changing schools must be very strange but I'm sure you won't want to miss our story time.'

It was almost home time again. Evie rubbed her eyes and looked up. Everyone was giggling at her. She'd fallen asleep.

In the weeks following their move, Kay gradually got used to having the house to herself when Evie was at school. It had been a hard decision to send her off on the bus each day but Mrs Snowden told her she was doing the right thing. One look at the school's Ofsted report convinced her that the child was in safe hands.

Evie needed friends of her own age and some stability while Kay sorted out her own muddled plans but it was hard to let her go, for she was all she had now and liked to keep her close by.

Some afternoons, though, she could not resist bringing the car down to the village to wait for her outside the school gate like any other mother. She would park up and walk around Wintergill village, admiring the sturdy grey stone houses with iron railings and slate roofs like fish scales. She

119

could see blue smoke spiralling from the chimney tops and the lamps already lit through mullioned windows.

It looked like a picture postcard of a toy village until she noticed how the cars were crammed in the narrow streets, the satellite dishes poking awkwardly from buildings while some cottages were empty.

The village clustered around the ancient church and schoolroom, which nestled under the hill. There was a narrow hump bridge over the beck, which tumbled down from the hillside, dividing the green in two halves. It was like stepping into a James Herriot film. She could almost hear its jaunty music echoing in the background as she admired the date stones over the lintels of many of the cottages.

She made for the little post office-cum-shop, dry cleaners, video store, bank and tuck shop, knowing Evie would pester for the penny tray if she did not buy some ammunition. The window was plastered with posters and information for the vanishing tourists and holiday lets, church time-tables, bus routes and village activities. 'Annual Charity Quiz Night!' 'An Auction of Promises with a Jacob's Join Supper.' 'A Rummage Sale.' 'Claiming Dates for the Christingle and Lighting of the Tree.' It all sounded Greek to her.

Yet she sensed a secret life going on behind these doors that as a visitor she knew nothing about: prayer groups, coffee mornings, reading circles, sewing clubs, local studies, dinner parties and drinks dos. The posters showed there was life in this village.

I'm just passing through, she thought, marking time, putting off the moment when I must step back into life and make my own decisions. Looking in through the cottage windows, she envied the settled lives inside that had a routine and purpose when she had none. Never had she felt more an offcomer and stranger than when standing at the school gate, knowing no one to talk to.

Pat Bannerman had rung earlier to suggest that they have a chat about Evie. Kay felt nervous all day, anticipating the worst, but the Head tactfully suggested that Evie must do her reading practice at home. Her maths was strong for her age but her reading was weak. She wondered if the frequent moves had disrupted the child's concentration and enquired if her father visited at all. Kay recounted their circumstances and instantly the teacher softened, explaining that Evie's grief was taking its toll.

To her surprise Kay found herself spilling out all her concerns about Evie's unwillingness to accept her daddy's death, her own helplessness on the subject and the real reason for this move.

'What goes on in a child's head after such a tragedy is a mystery but we can guess at some of the confusion, Mrs Partridge,' the teacher answered, and Kay warmed to her sensitivity.

'What would you suggest?' Kay said, desperate for advice, but the teacher shook her head.

'Our psychologist might be able to help but by the time we set up some sessions you will be long gone. Be honest with her and let her talk. I'm sure you're doing the right things . . . Now I'm aware of this . . . I presumed you were divorced.' She smiled, pausing, 'Like myself. It must be hard.'

Kay sighed and shrugged. 'It's like jumping into a no man's land. One minute it's all happy families and then wham! You are out in the cold, aren't you? There's no choice for me about separation or singlehood. People do look at you so differently when you are widowed. I think they expect you to be some saintly martyr, set apart by your grief and loss. No one sees the flesh and blood seething underneath, just longing to be loved and normal again. The world is full of couples and you feel an outsider . . . I'm sorry,' she croaked, finding herself crying, but Pat was listening and nodding, encouraging her to go on.

'I felt like a widow long before he died, if I'm honest . . . Work came first for Tim and family second. It took me a while to realise that. I tried not to resent it but things were not great between us. I was a company wife, constantly moving from city to city as Tim climbed the corporate ladder. I gave up my career as an accountant when Evie came along,' Kay confessed. 'You wouldn't think I once held down a senior post in Birmingham with Price Waterhouse, the accountancy firm, and now my brain feels like mush. Now I just feel a freak of fortune with no confidence in anything much, and Evie senses my weakness and holds all her confusion into herself. It's not fair on her.' She could feel tears welling up again.

'Why am I saying all this? I feel such a wimp. I ought to be out there earning my own living . . . not mooching around feeling sorry for myself.'

'It sounds to me as if you need some time to sort out your priorities,' said Pat. 'Look after your own needs and she will follow your model. When I came up here with my son, I felt so guilty about disrupting his world but kids are adaptable. He soon made his own life up here. Don't be so hard on yourself.

'Evie is bright and sensitive, if a little withdrawn and dreamy, but that will pass, given time and encouragement,' Pat smiled. 'And it sounds to me as if you are just the person we need on the team for the quiz night at the Spread Eagle. It's the annual charity quiz night in aid of farmers' charities. The PTA want to field a decent team. Would you consider it?'

Kay looked up in horror. 'I don't want to let you all down. I'm no Carol Vorderman. I'm not sure. Thanks, but it's ages since I've been out in my own right . . .' She looked up and saw the teacher smiling.

122

'So? Isn't that what you've just been talking about? Perhaps a night out on your own might help. You'll get to know some of the other mothers and I can promise you a good pie-and-peas supper with the best pastry in the district. Think about it.'

As Evie chattered in the car as they climbed the now familiar hill up to Side House, she was mulling over this unexpected invitation. Why all this soul-searching over a pub quiz? Surely she deserved a night out, and Mrs Snowden had hinted that she would always baby-sit if given enough notice.

Could she leave Evie? Would it be fair? Why was she always dithering over the simplest task these days? It was pathetic. There you go again, she smiled. Pat Bannerman is right. You are so hard on yourself. This time last year, she would not have thought twice about such an evening out. This time last year was another world. Now she was slowly creeping towards the final milestone of this bereavement year: their wedding anniversary in June, Tim's birthday in August, the move from Glenwood Close, and now the first anniversary of his death was looming. How would she cope?

Looking out over the bleak landscape to where the white walls of Wintergill House flashed brightly, set like a pearl on an emerald cushion, she laughed at her overblown image. You followed a dream, took a chance and found this lovely place, she argued silently. Surely you can take a night out with strangers in your stride?

No one here knew her past history or cared. They were too busy struggling to survive their own miseries. Why shouldn't she go?

Evie was on a greenery hunt in the wood by Wintergill Farm with Mummy trailing behind in a bad mood. There was a letter from Nanny Partridge that had her on the phone all morning and now they weren't going shopping but going out for a walk instead. Mummy was angry and said walks were better for them and muttered on about Santa being hard up this year. She always said that, but somehow Evie sensed she meant it this time.

They were gathering leaves and branches to make into an Advent wreath with special wire. Mrs Snowden was going to show her how to make one when she went to tea again. She liked visiting the old lady with her frizzy hair. She had the biggest hands, but her legs were thin and she sat down a lot. She was coming to baby-sit for Mummy when she went out with Mrs Bannerman, her teacher. They were going to do some knitting.

There was lots of dark holly but few branches with red berries on, and lots of ivy dripping over the stone walls. Evie was determined to collect a sackful. Mummy laughed when Mrs Snowden said it was 'trim-up time' but they had been learning all about Christmas customs when they sat on the rug in the school library corner, and she knew just what branches they should bring into the house and which were unlucky.

Mrs Bannerman said soon it will be the shortest day of the year when the sun hid from the earth and people used to light fires to welcome it back again. Evie knew about mistletoe and rosemary, and how Mary laid her purple cloak on a rosemary bush and stained the leaves for ever.

They were going to do a play about the trees of the forest. Mummy promised her a real one this year, growing in a pot. Evie wanted to choose one with Daddy from the wood but Mummy went red and said he couldn't come any more because he was in Heaven now.

Mr Grumpy showed them where to walk down steps cut into the rock alongside a stream that led into Bankwell village.

It was dark and slippery in the wood when he waved them off shouting, 'What goes down must come up!' which was a silly thing to say. He spent all his time out in the fields, building up the walls, and didn't smile much. Mummy kept saying he'd lost all his sheep and cattle in the summer and was very sad. They were not allowed to walk across the fields but skirt around the edges, down narrow green paths with high walls.

'Slow down . . . Don't slip!' yelled Mummy, but Evie darted down the steps searching for her leaves. They wandered down to Bankwell village over the humpy stone bridge . 'I used to play here when I was your age,' she smiled, pointing to the stream. 'It doesn't look much now but when it rains and swells up it's so dangerous.'

It was here she glimpsed the white-haired lady in the ragged cloak again, drifting over the field on the other side, and Evie waved her branches in the air to greet her. The lady was staring into the air and when Evie blinked, she vanished, just like before.

There was no point in telling Mummy. No one believed her and now there was nothing to see.

She would put it all in her special drawing book and make up stories about the Lavender Lady and the White Lady in the woods. Sometimes she thought she heard her whispering, 'Come with me and play,' or something like that. Grown-ups didn't believe in fairies, and the strange ladies weren't ghosts like in *Ghostbusters*. They were nice ladies who popped up just when she'd forgotten about them. She turned to the riverbank, hoping the White Lady would appear again. Perhaps she was trimming up for her own Christmas, and Evie wondered where she lived. Did ghosts like her have proper homes?

I stare up with yearning eyes at the craggy path that leads to Wintergill. The child is waving from across the water, but I have no strength to cross the water to reach her. The river has always divided Bankwell from Wintergill as Hepzibah separates me from my child.

It is time for the gathering-in of the green boughs, for the killing of geese and swine for all the yuletide preparations to begin. But why is my heart so burdened by such a once joyous task? I have decked my hall with garlands and wreaths; so many yuletides have come and gone and still she does not return to me. This season rolls again like dusty cartwheels along a well-rutted track, turning, turning over and over the same ground. I will keep my vigil for the twelve days of Christ's Mass once more, no matter what that silly priest says . . .

Quiz Night

Kay was looking forward to the quiz night, 'The Turkey Special' at the Spread Eagle. She turned to Evie, who was glued to their laptop screen, unsure if she should be going out. 'Do you mind if Mrs Snowden sits in with you? I can stay if you like . . .'

'Brill!' she answered. 'She'll let me stay up late.'

It had taken some persuading to get Nora Snowden to sit in. For some reason she was reluctant to take responsibility. 'I'd never forgive myself if anything happened while you were out . . . It's a long time since I did that sort of thing . . . but if you're sure you can risk it . . .'

'I'm only down the hill in Wintergill. She'll be no trouble and you can phone my mobile . . .'

Now she was in a flurry of indecision about whether to go or what she should wear. Definitely casual, but Midlands casual seemed country smart, she'd observed. It was only the village pub, not some city tapas bar. It would be smoky and draughty: perhaps her long skirt with a cashmere sweater would do the trick?

She came downstairs with a flourish, and Evie looked up.

'You're not going like that!'

Kay trooped upstairs to try on her black leather trousers and mini top. They were too tight and too suggestive and chilly round the middle. Out came the cords and chunky knit. She peered in the mirror, hoping for a miracle, for her hair needed a trim and her tummy was missing the gym. This was a little too casual. After flinging everything on in her wardrobe she settled for a quick shower and blowdry, a three-quarter-sleeved olive-green sweater and her black leather trousers with a long waistcoat to hide her lumpy bits. She piled her hair up and splayed out the ends and lacquered them to cardboard. This was her first night out solo. She was, after all, only a visitor, a tourist, and she could dress up how the hell she liked. She was nervous about leaving Evie, though.

It felt like an honour to be asked to step into the school team as if she belonged. She knew that quiz teams took their game seriously and they'd be out to win. She went downstairs once more, and this time Evie nodded approval.

'You'll do,' said Evie, rushing to answer the doorbell to see what Mrs Snowden had brought. 'Can we play Scrabble?' she asked but the baby-sitter smiled.

'Perhaps later, but I've brought you something to knit without needles,' she replied, producing a bobbin reel with nails in the top and some balls of wool. Kay hadn't seen corkscrew knitting for years and it took her back to her own Granny Norton. She relaxed, knowing Evie was in safe hands.

'You know I do recall your gran, Betty Norton. She was always very crafty with her hands . . . You do know they were once gentry . . . Bankwell House was theirs. It's a residential home now, the last bus stop before St Peter's Gate!' Mrs Snowden laughed.

'There was nothing gentrified about my granny's cottage: outside loo, two up two down. We only visited in the summer but I thought I might do some ancestry research on the Norton family.'

'Sir Kit Norton fought with the Royalists. The Snowdens

were for Cromwell. The History Group did an exhibition on the Civil War a year or two back. The house went to rack and ruin for a while, split up into smaller bits. There'll be stuff in the library to help you,' Mrs Snowden offered. 'But it's time you were making tracks, young lady.'

'Wish me luck,' Kay shouted, banging the door behind her. It was a clear night with a moon rising up across the moors. This time last year they had been packing up the house and settling into Tim's parents' house for Christmas and New Year. Life was all mapped, and then suddenly nothing was the same. Now she felt guilty to be driving towards the twinkling fairy lights of the Spread Eagle for an evening among strangers. How could she be enjoying herself when Tim was dead? She drew up the car, ready to turn around, but some stubborn part of herself made her drive on.

The Spread Eagle was an ancient hostelry untouched by brewery design teams. Its low black beams were smoked, not painted, the fire was red with coal heat, not imitation logs; the brassware was gleaming with polish, not dipped to a dull gold. There were photos in frames of ancient darts teams and batsmen: reminders that the pub was still the heart of any decent village. The Christmas decorations glistened worthy of a Chinese New Year party and the crush was noisy, beery and full of the thick flat vowels Kay was beginning to remember.

There was a bigger turnout than usual for the annual quiz; all the competitors determined to win themselves some Christmas goodies. Pat explained that this was not the usual pub quiz rules but a knockout competition with a Christmas theme. She pointed out regular rival teams from other villages, teachers from the public school, the local bank and the Women's Forum. There was a team from the golf club and the Young Farmers, and the proceeds would go to the Dales Recovery Fund.

Kay bought herself a lime soda, for she still found the local beer so heavy that it sent her to sleep and she needed all her wits about her to compete alongside the likes of Pat Bannerman.

It was at the bar she bumped into Nik Snowden. She hardly recognised him, he looked so smart. Gone were the grubby overalls, wellies and flat cap. In their place was a whiff of expensive aftershave, a tweed jacket and cavalry twills: well-cut and distinguished, the traditional garb of the country landowner. He looked up with surprise at her arrival.

'Didn't expect to see you here, Mrs Partridge,' he smiled.

'Why not?' she answered. 'I'm filling in with the PTA.'

'The brainbox team, is it? Us Yokels'll have to be on our mettle then,' he quipped, turning towards his own team sitting in the opposite corner.

She saw him eyeing her up with care. She was glad she wore her leathers and boots and a good coat of make-up. He was not the only one who paid for dressing.

Evie was having a wonderful time bobbin knitting, lifting the wool over the nails to make snakes of round coils while Mrs Snowden was busy counting stitches and clacking her needles. Evie had never seen anyone knit so fast. In fact, she hadn't seen anyone knitting before. She thought that jumpers were made by machines, not by old ladies who could talk, knit and watch television all at the same time. Mrs Snowden was making sleeves out of fine navy-blue wool and there was a swirly pattern of cream wool all mixed in.

'Is that a Christmas present?' Evie asked, knowing that Santa didn't come for old people. They had to give each other presents.

'I suppose so,' she replied. 'It's for me, if I can find the time to finish it. What do you think?' She held up the knitting for Evie to inspect.

'It's very big,' said Evie. It looked like a blanket.

'We're built big up here,' Mrs Snowden laughed. 'How's your knitting growing?'

Evie showed her the coil of coloured stripes. 'What do I do with it now?'

'The possibilities are endless,' said this new teacher. 'You can coil it into a mat or a tea cosy or make it into a beret or a scarf for one of your dollies.'

'I don't have dollies,' said Evie. 'Only Barbies, and they come with their own clothes.' She pointed to a basketful of tiny outfits.

'They look like stick insects to me . . . When I were little we had real dolls and prams to push them in, and we made little houses for them too.'

'Did Shirley have a doll's house?'

Mrs Snowden shook her head sadly. 'It was after the war and there weren't many toys, but she had a special one for Christmas once.'

'Can I see it?' Evie was curious for whenever she asked about her, Mrs Snowden's voice went all far away and whispery.

'I don't rightly know where it is now. It was such a long time ago when the Germans came to stay. We called it the Christmas House after that . . . Look – you're dropping stitches. Give it here or it'll all run!'

Nora could feel her heart missing beats all over the show at the thought of the Christmas House and the memories she was stirring up. How could she explain to this mite what a time that was? Each year as Christmas approached she could feel the memories flooding over her again: those happier far-off days when Shirley was little.

131

They played cards for a while but Nora couldn't concentrate and was glad when it was time for 'the up them stairs game'. She tucked Evie under the duvet with her knitting clutched tightly by her side.

It was strange how as she came down the stairs of the old barn she felt memories closing in on her. How could something that happened so long ago still have power to warm her stubborn heart? It was a time when winters were real corkers and went on for months, when railways ran to schedule and there were two deliveries of post each day in a world where men and women occupied separate worlds, despite two world wars, a time when Wintergill was accessible only down a dirt track. Cart horses were the mainstay of the farm and tractors were newfangled luxuries. Milk was ladled out of the can and the water had to be pumped from the artesian well: a time before television ruled the world. A battery wireless was their only connection to the outside world.

It was a time when a farmer's wife laid up food as if for a siege just in case winter would squeeze them with an iron fist, and kept a pigeon in her basket when she travelled abroad to send news of her safe arrival. Sometimes she longed for that black-and-white world, when everyone thought they knew right from wrong and you were either Church or Chapel. The war was over and won but the peace was drab and rationed, everything was worn out and hard to replace. Farm labour was scarce, men were still being demobbed and the only glamour came from the film shows in the local picture house.

How innocent we were, she mused, as she stoked the fire, content with homespun delights, nights around a piano, dances in the village halls. What would the child upstairs make of that old-fashioned world?

Nora caught a glimpse of her face in the mirror with a

sigh. It was a weathered, Dales-bred face with pink veins streaked across her cheeks: a faded careworn face that once was flushed with lust for life. How did I get to be this old? she sighed.

You were not always so staid and homely, Lenora Snowden, trussed up in your corsets and thermals. There was a time when passion brought colour to your cheeks when the Christmas House was brought to Wintergill. Love came rushing in like a whirlwind swirling you up in its grasp. Only the Christmas House knows your secret, and wooden walls can't tell tales.

She smiled, dreaming about those never-forgotten days when she was young and firm in face and body, when she could run upstairs two at a time and think nothing of it. Those were the days, her heart fluttered.

If only I'd known just what a price I must pay for such goings-on . . .

Nik left the Spread Eagle to its Christmas quiz. He was in no mood to join in his team. He always found his birthday depressing, just a card from his mother and bottle of single malt. Who wanted reminding they were in their fourth decade and creeping towards a half-century?

His team was no match for Pat Bannerman's table, with their quick-as-a-flash answers. The quiz was up to the usual standard but he could not concentrate since that session with his financial advisor in the morning. He wanted a clear head to think through the projected figures.

What did he care what Swedish saint was celebrated on 13 December? How did he know which was the busiest airport in Germany?

He was in no mood to get stuck in answering these questions when Jim's face kept staring over the bar at him. Jim was a great one for a quiz night, and without his friend

Nik's beer felt flat. The Yokels were struggling and Nik couldn't be bothered to join in now.

'It feels like doing A levels and pulling a tooth all in one go,' he muttered to the barman as he sipped the dregs of his glass. 'Let the brain boxes get on with it.'

'And you can't phone a friend or ask the audience, either,' the barman quipped, referring to the popular quiz show on TV. 'Not like you to leave us sober,' seeing Nik rise and make for the door.

Nik waved his hand, listening to the other questions as he walked out of the door.

'Spell Wenceslas of Czechoslovakia.' 'Who wrote the poem . . .?' 'Name three ingredients in Stollen.'

The windscreen was crusted over with frost and the sky was clear. He felt like Billy No-Mates, envious that the Partridge woman was obviously enjoying herself with her new cronies.

Not a bad looker, he had to admit, with quite a figure on her. She seemed a one-woman answering machine when she got going. It was not as if he was a total ignoramus. He was always good on musical questions. The composer of 'Silent Night' and 'The Ceremony of Carols' was no problem, or the lyrics of the *Messiah*. A Sunday school education came in useful when it came to the Bible questions but all that twaddle about the names of the reindeer on Santa's sleigh . . . He was in no mood for showing his ignorance before a bunch of schoolteachers.

It was just a village pub quiz, not an aptitude test for Mensa membership. Nik felt the chill in the air. What a sad tosser you are, he snapped at himself, fumbling for his key.

The sooner this Christmas was over the better. Then he could look forward to restocking the farm, reshaping his business, rethinking his position.

The road was well gritted as he cornered the bends up to Wintergill. He knew each bend personally, where the walls curved and bulged. He zigzagged his way home, the radio blaring to drown out his bad mood and he banged his hands on the steering wheel in time to the music. Then out of nowhere he saw the misty figure of a woman standing in the middle of the road, an old bag lady, by the look of it, and he stood no chance of avoiding her. Screeching to a halt, slithering on the bend, skidding into the stone wall, he ground to a halt. Then there was nothing but night mist swirling round the pickup.

He was stunned for a second, winded with panic as the truck lurched and crumpled under the impact. His heart was racing at the enormity of what he had done. A wave of nausea flooded over him and yet he knew he was stone-cold sober. Two pints, that was all, not his usual four. And he'd had a pie-and-peas supper.

His first instinct was to leg it over the field as far as possible from the scene of his crime like a delinquent, to hide from the consequences of his careless driving. If only he'd been going slower. There was an old biddy crushed under his wheels and he was over the limit. His future loomed up before him, banned from driving. How the hell could he survive without transport? Was there no end to this horrible year?

Nik found himself shaking with shame at his tears of self-pity and cowardice. There would be no witnesses if he scarpered, but the body underneath would tell its own tale. Nobody could have survived that impact. He could see her white face and staring eyes like fires in his headlights, the hand raised up to defend herself. What the hell was she doing alone in the dark at this hour?

Nik extracted himself from the wreckage slowly. He must do something, not sit feeling sorry for himself. His legs were like lead. His body was shivering from shock, cold and fear. He hadn't even a battery in his torch to search underneath. The worst must be faced and he steeled himself for bloodied, severed limbs or worse. He wanted to flee from the carnage but his legs were rooted to the spot and he bent over, vomiting his supper onto the verge.

He kneeled down to examine under the wheels. She must be dead, for there wasn't a sound. He grovelled on his stomach, holding out his trembling hand to touch her but she wasn't within his grasp. Perhaps the body was tossed into the air and landed across the road or over the wall. His eyes were getting used to the darkness. There was just enough moon to inch his way slowly across the road, calling softly, hoping against hope that she was still breathing. There was no sign of a body.

How could she have the strength to crawl out of the wreckage?

It was not possible that she had escaped injury but there was no one under his wheels or in the road or over the wall. She couldn't have walked far after such an impact. He called over and over into the black night, but nothing responded and he sat back in his car exhausted.

Is this some terrible nightmare and I'll wake up in my bed with a hangover? he prayed. The pickup was crumpled and not safe to drive. He'd bashed his head, his nose was bleeding and he could taste blood at the back of his nostrils. That was real enough. He had seen the white hair streaming behind her. He had seen her standing in the road.

Suddenly exhaustion overtook him and a sickening feeling that he knew that face of old, hiding behind the trees in the copse. There was not one bit of evidence that she was real. The old hag had played a trick on him again.

It was all some strange mirage. He felt the relief seeping into his limbs and his head was spinning. Why was she doing this to him? Who was she? Why me? he muttered. Why? Why? He could feel his eyelids closing.

Oblivion was beckoning until a tapping on the window and a voice was shouting from a far-off place.

'Mr Snowden . . . Nik! Wake up . . . Are you all right?'

There was a flurry of movement that stirred him from his strange dreaming. The door was open, a hand was on his arm and he jumped. He stared at the pair of grey-green eyes searching his face.

'It's only me, Kay Partridge . . . You look as if you've seen a ghost. What happened?'

What could he say? I saw the white lady of Wintergill and ran her over. She follows me but I know she's not real? Nik gulped.

'Would you believe it, a badger shot across the road. I thought it was a sheepdog and swerved into the wall. I'll try and get her started,' seemed a reasonable reply.

'Just get in my car and I'll drive you home. The van can stay there for the AA or someone in the morning. You need checking over.'

'I'll be fine. I can walk,' he answered, seeing the concern on her face.

'Don't be pig-headed. You've had an accident and you may be concussed,' she was insisting, and he hadn't the energy to argue.

'I've got to get this pickup on the road. I've got an appointment in Skipton tomorrow. I must go,' he could hear himself wittering.

'Stuff the appointment. It can wait. I can take you there myself, if needs be. It's about time I faced the Christmas shopping. Get in,' the woman insisted, and for once he was in no position to argue. He was so tired he could hardly move. By the time they reached Wintergill farmhouse he was asleep. He was woken up brusquely, blinking at the light.

'Good, at least you're not unconscious. Sweet tea and bed,' she ordered, but he was in no state to protest. 'I'll put the kettle on.'

'Are you always this bossy?' he muttered in feeble protest.

'Only when a man is being stubborn. You don't fool around with concussion. You're as white as a sheet.' She marched him into his kitchen and yanked the kettle to boil on the Aga. Nik was ashamed of the mess, the grubby dishcloth and towel. 'I'll be fine. It's only a scratch . . .'

'That's what they said about Tim when he crashed on the motorway . . . only a bang on the head. He got out of the car and walked around, trying to phone. Then he collapsed . . . no warning . . . gone . . .'

'Your husband?

'On Christmas Eve last year.'

'I'm sorry. I didn't know.'

'Didn't your mother say anything?'

'We don't talk much . . . I'm sorry.'

'You weren't to know.' He could see she was close to tears.

'That's why you've come up here then?'

She nodded. 'To get away from Christmas, sort of. But with Evie . . .'

'Not easy, is it?'

'You didn't stay for the quiz.'

'Too many memories in the pub tonight. My old school mate Jim ended it all with a gun just before you came. I didn't know how bad he was feeling. I could have done something.' Nik felt the sadness wash over him.

'You're not to blame.'

'That's what they all say, but you can't help wondering, if only . . .'

'I'm sorry. Sounds like 2001's been a rotten year all round. Drink your tea,' she ordered, flashing her green eyes.

'It's too sweet.'

'It needs to be, for shock, and then off to bed, but if you feel sick at all . . . I can run you to Airedale Hospital.'

'Good night, nurse, and thanks!' For once he meant it.

Nora Snowden looked up from her knitting. 'Had a nice evening?'

'Fine, thanks.' Kay was too tired for a post mortem but she knew she must break the news of Nik's accident.

'Did you win, Mrs Partridge?'

'No, we came joint second because I fluffed the last question, if you must know.' She was dying for a cup of camomile and honey. 'Please call me Kay. Everyone else does.'

'Did my son behave himself? He can be a bore in the boozer, especially when it's his birthday,' said Nora with a wink as she gathered up the bits of her jumper into a basket.

'Oh, I wish I'd known it was his birthday. I'd have bought him a drink.'

'He drinks too much as it is,' said his mother.

'Actually, there's been a bit of an accident with his pickup. He's fine, just a little shaken, but he may need looking at once or twice in case he's concussed,' she replied, seizing the moment.

The old woman put down her knitting with a sigh. 'He's a law unto himself. His drinking and driving's got worse lately. Serve him right if he'd been caught. I don't know what gets into him. I've no sympathy. I suppose the pickup's a write-off?' Nora snapped her glasses case shut.

'Oh, no! It was just an accident on the icy road. I don't think he'd drunk much and he left early. I really think you should keep an eye on him,' she insisted, surprised at the hardness in his mother's voice.

'If you say so,' came the curt reply.

'Has Evie behaved herself?' Kay asked, changing the subject swiftly. 'It seemed strange going out without her.'

'She's that sharp she'll cut herself.' The old lady's eyes softened. 'Had me rooting in my memory box. No trouble at all and a credit to you. Anytime you want me to sit . . .' she was offering.

'I don't think I'll be going out again,' Kay replied with a laugh, but her laughter was hollow.

As she lay in bed, unable to wind down, all those Christmassy questions were going round in her head. When the evening came to an end she was almost last in the car park, reluctant to go home. She'd enjoyed being part of a team. It was so long since she had been out with a group of women. How easy it is to feel a stranger in a crowd, she thought, when you don't know the gossip or the people around you, and they know little about you. She felt such a town mouse, a creature from a different planet, and yet she didn't like feeling an outsider. She was stuck somewhere in the middle, trying to fit in, but conscious she was trying too hard.

Then there was Nik Snowden, another puzzle. Why was his mother so unconcerned for his welfare, and why was she, Kay, even bothering to try to understand the two of them? It was none of her business how they bickered at each other.

Other people's families were always a mystery to the onlooker. She'd be going back south in a few months and this would all be just an episode in this strange year of her life. She lay on her back and tried out her deep-breathing routine, in . . . two, three, four . . . hold . . . out, two, three, four, and then Tim's face kept hovering in and out of focus in a mist above her eyelids. Just talking about the accident brought it all back and how furious she'd been when she knew he was late as usual. He was so unreliable. Somehow their frequent arguments had made his death all the worse and the recovery so painful. Living with his parents had been so difficult. They wanted to make an idol of him, turn him into somebody she didn't recognise. He'd always been letting her down. He hadn't meant it but he was so driven, and what good had it done any of them? Now her eyes were filled with that look on Nik Snowden's face, the hurt look of a little boy lost, so strangely appealing. Why was she thinking of him and not her husband?

Nora made her way up the wooden stairs to check on her son. She could hear his snores rasping through the door and sensed all was well enough. We're a funny lot, she sighed. Showing affection to each other was difficult and she always put it down to the hard life they'd lived.

Her eyes caught the framed sampler on the corner of the wall, a beautiful piece of stitch craft attributed to one of their ancestors in the time of Joss Snowden.

Snowdens might be simple country folk, she smiled, but when they set their hearts on something or someone, nothing was allowed to stay their path. She ran her finger over the gilt frame and saw the black dust and sighed. Everything has its price, especially in matters of the heart . . .

She smiled, thinking how she was warming to Evie, and teaching the girl to knit brought back such memories . . . *Don't go there, old girl. If you want to sleep just put all that old stuff out of your mind.*

How she longed for grandchildren by the hearth, but it was just not going to happen now, more's the pity. It wouldn't be hard for her to make a better stab at being a grandma than she had as a mother. Nik would testify to that if asked. She'd made nothing of his birthday; just a card and a bottle of malt.

Nora stared at the sampler more closely and sighed, seeing the name embroidered so neatly: Susannah Snowden. Every family had its secrets and legends, and this one was no exception. There were rumours that the family once owned a famous painting, a Constable or Turner or some such. Joss Snowden made a fine extension to the old house and it was a pity it'd come to this sorry state of neglect, but the family needed a thick wallet to keep the buildings in good repair. Upland farmers had not exactly had the best of times lately.

Nik's office had once been an elegant morning room in the old days but now wasn't a pretty sight to behold; crammed full of files and boxes. His computer took up all of the table – printer, manuals, stacks of mail and catalogues; the usual clutter of a busy life. He'd been glued to the damn thing for months, a lifeline and link to the outside world in the months when they had to be barricaded in like victims of the plague.

The fire grate was stuffed with his tobacco pouches and beer cans. He was in danger of letting himself go but the presence of an attractive woman around the place might buck him up a little. She knew he was worried about their finances and if she asked he bit her head off. It was a good job they lived back to back. Why did they not get on?

Come on, it's late. Don't go wittering on. Some things are better left unsaid, she sighed as she shut her door. 'Sufficient unto the day is the evil thereof' said the Good Book. Who knew what tomorrow might bring?

The moonlit track across the moor is slippery and coldness chills. There are lights and noises, and a horseless carriage tears through my path like a storm battering a windowpane.

Where am I . . . why do I wander so far and for so long? The darkness deepens but I must not stop to ponder on such matters when I have a child to find.

There is a maid asleep nearby who will guide me to my

Nonie. Children open the doors that others do not see; the maid who gathers greenery by the riverbank. She will light my path.

I cannot bear to see mothers with daughters. It hurts my eyes, pierces my heart with such anguish of soul. I have to step between them again, to save them from the sorrows that have bowed my spirit. They must be parted so the child can help me in my search. It is for the best . . .

A Stormy Forecast

'The figures are not looking good, Mr Snowden,' said the young accountant from behind his oak desk. It was their quarterly review of the farm accounts. 'I know you can't trade yet, but there's the compensation, the grants and rate rebates, they'll help to close up this gap. These recent cash injections are not going to cover your shortfall or your previous overdraft, however.' The warning was clear. 'Remember, you need provision for a pension fund.'

Nik sat glumly looking out of the window, wishing he was working on a stretch of walling. True to her word Kay Partridge had driven him down to Skipton, dumping him in the town centre while she got on with her own shopping. His pickup was towed away for an insurance estimate and repair. He felt legless without his own transport. His mother refused to give up her runabout to him. She was busy with some WI business and showed little sympathy for his plight.

If only they knew how confusing it was having the promise of cash and yet having none of it to spend. Everyone was giving him their pennyworth on how it should be used. His debt was like a hangman's noose drawing ever tighter around his collar. He was only robbing Peter to pay Paul.

This was going to be a morning of gloomy appointments:

first the accountant, then the summons to the bank for yet more financial advice. He was a farmer, not a stockbroker.

There was a time when he had sipped pints with his old bank manager, a friend of the family, but he retired early due to stress and was replaced by a series of faceless ever younger men, barely out of school, to whom he was just another difficult account to control; another set of figures that didn't add up. Nik knew his debt was mounting despite his compensation. He should be laughing all the way to the bank but there was dry rot in his coffers.

The accountant was only doing his best but he couldn't work miracles. Time was when Nik's father could look any bank in the face, paying up promptly, cash on the nail. Tom Snowden, like other Dales farmers, was careful with his money, bought only the best and bought to last. He wore hand-made tweed suits, expensive brogues and changed his car every three years. He never took a holiday, paid for Nik's private schooling, drank little and smoked even less. He would be horrified to see his son in this mess.

'We got out of last year's difficulty with the sale of the oak furniture, I recall.' The man looked up hopefully. 'Is there any other antique gem hiding in your attic to tide you over?' He laughed at his little joke. 'Or are we now thinking about selling the house to realise capital? It's the sensible option, Mr Snowden, given the facts. You'd have a good pension pot to fall back on. The compensation is more money than you'd have got for your livestock in the present climate.'

At least he had the decency to pause, seeing the look on his client's face.

'On today's buoyant market the house alone would fetch upwards of three to four hundred thousand, subject to change of use and planning permission . . . and then there's the renting out of your land, another steady income.'

'Wintergill is not for sale,' Nik snapped.

'I know how you must feel, but with a couple of acres and a paddock there must be a ready market for such a property. Have you had it valued lately?' The lad was not listening to a word he was saying.

Nik shook his head. How could this fresh-faced townie have any idea how it felt to be facing such an option? 'I was hoping that the compensation and extra income from the winter let would cover all of my previous deficit,' he argued, pointing to the figures.

'It all helps, of course, but the cost of the renovations swallowed half your injected capital, as I recall. Then there's the everyday living expenses for you both this year. Have you thought of moving into the barn conversion yourself and selling the house as a country house hotel or a tele-cottage business centre?' came the next hopeful suggestion.

Nik could feel his hackles rising but he swallowed hard. 'Not really. I'm sure I can come up with something to tide me over.' He was trying to sound confident. 'Once I restock.'

'It's all going to take time, Mr Snowden,' the accountant was muttering. 'Have you any other item to sell as a stopgap?'

Nik felt like choking him on the spot. 'We've sold the family silver but I can always sell the barn when the time comes.' He was trying to sound casual, swallowing his fury. 'I have some interesting Victorian memorabilia that may perhaps stem the flood, if needs must.' If only the rumours of the old family painting were true, he mused.

'I must advise you to realise as much capital as you can if your compensation is to stay in the bank. Selling the family silver is no answer to this dilemma. There comes a time when the options shrink. You'll have to rethink your position. This uncertainty must be worrying but you are now in a good position to retire and be better provided for than before. It's a good time to get out of farming,' the manager added.

'And do what?' Nik argued.

'I'm sure you have transferable skills,' the young man smiled. 'These are unusual circumstances. I'm sure your bank will say the same thing. I do hope so. We do sympathise. You're not the only farmer in this boat . . . not that that is of any comfort. Bad times. Who would have thought it would come to this?'

Mr Pinstriped-Suit stood up, bringing the interview to a close, and Nik shook his head in defeat. What did this boffin know about anything? He'd never taken a risk in his life, nor given a lifetime of hard graft to see it all tumbling around his ears. All he was worried about was making sure his fees were covered.

As he strode out into the High Street, lined on either side with market stalls, Nik was caught up in the bustling Christmas crowds; the Christmas trees stacked up on the pavements, the holly wreaths, the rolls of wrapping paper and tinsel, and the Sally Army brass band was playing carols across the road.

He felt like telling them to shut up. There was nothing 'God Rest You Merry' about this gentleman! There was just time to grab a pint and sandwich before he set off for the interrogation at the bank. There was some exhibition at the Auction Mart to look at successful diversification schemes, and a team of Defra experts on hand to talk about restocking and extra funding for hill farmers. He could do with some creative suggestions. His mind was a blank with worry.

Later, he sat exhausted, depressed and out of sorts by the fire in the Red Lion, waiting for his lift back to Wintergill. He was watching tired shoppers with their parcels and packages chattering like starlings on a rooftop. There were pensioners sipping bowls of soup, enjoying a day out.

Nothing he had heard or seen that afternoon had cheered his weariness. He was awash with leaflets and good advice, warnings and cash projections. He felt so flattened by failure, by the sadness of Jim's death, his mother's indifference and now there was the Christmas jollies to endure.

How he loathed the idea of Christmas: the meal eaten in silence, the pints or three in the half-empty pub, all the meaningless rituals of the season. What was there to celebrate but empty fields full of weeds and uncertainty? Even his night out had been a disaster.

Quiz night was always a bit of fun. It usually took his mind off things, like music and walling did. His vehicle needed repair and he could still see those icy staring eyes in front of the windscreen. What was all that about? Everything was going pear-shaped.

Then there was the two of them in the barn. His mother had taken to their tenants, especially the kiddie, but then she was always one for girls. It was strange having a kid about the place. He knew now about her father's car crash and understood why the mother had done a bunk. He didn't blame her at all if she wanted to give the festivities a miss. It was not every mother who took time out in the country to spend with her kid. He could have done with some of that when he was younger himself.

He was never quite sure how to be around children, whether to stay aloof or act daft. He had often wondered if he and Mandy had had a kiddie whether they would have made more effort to stay together. He wondered what she was doing these days. They'd gone their separate ways. He'd heard down the grapevine she'd had a baby. He sipped his pint and sighed. She'd be having a family Christmas, no doubt.

We were so ignorant, he thought. We thought that sexual attraction was enough to withstand the rigours of life on top of the Pennines. Where there was a will there must be a way. How wrong can you get? There had to be more to marriage than four legs in a bed. He'd never given her any proper time, lumped her with his parents, forgetting she was not used to his way of life. No wonder it ended like it did.

It didn't take long for Mandy's looks to fade, her eyes to lose their lustre, her interest in both him and the farm to wane until there was nothing left between them both but arguments over wedding presents. He'd been gutted but at least he'd never given his wife the satisfaction of seeing his wounds. That was something he had learned early at his mother's apron strings.

Whatever Mother felt about losing Shirley and then Tom, it was never discussed or expressed. He used to think that they had their own special Iron Curtain; a curtain that was drawn across the past as if the time before he was born never existed. There were no photographs, no references made to Shirley's childhood. Things were After Shirley or Before Nik.

Even her death was shielded from him. They thought he didn't know how she died. It took only a week at the village school for some tyke to knock him over in the playground and point to the churchyard. 'Shut up or you'll end up over there with yer sister!'

There was a baby portrait of him sitting on a mat with ringlets and one other photograph of a girl in a party dress, on his mother's dressing table. He knew which one got kissed every night and it wasn't him.

'Who's that?' he used to ask.

'An angel too good for this life,' came the reply like a door slamming in his face. Shirley was held before him as always good, well behaved, who never scuffed her knees or tore her trousers. He was a poor second in this race. How could you win against a shadow?

Sometimes he would linger after school and go to the

grave, but even the words on the headstone he didn't understand for a long time. He watched the pink-leaved maple growing taller and rounder. In his mind Shirley grew in that tree. She was not human at all.

Nik jolted himself out of his daydreaming, half his pint untouched; this was not like him at all. What's past is past, he sighed, and looked down at his watch. Kay was late. Typical woman. No sense of timing. There must be a way through this gloomy predicament without topping himself, like Jim, or selling out to Stickley, but he was damned if he knew what.

He put some money in the collecting box as the Sally Army officer came round the bar. Don't be a mean bugger, he thought, you've got some brass in the bank. Some have nowt. It was not their fault he was in this mess.

There was a time when the sound of a brass band outside took him back to carolling round the village by torchlight with the school, frosty nights and throwing mince pies like snowballs, with the usual clip round the ear from Mr Hampson, the headmaster.

Bah, humbug! He shook his head grimly. I'm turning into Scrooge. I'll give Christmas a miss this year, forget the whole business. Christmas was a waste of good brass, and they never did anything much. Mother was always odd around the season, and he just sat around the Spread Eagle out of her way. He might as well go and shoot some rabbits.

The accountant had got him thinking, though. Perhaps he should use the time to take down some of those boxes in the attic and sift through what was left of the memorabilia to see what might be sellable. Joss and Jacob were some of his most successful ancestors. There was talk of pictures they owned but no one had ever seen them. Perhaps there was something hidden up there that might cause a sensation at the *Antiques Roadshow*. Don't be an idiot. You're

150

clutching at family myths and legends to rescue you, he mused, draining the dregs of his glass. It was all a load of nonsense. How could Turner or Constable have ever darkened their door?

Joss Snowden and the London Painter, July 1816

Mrs Snowden's Yorkshire Drip Pudding

Take your eggs and whip them to snow.
Add plain flour and beat in until absorbed.
Thin down the batter with salt water until as thick as cream. Set aside to rest awhile.
Put in the oven at its hottest when the beef is nearly cooked and ready to be basted, and pour dripping into a hot tin.
Beat up the batter and pour onto boiling dripping.
Let the beef fat above drip onto it.
Cook until puffed up and brown.
Serve at once with gravy before the roast.

Young Joss Snowden ran out across the meadows chasing his big brothers' footprints in the hay meadow. It was the wettest summer he could recall in all his thirteen years. His bare feet squelched in the battered grass and the seeds and burrs stuck to his breeches. They were nowhere to be seen, being too old to bother with a knobbly-kneed bairn still at his school books and smaller than his mother.

This should be the time for haymaking, scything the fields, gathering the stooks into haystacks, but the rain was ruining the crop.

> Hay in June worth a silver spoon,
> Hay in July worth a peck o' rye,
> Hay in August not worth a peck o' dust.

His breeches were so sodden he might as well go paddle in the beck at the foot of Wintergill waterfall, and it was there he came across the strangest man, sitting like a gnome staring out across the water, with a book of empty pages in his hand: a short squat man with spectacles, a hooked nose and a red face.

This was no bogtrotter nor a farmer in thick breeches of woollen cloth. Farmers never had time to stand and stare at anything if it hadn't got four legs. His boots were quality leather, well creased with walking. On his head was a flat crowned hat, but the oddest thing was he was sitting under the shade of an umbrella making pictures at great speed. His knapsack lay by his side, full of pockets and straps. Joss had never seen such a carry-all.

He crept up silently, fascinated by the way the man's hand raced across the page.

'What is it, boy?' he snapped in an offcomer's strange voice.

Joss jumped back under the thicket of bushes, not sure what to say.

'You are making a likeness,' was all he could think of as the man rose, shifted his position and proceeded to sketch the tumbling water over the rocks from a different angle. 'I can show you a better foss than this 'un,' he boasted. 'This is nobbut a spray.' Joss knew a real waterfall, a foss, hidden from view up on the Snowden moors.

'Is it indeed!' the man replied, lifting his eyes to peruse this observer. 'And where might that be?'

'At Gunnerside Foss, sir, just a stride hence. I can show you, if you like, for the path is twisty.'

The artist rose awkwardly and closed his battered umbrella, packed up his leathery book into his knapsack and peered at his new guide. 'Who might you be?'

'Josiah of Wintergill, son of George Snowden, up yonder.' He was proud of his farm and the grand windows that his grandfather, Sam, had built onto the farmhouse to warm the stone.

'Why aren't you at your studies, or are you just a farm boy untutored?' The man stared hard over his spectacles as he was packing up.

'I have my letters. The school is out for hay timing but the weather plays us fast and loose. I came here to see if fish were jumping but I see none,' he found himself babbling on.

'I have a rod and line,' the man smiled, pulling a fishing rod from out of his umbrella as if he were a conjuror, and fixing his bait. 'Let's see if anything will take the bait.' He sat down again promptly and started fishing.

Joss had never seen such a traveller in all his summers. It was true there were strangers abroad: walking men were known to gad about the Yorkshire Dales just for the exercise, but to this farmer's son it was a mighty strange way to fill your time.

'You've come from afar to make pictures?' he asked.

'This is my summer tour. Before you is a painter from London who journeys abroad each season,' the painter whispered, hoping to make a catch.

Joss knew about pictures, for there was one in the old church, of Mary and Joseph, and the baby in the manger. He was not a churchgoer but a Methodist, and they had no chapel but met in a barn for Sunday worship. His father did not hold with the local parish church. Once he'd heard John Wesley preach at the market cross. This'd caused a heck of a stink in the family. His grandfather had all but disowned him for lowering his sights to be a Dissenter. But once Joss had seen the church picture in its gold frame through the open door, he was transfixed by its beauty and colour, and thought it very fine.

'Do you sell your paintings?' he asked, dangling his legs over the water but longing to have a sight of the sketching book. The only books he knew were the Bible and the school reader. He had never seen a book with empty pages before.

'Only if you have sixty guineas to spare,' the man replied. There was a silence. Only the buzz of the bees among the elderflower disturbed the air. He could not believe there was so much money in the world for a few daubings on a sheet of paper. How many prize tups would such a sum buy?

157

'Can I see what you make?' he was asking out of curiosity.

'Not with these drips falling off the trees,' the painter replied. 'These are only sketches to be finished off else-where. I don't show my work to just anybody.'

'Not even if I showed you a right wondrous fountain, sir? You'll happen not find it if I do not guide you,' Joss bargained.

'Impudent puppy! When you show me this wondrous fountain then I might, just might, show you a sketch or two, and only if the sky brightens, but first I must catch my supper, so silence, lad.'

'Aye, sir,' smiled Joss, youngest down the line of Snowdens, knowing full well when to stay silent and seize the moment.

Gunnerside Foss roared in full spate after heavy rain, spewing water over huge boulders, white foaming sprays crashing down into a chasm below, and the London painter stood as if bewitched. Joss sensed he must not disturb the moment or the man might send him away. He was curious to see what pictures he might conjure up from his battered sketchbook.

'Leave me be, boy. I never work before an audience.' The man ignored his companion, turning to his knapsack eagerly.

'But you promised to show me . . .' Joss felt cheated. Had he not brought him to this wondrous scene and now he was shooed away like some troublesome flea?

'Not now, laddie,' said the man. 'Take this fish to your mother, ask if she will cook it for my supper: plain with no trimmings, mind. If she has a spare bed for the night I will pay for my board and then I might show you a page or two of my book.'

'My mam will do you proud. Her drip pudding is crispest in the dale. We have many chambers in the house,' he smiled. 'The farm track is just a mile from this path taking the right fork. Our house is not to be missed with the biggest windows shining afire from top to toe.' He took the fish and made for the path.

'Be gone and leave me to the light before it disappears,' the London painter dismissed him with a wave of the hand but the boy was full of excitement. His mother liked strangers at the door with coins in their pockets. They brought tales of far-off places that she drank up like expensive tea, savouring each sip, rehashing to her neighbours what she had gleaned of the ways of the world. Tonight she would not be disappointed.

True to his word, as shadows fell across the fields, Joss watched the stranger making his way along the path. *There was a crooked man who walked a crooked mile . . .* His walking was lopsided and it was late.

Joss was weary of waiting, his eyes were heavy but he was determined to have his reward. The fish would not be put on the griddle pan until the stranger was through the kitchen door.

Father was at his class meeting. No London painter would keep him from his weekday worship and Bible study. Joss feared his mother would send him off to bed while his big brothers were allowed to sit and stare by the fire in silence.

Replete with fresh fish and vegetables, roast rib, drip pudding and a slice of apple and cheese pie, the London painter burped with satisfaction.

'Come on, boy, I suppose patience must have its reward.' The man lifted his knapsack to remove the leather-backed sketchbook onto the table. 'Wipe your fingers first.'

Joss needed no bidding as he sat down by the light of the candle to examine each selected page. They were wondrous scenes, just like those from an illustrated Bible that the preacher carried to Sunday services. Some of the scenes were tinted and coloured: swathes of sky and storm clouds, caverns spouting great waterfalls, castles on high mountains, pinnacles of rocks with lightning crashing down across the moors. There were scenes he recognised from his own district; Ingleborough hill and Pen-y-ghent, the riverside and the old corn mill near Settle. He had never seen anything so grand in all his born days.

'How do you conjure up our world as if by magic? And these are but a few of your works.' He pointed, breathless with admiration. Was each of these worth sixty guineas?

'This is not the full work but partial sketches, reminders for me to work from when I take them back to London. Here is where the inspiration begins, standing in the rain, on the top of the crag listening to the curlews and skylarks . . . You are indeed fortunate to live among such glory.' The artist turned to Joss's mother, who smiled and nodded.

Joss yawned, looking at one sunset that caught his eye. 'A've never seen a sunset like yon.' He spoke honestly with the eye of a tired child. The London painter stared at his sketch for a moment and smiled.

'No, young man, but don't you wish you had?'

Joss tossed and turned, scrunched up restless in his bed. How could a man earn such fortune for scribbling with pen, ink and paints? Even now he was lodged in state in the parlour bed with the curtains, like an honoured guest. He talked late into the night when Father returned and queried him further on the state of the world. He had lodged with the Fawkes family at Farnley Hall and was on speaking terms with Harewood House and other great houses of Yorkshire. Father showed him round his house with pride and viewed the sketches with mouth agape. In the morning the painter would be gone for ever.

The boy rose at first light, anxious to sneak one last look

in the knapsack. He tiptoed carefully into the parlour and peered at the pictures with longing. It was the scenes he recognised that stirred him most. This must be how God sees the world, he thought. So many repetitions of the same scene, surely one of them would not be missed.

Once this thought seeded itself in his head it would not be dislodged. How could he ever afford sixty guineas? The sketches were of his own country. The stranger was taking what was free for all to see, capturing God's world that could never be bought or sold for golden guinea pieces. Had not he shown the artist the very hidden beauty of these parts and found him safe lodging?

His hand turned the pages to Gunnerside Foss and the views from the Wintergill moorland crag. He counted five sketches and his fingers found themselves gently removing one sheet slowly and then another, silently until they lay loose in his trembling hand. He was shaking with the enormity of his sinning, but the London painter did not stir from his slumbers. He slipped one back, ashamed, but not the other. The book was shut and placed back.

He crept back up the stairs, remembering to tread the third step with care. He rolled the parchment into a tube, wrapped it in his best linen kerchief and stuffed it carefully behind the loose panel in the wainscot that held all his treasures: birds' eggs, a silver buckle, the silver coin he found by the water's edge. He did not want to think about what he had just done. His father would beat the skin off his backside if he knew.

He could not sleep for guilt so he dressed and ran out towards the rocky crag where he could watch the sun rise slowly. This was God's sunrise and it should be free. He would stay out of doors until the London painter was long gone.

'Be not forgetful to entertain strangers,' said the writer

of Hebrews, 'for thereby some have entertained angels unawares.' Joss wondered at this verse many a time in the months that followed, thinking of the stranger and of his own theft. It stood like some great boulder between him and his Maker and he didn't know how to make amends.

Then the lazy sun decided to put in a late appearance and seared the dale with blazing sunshine. They were out from dawn to dusk, mowing, stacking hay, loading it onto carts. Joss was too tired to think about his secret. The days grew hotter, and late in the afternoon he took to swimming in the river at Bankwell. It was here he first clapped eyes on Susannah Carr.

The Carrs didn't mix in the village, being more gentry than farmers, and their children were sent away to school. They were churchers not chapellers, and lived in the old house at Bankwell with servants and a carriage. Banker Edward Carr was a drunkard and a fool, so said Joss's father, but had built cotton mills with spinning machines down by the river and brought many strangers to work the machines. Now the new turnpike road from Keighley to Kendal carried wool and cotton back and forth to everyone's satisfaction.

Joss noticed a girl sitting on the riverbank dressed in white muslin and fancy frills. Her ringlets shone gold in the sunlight and her maid fussed over her. He'd never seen her before and stared across, but her maid was having none of it.

'Don't be rude,' she shouted at him. 'Come on, Susannah, we won't linger where rough boys lurk.' They rose up and gathered their picnic, making him feel uncouth and angry. At least chapel had taught him that all were equal in the sight of the Lord. This was the first time he had felt himself shabby, barefoot and lumpen in his homespun breeches. There was something about that girl that reminded him of

Mr Turner and his world of beautiful pictures when he slipped the sketch out of its hiding place in the wall.

Susannah Carr was lonely at Bankwell. Her father took little interest in his only daughter, shutting himself in his library with only his wine bottles for company. Sometimes Papa was too busy to bother with anything. There was the mill to oversee, and he was a partner in some new district bank. He rode with the local hunt and soon she would join them. She attended a little seminary in Scarpeton, but she hated all that singing and sewing and sitting around. There were no girls of her class to visit in the district, just Eliza, her serving maid, for company on the long dark evenings when they sat in the drawing room waiting for Papa to put in an appearance, but he never did, waiting for Aunt Lydia to write her a long letter, which never came. The servants had more fun and games in the village than they did, she thought as she raced across the fells, unchaperoned.

Her pleasure was to put on a riding habit, saddle her fine pony, and ride across the fields away from Eliza, astride her horse like a boy, her hair flying in the wind under her tall hat. Side-saddle was too sedate.

One day, as she was careering across the fell, she didn't see the deer shoot out of the thicket in front of them, startling Mercury, so he reared and threw her to the ground, then bolted off with an empty saddle. Susannah lay on the hard turf, feeling stupid, watching her steed heading off down the slope leaving her a long trek home. 'Damn and blast you!' she yelled into the wind.

Looking up, she saw the shadow of a youth staring down at her. He had appeared out of nowhere in his leather chaps and corduroy leggings.

'Are you injured?' he asked, taking off his broad-brimmed hat.

'Thank you, I'm fine, no bones broken just my pride . . . stupid horse.' When she looked closer there was something terribly familiar about his broad open face.

'Stay put, miss,' he ordered. 'I'll go and find your cob.'

'He's not a cob but a fine-bred hunter,' she corrected him.

'I like Dales blacks meself,' he continued. 'They do the job nicely on a farm.'

'Don't bother, Mercury will take himself home,' she sighed. 'It'll do me no harm to walk back.'

'Not after a tumble it won't. Wintergill's nowt but a stride away. My mam will see thee right.'

'I couldn't possibly,' she smiled, gathering her skirts to jump up, but her head was spinning and she wobbled.

'See, I told you. Come and have a dish of tea and we'll see you back down safe. Thy father'll be worried.'

'My name is Susannah Carr,' she said, holding out her hand as grown-ups did.

'Aye, I know, I've seen you before.'

He was blushing, not looking her in the face, and then she recognised that look. He was one of the rough boys by the river.

'Which farmer's son are you?' she asked, knowing it was polite to make inferiors feel comfortable.

'Josiah Snowden, miss, but everyone calls me Joss.'

They walked slowly towards the open gate and up the fell to the stone farmhouse and all the pungent smells of a busy farmyard. The farm boys doffed their caps at her presence and she waited on the doorstep as Joss went in to warn his mother of her unexpected arrival. She could sense the flurry of tidying and clearing away before she would be shown into their best room.

Susannah often went on visits with her aunt to the low-beamed stone houses to dole out alms and baskets of fruit and cakes. She had learned not to turn her nose up at the rough smells assaulting her nostrils, but she had never been on a working farm before: not one so high up the hill with such wonderful views over the valley. It had a better aspect than Bankwell House, which was closer to the river and darker, facing south and east.

'Come in, come in!' smiled Mistress Snowden in a fluster of welcome, straightening her mobcap and curtsying. She had a pleasant round face and bright blue eyes. 'I will mash a dish of tea and there are fat rascals straight off the griddle.'

Aunt Lydia trained her always to take a bite and a sip but no more, for she might deprive poor children of their supper, but here was such a pile of baking, bread and fancies on cream china plates. There was a wall dresser full of pewter plates and a wall clock ticking away. Everything sparkled in the firelight. The fire in the chimney blazed with such ferocity that she could feel the heat warming her through. Joss was standing dumbstruck, tall and fair like his mother, who clucked around her like a mother hen. There was a different warmth here, more like the chatter in the servants' hall before it fell silent when she walked in unannounced.

'I don't get much company passing the door, just pedlars and bogtrotters, but having said that, young Joss brought another visitor a while back: a London painter on his travels. He drew some bonny sketches of our district, didn't he, son? He said we had the best view in all Christendom and I didn't gainsay him,' she laughed.

Susannah sipped the tea and bit into the spicy cake, and kept on nibbling until it was all gone, not a crumb. She blushed at this boldness.

'That's what I like to see, a hearty appetite. Have another,' said Mistress Snowden, offering the plate again, but Susannah declined.

'I must be on my way before the light goes.'

'Joss and I will walk you back partway. It is only proper,' she said, reaching for her cloak hanging on the hook at the back of the door.

They walked slowly at first, with an awkward silence, but then Susannah fell back with Joss. 'Do you have a habit of inviting strangers to your farm?' she said.

'Mr Turner, the London painter, wanted lodgings for the night. We have upper rooms. My brothers and me, we bed down together,' he replied. 'They were really good, the likenesses. He showed them to me.'

'We have lots of pictures but I never look at them,' she confessed.

'You should if they are all like Mr Turner's. There was one of the Foss.' Joss hesitated, looking at her carefully. 'Can you keep a secret?'

She nodded eagerly.

'There were so many drawings, all of the Foss, I let one slide away out of his book and I have it still.' He bowed his head, looking at her through the side of his eye. 'There, 'tis said. It has worried me so long. You won't tell anyone, will you?'

Susannah stopped and looked him straight in the eye, for she was about the same age and height. 'Of course not, never. Ladies don't gossip.'

'That's all right then,' he smiled. As village boys went he was quite presentable.

'Are you ever afraid?' she smiled back.

'I will be if my father ever finds that piece of paper behind the wainscot, very afraid.'

She looked at him and smiled. She was fearful when Papa came in roaring drunk, shouting and cursing and then crying into his glass.

'Favour for a favour then, Josiah Snowden. Give me that drawing and I will hide it for you until you come to collect it. There are hundreds of hidy-holes in Bankwell. Cross my heart and hope to die but your secret's safe with me.' Susannah solemnly crossed herself and they shook hands on it like farmers over a sheep pen deal.

'Done,' Joss laughed.

'What's undone?' said his mother, turning round.

'Nothing, Mam, just a game,' he replied.

In the days that followed Joss wondered if he had dreamed the girl's visit, but his mother kept going over every detail of Susannah's fine appearance, the cut of her riding jacket, the quality of the woollen skirt and her dainty leather gloves. The servants had spread the gossip up the dale how the master was bereft of an heir and how the girl must now be brought out to make a fine marriage.

'She's a real little lady, is that one,' Joss's mother sighed. 'You did well to bring her here.'

Joss was lost in his own worries. Did Susannah really mean to keep his secret? Should he risk taking the sketch down to Bankwell? They had made no arrangement to meet again but the guilty theft was burning a hole in the wood panelling. He rushed up the ladder stair when everyone was out at their chores and fished it out, stuffed it in his waistcoat lining and made his way down the path.

At first his steps were bold and fast in the descent, and then he strolled through the village past the lich-gate of St Oswald's church. He dawdled over the river bridge in the direction of Bankwell House, not sure which entrance to take through the arched gate. It was the closest he had ever been to the manor house, with its golden stone and ivy-clad walls. One glimpse told him the stable yard and paths were not swept as well as their own yards. A groom came out to greet him.

'Now then, young Snowden, what brings 'ee down these

parts? Come a-courtin' Ellin Bargh in the kitchen?' he laughed.

'No,' Joss blushed. 'I've got a message for Miss Susannah,' he stuttered.

'Have you indeed? We'll see about that. And what might your business be?'

'It's private. I have something to give her. She did ask for it,' he added, not sure now how to proceed.

'Oh, I'm sure Miss Susannah will get it a plenty when she's bit older but she's a tad young for carrying on with farm boys,' the groom roared. 'Hey up, lads! Young Joss has come a-courtin' and him not thirteen summers. They start them early, up Wintergill. It must be all that fresh air.'

The men stood around gawping at him, and Joss wanted to flee from their teasing. He was wrong to have come and made a fool of himself. He turned to go just as Susannah trotted into the yard from her morning ride. There was a scurry of attention to horse and rider, but Joss bent his head and walked away.

'Joss!' She raced after him, waving her whip. 'I thought it was you.'

'I'll be off, miss. Sorry to trouble you.'

'No, wait . . . Did you bring it? The picture – did you bring it or is it discovered?' she whispered, her eyes burning into him with interest.

The girl had remembered their secret and his heart leaped that he was acknowledged. 'It's hidden in here,' he smiled, patting his long jerkin.

'We can't open it here,' she whispered. 'But wait under the river bridge on the path. I'll change and say I'm walking down to collect berries or something. Meet you there,' she ordered, and left him standing.

The men were watching them but then Susannah barked at them to get on with their jobs, and he was forgotten.

The two of them hid under the stone arch as he rolled out the sketch from its linen pouch. 'You know where this is?' he said, watching her face pale as she recognised the waterfall scene.

'He's captured that cold dark place. They say it's haunted,' she offered.

'Aye, I've heard that too, and sometimes I've felt it. Happen you don't like it much,' he sighed, making to roll it.

'Oh, yes, I do. I promise to keep it for you and I will. Are you my friend?' she said.

'Aye, I am that,' he replied.

'Then you'll have to learn to speak properly. Say "yes", not "aye", and "no" not "nay",' she ordered. 'And I shall be your tutor. This'll be our meeting place. I shall wait from the quarter-hour chime to the half-hour chime, and no more.'

'When?'

'Sunday afternoons, but don't be late.' Susannah waved the parchment in the air. 'Don't worry, I have a secret place for this.' Then she was gone.

It was hard getting away on a Sabbath. The cows and the hens didn't know which day of the week it was, so all must be prepared before chapel. Then there was the special dinner to eat that Mother took trouble to make. More chores and then Sunday class back down in the village. This was where they learned to read and write their names, copy scriptures and listen to visiting preachers. If he wagged off the class someone would tell of his absence. Joss hovered at the back, dashing out early to make the meeting place. Sometimes he waited and waited and she never turned up, and it was a long wet walk back up to Wintergill.

Then she would arrive as if nothing had happened, standing proud in some pretty taffeta gown that rustled as she walked, her ringlets bobbing, and they sat and talked and fished and she showed him how to pronounce words correctly.

He sat and listened to her worries. Her world was so different from his own. How he longed to be her equal, to ride and jump for pleasure, not necessity, to eat fine foods the like of which he'd never heard: pineapples, melons and other fancy fare.

He told her how he wanted to build up their breeding cattle and make Snowden's farm the biggest and the best in the district. How his big brother Ben was to marry a farmer's girl over the moor and Tom wanted to go into the town and make his fortune. His father was not well so he must stay to be about their business.

'I'm going to stay with Aunt Lydia soon and when I'm older she will bring me out,' Susannah told him.

'Out where?' he asked.

'Out into society, you bumpkin, to make a good marriage,' she laughed.

Her words brought a chill into his heart that soon their worlds would separate for ever. He was just a country yokel, a plaything to be picked up and dropped, a nothing boy. As he walked back that afternoon, he felt a rage inside him that there was no equality in this world. It wasn't fair. That was when he heard a voice ranting in his head.

'Then make thyself her equal, laddie. Learn thy letters and make summat of thyself.'

The Snowdens of Wintergill bowed to no man but their Maker, his father once said. Well, he would show her and all the Carrs that he was worthy to be her suitor one day, not her secret cast-off.

Joss never went back to the river bridge after that. He would not be at her beck and call. Sunday school was more important now for there was so much to learn and so little time. From that moment on Josiah Snowden was a driven man. One day he would make Susannah Carr not just his friend, but his bride.

Susannah waited and waited long past the half-hour chime, but still Joss didn't come. How dare he make her wait in the rain with her skirt all muddy and her ringlets hanging like rat's-tails? This was the last time she was ever going to meet him, the rude boy. There was so much to tell him. How Aunt Lydia had written with an invitation to attend seminary in York. She wasn't sure she wanted to go so far away from everything she'd known.

'I don't want to go to York,' she announced.

'You'll do as you're told,' Papa ranted at her. 'How else will I ever get you off my hands? Girls are expensive to marry off. The sooner we start, the sooner your aunt will find you a husband to pay for all your frills and falderals. There's no one here rich enough even to keep you in ribbons.' How Papa raved about the output of the mill and the cost of wages and new machines.

Well, Joss Snowden could go hang himself, for all she minded. What did she care for such a peasant? The fact that she missed seeing the look of pleasure in his bright blue eyes and even the way his rough speech was improving was neither here nor there. She was gentry and quality, and above such bad manners. What could you expect from a simple clodhopper? The thought of not riding Mercury over the hills did not bear thinking about, but Aunt Lydia promised that they would visit the shops and buy some new dresses. A whole new life was opening up and she ought to be delighted. The fact that she was not puzzled her.

The change in young Joss did not go unnoticed. His mother saw the small things at first: how he washed more often at the pump, how his head was always stuck in a borrowed book. He attended chapel school with more fervour than any of her other boys and she wondered if he had ideas of being a preacher.

He laughed, saying his mind was not set on such holy things, being more a plough boy than a scholar. He cajoled his father into making changes around the farm: to breed more stock and get better prices for their wool; to oversee the building of stone out barns to store the fodder for winter. He was all for overwintering cattle with the newfangled notions of feeding them turnips, fussing over which tup to set on the ewes for the best quality wool. He nagged the men to tidy up the yard and keep the milk cows clean, and began inspecting their cheese-making, fussing over machinery.

'What's gotten into you, lad?' Mother snapped.

'This is 1822, a new century. The Boney wars are over. There's money to be made in these hills if you know how to go about it. I hear old Collins up at Malham Water House mines coal, copper, lead and lime off his own land. I am thinking of opening up a seam or two. There's more to farming than sheep and cows.'

He stood there in the prime of his life, nineteen years old, tall, broad-shouldered and handsome in the Snowden sort of way.

'It's about time you found a wife to keep your feet on the ground,' Mother answered. 'And what's all this talk of you going to St Oswald's of a morning worship? Is it to see if that Carr girl's back from her wanderings?' She laughed, seeing him go scarlet. 'Mercy preserve us, don't go looking in that direction, Joss. Thee's getting above thyself.'

The spies had been out and about, and someone had seen him in the back pew of the church ogling the squire's pew for signs of the girl's return. He had caught a brief glimpse of Susannah once, walking out through the side door, erect and proud. It was she who had taken his eye and he would not be dissuaded from this path.

This thoroughbred filly wore a short velvet jacket and big bonnet, dressed as close to town fashion as to make all the other village girls look plain in their homespun finery. He had perused the pews, hoping some spark of passion might be aroused by one of the village girls but there was none. Susannah had grown into a thing of beauty, dazzling all others out of his fancy. There was a spirit in her gait and boldness in her eye even if she didn't recognise who he was when she drove past him in the street. She was to him a strange mixture of wildness and calm, like a summer's day brewing a storm. He must make a fortune and fast, raise his standing in the district if there was to be any hope of wooing her. To wed a Carr was aiming higher than most would have dared. To achieve this would mean a long and hard campaign but he was no shirker from hard graft so he set himself the goal of making the most of every penny he earned to improve his income, his profit and his land. His parents stood back and watched his efforts with wonder and not a little fear.

To this end he made himself available to the parish worthies for any duty no one else wanted to take on. Joss Snowden was a byword for reliability. He took dancing lessons secretly in the town, but however nimble his foot-work in the cotillion steps there was no entrée into the hallowed Bankwell House Assemblies.

When his intended was in residence he made sure that he was busy close by. There was a rhythm to Susannah's charitable expeditions into the village that wasn't hard to gauge. He took note when she rode abroad, hoping for another chance to rescue her, making sure he wore his best jacket and waistcoat and brown hat, but none ever came.

Of course, he guessed that she was destined to marry well and secure monies for the estate, whose walls were not in such fine fettle as his own. That was always a giveaway as to how well managed and prosperous a man's land was. There was talk that Edward Carr had expensive tastes in thoroughbreds and his vintner's bills went unpaid, and that shopkeepers in Scarperton despaired when fresh orders were demanded for Bankwell. Rumours of that sort of shortfall galloped up the dale and in the cattle marts. The Carrs were not now so high and mighty as they would like to think, not among the locals. Perhaps there was hope.

At Christmas he made an excuse to visit the house on parish business but still had to go first to the back entrance, not the front porch. He hovered around, hoping for a glimpse of Susannah, but of course there was none. Then the freezing weather came and the mill pond froze, and everyone took to the ice for fun, careering around arm in arm. He hovered out of sight, watching Susannah skating while her maid sat on the bank with her hands in her muff. If only he could have dazzled her with his prowess, but he was hopeless on blades.

Sometimes Joss thought he caught her staring in his direction but that was all. He hoped he cut a dash in his corduroy jacket and worsted breeches, his boots polished to glass. His mirror told him that his figure was lean and long-limbed, his shoulders were broad and his hips well tapered. He would be a catch for any of the farmers' daughters who eyed him eagerly when dancing a jig. He was honest and hard-working but too low born to turn this one particular head in his direction. In his despair he turned to Parson Simey, whom he knew had the ear of old man Carr. It was after a parish poor law meeting that he sat sipping port in the parson's small study.

'What ails thee, young Joss? You've been hovering around

Bankwell of late, like a bad smell. Who is the maid who's captured your heart?'

Joss took his courage in hand and declared himself.

'I have a great affection for Miss Susannah Carr. She's caught my eye with her beauty, her horsemanship and kindness to the poor.' He galloped it all out in one breath. 'I'd like to make my intentions plain to Squire Carr.'

The parson shook his head. 'Oh, dearie me, this is bad news. What gives you the notion that he would ever entertain the idea of his daughter being passed on to some twopenny farmer from up the dale?' He eyed Joss keenly for a response.

Joss was not cowed by these words. 'I don't intend to stay in this station for ever,' he argued. 'I've got plans to buy more land, renew our stock with finer breeds, and remodel the farmhouse in a grander design with rooms suitable for any lady; a parlour with sea-coal fireplace, bedchambers, a little park outside with a walled garden away from view. My eye is so fixed upon her I will do anything to set her like some precious jewel in a grand setting.'

'Will you now? Thy plans are ambitious indeed, but have you spoken to this jewel of your intention?' asked the parson, sucking on his pipe with interest.

'Nay, no . . . sir. It would not be seemly without her father's consent. I'd not presume such boldness for although I may not be a gentleman by birth, I will behave as such.'

'I'm glad to hear it, young man, for I fear you will face a grievous disappointment. Edward Carr will not waste his daughter on sons of the soil. She's destined for higher men than you, but I admire your courage. Without dreams, Josiah, we are nothing. Aim for the stars and you might reach the sky but don't overreach yourself in that direction. She must marry a man with money and estate and soon . . . however her heart may be fixed.'

'But if you could but speak on my behalf to the squire, and tell him I will do exactly as I promised, plus mend his walls and see to his broken barns, perhaps that will help . . .'

The parson laughed aloud. 'Oh, Joss, go find a farmer's daughter of your own sort. The Snowdens and the Carrs are stations apart. Don't be a fool!'

'Not in my great-grandfather's day, they were not. Were not the Carrs and Snowdens equals in Cromwell's day and are we not all equal in the sight of the Lord?'

'That may be so but I don't think our squire sees it in such a light. I will make such delicate enquiries that are befitting a humble man of the cloth. Better to set your sights lower and you'll do better for yourself. It doesn't do to stir up the proper order of things. Be content with your station and all will be well.'

Thus was Joss dismissed and denied hope of furthering his cause with the family, but the Snowdens were by nature a stubborn stock, no quitters in affairs of the heart, and he rode back under the stars all the more determined to win his heart's desire whether he had the squire's consent or not.

He lay in bed composing the most delicate letter to Miss Susannah, brimful of all the admiration and praise he could muster, enclosed with a special poem he had copied to plead his cause. Perhaps if she knew of his regard, she might give him some sign of hope. He asked her if she still kept his guilty secret safe. The missive was delivered in the dead of night and was duly ignored, lost or undelivered, he knew not which.

Undeterred by the deafening silence Joss decided that, come what may, he would set about achieving all that he had described to the parson on that winter's night. He would wait like Jacob for his Rachel, seven years if need be, until the Carr resistance crumbled under the force of his love.

As if to deter him further Susannah was suddenly removed once more to some relative in York to further her education in the seminary. This much was gleaned from servant gossip. But her absence spurred Joss even more to set about the monumental task he'd set himself. When she returned to Bankwell House Josiah Snowden would not be so easy to ignore.

'Who's that letter from?' asked Eliza, peering over her shoulder.

'No one.' How dare that silly boy write such a letter to her, thought Susannah as she threw it with disdain almost onto the fire but then drew it back, shoving it into her reticule. It was the first billet-doux she'd ever had, even if it was from that rough cowherd Joss Snowden, who was growing so handsome and strong. How many times through the corner of her eye had she caught a glimpse of him watching her movements? Who did he think he was even to address her in such an intimate manner?

If Papa had known of such impudence he would've had him whipped or dismissed, but you couldn't stop a free man from going about his lawful business, and Joss was no man's fool. His name tripped off the tongue of many a housemaid as being the finest beau in the village.

If only she could've laughed and told them he was ordinary, but the young bucks she'd met in York through Aunt Lydia were silly dumb dogs or foppish mincing minions. Now she was going back to the seminary with its chaperones and dull deportment lessons, soirées and recitals. The city air was rank after the moorland freshness, the smoke and muck brought a different sort of smell. The poor were poorer and more threatening. The hovels they visited were beds of sickness and death. This time they must make an effort and be seen out in good society like prize heifers up for auction to the highest bidder. Papa was expecting a result, but how was she ever going to find a suitor for herself when there was no one that pleased her eye as much as Master Snowden?

She still had the picture of Gunnerside Foss safely hidden in the secret drawer at the back of her writing bureau but it had languished long forgotten, like poor Mama in her grave.

Aunt Lydia was losing patience with her niece for being too particular. 'There are girls biting at your heels for a chance to show themselves at the Assembly Rooms. You've spent too much time up in the hills. It's coarsened your skin and flushed your cheeks like a dairymaid. A little more restraint at the dancing and the singing, Susannah. A gentleman doesn't want a milkmaid for a wife but a delicate flower.'

From what she gleaned from back-stair gossip, gentlemen with roving eyes grabbed milkmaids wherever they could after the hunting. There were girls dismissed for carrying bastards or being caught with their skirts high up in the barn. Once in Papa's library on a wet afternoon she discovered a leather ledger full of pictures that left nothing to the imagination as to how children were begat: Eastern maidens astride men in positions that defied her understanding but stirred her loins strangely. She smiled, thinking about stallions and mares, and then of Joss Snowden and going hot at the thought.

As they bustled through Spurriergate that afternoon, tripping from shop to shop, browsing, sipping afternoon tea, little did she guess how soon her world was to be turned upside down with a letter from Bankwell in the morning's post that had her aunt in tears.

'You must return at once.'

'What's happened?' Susannah asked, feeling a stab of fear in her chest. 'Is Papa dead?'

'Would that he was . . . he's ruined. We are all ruined . . . You must go back to comfort him.' With the fearful news came a strange relief. The tall town house was empty and stale. She was safer at home, whatever the outcome. Thoughts of the high fells and the gracious old house were comforting. Perhaps it wasn't too late to rescue their fortunes after all.

Joss was up on the roof of his new extension, inspecting the slate and the lead flashings, checking that the hired mason had finished everything to his specification. His mother stood back, scratching her head at all the mess cluttering the yard. 'You'll beggar us ere long with all this nonsense. Three of us will be rattling around in this empty barn. The laughing stock of Wintergill, you are, with your fancy notions!'

'Have faith, Mam. I know what I'm about. My overseer says our calamine mine is not exhausted, and the lead seam's brought us in good brass. I said I'd make us a fine homestead and that's what I'm doing,' he shouted down as she shook her head and walked away.

His next visitor had him down the ladder in seconds. Parson Simey was striding past the farm, stretching his legs in the bright sunshine. He waved to his protégé to come down.

'You've done a fine job, Josiah, but I fear all to no avail,' he whispered. 'I have kept my ear to the ground on your behalf, as I promised, but the news is not good.'

'Miss Susannah's betrothed in York?' Joss whispered, his heart leaping at this terrible news.

'No worse, I fear. The Carrs are ruined. The bank has failed and the squire is disgraced,' said the parson.

'What can I do?' Joss cried, stunned at such news.

'We can do nothing but pray for all those who've lost

179

their money. The squire has taken to his bed with a bottle, blaming himself. I told him matters were in higher hands than ours now, and he threw me out of the chamber.' He bowed his head.

Joss felt his spirit lift at this unexpected news. There was no hope for him if Susannah was not in his world. In York he was in danger of losing her, but now there must be no delay. If she returned nothing would prevent him from making her his bride.

Into the dark damp recesses of the foss, he gazed down at the tumbling spray, willing himself to have one of those funny turns that sometimes gave him a slip second into the best way forward, but nothing came. He sat there until it grew dark, praying she would return home. There must be hope, and to this end he must continue his good works, set about his rebuilding with renewed vigour. It would have to sustain him for many a month more.

The news of the Carrs' ruin was all over the village, carried from Bankwell House servants to all who would hear. The house must be sold and Miss Susannah must go as governess to some household to earn her keep.

'The squire's a broken man and quite weakened by these sufferings,' whispered the parson. 'I fear the family'll be much changed by sorrow and needs to be left to recover when the girl returns among us. I don't want to hear of you pestering her. Be patient, young man. Time is a great healer.'

How could he be patient when she would soon be living only a few miles down the valley? How he longed to comfort her and see her beautiful face once more, but first he must write a letter of condolence in his best copperplate hand-writing, hoping against hope for a reply this time. Now was the time to make the final assault on the farmhouse renovations.

The parson restrained every sign of Joss's eagerness to make contact with the family, saying he must make no demands but prepare the ground for his proposal only after many months had passed and it was seemly. The Scarperton bank, in which the squire was a partner, had overstretched itself in some foreign venture and closed its doors. The *Gazette* was full of the terrible news and many a good man lost all his capital from this collapse. As a man of honour Edward Carr must pay off his debts by selling off land and assets, or be shunned. Suddenly the tables were turned and Joss knew that the moment had arrived to make his bid for happiness.

He chose a fine summer morning to ride his finest horse, in his best apparel, to the front entrance of Bankwell House and this time he would not be denied access. The squire welcomed him, if a little hesitantly, into the drawing room. Suffering, disappointment and the effects of strong wine had etched lines on his once handsome face. His reception was cautious but civil.

Joss sat, trying not to be overawed by the sumptuous draperies and dark panelling, the portraits hanging on the walls, the fine porcelain in cabinets making his own efforts at decoration seem shabby. His longed-for dream was coming true but he must be patient. He gave his condolences as best he could. His courtesies were accepted with a brief nod.

Then it was time to assault the squire's ear with all he had achieved over the past year and how the plans for a new wing to Wintergill were almost complete. He talked about his breeding stock and the mineral deposits mined from his moorland. How his calamine ore had been bought by a Bond Street firm for brass making, taken by canal from Gargrave to Leeds and down to London. Supply was keeping pace with demand.

'It is no secret in this district that I have long since held Miss Susannah Carr in high estimation,' he continued in his best Yorkshire accent, adding how, for many years, he'd wished to make his humble affection known. 'Until now I have felt unable to pursue my suit but I hope in the past years I've bridged the gap between our stations in life by honest endeavour and enterprise.'

'And now you want to kick a dog when it's down?' snapped the old man.

'Certainly not,' Joss argued. 'This is no fly-by-night affectation but a genuine desire to make Miss Susannah my wife and give her the honour she deserves. I will wed no other,' he said with all the conviction he could muster, but wondering if he'd gone too far in his enthusiasm, expecting to be shown the door any moment.

'I like a fellow who knows what he wants, young man. Susannah is not to be fooled with. She's all that's left now. I have no fancy dowry, if that's what you are looking for?' Edward Carr pulled the bell, summoning his beloved to the room. Joss's heart was thumping in his chest like a hammer, knowing there must be hope in this gesture.

She came, sitting down quietly, listening again to his condolences, not saying a word. Susannah was much altered by suffering, thinner but still a thing of beauty in his eyes.

She heard his stuttering offer without a word. He asked her to take a turn around the walled garden. Susannah nodded and rose, embarrassed, striding in front of him. It was high summer and the roses were dripping over the walls in pink profusion, in cascades of blooms with a delicious scent.

'This is all very unexpected. I can't make a hasty decision. I fear you may make a poor bargain . . . I am no farmer's girl. I know nothing of hard work.'

'I'm not asking you to be a servant.'

'I will have to think about this . . . but you will get your answer by the end of the month.'

The days dragged into weeks and still there was no word. Joss began to believe all his hard work was in vain; that his embellishments were wasted, fruitless, an extravagant gesture to his own vanity.

Sometimes when he was struggling with his accounts, trying to balance the mounting expenses, he laid down his pen and sighed that his beloved was not keen to wed beneath her. Then he chastised himself for being so unfeeling. Had she not been bereaved of her rightful future? It was too early to expect some brightness in her spirit. He took comfort from the parson's words: time was a great healer. It was only natural that she was hesitating now. If she consented she must have everything in the way of fabrics and furnishing, no matter what they cost. Even her bed and its furniture would be transported from Bankwell to Wintergill, everything replicated so she would feel it was just as it always had been.

As he worked tirelessly to this end, he prayed that everything he had striven for might come to fruition, but still she didn't come. The month dragged on until one dark afternoon, she came alone on horseback, dressed in plain grey wool with a veil over her riding hat.

Joss was busy in the yard, his gaiters covered in cow muck. He looked up in shame at the sight of himself, hardly daring to believe she was here.

'I've come to visit with your mother,' Susannah announced as if this was a regular occurrence.

'Oh, aye,' he croaked, knowing they were unprepared for this honour.

She looked up at the building with surprise. 'I scarce recognise the farm. It is so enlarged.' Joss pulled off his hat and grinned. 'Come on round the front and see what we've done to it. Of course, it lacks a lady's touch yet . . . Mother, Miss Susannah has paid you a visit . . .'

His mother was unperturbed. 'Come in, lass, and sit thee down. To what do we owe this honour? Are thee well? 'Tis been a sad do these past months.'

Susannah bowed her head. 'I am here to reply to a request. If I am to contemplate being a farmer's wife, I must needs learn how to use a kitchen and dairy,' she smiled, blushing, looking up at him, and Joss's heart burst with love, sensing the courage it must have taken to take such a downward step.

They were married at Christmas as soon as the banns were read, and Joss was bursting with pride as his new bride crossed the threshold of her new home. On Christmas Day he found a parcel wrapped on the new mahogany table in the grand hallway. Surrounded by guests, he opened the gift in high excitement.

'How did you come by this?' asked Parson Simey with interest at the framed picture. 'It's in the style of Mr Turner . . . the most sought-after artist in the country.'

Joss peered closer, his pink cheeks blushing with surprise.

It was Susannah who recounted the London painter's visit all those years ago, emphasising that this was in fact a sketch drawn from somewhere on Snowden land. Everyone was impressed that such an illustrious artist once graced the area with his patronage, presuming the picture was a gift, and Joss knew better than to disillusion them. What the eye does not see . . . And most of her story was true. No one would ever suspect the true origin of the sketch.

It took pride of place in the upstairs parlour for all to comment upon. It added a stamp of authority to Wintergill; that such a famous man should paint a scene so close to them. It was right that his wife should have fine things around her. Her price was above rubies, she gave him sons and graced his table with silence and good manners.

If sometimes he found her shop purchases extravagant and a little showy, he said nothing. She repaid him many a time by pious acts of charity and thoughtfulness among the poor, and she was a good housekeeper. She supervised her maids in all things so that the dairy was spotless and the kitchen a hive of industry and good baking.

Sometimes he found himself staring up at the sketch with awe. It spoke of the grandeur of the Lord's creation, of Yorkshire's beauty, of Joss's prosperity and a sixty-guinea theft. On the Day of Judgement he would have to account for this deceit, but not yet, not yet . . .

Susannah couldn't settle through this never-ending Advent sermon endured in the draughty chapel. She ought to be at home, her stomach was churning with fear, and she wished she'd stayed home with her sick boy. William was not responding to the apothecary's bottle or the leeching this time.

Her firstborn son was born nine months after their marriage. He'd made their happiness complete, even if he had grown weak, easily puffed, and only when her other sons followed quickly did she see how weak and under-nourished he was and it was all her fault.

If only she'd not gone riding that winter morning in her delicate condition, but to sit astride her horse gave her such freedom, out on the hilltops in the fresh air. She was not bred for confinement, even if she had adapted to her new circumstances and Joss was everything she could wish for as a master.

Her home was full of light and pretty things. There were others to do the rough work but she took pride in her fine cheeses and butter pats, which were sold at market. She supervised the dairy maids with a keen eye. If only she'd not gone riding in the mist and fog, losing her way, but she'd been curious to see for herself what one of the dairy maids was talking about.

One of her girls was fetching water from the covered well sunk deep into the rock when she'd seen a figure waving as if in distress. In her haste she'd lost her balance and almost tipped into the chasm. Only the arrival of one of the stable boys had saved her from the deep. There were other sightings of a beggar woman lost on the hills and always talk of a local white barghest, the hound of the hills let loose on the rocks. Stuff and nonsense it was, but she was curious. Someone was playing tricks on them and she was determined to squash their superstitious talk.

Mercury was old now, gentle and steady afoot, growing fat and in need of exercise. They were plodding forward when suddenly he reared up in fright, ears pricked, nostrils flaring, and Susannah was thrown onto the rock.

'Who's there?' she yelled pulling herself up, feeling shocked and dizzy. The mist swirled round her, cutting her off from all sounds, but she thought she caught a glimpse of a grey cloak with a fur hood. There was a chill in the air and such a sickly smell but then it was gone. Mercury stood, ears pricked, unsure and suddenly Susannah was afraid for both of them. 'Home,' she commanded, gathering the reins to guide him back down the rocky outcrop of limestone, trusting his sense of direction to bring them to safety.

It was a downhill trek, and her back ached from the bruising and her stomach tightened under her loosened stays into a knot of pain. By the time she staggered back to Wintergill, the pains were gripping her and she knew she must make ready for her lying-in.

William was born early, so small they feared he'd never breathe at all, but nursed by the warmth of the hearth in a cradle packed with lamb's wool, he struggled into life.

She hid the fall and what she had seen even from Joss. William survived but was never strong, and she would always blame herself that she'd caused him to be born too soon.

Now she sat with three fine sons who worshipped with her: Samuel, Jacob and John Charles. All but one of her boys were now strapping lads, sturdy oaks, built to last the century out.

Will, the eldest, was always her favoured child, but she sensed he was only borrowed for a season. She'd felt him hovering between life and death each winter. The greedy ones were out there ready to snatch him from her but she'd kept him safe for seven years now. His heart was never strong but she'd gleaned such knowledge from the apothecary and the conjuror's herbals as to keep him by her side. Despite all her efforts he was growing pale, listless, until he could only watch the others at play.

How her heart ached to see the boys outstrip him in size and vigour. She sensed the firelight in his eyes waning dim but he stayed because she willed him. 'I could sleep for a month, Mam,' he'd smile.

''Tis nearly Christmas, hang on. What larks there'll be when your father lets the season in,' she pleaded, but his eyes were growing glassy and his breathing laboured.

She woke from her daydreaming, looking around the congregation feeling sick. What was she doing here when Will needed her? She jumped up and ran out of the church, sensing something was wrong.

Lucy Snowden, her old mother-in-law, was wringing her hands when Susannah arrived back. 'Thank the Lord you've come in time. I've sent for the doctor in Settle but I don't hold much hope . . .'

William fell asleep in his mother's arms that very night. There was no Christmas that year and she mourned his loss for the rest of her life.

There was such a ferocity in this mourning that it kept folk from her side, an anger in her voice, the choking haltering bitterness that all but consumed her for a while. Joss found it hard to reach her broken spirit and withdrew his company, unsure what to say.

'You never rear all your children,' the parson said as if to comfort them. 'The hand of God has been heavy on you of late, but 'tis His way of testing yer mettle. William's in a far better place.'

She wanted nothing more to do with such a selfish deity. How she yearned to know her child was happy out there, free of sickness. Over the years his gentle presence was fading but he was tethered to her heart on a leather rein. His absence now made an ache in her heart no doctor would ever cure.

'Oh, Will,' she cried, 'where've you gone? I'd follow you myself but now you're in a place I can't find . . . a place I can't go. I have to find you again.'

So she lost herself in work. She filled her days with baking, visiting the poor and supervising her household, but it was never enough. Each season brought its own pain, especially Christmas-time. While Will was alive it warmed her heart to see her children enthralled with presents and games, but once he left them she found it hard to have any enthusiasm for their antics. Joss's festivities grew more elaborate each year as if to compensate for the loss of his child and to chivvy her out of her mourning clothes.

She blamed some malicious force in nature for taking her son. Folk talked of a spirit that haunted the hills around Wintergill but she felt powerless in the face of such elements.

If only she could turn back the clock and not have taken that ride, Will might have lived.

She found solace in her green patch, such as it was. She asked Joss's men to build a wall to protect her plants from the hungry wind that burned the leaves off the stalks. She bought liquorice and sugar loaf, spices to make cough tablet and hard-boiled throat soothers. She wrapped her sons in flannel until Joss protested she was making weaklings of them. Her elderberry cordial kept many a chest clear in the dark months when the cold blew in off the moors but she longed to know more.

Sometimes she heard a crying moan on the wind, a piercing wail of grief outside in the blizzard, echoing the sadness at her own hearth, and she wondered if it was Will trying to contact her again.

There was an ally of sorts lurking nearby, a kind enough soul who watched her at her labours in the house. She had heard tell of the lady who lived within the walls. One morning when she was busy with chores she felt the presence of a woman standing by the door, watching her at work. She looked up and caught a fleeting glance of a black skirt and then nothing. They had no need of words to each other for they were both of one mind, resolved to protect this house from more trouble and sickness.

It was this sickness she feared, which always came with the snow and the darkness; the veil of mist that separated her from her child had thickened with the years. How Susannah wished she could hold him in her arms once more and sniff his head and bury her face in his hair.

She trod many strange paths in search of a truth, visiting preachers who fell into trances of ecstasy in the pulpit and spouted out strange burbling tongues; transient showmen who set up tents by the river and promised all sorts of tricks. Most were quacks, charlatans, stripping the gullible

189

of hard-earned silver for little return. If only she could hear the truth, sense the genuine from the fake and begin her own journey to find peace of mind. She longed to discover a pathway through her suffering, the forest of brambles snagging her spirit. She owed it to Joss and her boys to start living again. On the dark days it was all she could do not to hurl herself down the ravine at Gunnerside. There had to be a better way than ending her life in the view of the very painting that had brought them such happiness in the past. If only someone could soothe her broken soul.

Christmas Shopping

The crowds were pushing and shoving down Skipton High Street, the market stalls twinkling with fairy lights as Kay rushed to finish the last of her shopping. At the top of the street the ancient church and castle made a romantic backdrop to the Christmassy scene, but she was in no mood to linger at the floodlights. There was her list to consult. Tim's parents were sorted, the stocking fillers for Evie and the book for Mrs Snowden were in her bag, along with some spare boxes of chocolate mints from Whitakers in case they were invited anywhere unexpectedly. She had got the tinsel to finish off Evie's angel outfit for the school play, but her most important quest was unfulfilled: something for Evie's main present.

She was not going to set up Evie with loads of compensations for taking her away from her grandparents. She was too young for CDs and most computer games. She wanted something thoughtful, something creative, and as if in answer to her prayer there it was in the window of the art shop: a huge box of paints. It was a compendium of chalks and pastels, poster paints and watercolours, with sketchbooks and palette.

Evie had stuffed a letter up the wood-burner asking Santa for something to do. Surely this would give her hours of pleasure. It wasn't cheap, but it would wrap up well into a big parcel. The shop was an Aladdin's cave of arts and crafts and it took her back to the days when she lived as the headmaster's daughter in the grace-and-favour house of a small public school. She had amused herself with Fuzzy Felt and Lakeland pencils, Plasticine and stringing up beads. She enjoyed making things then.

Now there was a long queue at the till and she was tired. Her feet were used to comfortable trainers now, not tight boots. She longed to sit down with a glass of red wine. Then she heard the music wafting from outside, the haunting carols of childhood played by the brass band, and she felt her chest tightening and her heart thudding. She would have to get out into the fresh air and run as fast as she could away from the sound of the horns.

With tears in her eyes she rushed for the door and out down a side street into the nearest teashop. Her hands were trembling as she ordered strong coffee and poured in spoonfuls of sugar to calm her jagged nerves. It was all flooding back: the memories of last year, of shopping in Sutton Coldfield, hearing the band and thinking what a wonderful Christmas they would be having. There were to be parties and drinks invitations galore, an outing to the panto in Birmingham. Her arms were full of groceries, all Tim's favourites: chocolate gingers, sugared mice, tangerines and spiced tea.

'Be kind to yourself,' said her grief counsellor. 'Let the pain flood over you. It cannot harm you if you let it flow in and out. Breathe deeply. Give it space and let the pain pass over.'

Every minute of last Christmas unravelled slowly before her – first the excitement and anticipation and then the terrible drama. Scene by scene she relived her shock, her disbelief, her numbness, her panic. When the whole world was celebrating they were struck dumb with numbness and the tinsel music on the television rattled on accusingly over their heads. The warmth of the drink settled her. This was what she was told to expect but words could not prepare her for this sadness. Already she felt steadier, calmer. These were different shops in a different town. The band was playing for joy, not sorrow. It was time to go back and get Evie's present. Why should the child not have her wish? It was only for one day. She would cope. Other people faced lonely Christmases, full of bad memories. She was lucky, for she had a child and she had made choices in coming north to protect them both. It was time to retrace her steps. She glanced at her watch in horror.

Nik Snowden was waiting in the Red Lion and she was already half an hour late!

'I'm so sorry.' Kay rushed into the pub with hands full of carrier bags. Nik could see she was out of breath and her eyes were full of tears, in a right state. How could he be angry with her?

'Sit yerself down,' he ordered.

'I'm so sorry. There's so much on my list. I forgot the time. I don't know what's got into me.'

'There's no rush. What'll you have?'

'Oh, I can't drink, I'm driving . . .'

'I've only had a half so I'll drive you home.'

'But—'

'No buts, sit down and sup up. You look done in.'

She promptly burst into tears.

'It was that wretched brass band, it brought it all back . . . last year. I'm sorry.'

'What's there to be sorry about? Sit down here by the fire. You need something inside you.'

'But . . .' Those green eyes flashed up at him so he gave her one of his steel-eyed looks and she smiled through her tears. 'Thanks, Nik. That's a Christian act.'

193

He could see that she was really upset. Her hands were shaking. He was used to seeing her brave face; now she looked like a frightened kid and he knew how that felt. When he'd heard about Jim's suicide, when the sheep were slaughtered in front of him, he'd howled in the barn like a baby out of everyone's sight.

It was hard to pin your face up all the time, and she had such a striking face, when she smiled. She needed company just as he did. Suddenly the pub chatter cocooned around them, the log fire flickered into life, warming him as he took over the glasses. It was like old times on a date with a pretty woman. To onlookers they were just another couple wrestling with a pile of Christmas shopping, taking stock of their purchases, part of a happy family, no doubt.

If only they knew the real truth. Nothing was as it seemed on the surface, and yet his heart was warmed as he sensed her misery and he drew his chair closer towards her.

'There, get that down you and we'll order some soup. Might as well make a day of it now.'

'How did you get on with your accountant?' She changed the subject quickly.

Nik shrugged. It would be easy to fob her off but he needed to get stuff off his chest too. He told her everything. 'I got all the usual warnings but he did have one or two useful things to suggest. When I get back I'm going to root around . . . on a treasure hunt. If only we could find the lost heirloom my gran used to say once lived in the upstairs parlour – a Turner, no less. That would help things out no end,' he laughed.

'You do love your farm, don't you?' Kay was peering at him with concern, making him go hot under the collar. For a second their eyes locked. He swallowed his emotion and looked away as he spoke, trying to keep the tremor out of his voice.

'I'm not giving up Wintergill, not ever, no matter what Mother thinks. There's got to be a way through.'

'You'll make it work. I can see that from what you've done already.'

'I hope so.'

'I know so.' She reached over, patted his hand and held hers there. Then she laughed. 'Listen to us, like a couple of old agony aunts. What's the soup of the day?'

'Never mind soup, I know another place round the corner,' he said, standing to help her with the bags.

'Fish and chips at Bizzie Lizzies?' she asked.

'No, there's a wine bar I've been meaning to try out. Come on, this is on me.' The sun was shining down the High Street and the crowds jostled, but Nik guided her through the side streets. His world may have collapsed, and hers too, but it was easier to face things as a twosome than on your own. The trip to Skipton was turning out better than he'd thought.

Nora was sitting in the Village Institute, putting dolly mixtures on cocktail sticks to decorate the Christingle oranges. There was a force nine draught coming under the door that no curtain could quell. She could not shake off her bone weariness or the sore throat burning the back of her mouth. She ached from head to toe but a promise was a promise. She felt mean not lending Nik her boneshaker of a saloon, but the thought of walking back uphill to Wintergill House was unthinkable. There was no use telling him she felt unwell. He would just tell her she was stupid to be going out. There would be no sympathy from that quarter.

The Christingle service was an annual event guaranteed to fill the old church and raise funds for charity. The WI had over a hundred oranges to put together on their

195

assembly line, and it was all hands to the task. She was glad the Partridges would be involved with the school play too. There should be a bit of religion at the heart of everyone's Christmas, especially in these troubled times. It was no use hijacking a Christian festival and not giving it some respect.

They were a motley bunch in their WI, young and old, locals and offcomers, professional women and housewives. The village would be the poorer without all their activities, especially in the winter when the gloomy grey days and long nights made for depression and isolation.

It was a fiddly business for old fingers, wrapping ribbons around the oranges, threading nuts and raisins and sweets onto spikes, inserting candles. If Health and Safety could see what the kids got up to with those lighted candles, the Christingle would have been banned years ago. She smiled to herself, thinking of last year's service when one toerag lit his sister's hair and singed it. Only the smell of burning stopped her from being scalped!

Lighting candles in the darkness still had the power to enthral youngsters into silence. Spoiled brats needed to know about those less fortunate than themselves – the refugees, the abused, those bereaved, neglected children all over the world.

Christmas had ceased to have any meaning for years now, she sighed. The annual customs were upheld for old times' sake. If it were an optional extra she would duck out, but she usually cooked Nik a turkey breast, bought back one of her own puddings from the WI stall and did her duty. No more goose extravaganzas or drinks parties. They exchanged tokens: a new CD for him, a book token for her, with a glass of sherry and a truce for the day.

There were still a few cards she exchanged with distant friends, but she refused the myriad invitations for drinks around the village because she couldn't be bothered with small talk and false bonhomie. One of the advantages of being old was that she could do as she damned well pleased and didn't have to justify herself to anyone.

Making Christmas happen when there were children in the house used to be a labour of love, however flat she felt underneath. Yet Christmas promised what it could never deliver to her: peace, joy, goodwill and wishes fulfilled. All it seemed to bring was quarrelling, disappointments, and hangovers.

Christmas used to be a truly riotous festival with open house and children, babies and parties. But after Shirley's accident, it was hard to celebrate the season. It became a meaningless ritual done for Nik's sake. An attempt was made to honour the day but it always fell flat somehow.

Nora found her coat in the passageway. She wanted to slip away quietly now, having done her stint with the oranges. She wanted to put something in the churchyard. It was time to pay her respects with a bunch of garden flowers. Funny how there was always some bloom to find even in winter: some *Vibernum tinus*, winter jasmine, and a few Christmas roses tied with greenery and ribbon into a makeshift posy.

The other graves were bedecked with holly wreaths with plastic flowers stuck in and they reminded her of graves in France, gaudy with waxy blooms. It was bitterly cold as she bent down to replace the dead flowers and she felt her head swimming in a cloudy fug. The ground rose up to meet her and now she was sitting on the chippings with the sky above dancing round her. She felt so sweaty as the first spots of sleet and wet snow cooled her cheek.

It was time for a swig of Granny Aggie's firewater from the medicine cupboard: that pungent mixture of elderberry cordial, herbs and alcohol that took the roof off your mouth. That would knock this cold on the head, and a hot bath would soothe her cold bones. She wanted to see Evie at the service and watch her face at the Christingle. It would do the girl good to stand in line with children of her own age.

Evie watched the candles twinkling on the windowledges of St Oswald's. It was magic, sitting in the darkness, and she was not a bit scared, watching all the audience waiting and the children dressed up for their play. Her tinsel was scratching her ears but her wings were strapped around her shoulders and she felt so important.

Mrs Bannerman explained all about the Christingle: the orange was the world and the ribbon was the cross and the candle was the light of the world. The sweets and nuts were God's gifts to be shared. She was dying to sink her teeth into the dolly mixtures, and hoped she didn't get a jelly baby on a stick. She hated them. Mrs Bannerman was busy organising the infants, who had rugs on their backs and sheep faces.

Evie's wish had come true to be one of the angels dressed up with tinsel crowns and real wings. Granny Partridge would be sad not to see her singing but Mummy promised to send them a photograph. Her friends Karly and Millie were playing recorders and guitars, singing solos and carols. Evie wished she was up there at the front, not stuck at the back, but singing didn't come out right when she opened her mouth. It sounded all funny. In the twinkling candle-light she could see Mrs Snowden, who kept coughing and sneezing.

They had all come together in the Freelander as it was beginning to snow, just in case it blew a blizzard. Magic.

Only a week until Santa came to Wintergill. She made sure her letter was stuffed up the wood-burning chimney pipe. Already her green trimmings were dried up and curly. The pine needles were dropping off their little Christmas tree in a pot. Mummy said it was too warm for a tree in their sitting room. The tiny tree would do, she thought, until Daddy brought the big one back on Christmas Eve. She hoped he knew where to find them.

They made lots of decorations in school: a Father Christmas with cotton wool trim, stars made from baked pastry. Mrs Snowden helped her make paper chains and gave her an Advent calendar with windows to open. She had opened them all in secret and stuck them back again. It was so exciting when the cards started arriving read-dressed from Sutton Coldfield, and there were now two parcels waiting under the tree. She was disappointed when they went to collect Mrs Snowden for there was no Christmas in the big house – no decorations, no tree, no parcels or anything. It was all very sad. Did Santa not come to old people too?

Wintergill village had its very own Christmas tree and she had gone down to see the lights switched on, and one of Santa's helpers, who stand in when he's too busy, had asked them to count down from ten, and suddenly there were lights all around the village green hanging from the trees, and fairy lights in the windows.

She knew about lights and the longest night of the year. She knew about Swedish crowns of light and the Christ Child's candle. Now that the schools were breaking up for the holidays Mummy said they must keep up her reading lessons for a couple of weeks but she still kept her secret drawing journal up to date and hid it in a bag under the car seat so Mummy wouldn't read it. It was fun drawing pictures of her secret helpers, and how she sometimes saw the White Lady by the old wall on the footpath.

Soon they would be going back to Granny's house and there would be another school, but Evie didn't want to think about that now. She could see Mummy watching her in the darkness, smiling, and she wished Daddy was there too but he was always busy somewhere else. She wondered where he was, for he never rang to leave a message. Sometimes she wondered if he was ever coming back, but a promise is a promise and he promised her she could choose a big tree. Mummy kept telling her his spirit was in Heaven and he didn't need his body any more. It was buried in the churchyard near Sutton Coldfield where they took flowers sometimes with Granny, but Evie didn't like going there.

When they were carrying the Christingles out into the darkness it was snowing hard. Evie looked out over the snow and twinkling lights and thought it was just perfect, but poor Mrs Snowden started to shiver and Mummy said she wasn't well and must go home. So they did not stay for the mulled wine and mince pies, though Evie grabbed a Christmas biscuit decorated with silver balls.

The school children had made all the refreshments for their nativity play, rolling out the pastry for the mince pies, cutting out biscuit shapes. She was having much more fun than she ever had at her other schools.

By the time Mrs Snowden got into the car, Mummy had to go slowly up the hill, struggling with the gear stick all the way back. The snow was turning back to driving rain and the magic was gone.

'You shouldn't have come out with us tonight,' said Mummy to the old lady. 'You aren't well.'

'I'll be sorted once I've had a good night's sleep. I'm fine. I hope you enjoyed it all, Evie,' Mrs Snowden asked.

Evie nodded. 'Can we make Christmas biscuits?'

The two women laughed. 'Not tonight, love, another day perhaps . . . if you behave.'

* * *

The next morning when Kay and Evie called over for some eggs at the back door, Mr Grumpy looked very worried and said Mrs Snowden was in bed with flu.

'Stubborn old mule, she won't be told! She won't have the doctor and didn't get her flu jab this year. Serves her right.'

Mummy went up to see her and came back with a list of stuff from the chemist. 'I don't like the sound of her chest, Nik,' she added. 'I think it needs to be checked out. She's too old to leave it to chance.'

Evie didn't like to think of anybody in bed for Christmas. 'What will she do on Christmas Day?'

'That's a long way off yet,' said Mummy. 'If she gets antibiotics I'm sure she'll be fine by then.'

Evie was not to be thwarted. 'Can we give her Christmas?' she offered hopefully, looking at Mr Grumpy. Why was he always sucking his pipe like a dummy?

'That's kind of you,' said the farmer. 'but Christmas is not one of Mother's favourite seasons. She'll be glad to give it a miss, I expect.'

She looked up at him in amazement. 'But everybody has Christmas,' she argued, but the farmer just laughed.

'Not at Wintergill, they don't,' he replied. 'Not for a long time.'

Evie's jaw dropped and she turned to her mummy, puzzled. 'We're having Christmas, aren't we?'

'Don't worry,' she winked. 'We'll leave the Scrooges to themselves.'

Mr Grumpy laughed.

Nik spent the next morning sifting through the boxes of junk in the attic cupboard. The dust was getting up his nose but he knew what he was looking for: a set of old leather hatboxes full of Jacob Snowden's Christmas collection.

201

He sifted through the papers with interest. It was years since these boxes had seen the light of day, and memories came flooding back of his own father proudly going through it all with him, explaining some of the long-forgotten occasions in the district that Jacob had documented so meticulously over the years as senior Circuit Steward of the Methodist chapel.

There were photographs, programmes for concerts, testimonials, chapel anniversaries, invitations to weddings and funerals, ornate black-edged orders of service. The whole life of Wintergill village and the dale lay before him. Sadly he calculated none of it was worth much. It would be better donated to some local archive. He felt mean to be even thinking of selling such a heritage, but instinct said there was something he recalled in here of value and then he found them.

Wrapped in tissue paper was a series of the most beautiful Christmas cards he had ever seen. Some were hand-painted Valentine cards to Joss's wife, Susannah, and they were executed with such an eye for detail, exquisite in their sentimentality, innocence, and signed in a spidery copperplate from Joss himself. Others were overprinted commercial cards, showing the Dickensian Christmas in all its glory: a coach and horses in the snow, the church spires, glistening with hand-painted gold dust. There was a fine pop-up card in the shape of a flowery bower of roses with two turtle doves on the roof and posies of flowers with a sliding tab that said:

> Neath love's sweet bower,
> O may you spend a very merry Christmas
> Friend!

Another world, another planet, Nik thought to himself sadly. Those long-gone days when Wintergill House was in its prime, filled with Snowden treasures. Jacob, Joss's son, was renowned for playing tricks with parcels and conjuring displays. He was a man who saw only goodness in folk, his father had once told him. No tramp ever left his back door hungry, no plea for alms went unanswered. His view was a simple one. His wife was another matter, a gypsy's child, by all accounts.

Nik smiled to himself as he looked at their wedding portrait on the hall stairs, Agnes peering down with her strange white features and piercing stare, Jacob all whiskers and bonhomie. He must have had his work cut out taming a gypsy, he thought. No one mentioned her much. Was she the shadow to Jacob's brightness? Apart from the Christmas cards there was nothing much to the collection. How could he think of auctioning such a family treasure? In a trunk there were old costumes packed tight, Victorian day dresses by the look of them, shoes flattened, a musty smell of decaying silk, nothing of interest but a strange cotton quilt made up of patchwork moons and stars, hand-made, frayed at the edges, as he pulled it out. Perhaps Kay and his mother might like to see such a motheaten object.

As he lifted the cloth, something fell out onto the floor amidst a flutter of dried leaves; a small leather-backed note-book. In the fly leaf was handwritten:

Privet
Agnes Snowden. Her Herball.

Nik plonked himself down on the dusty floor and began to read the copperplate handwriting, first with curiosity and then with amazement.

Agnes, 1869

Her Herball

For the opening of the mind drink first, rosemary, thyme or yarrow tea. The burning of the bay leaves, mugwort and wormwood to transport the spirit whither it must go.

For the cleansing of a room from evil, an incense of pine, juniper, and cedar is best. For protection from evil take fresh marjoram or dried to every room of the house and renew at each new moon rising.

Restoration Jelly

Pack a cow heel into an earthenware pot with 2 quarts of new milk, 2 ounces of isinglass and 2 ounces of hartshorn shavings.

Put jar in brick oven, just after the bread has been drawn out, let it remain until half consumed.

When cold, skim off the fat, drink a small cup warmed, morn and night.

Regular pursuance for six weeks is necessary to render this restorative thoroughly efficacious; therefore should a housewife be in the habit of visiting the sick from house to house, she must make a point of taking a supply with her.

Time to head for the hills again, smiled Agnes Lee. They came to Wintergill every year for haytime but there was still no sign of her brothers ahead as the lanes narrowed. The Snowdens would find fewer hay-cutters this year since there'd be better paid work building the new Settle-to-Carlisle railway through the mountains.

Agnes and Granny Bones were following the old droving route, hoping to catch up with Jesse and Rufus and their cart. It was looking like they'd not bother to turn up after the rowdy gatherings at Appleby Horse Fair in June. Now they must make their way straight to the new camp at Batty Wife Green instead, to sign on for navvy work.

Granny wanted to linger round the campfires listening to the craic, the gossip, admiring the new brides and the families joined in the gypsy ceremonies. Agnes always held back in the shadows, aware she looked different from other girls, with their black curls and flashing jet eyes.

She had seen the growing patchwork of white and brown on her arms and neck, the white streaks in her dark hair, her pale eyes blinded by the ripples of bright sunshine. Children pointed and laughed and called her 'the badger'. Sunlight hurt her eyes.

Winter was her season, and darkness gave her better vision. Ma once told her she was blessed with special powers and to give no heed to ignorant folk. She had stuffed her head with the growing of herbs and knowledge of potions since she was a small child.

'We must pass on our remedies to anyone who will listen. Make an honest living and you'll not go far wrong in this world.'

Pa called his wife a heathen witch and beat the daylights out of them with his belt if he caught her with her candles and signs. In defiance Ma had sewn all her knowledge into a patchwork quilt, each square an instruction, a recipe like a book. It was all Agnes had to remind her of those special times they shared before Ma and Pa caught the fever and left them orphans at the mercy of Pa's mother, Granny Bones.

Now Ma was gone, they were back on the open road in all weathers, knowing that Jesse and Rufus would want Granny up at the navvy camp to cook and wash for them. The makeshift town, high up in the rough hills, was growing, despite little shelter under the three high peaks of the Yorkshire Dales.

Granny Bones was sucking on her clay pipe, chuckling as they neared the farm track. 'There's gold in them hills, I've heard; rich pickings, fortunes to be told, palms to be crossed with silver, baccy to chew, beer huts and farm doors to knock with lucky heather and pegs. Happen you'll jump over the brush with a strong navvy man, keep his hut and take in lodgers. I don't know why yer driving this poor old horse up the lane to the high house again. They don't take on women at haytime.'

'It's worth a try, and I like it up here. The air is clean, the green lanes are quieter than the turnpike road. The Snowdens will not see us go without.'

Agnes knew some farmers' wives set the dogs on them if they knocked, others bought in fear of curses. One look at Granny Bones in her black boots, shawl, her flat cap and her pipe, and the maids fled. Others sifted through her basket of hat trimmings – lace, ribbons and feathers – shaking their heads and closing the door.

There were markers left by tramps on the gateposts, secret signs that showed who would welcome them and who would see them off. The Snowdens never turned a genuine pedlar away. The mistress was a fine lady who liked to dress her bonnets in the latest fashions.

Haytime was a good season to call. It was all hands to the fields, any help was welcome and field workers were fed. If they were short of labour, there was a chance that Agnes would be hired. She was all sinew and bone, not afraid of hard work. She wore her ma's sun bonnet with a wide brim to shield her face from the sun and a deep neck shield. Her sleeves were never rolled up to reveal her patch-work skin.

They would feed from the farm kitchen, pasties and cool lemonade, flatbread with cheese and fresh berries. She would share it with Granny. It would make a change from rabbit pot, and hedge greens.

Ma was right about one thing. Light and shadow, goodness and evil, kindness and malice she could sense in other souls as clearly as her sight in the darkness. There was something about Wintergill that drew her back each season. Strange, since she came from travelling stock, who moved with the seasons, not fixed in one place for generations, but that too held its own mystery and power.

Sometimes she felt a grey mist of sadness around the place, some unquiet spirit like a force of nature at work, a danger in this windswept place. But if she was honest what drew her most was the sight of Jacob Snowden in his breeches and boots, striding the fields like a lord in his glory. She had worshipped from afar for years and dreaded the moment she might find out he now had a pretty wife by his side.

Granny apologised for her grandsons' absence. Agnes offered her services. They had been welcomed back and found a corner by the hedge to park the vardo and rest the horse. She was given lighter work with the other village women, gathering up loose hay, and Jacob had smiled at her, asking about her brothers.

In her bodice she was carrying a posy of fresh herbs and charms she hoped might open his heart to her. It was guess-work since Ma had thought her too young to know about the love charms and incantations necessary to secure a lover. But midsummer would work its own magic if only she could recall the ceremony. There was a bonfire and words to be said but how could she get a lock of his hair?

Suddenly the skies were darkening and everyone was rushing to get the hay under cover. Jacob was shouting to his brothers and men to drag the bales to the far barn while he was loading the cart high. Agnes didn't want to be in the way but something made her hover by the gate, an instinct felt deep in her belly that something was about to happen and she might be needed.

Granny was already packing, restless to be on her way north to the railway settlements. Agnes's brothers would want a roof over their heads, and one they didn't have to rent. It was going to be a hard winter and she would have to find servant work. Most girls of her age were long married, but who would marry a badger who needed spectacles to see, a girl with no schooling except as a hedge woman . . .? Then she heard the scream and shouting.

The haycart was on its side and someone was trapped by the leg underneath, in agony. Men were muscling up, straining to lift the weight off the man to drag him clear. 'Send for the master and the doctor!' A crowd stood not knowing what to do, and the lad was lying as if dead.

Agnes tore across the field, her heart racing with fear,

pushing her way forward. 'Don't move him now . . . give him air!' No one let her pass, eyeing her with suspicion. 'If you move him you will crack his back!' she ordered 'Give me a belt . . . a necktie to stem the bleeding, and a bucket of spring water to cleanse the wound.'

'Who does she think she is?' said a village wife. 'It's a job for a doctor not a dirty thing like her.'

Agnes didn't hear her words. She saw that Jacob was in danger. Doctors lived in towns and it would be hours before he would come. 'Please,' she begged, 'let me treat him here and find a board to carry him back to the farm.' She peered down, relieved to see his eyes were open though he was staring in shock. She asked for a jacket to cover him while she searched out where the bone was crushed. She could stem the flow of blood, clean the wound and get him to safety.

She knew about shock. There were always accidents on the road and the injured needed sweetness, honey and warm drinks to stop the shakes and weakness. She was thinking on her feet, reeling off all the herbs needed for healing: knit-bone, poppy juice and cleansing poultices. Still hiding her face under the sun bonnet she barked her orders like a fishwife on a market stall and the onlookers were too stunned not to obey. She felt over his body, trying not to shake. Ma, please help me do it right, she prayed, and then out of her bodice slipped the posy and she blushed, hoping no one recognised what she had made.

'Get the hay in afore it rains . . .' Jacob groaned.

Agnes smiled with relief at his words. He was alive enough to be worried. The pain had not kicked in yet but it would come later.

'Can you feel your legs?' she whispered, touching his other leg with a pointed finger. He nodded. Only then did she let them lift him gently onto the barn door.

'The hay . . .' he groaned.

'Never mind the hay!' Agnes screeched. 'Get him to his ma's kitchen. I'll go and fetch my healing box.'

She ran across the field to where Granny was packing the last of the cooking pots and dousing the fire. 'We have to stay. The young master's in trouble.'

She reeled off what had happened but Granny sniggered. 'Just like yer ma: one drop of blood and you've got your sleeves rolled up. Come on, let's be off before you get lumbered. He'll be fine.'

'No, Granny, I have to stay . . . I just know it.'

'It's none of our business. They don't want the likes of us hanging about once a job's done.'

'I'm not coming . . . I'll follow you on foot when I'm done.'

'Don't be daft. It's miles from here. This be no place for a lass on her own.'

'I'll be safe with the Snowdens . . . I can find a bit of the barn to rest in, but I'm staying. I don't know why but I have to. The place needs me,' she argued.

Granny put on her cap. 'May all the blessed saints preserve us, and pure St Agnes, yer namesake. What would yer pa be thinking of me to let you abide with strangers in a stone house?' She crossed herself three times and climbed up on the ledge to leave.

'I'll be needing Ma's chest – the wooden one,' Agnes called.

'I suppose you'll be wanting her quilt for your witchery, an' all. They'll show you the lane end if you show those heathen things to good Christian folk.'

'I just want to see Master Jacob back on his feet.'

'So he'll make a bride of you? Who are you fooling, Agnes Lee?' Granny chuckled again. 'I'm off bogtrotting. You know where to find me when you come to your senses. You're on a loser there. Who wants a witch for a wife?'

*   *   *

212

Susannah watched the field girl washing down the wound without flinching. It would need stitching up. She'd never seen her mottled arms before, patches of white skin and brown, and that thick streak of hair down the centre of her parting like silver ribbon. They'd given Jake sleeping draughts to ease the pain but the poor lad would not take to his bed kindly. Already the storm was abating but the hay was dry inside now.

There was something about this strange girl, the lilt of her voice with the hint of the Irish twang. She was no beauty but striking in a different way with fierce pale eyes and a quiet manner. She talked of garden remedies with a knowledge that belied her years.

Later, as they took a stroll around Susannah's walled patch, the girl surveyed the distant hills, the far peaks, the sky and then her straggly herb garden with interest. She stopped and looked into Susannah's eyes as if she could read into her very soul's anguish.

'You'll not have far to find your sorrows or your blisters here,' she whispered, eyes flashing with concern.

'Yes, it's a wild place, but the farm yields a good crop of lambs, and the herd fine cheese and butter. Our children thrive in the fresh air better than any town bred,' Susannah replied.

'It's not of this world that I speak,' Agnes said, looking straight into Susannah's eyes as they blinked. 'My eyes are better suited to darkness than sunlight. My ma says guard what is yours from the danger.'

Susannah made no reply as the girl continued, 'Fret not, the old ways have the best remedies. There's so much you could grow in here, mistress. This be not always a happy place,' she added, bending over to examine a patch of scallions.

'What do you mean?' Susannah snapped.

'Forgive my plain speaking. I talk not of this world but

213

the next, and the poor restless souls who find no peace, who gather with the winds in your corner. My ma would say you need protection from their menace.' Agnes's face was blank as if transfixed by some force beyond her.

I've prayed for such guidance, Susannah thought, hearing her worst fears realised. Was this child sent to give answers wise men couldn't, this common field worker? Her words sounded so matter of fact, so calm and confident, as the two women sat on a bench sipping yarrow tea.

'All women have powers, if you know how to use them, but the skills need a fine grinding on the rocks to sharpen them. How do you protect yourself?' The Lee girl looked up.

'I say my prayers like any good Christian.' Susannah sensed they were on dangerous ground.

'My ma used to say summon the four angels from the four corners of the earth to your aid: Raphael from the east to be your front, Gabriel from the west to your rear, Michael from the south for your right side and Auriel from the north to guard your left. When you feel yourself in danger summon these great forces to protect your home. Let their names sing around the clock, over and over for your protection, until the attack is over.'

The girl stood to leave in the gathering dusk light. She turned to face Susannah.

'Sleep within a circle of light,' she said. 'Carry the herbs of protection with you always, sew them into your cloak, as I do. I see you have a little rowan and elderflower by your door. Are there hag stones in the byre?'

She is talking witchcraft, Susannah gulped, knowing that only the superstitious hung stones with natural holes in them over their cattle stalls. I am talking to a hedge witch, she thought, hardly daring to breathe in case she cast a spell. 'These are heathen ways,' she snapped.

'My ma said these are the old ways, ancient as the hills,

and nature has a cure for every ill. I'm sorry, mistress, if I've upset you . . . My ma says there's nothing wrong in using nature's forces to fight darkness and ignorance.'

'Where is this ma of yours?' Susannah said.

'She's passed over to where no harm can befall her again. I've missed her many a year but never forgot what she told me.'

'It's hard to let our loved ones go,' Susannah sighed. 'You will stay on with us?' she found herself saying. 'I could use you in my garden.'

'Thank you, mistress, and I could teach you what I know, if it suits.'

'I want no witchcraft in this house. The master would not approve of anything heathen.' She could feel herself going hot and cold in case anyone should come and overhear such words. Yet she was intrigued. 'But do tell me what your mother taught you about the seasons.'

'There be things we do to help the crops grow, to heal wounds of body and heart . . . By the light of the sun, moon and stars, things handed down from one to another for the good of others . . . I can pass on only what I've been taught. I can go no further than that, but perhaps it's time I took my leave.' Agnes made for the gate. 'The master might take the whip to me.'

'Leave the master to me . . . If you help with my green patch, you can write down all the remedies for me to learn. I will find a room for you over the back yard.'

There was a pause and the girl bowed her head. 'I don't have any lettering . . .'

''Tis no matter. I will teach you and you will teach me your cures. We will both learn. There is something in your words that speaks to me or we'd not be talking like this.' Susannah was looking up, trying to sound brisk and in control. 'I have lost my dearest child. All I wish is to know

215

that he dwells safe, like your mother,' she whispered, hesitating to voice her deepest yearnings.

'Ma told me once that there are pathways to the dead so we may speak with them but it needs special powers. It be dangerous work and I was never to meddle,' came Agnes's guarded reply.

'How do you learn that?' Susannah asked.

'I can tell you all I know of such ceremonies, how to cleanse this house of all that ails it. There is a right way and a wrong way to go about the task. That I do know. You will write this down?'

Susannah nodded. 'It's just like making new recipes.'

Agnes smiled and her face was transformed into sunshine. 'If you say so, mistress, but all I have, I carry in my head. There are herbs and flowers, tools and a sharp eye, and moon time.'

'Can I write down the instructions, step by step?' There were so many questions bubbling up in her head like jam on the boil. She would feel safer if it was all written down.

'My ma says, hide them away for they might bring trouble. There is a great fear of the old ways, of ancient rites and talking to the dead.' Agnes shivered, grasping her shawl around her. The rain had long passed but the wind was rattling through the open gate.

'Talking to the dead – is it possible to hear my child again?'

'I don't know about that, mistress . . . Ma said it be the unquiet soul who causes bother,' Agnes answered. 'To reach out and show them the way towards peace, to conjure up soothing dreams to tired souls, to calm the terror of their empty grave, is beyond me.'

Susannah felt her heart thumping with terror at the thought of such responsibility. Be careful what you wish for, she mused, for it may come true. 'Come, time enough to talk more another day. I will find you lodgings.'

'My ma says, "Life be but a journey, a circle from maiden through mother to old woman. We are but wheels turning with the seasons, ever forward into the light."'

Susannah nodded suddenly full of hope. 'Then you and I, Agnes, and others like us must work to bring light into darkness so that the light shines over our children and children's children, however long it takes to learn the art. Your ma was a wise woman. A pity she isn't here to guide us,' Susannah sighed.

Agnes smiled. 'But she lives, here in my heart. I hear her words in my head guiding me. She made me stay on here for this purpose.'

What words this girl came out with. Susannah didn't know what to believe. But of one thing she was certain: with such a canny spirit around the kitchen door, no one would come to harm, though she must know her place and not take advantage of their secret. One step out of line and the Lee girl would be sent packing down the lane.

Agnes never did get herself up to the shanty town at the head of the Ribble. There was always some piece of the garden, some lesson, something to stop her going. Susannah was a hard taskmistress when it came to tidy dress and house-cleaning. She would brook no slackness of effort and little by little Agnes found her wandering ways changed by indoor living.

At harvest home and Christmas she performed the old ceremonies in honour of her ma and sometimes Susannah looked on briefly and then disappeared, but Jacob, once recovered, treated her as he did all the dairy maids – with distant politeness. He had thanked her for saving his life but nothing more.

Her heart saddened when it came to Midsummer Eve once more. She climbed to the hilltop, to the ancient wall she sensed was a sacred place in times gone by. She carried a sack of kindling, making a ring of stones to fix her fire. Round her loosened hair she wore a garland of flowers but nothing else to hide her body from the moon. She circled the stones and struck the tinder to set the fire ablaze. She said the old words. In her hand she held a lock of Jacob's hair, strands she'd cut with a knife when tending his wounds. It was all she had to secure him for herself.

'Oh Ma, I'm trying my best but nothing is working. What am I doing wrong?' she cried, throwing the hair onto the fire in desperation, trying to dance sun-wise as she was taught.

What's that fire on the tops? Jacob was walking the fields in the half-light when he saw the flickering flames. You could see a candle burning for miles on a clear night, and he feared the worst. It had a been hot June and the grass was as tinder in parts . . . He must find a fire brush and stamp it out before it set the whole moor alight.

He tore up the fellside cursing, his leg still stiff and aching from last year's accident. Hot and sticky from a day's labour, he was in no mood for smoke and destruction, but when he drew closer he saw a figure dancing in shadow, the lithe body of a young girl. Was he dreaming? Who was she? Was it the White Lady of Wintergill up to her old tricks, tempting him over the edge of the rocks with her wiles?

He hung back, hiding behind a rock, ashamed of his arousal. He'd never seen a naked woman before, and one dancing like a savage. She looked so beautiful as she sang up to the dark sky. Why was she up here at this hour?

It had to be some apparition, and yet he recognised something in her voice and smiled with relief . . . Who'd have thought it! It was little Agnes, his mother's helper . . . So this was her game.

Should he storm up and demand an explanation and tell her how dangerous it was to bring fire onto a dry moor, or should he stay and watch?

That would be cruel. Whatever she was doing, she was doing it in private for a purpose and Mother spoke highly of her work. His presence would give her such a fright and shaming, so he tiptoed back grinning at the vision of her loveliness in all its glory.

By heck, she'd filled his breeches and no mistake . . . He'd never really noticed her in that way before. It was little Agnes who'd dressed his wounds and made him comfortable. She'd got his mother smiling again and sorted the cow with the swollen udder. She might be a witch but she was handy round the house. She would warm his bed and all . . . Who needed some prim farmer's daughter when he could have a home-grown wife who knew the chores and a few other tricks besides? Jacob could do far worse . . .

Agnes couldn't believe the change in Jake that summer. He sought her out on any excuse, blushing when he spoke and made his intentions plain. The household waited for a furious uproar from his parents but none came. How could a Snowden go courting a field girl and a gypsy? Agnes smiled and thanked her mother for giving her the secret knowledge to bring him to her side.

On the eve of their wedding, when the house had finally retired, Susannah knocked on her door, bringing the bride a pretty veil of Brussels lace that had once belonged to her mother. She sat down at the end of the bed, and Agnes saw the deep frown lines that made a ditch in her forehead were smoothed over.

'He came to me last night . . . my dear little boy,' she whispered. 'I drank the yarrow tea with the rosemary as I have on many a night but this time I dreamed such a dream.

It was as if he was there by my side, smiling. I felt his hand in mine. Then he was on this tall sailing ship, waving from the deck, and I saw it slip slowly down the river until it was a speck on the horizon. I woke up with tears running down my face, not of sadness but of peace. He was saying goodbye and I know he is safe out there waiting for me when my turn comes . . . How can I thank you?'

Agnes bowed her head. 'You already have. You took me in and made me welcome when many another would have shown me the door. You taught me my letters and numbers and much more besides. I should be thanking you.'

'You will take care of my son . . . and those that follow after. You know what I am saying.'

'No one will harm my bairns . . . be sure of that or they will have me to reckon with.'

'I thought as much,' Susannah smiled. 'Now get some rest. Tomorrow you'll be taking up a new position at Wintergill and I'll be glad to put my feet up in the upstairs parlour for a change. Neither of us was bred for this farming life, but I reckon we both are up to the job in our different ways, don't you? Love evens everything out in the end.'

1874

On Christmas morning the wind carried the church bells high across the valley to the tops but Jacob woke at dawn with excitement long before their peals filled the air with promise. This was the day when it would all begin, when all his planning would come to fruition.

Ever since he'd attended the penny readings at the navvy camp, he'd been bewitched by Mr Dickens's serials of *Pickwick Papers* and *A Christmas Carol*. He was determined to make this day special for the miners, diggers, workmen and their families, who were straddled across the hillsides close to the farm. It must not be just another boozy blowout when everyone got roaring drunk, ending up in terrible fisticuffs with bloodied noses.

This day was sacred, not only because it was the Lord's and his baby daughter, Mary's, first birthday, or because it was a dedicated day when folks could wear their best clothes, stovepipe hats, tweed jackets, rustle in silken dresses, and show off new kid gloves in church, but because they must show goodwill to all men, rich and poor, rough or comfortable. It should be a day when the smell of roasting birds and spiced breads, puddings and fancy trifles should reign all over the house-place, a day when they could worship the Lord whatever day of the week it was. The mill gates were shut, the shops shuttered in town, and he hoped

221

the Midland Railway would silence its engines in honour of the season.

Preparations had begun earlier in the year with the fattening up of their best shorthorn for the Christmas stock show. He could never hope to rival the Reverend Mr Carr's famous Craven heifer, which weighed in at over a ton, but Jacob's beast was prepared for the show, preened and pampered, dusted and her hoofs polished to a finish. Then after the parade, with a fine rosette on her horn, he commissioned a proper photograph of the successful day. In fact, he was so proud of this creature he asked the local artist to make her likeness for him to frame.

Agnes had been on at him to replace the picture on the mantelpiece, the one his late mother had been so proud of. She thought it a poor affair, lacking in colour, and he tried to explain it was only a sketch by a famous artist but she'd have none of it and said they could do better than a few charcoal scribbles, so he decided to put the beast in the foreground of Wintergill House as a surprise present for his wife.

He tried to make sure all his servants and Agnes's dairy maids were given time to visit their parents down in the village. He saw to it that the navvies, camped close to the track, got some time to celebrate too although some of the navvy families living further out would be left to their own devices.

Christmas Day was always set aside for visiting and feasting, but it must begin with worship, and the bells would ring out to remind the parish to gather in celebration. In Wintergill you were either church or chapel, Anglican or Methodist; black or white, sheep or goat. There were no half measures when it came to allegiance. Few changed sides once baptised into their specific corner, but the navvy camps strung along the new rail track were another country, a jungle of heathens and wild fighting men. They didn't care what label the preachers went by, so long as they dolled out comforts, sat with the dying men to the end, and their children got some schooling.

Everyone should have some Christmas cheer, Jacob thought, before they drank away precious wages, leaving their family without. What the navvies needed was something to brighten this special day: a procession of witness on Christmas morning, something to wake the world to the birth of Christ. His idea grew from a tiny mustard seed to a mighty tree of conviction over the months and now they would spring their surprise this very morning.

He chivvied his own household to dress early, crack the ice on the wash bowl, stir the lazy from their beds with the best porridge oats, dressing warmly for the cold, and get the carts saddled up for the journey up to the nearest camp.

'Do I have to go?' yawned Agnes, reluctant to budge from her feather counterpane. 'There's so much to be doing on Christmas morn if we are going to eat before dusk.'

Jacob would have loved to indulge his wife but she must set an example for once. Lately she was a sluggard about her attendance in the chapel. He asked no questions when she claimed to have the headache or sickness. He knew she was the fittest horse in his stable, walking out in all weathers on her strange expeditions, but he said nothing.

'Rise and shine, beloved. We'll stir the hearts of Wintergill camp with our praises today and I need you by my side. The chores can wait this merry morn,' he said. 'Besides, I have a special surprise for you in the hall; something to give you and young Mary a deal of joy on your walks.'

'What is it?' Agnes smiled, coiling her black and white hair into a twist around her head.

He loved to watch her at her dressing, all that lace and ruffles, the tinctures of musk roses on her piebald skin.

There were some in the chapel who thought her flighty in her choice of bright colours, her flamboyant cloak, her hats and parasols. She did not look like a country farmer's wife, and that was one of the joys of his marriage: he never knew what she would do next, what enthusiasm would overtake her. She'd borne him sons, Tom, Joseph and Will, and now there was little Mary to add to their joy. Much to his surprise his own mother became her ally and the two of them took care to keep the walled patch of garden full of hedgerow medicines. He did not agree with some of her strange rituals but he put it down to finding cures for woman's complaints and didn't pursue the matter.

Agnes sped down the stairs to find her present and stared at the gift, shaking her head puzzled. It was a little truck with spoked wheels and a padded seat for a small child to sit on, covered with a sturdy canopy.

'Do you like it? I had it copied from the *Illustrated News*. The Queen herself couldn't have one better . . . Mary can sit in style and you can push her on your walks.'

Agnes smiled. 'It's . . . grand, Jake. We can take longer hikes along the footpaths. It would be good for carrying greenery and plants for the garden.'

'Whatever you like. Merry Christmas! You'll be the first in the dale to have a baby carriage,' he laughed, relieved she liked his unusual idea.

'I shall walk down to the camp with it later, if you don't mind. There's much to do this morning if we are to dine on time this afternoon.'

His party set off in the darkness, a line of carts plodding along the track as the dawn light was breaking; streaks of lemony, mauve stripes heralding some settled weather, for a change. By the time they reached the navvy camp, the fires were choking the air, the cocks were crowing and chickens darting amongst the wooden huts. None was stirring behind the wooden doors but the fierce barking of the dogs huddled in the lee of the houses sounded a warning. There were a few stalwarts huffing and puffing, stamping their boots: the mission faithfuls wrapped against the cold with shawls around their heads; men in hobnail boots and flat caps holding baskets of hymn sheets, children already playing tag across the muddy tracks lining the makeshift street.

The last to arrive, of course, was Mr Jagger, the site manager, in his stovepipe hat and best frock coat. It was nearly eight o'clock before the most important arrival showed his face out of the door sheepishly. The Fothergill brothers flourished their instruments – trumpet and drum. They were going to lead the proceedings.

'Are we all here?' Jacob did his head count. It was going to be a poor show from the village chapel.

'Hurry up, I'm starving,' muttered someone from the ranks. 'What's the first hymn?'

'"God rest ye merry, gentlemen"?' shouted one wag at the head of the procession.

'Gentlemen, my foot,' laughed another. 'I don't see why us have to wake that lot up. There'll be a riot! You want something cheerful to get this lot out of bed.'

'I know summat cheerful,' said the trumpeter, smiling, and he turned to the drummer with a wink. There was a drum roll, a tuning up of the trumpet spit, and they were off to the tune of 'Wassail, wassail all over the town'.

'That's not the sort of carol I had in mind,' Jacob whispered to his father. 'They can't start drinking already.'

'Don't be such a sobersides,' said Joss. 'Do it this way or not at all. Christmas isn't all church and praying. It's the light in the darkness, a bit of cheer in the depth of winter, dancing and fires to stave off the bleak. No one wants sermons but food and dancing. Besides you catch more flies with honey . . . Come on and lighten your step. "Here we come a-wassailing Among the leaves so green . . ."'

Slowly valances twitched, a few heads appeared at doors and windows, curious about the racket.

'Happy Christmas! He is born!' Jacob shouted to anyone who appeared looking puzzled by the noise.

Finally they assembled outside the stone bothy with the sod roof, the drinking den where fights flared up each Saturday night. For once it was empty and silent and the cart drew up with a trestle table and baskets of Christmas food, which Jacob had gathered in over the last few days from the village and farmers. It had been a struggle to get them to give to the navvy mission. Village and camp didn't mix much, and the coming of the new railway line was seen as a mixed blessing.

Children gathered round, eyeing the food with interest. 'Who needs John Barleycorn to lift the spirits on such a day?' shouted the railway mission parson.

They managed one carol and a prayer before the children started to make a grab for the buns and pies.

'Suffer the little children . . .' whispered the manager with a sigh and a wink.

Jacob was standing outside the wooden hut looking around the camp in the murk of the morning wondering how he could brighten the lives of these workers, when the idea of a community choral concert came to him. Perhaps next year he could organise a mission choir with extra singers, an augmented band that would join villagers and navvies together in one big blast of Christmas music. Why wait until Christmas, though? His head was ringing with ideas as the crowds pushed into the little hall, devouring his pies and spiced cakes, biscuits and buns.

Food's a great leveller, he mused. It hadn't quite been

Christmas in Dingley Dell but it was a start and better than a punch on the nose.

It was hard pushing this new contraption along the foot-paths. Will and Jo wanted to have a ride too and Mary needed tying into the seat as she was still a little small for the chair. It was sturdy enough to cope with the bumpy metalled track down to the camp but first they must push it uphill past the boundary wall to the wonderful view down the valley.

Agnes loved this place. It was here she had first danced at midsummer, and it was here that Jake had asked her to be his wife. It would be good to sit and rest awhile before the downhill trek to the navvy camp. She was happy to let Jake and his father conduct their services without her having to tag along.

It had been a sad year when Susannah took sick and passed away quickly. Joss had aged, bereft of his beloved, but Agnes knew that she was at peace. They had named their son, Will after his lost uncle.

She ought not to be dawdling on such a busy morning but she felt in a playful mood, and Will and Jo had hoops and stick they were determined to whip along. 'Look at me, I can do it!' Jo shouted, and Agnes parked the carriage to give him chase while Mary looked on. It was only a gentle slope and her eyes were only turned for a second, but she felt a stab of fear in her chest. She was not alone; someone was spying on them from over the wall.

'Come out, whoever you are, and show yourself!' she yelled. The boys stopped their game and shot back to her side, hiding themselves in her cloak, sensing her fear. 'I know you're there. You don't scare me.' It was probably a drunken navvy sleeping off his booze but they could turn nasty.

She heard herself chanting the old prayers of protection under her breath. You mustn't feel fear . . . Make a shield . . . stand firm. She heard her ma's voice in her ear. Go to the bairn . . . She started to run towards the carriage as she watched it begin to roll gently down the slope, gathering speed . . . She flew like the wind after it, heart racing with fury. There was no wind, not a breath of breeze. It was as if an invisible hand was pushing her baby down towards the stonewall and certain death.

'Stop, in the name of Christ and all the Angels! Let my baby go! I will curse you to the end of time if you harm my child!' She was screaming and running, knowing every second was bringing Mary closer to the rocks and destruction. 'Hold her back. You don't belong here . . . go back where you belong . . . to your own time . . . I know who you are . . . Go home. Don't harm what isn't yours . . . I will not let you take what is mine!'

She was helpless, watching as, as if in slow motion, the cart reached the barrier, the ancient wall held firm against the force and the cart collided into it. Mary slid from her moorings, rolling over and over like a ball, landing on the grassy mound.

Agnes screamed a scream that pierced the air with anguish and dread, not daring to look, but then she heard her baby howl in shock and fear, and she raced across, fearing the worst. Mary looked up with surprise, covered in bits of straw and grass: her landing had been cushioned by all the padded layers of clothing – gaiters and leggings, a thick coat with fur trim, and a thick bonnet. They had protected her fall.

Will and Jo were howling and Agnes was howling, and Mary added to their noise. Agnes hugged her child to her chest, feeling her for any injury, but there was none to see.

'Thank you, thank you,' she prayed. She'd won this battle

of wills. The spirit had fled. The wall had stopped the cart, chipped a few corners, dented the paintwork, but no matter. What mattered most was wrapped close to her chest and holding her hand. She was shaking, exhausted but elated. She would make sure that tormented soul never got a chance to try another trick.

You must write it all down, she thought. Susannah was right. She must protect future Snowdens from such dangers. Mary, Tom, Joseph and Will were safe, but what about children to come?

By the time Agnes arrived it was time to load the carts for the return journey. She was pale and very shaken. There'd been some mishap on the way with the cart, and she refused to put Mary back in it, but Jo and Will fought over whose turn it was to take a ride.

From farm to farm they went making visits until Jacob was 'brossen' with roast and pie, pound cake and puddings. No one could say they didn't know how to entertain in the dale.

Jacob was proud to be one of the first to sport a magnificent Christmas tree, with candles flickering on the branches, and a bucket of water just in case. He had cards printed and posted around the district, cards with beautiful scenes of coaches and horses in the snow.

The feast itself was a right rib bender, and the cordial flowed all night, while the dancing in the hall shook the pictures on the wall. Agnes was quick to hang up the new portrait of their prize-winning heifer in place of the Turner sketch. Joss looked on, saying nothing, but Jacob hadn't the heart to stop his wife and gave the painting back to his father to keep in his room.

Funny how every year he woke up on Boxing Day with a belly like a pig and his tongue feeling like a scrubbing brush, but it was all worth it. To see his children's faces when they fished in their stockings for penny whistles, tangerines and coins was his joy. There were wooden toys for their farm and Noah's Ark. For Agnes, there was always some trinket from the jeweller in town – a brooch, a pin or a bracelet of coloured stones. He would have given her the sun and the very moon from the sky.

When the children were asleep he found her outside pacing across her patch, shrivelled with frost, looking up at a stretch of stars in the night sky.

'The darkness is broken and the new life is reborn,' she sighed. 'Blessed be.' Then turning to him, she smiled with twinkling eyes. 'Come and sit by the yule fire with me, my own Mister Christmas, and let's sup a cup of cheer.'

'The cup that cheers but does not inebriate,' he added, thinking of tea, and she smiled and sighed.

'This night calls for something special. I want you to try out one of my new recipes from our beehives,' she said, and he nodded. How could he refuse? Her experiments were always exceedingly tasty, even if they did give him a splitting headache the following morning. He could never understand just why. Perhaps it was better not to know but he was sure the Lord would not begrudge them high jinks and spirits on this day of days.

Nik woke from his dosing. He looked at the spidery writing. So my great-grandmother was really a witch. There were pages of instructions and recipes that might fetch a bomb on the occult market. Yet he felt protective of this stuff. It had been handed down, hidden for a reason, and not burned as could so easily have happened with his pious ancestors. He scanned the pages, taking note of the recipes.

'How to settle an unquiet spirit.' So the old hag had plagued them too.

'How to make a circle of protection when awake . . .' How long had these hauntings been going on? For centuries, if his forebears were dabbling in this stuff. No wonder Agnes and Jacob looked so forbidding in their portrait on the hall stairs. There was even a drawing of a place he recognised. What had the Celtic wall got to do with anything? Why had she ringed it round with a pointed star? When he had more time he'd examine this more closely. Not that he believed a word of it, and yet . . .

Hepzibah watches the boxes slipping out of sight with a sigh. Bit by bit the master of the house is stripping the house of all he holds dear. Perhaps for family gain, but some things ought not to be meddled with. A few trinkets may fetch a mickle of coins, but the old mistress's receipts should not leave this place. She served here in her own way. In Hepzibah's own day she would be burned at the stake for her troubles.

We all leave signs of our presence, she thinks: oak chests, settles, pewter, pictures, fresh chambers and hearths. The gypsy girl was a wild spirit who, like moor-bred horses, needed a tight rein from her sire but she kept her kin safe for many a year.

Snowden men have a taste for pickling-spiced brides, sweet or sour, easily befuddled by a fine head of hair. One thread of wild tresses can draw a hundred yoke of oxen, they say. This master be no different, methinks, she chuckles.

Now the old mother is abed with sickness, the son unheeding and a child sleeps in the byre. This is not the time to be off watch when a hungry ghost roams abroad.

She wonders why Cousin Blanche has not come calling, for the Twelve Days of Christmas cannot be far off.

She makes the sign of the cross, sensing that Blanche will be out there somewhere, hiding in the scrub, bushes or in the copse. She is trouble on the wind, keeping vigil with eye ever watchful.

It is allus maids, young maids, Blanche seeks out. Surely it's time this mischief must end and peace return once and for all, Hepzibah prays.

In the days that followed, Kay found herself running to and from the Side House Barn to check on the old lady, who lay limp, racked with coughs, hardly able to breathe. The doctor came and went, and Nik did what he could but a man never saw what really needed doing.

She lit a fire in Nora's bedroom to air the dampness. She changed her sweaty sheets, brought tissues and sponged her down, making sure there were plenty of drinks by her bedside table. She lit an oil burner with eucalyptus and tea tree oil to freshen the room.

Nora Snowden slept in fits and starts, and needed persuading to eat a little soup. But slowly, she began to pick up and listen to her radio while Evie wandered all over the house, looking for her imaginary friend, the Lavender Lady.

Kay was glad Evie was out of her hair, for the child's excitement was mounting by the hour and it was very wearing. They needed to be stocking up food for when the shops were shut over the coming holidays. This was the downside of living up a track miles from anywhere. She just couldn't be bothered. She couldn't face the crowds or the bustle and Christmas shopping brigade jostling for bargains.

It was enough that Evie was plastering the walls of the barn with cards and Christmas clutter. Soon she would be too old for all the Father Christmas malarkey but now she still believed in ghosts and fairies. Now was not the time to spoil her innocence.

Why did Christmas evoke such strong emotions? All over the world there must be people just like herself, counting the days until it was all over.

* * *

Blanche thinks she hears music through the walls of the old byre, the tinkling of a spinet, music and laughter. Her child is within and she bangs on the door but no one answers.

Her strength is failing, weary of travelling in circles down the centuries of time, stumbling like a lame hound, her resolve weakening. There are strange apparitions before her eyes, candles flickering, loud noises ringing in her ears, faces she no longer recognises, and the ever-changing shift of familiar buildings reshaped by time. She is losing control, losing power, losing the white heat of her fury. It has grown cold, crippled by age.

It takes so long now to shuffle from hill and dale, barn and cottage even by the simplest paths. Her power fades like the slowing hands of a timepiece unwound grinding to a halt. She can no longer measure the passing of the seasons, her mind uncoils like a rusty spring.

There must be no rest until I find my child, let these bones creak and stiffen, these eyes dim and mist over, she sighs. A beggar's life is a wearisome living. I creep where once I ran, chasing phantoms in the snow. I no longer know what path to take . . . the fight is gone out of me.

One last time, she cries. I am ice and fire, summoning all my angry grief that cannot be consoled. I call her name but she will not come. My hackles rise in a roar of pain that spews out from me like dragon's breath shooting flames into the night air. Sparks of blue light crackle over the rooftop like forks of lightning rending the darkness.

The barn house sleeps, the heating clicks off, the log fire guarded by a rail and the lights on the little tree are dimmed. Holly curls over the wooden shelves. Christmas garlands hang limp, the wind is silent. Only the owl hoots from the sycamore tree. Then a surge of energy bursts through the plug, a flash, a crackle of electricity, surging like a gush of wind rustling through the wires. Sparks are showering over the room,

*alighting on the crinkled edges of a paper chain, and it smokes
into life, feeding on the dry air.*

*The flames creep along the chain, link by link, and the
paper Santas hanging from the branches with cotton wool
beards curl and bow to the heat. It lingers, devouring stars
and angels, dried pine needles, and reaches out to touch the
curtains and Christmas cards dangling from the low beams.
Flames rush down the walls, gathering power, magazines,
books and newspapers feeding its frenzy. The room is ablaze
and the hungry smoke curls under the door into the hallway
where draughts fan its fury.*

*Blanche can see dancing fire, mischief and destruction. She
smiles, seeing that her breath has still the power to consume
all before it.*

Shadow Fire

Kay could hear a strange buzzing in her dream. She struggled awake, knowing that the sound was outside her. The buzzer was loud and urgent, and suddenly she recognised the alarm. She could smell smoke and was out of bed in seconds. The smoke alarm at the foot of the stairs was on alert. She opened the door to a gush of smoke swirling up the stairs. No time to think. Instinct took over as she leaped into the second bedroom and grabbed the sleeping child from her duvet.

'Wake up! Fire! Come on . . . into my bedroom.' Close the door, plug the gaps, wet towels by the entrance. Windows . . . windows, open the curtains . . . open the window and get the hell out! Keep calm! Wrap Evie in the duvet. The mobile . . . dial 999, but her fingers wouldn't hit the right pad. Stay calm and ring for the fire brigade.

Years of living without Tim at her side made a habit of having a phone by her bed and she prayed the signal would work. What was the number of the big house? Damn it . . . it was stored somewhere in her phone. She pressed the buttons on her mobile almost at random. There was a connection.

Answer the phone, please.

There was a voice barely conscious, but a voice.

'Nik! The Side House is on fire. Help us. Bring a ladder.'

Kay's voice sounded calm and cold as she heard the roar of flames and the sickening stench of acrid smoke. Then she was flinging everything she could soak by the door, throwing everything in her room of any value out of the window. Evie was watching wide-eyed with terror.

'Darling, we'll be fine. See, we can still breathe. Nik is coming and you must get out of the window when I tell you.'

Thank God for an en suite bathroom, she thought. There is water to fight the flames if the worst comes to the worst, and a vase full to the brim to sprinkle down the door before it bursts.

Where is he? She was standing on a chair, pushing at the window, seeing Nik running in wellies and boxer shorts.

'Hold on! Stay calm!' he yelled, but she was beyond instructions now. Her only thought was to get her child out of this inferno. The ladder was short but Evie must be pushed through the Velux like a snake. It had an up-and-over window, hard to budge but it yielded to her effort and she pushed the child to the opening.

'Come on, Evie, slide through,' the farmer called.

'I can't.' Evie was hesitating.

'Just get out of that window this instant!' Kay yelled, her adrenalin pumping an icy calm into her voice. 'You can do it. Nik will help you. See, he's waiting at the top of the ladder.' There were blue lights flashing over the moorland top road. How quickly they were responding. It gave her the courage to force her child through the window into Nik's waiting grasp.

He climbed down carefully before bundling Evie into a duvet on the ground and shouted up, 'Now it's your turn.'

Suddenly Kay froze with fear at the sound of the fire, the smoke and her natural fear of heights. This cannot be happening to us. But the smoke was seeping through the walls and she had to go forward to survive. Shutting her eyes, she edged forward, wriggling under the window as best she could, gasping for air. The siren bells were getting closer. It gave her courage as she stuck, wedged tight in the gap. 'If only I was a size ten not a fourteen,' she heard herself murmuring.

Suddenly there were hands and voices and arms, and a lift and the coolness of fresh air. There were bursts of tears as she was bundled up like a parcel, manhandled down from the firestorm towards the safety of Wintergill House.

The rest was a blur of sweet tea, being checked by the paramedics, a gentle man testing her chest and her pulse and her reactions, asking her questions. She was reunited with Evie, who was sitting with a black face and white eyes like a Pagliacci clown. They sat hugging each other, unable to speak while all the fuss went on around them. The firemen struggled to control the blaze, soaking the building with bursts of water, hosing down her car, the stone walls, smashing windows and doors, opening up the flames to their hose pipes.

Nik was doing what he could to help, rushing from house to fire, blackened from head to toe like a chimney sweep, his legs sticking out of his wellies. It was all so ridiculous, sitting wrapped in blankets, with hardly a stitch of clothing between them in the middle of the night. Only as the shock began to kick in came the shivering awful realisation they could have been burned alive. Only then did the shakes begin and she crumpled. One simple battery-operated alarm had saved their lives, giving them precious minutes to defend themselves against the fury of the flames.

Everything was gone: laptop, furniture, handbag and credit cards, and all her Christmas shopping hidden under the cupboard stairs.

They were safe now, but what if she had had no phone?

Would they have jumped to the ground in panic? It was strange how she had been on automatic pilot, going through some fire drill, as if in a dream. The Side House was almost burned to the ground with only the stone walls left. How did it happen?

Kay was trying to check over her night-time routine: lights off, fire guard, door shut, or had she . . .? The aromatherapy candles, her constant companions, were blown out or were they? A familiar shaking panic began to creep over her. Had she left a pan on the hob and caused something to catch fire? No, she was sure she had had a blitz in the kitchen and everything was put away. She was always nervous in someone else's kitchen. Had Evie been playing with matches? How easy it is to be careless and cause a catastrophe. But her mind wasn't clicking into gear any more.

She felt so bone weary that she was almost asleep. She felt punch drunk, flopping on that saggy sofa in the kitchen full of dog hairs, and crumbs scratching her bare bottom.

'It's under control now,' said a grim-faced Nik Snowden. 'Are you OK?'

At the kindness of his concern she promptly burst into tears. He put his arms around her and she sniffed the warmth of the smoke and sweat on his fleece. 'What are we going to do? It's almost Christmas – where shall we go?'

'That's the least of your problems,' he smiled. 'I've made up a bed in my room for the two of you. Upstairs now. It's a bit of a mess in there but I don't suppose you'll notice tonight. Ah, here comes the doc . . .'

A cheery young man not long out of short pants plonked his bag on the table and proceeded to examine them both carefully. He pronounced them remarkably unscathed from their experience and said there was no need to send them thirty miles to the nearest A&E, but what they needed most was rest. Somehow they were escorted up to a bedroom with a huge double bed that swallowed them both whole and they fell into a deep sleep.

Kay awoke late in the morning, looking up at a damp patch on the ceiling stained like the map of the world. This was not the sloping barn roof or Glenwood Close. Where was she? Then a panic of sensations seized her limbs, paralysing her for a second with fear. Fire! She was out of bed searching for Evie until she saw her golden head tucked under the air cell blankets.

It was the old-fashioned sort of blanket bed. The bedstead was mahogany inlaid with mother-of-pearl leaf scrolls, with a matching tallboy and wardrobe. The gracious room had a fireplace and marble surround, and long velour curtains on a pole. The rest was a clutter of clothes and *Farmers Weekly*s, CDs and books. There were dirty shirts hanging over the chair and a basket full of laundry. A bottle of Lagerfeld aftershave and a tortoiseshell brush set sat on a dressing table cluttered with pipe cleaners, cufflinks and a photo of Nik in his youth, scowling like James Dean on a motorbike.

Thank God for his bedside phone and her mobile. She could sense again the long night's terror flashing before her eyes, the smell, the crackle of flames. Now their stay was over. This house for winter was yet another disaster in this horrible year. What on earth was she going to do now? They would have to return to Sutton Coldfield, back to all the fussing and 'I told you so's, but it was not a prospect she had the energy to contemplate.

Nik was pacing outside the shell of his old barn, his heart thumping at the sight of the mess. The inside was blackened with smoke and charred beams, the walls hosed down to curtail the fire's path. He could hardly bear to look. The cause of the blaze was still a mystery. It was not one of the usual suspects in a domestic fire: burning chip fat, lighted cigarette, a fallen log, or spilled fuel. It was beginning to look like an electrical fault in the wiring that had sparked off a small fire, aided on its way by the Christmas clutter and perhaps the tree lights.

But the lights had been switched off when he went for his late evening stroll across the field with the old dog the night before. He could see through the open curtains that Kay and Evie were in bed. The fireman said Christmas was a terrible hazard with all those candles and floating decorations, not always fireproof, but their regulation smoke alarm had done its job.

Nik felt sick when he thought of what might have happened to their guests. The barn was a ruin, his pension gone up in smoke, but at least he didn't have two lives on his conscience. The worst of it was he had meant to renew his insurance policies for buildings and contents together. Wintergill was on a separate policy and he had paid that promptly, but as for the rest of them? There was a pile of bills waiting to be sorted out, but with the upheaval some stuff got forgotten. He had simply shut his mind to them all.

He looked up at the ruins, the blackened stone walls standing and most of the roof. The upstairs was charred and gutted. He was looking at the end of Wintergill. This venture was supposed to have seen them through. It had earned nothing all summer. Now it would earn nothing until it was refurbished and restored. Now was not the time to contemplate how that might be achieved.

'When will my luck change?' he muttered out loud, staring down the valley to the river plain and up to the empty sky. God knows, I've tried, but we're finished now.

* * *

'What's going on?' Nora came staggering through her front door, still weak from the flu. She could smell smoke and rushed out, seeing the mess scattered everywhere. 'Oh my holy aunt, the barn . . . Evie! Kay! Oh, no! Nik!'

'Keep your hair on, Mother! Everybody's safe. It was an accident in the night. The fire brigade did us proud. The building's ruined . . . Don't look inside, it'll break your heart.'

'What happened? Where are they?' she cried, rubbing her eyes in disbelief. 'And I slept through it all? Why didn't you wake me, son?' She was standing in her carpet slippers, her hair like coiled wire standing on end at the back.

'You slept through sirens and engines and shouting and smoke. You could sleep through a blitz! What was the point of waking you to all this?'

'I could have made tea like the WVS,' she snapped. 'I must see to the guests, poor mites! Oh, Nik! What'll we do now? Four days before Christmas . . . poor little mite! Are you sure they're OK?' She could feel her heart thumping through her chest.

Nik shook his head. 'Don't fuss, Mother. The doctor's been. They're fine, thanks to the smoke alarm. It's happen an electrical fault sparked it off. All their clothes and stuff's gone, though. They've only the nighties they're standing up in. I put them in my bed.'

'Did you change the sheets?' she asked.

'No, and I don't think they'll notice,' Nik snapped back.

'Little Evie was so proud of her decorations,' she said, staring at the blackened building.

'That's what did the bloody damage. It sent the whole room up in smoke.' This was no time for sentiment, thought Nik.

'Still, we are insured,' Nora sighed. 'They won't lose out. We can make it all straight. Better get on to Laytons

Insurance brokers this morning. They can come and see for themselves.'

Nik nodded. He would have to bide his time to break it to her gently. What a bloody mess!

So it begins again, sighs Hepzibah, sensing alarms and excursions in the night: a night of shadows and a fireglow like Hallowe'en bonfires. The sun is dead and the moon is hidden, but the shadows dance across the house. It is a night of mischief and all Blanche's work. The time is come at last.

She watches from the copse as the flames lick over the stones, satisfied. The orange golden light of the flames warms her. They do not heed my pleas so they must learn the hard way. I am fire and ice, shadows and brightness. This is my terrain and I will do as I please.

She sees the man running, she sees shadow figures in the darkness silhouetted against the flames and cannot comprehend how men can fly on the wind to make such a rescue. There was no one to save her child in the night from the wolf's claw, no guiding hand for Nonie to hold.

She does not understand what is happening but senses her will has been thwarted and turns away into the darkness, sniffing the night air and a change of weather, her eyes sparking like flints on rock.

If not by fire, then by ice.

Refuge

Kay stood in a daze, sifting aimlessly through the wreckage of Side House. Everything was ruined. It looked as if a bomb had hit the building; an empty skull with windows like blackened eye sockets. The stench of burning singed her nostrils. Even though they were temporary residents, the place was full of their belongings. Now she was standing in borrowed clothes: a thick sweater of Nora's that drowned her, and some baggy pyjama bottoms with Wellingtons that made her look like a refugee.

Evie was subdued, still in shock, wearing an old-fashioned Fair Isle jumper and a kilt that Nora produced out of tissue paper, making her look like an evacuee from the Second World War. They would have to go into town and kit themselves out, but Kay hadn't the energy to drive that far. The sky was glowering overhead and the forecast was for snow.

Part of her just wanted to get down to the railway station and catch the first train south. The thought of negotiating motorways and traffic in bad weather, returning to another borrowed bed, was too awful to contemplate. I just can't do it, she cried. I can't move. We're trapped. What on earth shall we do?

News of the fire was wafting like a bonfire across Scar Top moor and down into Wintergill by police, postman, milk lorry, and within hours the local reporter was at the gate, wanting to make a big Christmas story out of their plight. He made Evie pose looking disconsolate outside the old barn. It was amazing just how much he had picked up from Stickley's about them; that Kay was a widow whose husband had died tragically last year at the same time and that all their presents were burned.

Evie was gabbling on about Father Christmas finding another chimney to come down and Kay felt sick, knowing that all her presents so carefully hidden in the under-stair cupboard had melted in the heat. She should have locked them in the boot of the car but it was too late now.

'What will you be doing for Christmas now?' the reporter asked.

'I don't know . . . back to the Midlands, I suppose. I really can't concentrate on this,' she said briskly, hoping he'd go away, but he stayed rooted to the spot.

'Just a few more questions, love. This will make a good human-interest story. Locals will be very generous to the kiddie, just you see.'

'If you have any Christmas spirit at all, just leave us out of your newspaper. The fire is public knowledge. The rest is personal to us. Don't make it any worse for my child either. It's the Snowdens who you should be interviewing. Nik saved our lives. You can remind your readers to buy smoke alarms too. Thank you.' Kay walked away, suddenly exhausted.

'I'll see what I can do,' the reporter promised. She sat nursing a mug of strong tea, shivering at the thought of what might have happened, wondering: when is this run of bad luck going to end? What have I done?

Why were her dreams turning into nightmares?

The phone at the farmhouse never stopped that morning as everyone in the district wanted a blow-by-blow account of the night's excitement. It reminded Nora of the phone calls after their stock was 'taken out'.

Nora was not surprised that the local farmers' wives wanted it straight from the source. Ringing in for a good craic on the phone just to while away minutes between chores after breakfast was something she was guilty of herself. She was ready for all their enquiries. If they wanted the lowdown then they must help out, and she began to galvanise action to support her guests.

'The poor lass has nothing but her nightdress. The bairn hasn't a toy or stitch to her name. They've lost the lot, all their Christmas gone up in smoke . . . We shall take them in, of course, but I've been laid up with flu and not a thing prepared for an invasion. Nik's rushed off his feet trying to sort out the insurance inspections before the holiday shuts everything down.' She made a big sigh into the earpiece.

'Days before Christmas is not the best time to have a blaze . . . so if you can find your way to helping these poor souls, I'd be most obliged . . . Ethel, Audrey, Kirsty, Pam . . .' Soon she was hoarse repeating her message.

She finished each phone call with a smile. Don't let me down, girls. I'm relying on your good-hearted generosity to show these offcomers a right Yorkshire welcome, she thought.

Then the sight of the ruined barn caught her eye. If truth were told there was a little part of her heart that was glad it was derelict. It had such a place in her own story. How strange to see Evie wearing Shirley's clothes; the ones she had kept by for the Christmas her daughter never got to see. She had kept them wrapped like a relic in tissue paper in the back of her bottom drawer, but now they could be better used. Evie was so unlike Shirley and it was all that could be found in an emergency. It wasn't morbid but oddly comforting to see the kilt swishing on a living child.

If her refugees were coming to stay then a bit of dust and clutter would have to be shifted to give them an aired bed and some privacy. There were meals to prepare, food to be bought in, and she was still too wobbly on her pins to drive into town. She would give orders, make lists and do sit-down jobs like chopping vegetables. She could keep an eye on the youngster and try to take her mind off the shocking experience. Kay must have a hundred things to do so Nora decided to ring Pat Bannerman and put her in the picture. She was proving a good friend to Kay and she would help Evie come to terms with the event.

Perhaps it was not too late to salvage something from this mess if they all pulled together.

Nik ran Kay down to Settle to buy some clothes for Evie. She would have to sort out credit cards and inform Stickley's, but she was working on automatic pilot, silent, sad-eyed, close to tears at the slightest sympathy. Nora had made them a list of essentials: toiletries, underwear, warm clothes and boots, and he left her to it. He had his own mess to sort out at Laytons Insurance brokers.

His mother was doing her best to cheer up the child. She ought to be convalescing, not baby-sitting, but it was all hands to the pump in this emergency. This is what happened when you let out your house to strangers . . . Hang on, he thought, they're not strangers now. This was Kay and Evie, who'd had a bellyful of bad luck. They'd brought life back to the yard, Evie dancing about with Muffin. She'd softened his mother's eye these past weeks, and as for Kay . . .

They'd had a great lunch in Skipton. She'd told him about her accountancy career and how successful Tim had been, and for a second he found himself jealous of a dead man. They'd talked through some of his confusion about compensation tax relief until their lunches were almost cold.

When Kay laughed he felt a glow of satisfaction. Here was a woman he could really fall for, but now she was homeless and would leave Wintergill with only bad memories. He couldn't have that. Mother and he were responsible now for their welfare. Neither of them would walk away from the enormity of what might have happened.

If only he had left the barn untouched, spending so much money in the hope of a good return. Now it was a write-off. What on earth was he going to tell his mother?

'I wish I could put you both up,' said Pat Bannerman as they queued in the supermarket. 'I'm sorry, but I've just the two rooms. You must come for dinner, though.'

'Thanks but no,' Kay smiled. 'We ought to go back to Tim's folks after all this, but I just can't think straight.' She was desperately trying to clear her head. 'I've just been into the shop to buy some clothes for Evie but I couldn't even remember her size! My mind keeps going blank. I'm sure I've bought a load of rubbish.'

The bank had been sympathetic issuing an emergency chequebook, phoning her branch in Sutton Coldfield and transferring cash straight away. She found herself standing in the cobbled marketplace amid the Christmas lights, and wanting to howl.

All around her were excited faces with their bags of presents and holly wreaths. All those families together, and never had she felt so alone.

They don't know about us . . . They don't know what happened. She could feel the tears spouting from nowhere again. It felt as if the whole world was against her. No one cared that we nearly died, she thought, sniffing into a tissue, pretending she had a cold. It must be the shock.

'Have a good cry, let go of it all. Release the energy.' She could hear her grief counsellor whispering in her ear. 'You've

been so brave and courageous. Good times will come again
. . . Keep battling on . . . All shall be well.'

How could all things be well when they'd no clothes, no
roof over their heads and not one present to give Evie for
Christmas? It was a stupid idea coming north and now
she'd lost everything! She drove back to the farm in a daze
of misery and confusion.

'I'd better start packing,' she sighed, knowing there was
nothing left but the car. 'We'll get out of your hair,' she
added as Nora hovered in the hall.

'Nonsense. You're staying here for Christmas and that's
an end on it,' Nora ordered. 'There's no blame on you for
the accident. It was just one of those things. I wouldn't
dream of letting you go to some hotel. We've made a start
already. Edna Danby's been round to give me a hand clearing
out a guest room for you both with twin beds. She's left a
big apple pie with mincemeat. You'll have met her husband
at the quiz show, I expect.'

Kay nodded, not having the foggiest clue who this Edna
Danby was, feeling much calmer now after the tears.

'Karen Grimoldby, who'll be having her own sad
Christmas since her husband died this back end, sent some
anoraks and sweatshirts her boys have grown out of for
play clothes. Pat Bannerman rang and will send up a pile
of books and bits for Evie to amuse herself with over the
holiday. The Pringles from Dry Beck called in with a plucked
goose and some sloe gin to take your mind off your troubles so you won't go hungry.'

'How kind,' Kay sniffed, humbled by all this concern. 'That's
how we do things in the dale,' said Nora. 'We help each other,
good times and bad. A bit here and there – it all adds up.'

'Thanks, I shall write and thank them,' Kay replied. 'We'll
stay on condition that we help out too. Keep me busy.
It'll take my mind off it all. I keep seeing the flames rushing

up the stairwell.' They were sitting in the little snug with a roaring fire, and the flames licking the logs looked so harmless.

'If you'll see to your own sheets in the linen cupboard and sort out your beds, that'll be a help.' Nora was giving her orders for the day. 'There's no central heating in here. I don't hold with it in bedrooms. I think it causes all sorts of ailments but we've got hot-water bottles somewhere. Put on your socks in bed and pile on a sweater.'

'There could be just a bit of a problem with Evie's bed,' Kay whispered, knowing she'd have to confess now. 'She's still a bit unreliable at night, and after all this, I'm expecting a setback in the wee department.'

'There's a rubber sheet somewhere at the back of the linen cupboard. I'm not that reliable myself some nights. Coughing plays heck with your bladder and getting old is no picnic!' Nora was laughing away any embarrassment and Kay could have kissed her. 'This place is too big for the both of us. It'll be good to have some noise around the house, like the old days. Evie's a breath of fresh air.'

'We must do our share, though,' Kay insisted, wanting no charity. 'But I don't know how to thank you both, Mrs Snowden.' She touched the old woman's arm.

'Then start by calling me Nora,' came the reply.

'Mrs Nora feels more respectful after all you've done.' Kay felt such relief not to have to pack up and head south. The decision was out of her hands.

The older woman rose slowly to her feet and made for the door. 'If that's what you wish to call me, then Mrs Nora will suit me fine. Come on, let's get stuck in. Christmas is coming and the geese are getting fat.'

Nora was sure that the insurance bumf was in the concertina file under the letter L for Laytons but Nik must have removed the policies when he went into town. She tried ringing their office but got some dreadful musak and slammed the phone down. Nik was out doing some walling on the fells and not due back until dusk. Trust him to disappear when he was wanted. She needed to know where they stood as regards the Side House so she hovered in his kitchen sorting out the mess until he kicked his boots through the door and put the kettle on the hob, ignoring her.

'Well?' she asked. 'How did it go?'

'How did what go?' he muttered, banging his mug on the stove.

'When are the insurers going to pay up? I saw the reminders myself.'

There was a silence and she noticed he was trying to be busy with his tea, not even bothering to answer her concern.

'There's been a bit of a complication,' he said in his 'no nonsense now, Mother' voice.

'Why's that? We've paid our premiums for years, buildings and contents, one after the other. They always come before November. What's the problem, son?' She didn't like the way he was avoiding her eye.

'The contents are fine . . . It's just the buildings that have lapsed.'

Those words poured over her like a drenching in cold water.

'I forgot . . . I thought we had the buildings sorted, not the other way round,' he said as he cut a crooked slice of bread.

There was another icy silence and she found herself gripping the table for support.

'Are you saying we're not covered for the Side House? All that brass we spent doing the damned thing up and it's all for nothing?' Her chest tightened in a spasm, her breath mangled up by the pressure. She sat down with her head in her hands. 'You bloody fool!'

'It's not that bad, Mother. The contents are covered, furnishings and stuff. There was a pile of reminders and I meant to sort it out. I thought they could wait a while longer,' he said, sitting down with his tea and shoving a mug towards her in a gesture of contrition.

'What good's carpets and curtains without a room to put them in? Have you seen the state of the place? It's just an empty shell.' She could hear herself shouting. How could her son be so useless?

'We've got a new-for-old policy with our contents. We can rebuild the shell somehow.' He was trying to sound optimistic.

'So we can refit the kitchen and bathrooms and everything?' Perhaps it was not so bad after all, she thought. 'Just when were you going to tell me all this . . . in the New Year?'

'I'm afraid the kitchen and bathrooms are considered a fixture . . . so they come under the buildings policy,' he mumbled into his tea.

I need a stiff whisky to take in this bad news, Nora thought, not a mug of weak dishwater.

'Well, you've done it now, our Nikolas. That's us in Dicky's meadow and no mistake! We're finished! How can we stay here with no stock, no income and a ruin on our doorstep? How could you?' She was screaming for all to hear. All the pent-up frustrations of the last six months came bubbling out of her mouth.

'I forgot . . . Anyone can forget, Mother,' he answered, gazing down at the floor, utterly dejected like a five-year-old that had punctured his balloon.

'You did not forget. You just did what you've been doing for months . . . putting off paying our bills when there's no need. We had the brass for once. I should have done it myself. I trusted you and look what you've done by burying your head in the sand. We're finished here . . . We have been

251

for years but you're too pig-headed to see it. Just like your father when he was thwarted, always wanting to go your own gait!'

'But there's the compensation . . .' he offered.

She burst into a fit of coughing at this. 'Comp, compo! I'm sick of hearing about compo! We'll spend it ten times over, repaying overdrafts and barn conversions that never get let. You're so mean keeping it in the bank, hoarding it when the whole place is falling over our heads. That family could have been killed and we weren't even insured. I can't believe I've got such a daft in t' head son.' She stood up, pacing around the table, hugging her chest with her arms.

'I just want out of here . . . out of this mess. I want my own fireside, some peace and quiet and no more money worries. I want my share of the bloody compo while I've breath left to enjoy it. What's so special about these bricks and mortar that we have to freeze to death living in this draughty old barn? We rattle around like two peas in a barrel. It's ridiculous.'

'Shut up, you've said enough,' snapped Nik. 'You don't understand, you never did. This is my house. I was born here . . . all I've ever known. This is my life and I'll decide whether I sell up or stay on. It's my compo.'

'Like hell it is!' She was blazing now with indignation. 'I were foddering the sheep years before you were born. I had to stomach this draughty house, nurse your dad in his last illness. I have a say in this place and its future, and I say call it a day, right now before it kills us both.' She stood staring at his dejected face, her cheeks on fire. 'Wake up, lad. You're living in some dream world. It's never-never land, you inhabit. Farming's never going to be the same after this lot's over, this government will see to that. They want the likes of us out and gone to our little bungalows in the town. That'll suit me fine. I'm going to phone Bruce

Stickley after Christmas. He can sort out this property and get it on the market. He'll give us a good price. You've gone too far this time losing money we haven't got. Grow up!' She stabbed her finger at her son.

'Don't you point the finger at me! You've never understood how I felt. I'm not the only one who lives in the past, or hadn't you noticed? When could I ever talk to you? You've never cared for me. Don't you think I don't know I'm a poor second after the blessed Shirley?'

She could see the pain in his eyes as she lifted her hands in protest, shaking her head up to the ceiling.

'That's right, look away,' he continued. 'I mention the sainted Shirley: the little angel who did no wrong. Father told me you never wanted to stay here after she died. Boy, have I had to live under her shadow all my life. You've never expected much of me so why are you disappointed now? I'm just a chip off the old block, and you never loved him.'

His blue eyes were blazing out at her and she felt herself flushing at his emotion.

'That's not true. How dare you say such things?' she hissed back.

'Oh, you did your duty by us, fed us and clothed us, but we weren't Shirley, and as for Dad, poor sod, you never loved him or me for not being another little Shirley. There's no use denying it. You should have left years ago and let us get on with it in our own way.'

She watched him slicing himself some more bread with a shaking hand, unwrapping some stinky cheese without looking at her. All these years she'd been living with such resentment. Suddenly her legs were trembling and she felt herself crumpling with exhaustion and the pain of uncovering such long concealed wounds.

'It's nearly Christmas, Nik. We've got guests, we've got to keep going.' It was all she could offer him. 'We can talk about this later without the whole world knowing our business.'

'Oh, aye, put on a united front, is it, as we've always done? Hide the mess. Don't expect me to be joining in any jollifications,' he shouted.

'When were you ever jolly, son?' The gloves were off now but she was stung by his accusations and couldn't leave it there. 'No inheritance of Mr Jacob's Christmas spirit in you – you're more like his miserable wife . . .'

'And whose fault is that? You were never sweetness and light around the turkey either, with a face like a wet weekend. You've spoiled every Christmas I've known.'

'May you never see your child die before your eyes, son,' she said.

'I DIDN'T KILL HER!' he shouted back. 'It wasn't my fault. I wasn't even born!'

'I know,' was all she could reply.

They were retreating from the brink of a black cavernous pit.

'No one can sue us for negligence. The fire wasn't my fault. It was a brand-new conversion with state-of-the-art wiring. There was some strange surge of power, some freak winter lightning that caused a spark or something. I'm not to blame,' he said, biting on his sandwich trying to act normal.

'We can't carry on now, this place is killing me,' Nora sighed, snatching the conciliatory moment. 'If you restock, I will go. I'm not fit for farm work. I'm getting too old. I want some time to enjoy my life before I peg out. You have to understand my point of view.'

'I do. I know it looks impossible . . . Let's just see the season through. I'm sorry,' Nik said.

'By heck, you know how to pack a punch, son, straight where it hurts. Children always do. I'm fair knocked back by your words,' she stammered, standing in the doorway, breathless.

'Then say no more. Happen we've both said enough. It alters nothing. One careless slip and we're up shit creek without a paddle and it's all my fault,' he said. 'If you don't mind, we'll leave it there. I have to think it through.'

How did we come to this? she thought. Mother and son so distanced by grief and misunderstanding, so out of touch with each other. Nik's outburst was like a knife piercing her heart, straight to the guilty target.

All his life had he grown up thinking he was second best to the sister he never knew; second best to a child snatched from life, leaving a gaping hole, a ravine across which no other sibling could ever leap? Her death blasted a quarry between husband and wife, between mother and child.

How it must have puzzled a little boy, sensing such a mighty barrier. How he must have ached when she turned from him, distanced herself from his needs.

She fled to the safety of her sofa, burying her head in the cushion, breathless, her heart throbbing. I ought to have rejoiced that he was a boy and made no comparison, she wept. Surely each new child was a unique gift, but poor Nik was cast adrift in turbulent waters. All these years, she thought sadly, we've been living side by side politely, never sharing what really matters deep in our hearts.

How quickly resentments bubbled to the surface just now, rising like bitter damson stones out of the jamming froth. Suddenly she felt utterly bowed down by her guilt and sadness, a great ache in her heart for this lonely son who had been so neglected by her grief. She was stabbed with shame. How can a mother get it so wrong?

If only it wasn't Christmas, the saddest time of the year. If only there weren't guests to entertain. If only she could swallow her pride and bake him a cake, show him she had heard his anger and hurt, but all she could do was flop down on her sofa and weep like a limp rag. If only she could turn back the clock and do things differently. Why does truth always hurt?

If only she'd had some psychology to help her in those terrible years after the war. It was in its own infancy when Nik was young. They didn't have the words for how Shirley's death would affect the whole family. If only someone had warned her what damage she was doing by bottling things up. Tom had made noises but she was deaf to his hints. It was easy to be wise after the event.

Nik cut another slice of bread and nearly the tip off his finger, cursing as he ran it under the cold tap and found a plaster. He wasn't really hungry now. The crumbs were sticking in his throat. He had said his piece, told her the score but all that stuff about Shirley came out of nowhere. Why was he so angry after all these years? How could he be jealous of a little kid in a photograph, a Latin name on a tombstone, that shadowy presence around every Christmas? It went deep and it was a surprise just how much it hurt.

He felt sick that he had shouted down a sick old woman. What a bloody mess! She was right about him living in the past. That was what the bloke at the diversification lecture had said in his speech. There could be no more harking back to the glory days of hill farming, the post-war boom in agriculture.

Now was the time to go forward in faith, facing whatever the future held. It was time to think laterally, not on tramlines. It was time to try out new ways of using land and resources, less production, more marketing and service, giving the customer a specialised product – organically grown, quality lamb. This was a new age for farmers with time to think the unthinkable.

The implications of changing direction were legion and he could feel panic rising at the effort it would take to retrain. It did not alter what Nik felt about Wintergill. Oh, no. It was making him ever more determined to hang on and make his farm viable once more. He did not need his mother to tell him he was stubborn and pig-headed.

Was he not hefted to these hills as much as his dead stock? Someone had to continue the tradition of Dales life or it would be lost for ever. Cash was not the problem for once, but he had jeopardised some of his precious savings by this oversight.

Any road, he mused, stubbornness was not a bad quality to have if he was facing a battery of opposition. What bright spark said your problems were only opportunities in disguise? He could do with some enlightenment on that score. If only he could see into the future and not into the past.

He could still see that white ghost on the hill, her eyes staring at him in the headlights. Now there was the accident in the barn. That strange vision always brought bad news. Was there any connection? Perhaps he'd better pay closer attention to old Agnes's herbal after all if he wanted that spectre off his back. Witchery or no, he was going to need a clear head to make the biggest decision of his life, and that was fact, but first there was a stone wall to mend and it wasn't down the field but in the other room.

He stood in her doorway with a glass of brandy in his hand. Nora looked up, expecting another rant, but took the glass from him with a sigh. 'I want to know what it's all about, Mother . . . It's about time I knew the score. What happened all those years ago to make you . . .' he paused, '. . . to make us the way we are with each other? What did I do wrong?'

Nora flopped down, not looking at him but staring at

the photo on the mantelpiece. 'You did nothing, son. It was me . . . I did a terrible thing . . . After the war. It's not a pretty story but I suppose I owe you an explanation. I don't know where to start . . .' she sighed.

He shut the door and sat down beside her. 'From the beginning will do,' he replied.

Shirley and the German Christmas, December 1946

Uses for goose grease

Beat with cream and vinegar, lemon juice, finely chopped onion and parsley for a sandwich filling.

A hot flannel poultice of grease to be rubbed on chest to relieve a troublesome chest.

An ointment for the dairy maid's hands or on the udders of the cow or child's lips to prevent chapping in cold weather.

Rub on leather, leave overnight to soften and preserve. Rub off with saddle soap or dubbin.

Warm the grease and smear the sheep dog's ears and between his pads to ward off rawness in wet snow.

To buff up horns and hoofs, beaks of any animal going to a show and enhance the natural colour.

'We're not having any Germans in this house! It's not right,' Mum snapped. 'That's right, Shirley, you keep stirring the bowl with the wooden spoon.'

Shirley was nearly seven now and loved standing on a chair at the kitchen table, her fingers licking the mixture with relish. They were getting ready for Stir Up Sunday, when Miss Lane in Sunday school said 'Stir up, O Lord, our hearts . . .' telling them it was time to get the Christmas puddings on the boil. Mum had been hoarding dried fruit for months to be sure of a decent sprinkling of currants alongside the grated carrots, dried berries, nuts and treacle.

'You can make a big wish. Then Santa will bring you something in his sack,' she promised, smiling down.

Shirley couldn't wait, scraping the bowl so her pigtails got a coating of goo. 'I want a—'

'Shush!' Mum replied, putting her hand over her mouth. 'Say it out loud and it won't come true, love.'

Daddy was standing in the doorway smoking the last of his baccy ration. Just the person she wanted to see.

'How could you put our name down without asking me?' Mum whispered. 'As if we've not enough to do without having to entertain strangers as well. Whatever put such a notion in your head?' she argued. 'I thought that we're not supposed to fraternise with the enemy.' Her accent always broadened when she was angry.

Daddy paused from his tea break. 'Well, we can now, after the twelfth of this month. It's about time we treat them German lads a bit fairer. They've worked hard round here mucking out, building walls, out in all weathers. If ever there was slave labour . . .' he continued, seeing Mum shaking her head. 'It's only right and proper to show a little Christian charity to lonely men over Christmas. Come on, it's only for a day. Where's yer Christmas spirit, Lenora Snowden?' He grinned a big smile and winked at Shirley, but Mum was not for giving in.

'I don't have any for Germans. Not after what Hitler did at Belsen and what happened to my cousin, Gilbert . . . They've taken enough from us. Gil got no Christmas presents when he crossed the Rhine, only a bullet in his head.'

Uncle Gilbert lived in the sitting room, smiling in his uniform from a black frame. Mum banged the pudding bowl down on the slab in the pantry. 'There,' she said. 'It can stand for the night with a drop of brandy from the medicinal cupboard to perk it up. I think I'll be needing some myself to swallow the pill you've just brought me! Come on, Shirley, perhaps a kind fairy will cough up some silver charms for our plum pudding.'

Dad didn't budge but folded his arms just as he did when it was time for her to go to bed and she wanted to listen to the wireless.

'Anyroad, how can we entertain prisoners of war? They won't speak any English and my school German is long forgotten.' Now she was banging down all the dirty pots in the stone sink. 'We've heard enough of that language to last a lifetime. It's not fair, springing this bombshell on me. Don't I have a say?'

When Mum was angry she rattled everything in the kitchen, her blue eyes blazing.

'You've grown hard these past few years . . .' he began.

'What do you expect? I know we won the war but it doesn't feel like it to me every time I go into market with my basket. I keep getting less and less for my brass and keep giving up more coupons. You try finding something for Shirley's birthday in the toyshops. The kiddies must have the treats, not grown men who pointed guns against us.'

Daddy put his hand on her lips. 'That's enough, lass. Walls have ears. Don't spoil the little one's surprises. Shirley won't go without, she never has. Santa Claus won't miss her on his rounds, now will he? I know it's been a grim two Christmases but let's give it some rip, kill a goose this time and let's share it with others. Make some stranger's Christmas one to remember. Yon camp on the moors is no hotel de luxe. They're all caged in like animals in a pen. POWs have paid their dues, love. They ought to be sent home by now, not cooped up in this cold. Have a heart, our Nora!'

Shirley didn't know what to think about all this argy-bargy. She didn't want Mr Hitler coming through their door but everyone said he was dead and the war was over so it was time to make friends like she and Vera did when they fell out in the playground.

'You're too soft,' Mum snapped. 'If I had my way they'd be made to repair every bomb crater and kept here until every brick was back in its rightful place.'

They'd watched the newsreels on the Pathé News. Shirley didn't know what war was like. The worst they'd known was a few stray bombs frightening the sheep and a busload of evacuees in school who didn't stay long.

'I never took you for a bigot, Nora,' said Daddy, frowning.

Shirley didn't like it when they quarrelled and said nasty things to each other. It frightened her.

'Those lads here have been willing workhorses, polite and no trouble so far. Let's be gracious in victory and make friends with our enemies. Think on, Nora, give them a chance. Come to church and see for yourself what type of men they are. You'll be surprised.'

Mum shrugged, trying to ignore his arguments. She hardly went to church these days. 'If you say so,' she sniffed, and turned back to her chores. Shirley slipped out into the yard to play with the dog, glad to be away from them. This was the time she wished she had a brother or sister to play with, but she had some imaginary friends and sometimes when she was playing in the copse, she caught a glimpse of the white fairy who looked a bit like the good fairy Glinda in *The Wonderful Wizard of Oz*. They played games of hide-and-seek around the trees until Shirley grew bored and ran back to the yard.

The following Sunday they saw the prisoners processing down to the front pews of the Methodist Chapel in dark suits, carrying their overcoats on their arms, shuffling into the left side with caps tucked in their pockets. Shirley counted thirty of them, staring up at the oak pulpit and the pencil stems of the organ pipes. Mum had come out of curiosity just to see what the mighty vanquished looked like. They sat in silence, stony-faced, not sullen but slightly puzzled by the occasion, aware of fifty pairs of eyes boring holes in their backs.

Shirley had to admit they didn't look like frightening bogeymen in their shabby uniforms but their voices cheered up the usual singing as they pored over service sheets typed in both English and German. They behaved politely and were ushered out before the end of the service, out into the morning chill to be marched back up the hill to their barrack huts. Shirley and the Sunday school gang came racing out of the schoolroom to watch them and some of the boys called out rude names. She felt a bit sad that she would be tucking into a roast with all the trimmings while they would be marching back to barracks in the sleet.

'No one should be turned out of the House of God, should they, love?' whispered Daddy to both of them. 'Just look at them, they're broken men now, their whole world's collapsed. You have to feel sorry for them: young lads far from home who don't know who they are any more. We have to show a bit of forgiveness.' Trust Daddy to have a good word to say.

'Are we having one? Sally's having one . . . Can I have one?' she shouted from the church porch.

'Having what?' Nora asked, straightening her daughter's plait. 'Where's your ribbon . . . they don't grow on trees!'

'Can I have a Jerry for Christmas?' Shirley knew about pestering and noticed Mum didn't say no.

'We'll see,' came the unexpected reply. That was as good as a yes . . .

Why on earth did I say that? Nora mused. Perhaps it was because it was such a December dog day, the rooks were cawing overhead and she looked up to see the column of drab men marching upwards round the steep bend in the road. It was a bleak prospect, a long march, and she ought to feel triumphant, but there was a strange sadness melting her icy resolve. Not much of a welcome on a bleak hillside, but whose fault was that? If they'd stayed in their own country none of this would be happening and Gilbert would still be alive.

Tom was right, she had grown hard, as if she were carrying herself rigid, tight-laced, corseted, unbending. It was her way of getting the work done when they were up against the enemy. Now the enemy was sitting in the next pew praying to the same God and it made no sense. What was all the sacrifice about then?

It was time to get a move on if they were to have any dinner. She fingered her gloves and went to look for the tartan ribbon. It wouldn't find itself.

The strangers were to come on Christmas morning after Morning Service when a group of POWs sang 'Stille Nacht' with such sincerity and sweetness there was hardly a dry eye in the congregation. Even Nora was resigning herself to their visitation, knowing they were thinking of home and family. You couldn't begrudge them some proper Yorkshire hospitality.

After the service, when everyone in the congregation shook hands with the men and gathered the groups ready for their visit, she was introduced to Hans Braun and Klaus Krause but she did not look them in the eyes. It was awkward trying to fit Hans's long legs into their saloon car. He sat in the front with Tom while she was squashed in the back with the other man and Shirley as a buffer.

The men stood outside the farmhouse front door stiffly. Hans had to stoop to avoid the lintel. The other prisoner stood clicking his heels with a parcel tucked under his arm. When she looked up at him she saw only a pair of sad eyes, the colour of dull slate, and felt a stab of recognition. She had to admit he was handsome in a Germanic sort of way. Those eyes were the fiercest she had ever seen on a man, and the impact of them was like a blade cutting steel. He did not look like the Hun as she imagined at all, but a world-weary soul lost in a world he did not understand.

'Thank you for Christe . . . mass *Willkommen*.' Klaus Krause spoke haltingly and Tom shook his hand warmly.

'Come in! You are welcome. This is Lenora, my wife, and this is little Shirley,' he added as his daughter hovered excitedly around the parcel under Klaus's arm.

The minx, Nora thought. The parcel was wrapped in old

266

brown paper, and she felt touched that they had bothered to bring anything. Klaus could see the other gifts set around the tree and quietly put their offering with them. Shirley was bursting to open the presents but she had had her stocking and her big present from Santa so she must wait. It didn't do to spoil a child, even on Christmas Day.

The table was laid in the dining room, with the best damask cloth and home-made crackers and paper hats. If she was going to do the job then it would be done proper and no shirking just because these men were Jerries.

She could see the men looking round nervously and the silences were embarrassing. Give them a job and perhaps they would feel more at ease, she thought. Tom had other ideas and brought out a dusty bottle of parsnip wine saved for high days and holy days. It was a pre-war vintage. You could fuel a Spitfire off its fumes, packing a punch that would soon take the lid off everyone's stiffness.

The cook was far too busy with her preparations to join in the fraternising. She left the men to their drinking and busied herself in the kitchen when Klaus came in offering to help; a man in the kitchen willing to lift a finger was unheard of in the Dales so Nora kept him busy ferrying cutlery and glasses to the dining room that had been cleared out especially for the occasion, festooned with faded paper chains and bells and a coal fire lit in the grate. She did not want any Germans thinking the English were uncivilised.

There was a bunch of Christmas roses in an egg cup, home-made crackers and paper streamers at each place setting, and Shirley was jumping up and down with excitement. The smell of the goose was tantalising. Her Yorkshire pudding batter was resting to be served as the starter, traditional fashion. She was hoping each portion would rise like boxing gloves.

'Thank you . . . you give us *gut Willkommen*.' Klaus's

English was as stiff as her schoolgirl German but they made themselves understood. His anxiousness to please was unnerving, making her all the more nervous. This was her big moment to show these foreigners just what Yorkshire cooking was all about, and she wanted everything spick and span and no messing, but it was time to shoo him out and see to the meal without those fierce eyes staring at her.

'Christmas is coming and the geese are getting fat . . .' Shirley was dancing round the kitchen. The goose was rich and succulent and the men tucked in as if they were half starved. The Christmas pudding was up to scratch with brandy sauce and Shirley found the silver threepenny bits, and everyone laughed when Daddy did his usual gasp and produced a pound note from his mouth.

Over the last of the parsnip wine, the big one who had no English tried to explain what they ate in Germany on Christmas Eve and the other one translated carefully.

'On Christmas Even, we light candle in window for Christkinder . . . the Christ child. How you say? We have big tree and many fruits and Stollen . . . Christmas breads.'

'Can we do that?' Shirley was very keen on baby Jesus in the manger.

Then the big one brought out well-worn snaps of his wife and girls, rubbed bare with fingering. They looked very pretty with hair in plaits coiled around their heads. The other one brought out a picture of his mother and father. Dad asked where they lived.

He shook his head. 'In Dresden, but no more. I fear they are killed.'

'You must want to go home,' Daddy answered.

'I ask and ask to be sent home but Dresden is with Russian soldiers now. I want to find my sisters,' the other one answered.

They were very careful with their table manners and watched what she was doing, making Shirley feel important. The other one looked like a film star on the screen of the Picturedrome but he had a scar down the side of his ear and she kept staring at the ridges on it. He saw her looking and fingered it with a smile.

'I jump from the window . . . I was naughty little boy!' he smiled and she blushed knowing it was rude to stare.

As the afternoon drew on the noise at the dining table grew more raucous and when the teatime visitors arrived from the neighbouring farms they were still at the table with not a thing cleared away, the afternoon had vanished.

The local farmers had brought with them their own contingent of POWs and in no time everyone cleared away the debris ready for the real party to begin. They crowded into the hall for a singsong and party games: pin the donkey, winking murder, blindman's bluff.

Shirley liked cadging piggy backs. She felt like a princess in her pink crushed velvet party frock with the smocked bodice and the big one kept bumping his head on the beams and roaring like a lion. Everyone was enjoying themselves but soon it was time for Daddy and the men to do the foddering and farm chores. The prisoner men all lent a hand so the jobs would be done quicker.

Shirley joined the willing helpers making up a supper fit for the King himself: cold meats, Wensleydale cheese, trifle and Christmas bread; Mummy was humming to herself, which was a good sign.

'Frau Snowden, I want thank you, you are, how we say, *gemutliche Frau*, a warm lady, my heart is full. We not expect such *Willkommen*. English are not what we expect. I salute you,' said Klaus, clicking his heels and bowing his head, and Nora felt her hands trembling as she lifted the glasses from the tray.

There was a fizzing inside her like bubbling pop. In the bustle of her own cluttered kitchen something so unexpected was happening she could hardly breathe. How could she be feeling such sympathy and warmth to total strangers, men she had met only a few hours ago? It was strange to feel the bitterness evaporating like the brandy fumes on the pudding. She didn't know either of them or what they had done. They could've slaughtered women and children, shot their neighbour's son, murdered Jews, and yet when Klaus was looking at her with those flint sparkling eyes she sensed only a flicker of pity, not hatred. All she wanted was to stare back and that wasn't right. What would poor Tom make of her change of heart?

She fingered her winter best clothes, glad she had made the effort. Her rusty wool crepe dress, rich as shiny conkers in colour, shaped her body neatly, outlining her full bust and neat waist. She was built square but everything was in proportion. Her hair was coiled up at the front and hung loose at the back, bouncing with health. Her best stockings were neatly darned and she wished they were real nylons not thick wool.

Someone sat at the piano in the hall and they pushed the hall table aside to clear the floor for a dance. Tom and Shirley jumped around the room and Big Hans danced with the daughter of their next-door neighbour, who lived three fields away.

Klaus took his place at the keyboard and the POWs linked shoulders and started singing carols. Then, in honour of the day, Nora pushed in beside him and played the famous tune 'Lili Marlene'. She could feel his breath, the scratch of his uniform. The smell of him was sweet to her nostrils and she could feel the closeness of his lips as they all joined in the song.

Suddenly she was afraid. Something strange was happening.

270

Her cheeks were on fire. For a second they glanced at each other and held the gaze enough to register what was happening, a brief moment of recognition, an exchange so swift but so meaningful, so utterly all shaming that Nora could not believe the whole room could not see that there was more on the boil than the kettle!

'I must see to the kitchen,' she croaked feebly, and Shirley bounded across the hall. 'Dance with me. Dance with me, Santa Klaus!'

Everyone laughed at the mistake but Nora stood in the doorway transfixed by the sight of him spinning her child off the floor. He was lean and long-limbed, with an aquiline profile more Grecian than Nazi. For one brief second she was almost jealous of her own child. Then he looked up and smiled and that jealous aching was gone.

This is Wintergill, not Hollywood, she sighed. The war was over and this man was far from home, starved of female attention. He was not Errol Flynn and she wasn't Carole Lombard. This may be wild Brontë country but that sort of romancing was thin on the ground. Klaus was just enjoying his freedom for a day. There was nothing more to it than that. And yet . . .

Tea was served upstairs in the old drawing room, scene of many of Joss and Jacob Snowden's famous Christmas celebrations. Jacob would be looking down from his photograph by the door, glad that Christmas had come to 'Dingley Dell' once more. Sandwiches were passed round, bowls of trifle and a tin of Sharps toffee. Nothing was on ration for Christmas Day. Coupons and rations were forgotten when Wintergill House had a 'blowout'. Belts were loosened, ties undone, corsets unhooked as the heat of the fire, food and drink took its toll. Neighbours, soldiers, children all sitting on the floor, squashed together in the silence of satisfaction, in a silent reverie of nostalgia for the better times before the war had made them enemies. Klaus had saved Nora a place on the floor as someone began a ghost story about the barghest, the mysterious white dog that roamed the Dales, omen of death and destruction. As they sat on the floor by the fire she felt her hand aching to touch his, to caress his fingers, but pushed them under her skirt to avoid such temptation. She must be drunk.

How can I even think such thoughts in front of my husband and my bairn? she mused. The man was a stranger. She was bound tight by duty and loyalty. Passion and adultery were what happened in books to Emma Bovary and Anna Karenina, not to good old Lenora Snowden, farmer's wife, newly appointed Minutes Secretary of the Women's Institute.

'Can we open the presents around the tree now?' whined Shirley who'd been eyeing them all up impatiently. She was tired, overfed and ready for bed.

'In a moment, love,' Mum whispered. Her cheeks were all pink. Shirley didn't like her sitting down with Mr Klaus. He wasn't Santa after all just a soldier who kept looking at her mum. She sensed him distracting Mum so she tugged her sleeve.

'Come on, Mum . . . I want to open the presents.'

Daddy nodded from across the room and Shirley ran downstairs to the big tree in the stairwell to fetch the brown parcel tied with string. 'Can I open this?' she asked, tearing off the paper to find a beautiful little carved house, like a cuckoo house chalet, painted in bright colours.

'It's a gingerbread house! Can I eat it?' she cried, and Klaus shook his head laughing.

'It's a little Christmas house for your dolls, Fräulein Shirley. See, the front opens. *Ja?* It is house of *meine Heimat* . . . fatherland.' The soldier smiled, proud of his handiwork.

'It's beautiful, like Hansel and Gretel's gingerbread house,' Mum said. 'Thank you so much, but it wasn't necessary.'

'*Ja*, but it is so,' Klaus argued. 'At home before Christmas, we have many markets, to sell wooden toys, *Glühwein* – hot wine and . . . herbs – but it is all gone now, I think,' he replied as if he was talking only to Mum, ignoring Shirley.

'Say thank you, Shirley. It's a grand little house, is that. Go and fetch the stuff for our visitors,' Daddy ordered, and she went down again for their parcels, giving one each for the big one and the other.

'For us . . . *Hans, danke . . . danke.*' They opened their presents as if they were made of gold. There were just two pairs of rough woollen mittens and a scarf. 'You knit for us?' They looked so pleased. How could anyone be pleased with such boring gifts?

'No she didn't, they came from the WI,' Shirley snapped.

'Now I've met you, I will knit something for both of you,' Mum said, pointing at Daddy's jumper. 'One for you and you, *ja*?'

'You can't knit,' Shirley whispered.

'I can if I want to,' Mum snapped back, and Shirley wanted to cry.

Everyone laughed but the Germans looked at their gifts with tears in their eyes. '*Danke, danke*, merry Christmas,' stuttered Big Hans, the gentle giant, with a grin on his face.

'You are very *gut* to us, you shake our hand and give us *gut* things. We never forget,' said the other one.

'None of that, let's have another singsong round the piano,' Daddy called out. They sang until they were hoarse, more carols, German and English, patted each other on the back and Shirley felt sick watching Mum being silly. She was glad when the clock spun round until it was time for the lorry

273

to pick up the men again. Tomorrow she could have her parents all to herself.

The sky was bright and clear. Shirley's Christ candle sitting in the draughty window was burning low. The day was over and Nora slumped with exhaustion.

'I think we should ask for those two lads to be sent to work here,' said Tom, sucking his pipe. 'They've fitted in right grand, don't you think?'

'I'm not sure,' said Nora, suddenly wary.

'You could teach them proper English.'

'They can't stay in the house.'

'There's the room over the Side Barn where the Irish stay at haytime. We can make it sound, give them a bit of privacy. I never like to miss a bargain and Big Hans will do the work of two men,' he laughed. 'What do you think, lass?'

What could she say? He was the boss in the farm matters. They could do with more help but there was danger in the POWs coming. She ought to suggest another gang but she found herself smiling and nodding.

Meeting Klaus had stirred up such strange feelings, as if her guts were churning over in a silly schoolgirl fashion. There was nothing wrong in a bit of romantic temptation. It was the yielding to it that was wrong. She was a wife and mother and good Christian woman. Surely there was nothing to fear from such an arrangement, was there?

In the weeks that followed Shirley watched her mother knitting those jumpers with lightning fingers, a simple style in unravelled old wool, hand spun and dyed. Big Hans, as she called him now, was so huge he took a whole fleece. Every second she had free she was clacking those needles, lost in her thoughts with no time to play ludo or snakes and ladders. 'I must get on,' she kept saying.

Then the snowstorms came, and Shirley couldn't go to school, and the snow was so high they had to keep digging themselves out of the track. The postman walked on the stonewalls and gangs of diggers were out trying to keep the tops clear for the milk lorries. They were fast in with the two soldiers living in the barn until they sent for Big Hans to go home. He was that desperate to leave, he took snow shoes and poles and skied his way back to the road, taking their post on his back and some butter for the shops.

Then the blizzard took hold and it was all they could do to keep watering the barn stock and trying to rescue the stricken ewes sheltering under the drifts. Dad and Mr Klaus returned frozen each morning with the farm boy. All she could see were their eyes peering out of icy lashes like snowmen wrapped in scarves, and Mum fussing over them.

'Come in, get yerselves warm,' she cried as Shirley jumped up into her dad's arms. Mum was busy trying to warm them with hot broth.

'We'll need a warm-through,' Tom ordered. 'Get the kettle on the boil and let the lad soak in the tub in front of the fire. He can't go back to his billet until he's thawed out proper.'

Shirley thought it was all a game, filling the bath. Mum started shooing her out of the door when Klaus peeled off his layers. 'This is no place for the womenfolk,' she whispered, but Shirley noticed Mum kept nipping back into the kitchen for stuff she'd forgotten, pink-faced and all hot and bothered; not like her mum at all.

Nora drank in a glimpse of his nakedness in one draught. He was a fine figure of a man. His bare shoulders were still tanned from the summer sun, his muscles lean and defined, his hips narrow where Tom's were thick and fleshy. She grabbed the towels and fled into the hall, away from any further revelation. He was beautiful and she mustn't look any more.

'Stop it, you're hurting me,' Shirley snapped, and she realised she was gripping her arm tight.

'Sorry, love,' she croaked, feeling light-headed and silly.

As the days turned into weeks, Tom insisted she gave Klaus proper English lessons, and in the evening he sat stiffly at the kitchen table while she tried to engage him in conversation and some written work while Shirley kept butting in with suggestions. It was no surprise that he didn't make much progress and the blizzards howled round their heads, blowing drifts that cut off even the Side Barn from the house, and Tom suggested she make up a bed for Klaus in the shelter of Wintergill House.

Nothing was said, not one intimate exchange between them had ever taken place, but as Nora climbed the stairs that night she knew that somehow she would make sure they were alone. Lying in bed she waited for the house to go silent and for Tom to be snoring, slipped into her dressing gown and made for the stairs. She coughed outside Klaus's bedroom door and made enough noise to waken the dead but no one stirred. She waited and waited on the off chance with a sickening heart, and slowly made her way up the stairs back to bed with a terrible feeling of being utterly stupid.

Then she noticed a flicker of light under the door of the upstairs parlour and opened it softly. Klaus was there waiting, his hands hugging his knees. He looked up and smiled. 'Frau Snowden – Lenora – I have to speak with you. I am thinking of you all times, night and day. I must go!'

'And I of you,' she whispered. She sat by him shivering in the darkness.

'Never will I forget your kindness and your husband . . . This is bad thing, I know.' He bent his head onto his knees and she sensed he was weeping. Her arms were round him in seconds and she cradled him tightly as they rocked together and she wept for the hopelessness of their loving each other. In the darkness and the flickering candle, in the icy chill of the parlour, they clung to each other and found their lips crushing together, their bodies straining to express all they felt. What happened between them was as natural as talking and breathing. Why waste precious moments in words when bodies can express so much more?

In the days that followed, there was no shame, only desperation and the seizing of the moment. Klaus returned to the Side Barn room despite Tom's protests that it was too chilly. Nora made every excuse to visit him there. In the closeness of his embrace, all her scruples vanished in this primitive surge to surrender. It was only later, in the cold bed with Tom snoring by her side, that she realised what she had done was reckless and unforgivable. In the chill dawn light she knew she was betraying her family but try as she might she could not feel guilty, only sad and desperate that Klaus would soon leave and she might never see him again.

'Go and find yer mam,' Dad called. 'She'll be in the Side Barn giving Klaus his lesson.' The snow was giving way now and the yard was clear enough for the German to go back to his own place in the camp. She didn't like him any more and she didn't know why. He didn't play with her like Big Hans. He'd rather play cards with Mum and have stupid lessons, and go for walks in the woods and down the river gathering sticks. Mum was always humming and being too busy to play cards with her or read stories like she used to do. Dad was busy trying to fodder the beasts that had survived the blizzards and she had to go back to Wintergill School again.

No one was bothering with her much. She pretended to be invisible so she hid behind doors, listening in to grown-ups talk when she shouldn't. She peeped and tiptoed and crept about like the funny lady who walked through the walls that Mum said was all made up.

Shirley slithered across the cobbles to the side door of the barn but it was shut. She shouted but no one was there so she decided to go in and root round Klaus's room just to be nosy. She crawled up on her hands and knees, giggling, and when she peeped through the door, there was no one there but his bed was all rumpled and on the floor was Mum's pretty lace handkerchief. She picked up the hanky and shoved it up her sleeve, for some reason. She just knew it was important not to leave it there by the bed. Where were they?

'I can't find them,' she shouted back to her dad.

'Out gathering kindling to dry off . . . It doesn't matter, love. Happen they'll turn up soon,' he smiled, and carried on with his work.

It was then that Shirley decided to be Dick Barton, Special Agent on the wireless and go in search of them. Mum should be in the kitchen making their tea, not gallivanting in the wood with Mr Hitler's soldier.

Klaus made a bed for them further down by the frozen river. The trees had thawed the ground, and with their macs they could lie undisturbed, hidden by the evergreens, making love as if for the very last time. She had never known such passion and every touch thrilled her body, every kiss brought such sensations. It was as if she were on fire, even on the coldest of days. To make love under the skies was something she and Tom had never even contemplated. It was not their way, but she had never felt for Tom what she was feeling now. It was like some potent drug that she must swallow every day or suffer such withdrawal and hunger for more.

All the weariness of war and want, blizzard and cold disappeared for those few stolen hours when they were alone. There was this desperation in their lovemaking that drowned out all guilt and shame. 'You are he and I am she and we are one,' she whispered in his ears.

Then Nora heard a curlew crying as it flew up the river. The birds were returning. It was almost spring and the worst of the winter would be over soon. Her heart leaped at its bubbling call. Her eyes filled with tears of relief. They had survived this terrible winter unscathed and she was in the arms of her lover, safe from the world.

'It is time for me to go,' said Klaus. 'Soon they will send for me to leave.'

Nora felt such panic, and drew him back into her embrace. He mustn't leave the farm, not when they had found each other. Nothing mattered but these stolen minutes.

'No . . . no, I'm never going to let you go.'

'Come with me . . . and Shirley?' he whispered.

Nora sprang up as if splashed with ice water. 'We can't . . . Don't say another word, Klaus.'

He pulled her back roughly into the heat of his arms. Nora lost herself in him again.

Shirley followed their soggy snow tracks down the path passing Gunnerside Foss, which led to the riverbank. She was being an Indian brave now, stalking the cowboys like they did at the Picturedrome. She had on her wellies and her winter coat and beret. She was going to find Mum and Mr Klaus and tell them off for going on a walk without her.

She slithered down the thawing track, and the water went

down her boots and her knees were chapping and raw, but there was still no sight of them. But she could hear strange cries like an animal in pain, and followed the noise into the copse. It was darker and scratchy, and the branches snagged her path until she came to an opening.

Then she saw them fighting on the ground, rolling round together, making noises and kissing, and Mum's skirt was up and Shirley screamed and they looked up and saw her but she ran away because she knew they were mating like animals when the boar went to the sow and the bull to the cow. She ran and ran down to the frozen river. They were doing something wrong and she knew, and what would she tell Dad?

It was then she thought she saw the nice white lady waving to her across the riverbank. She would know what to do. There were stepping stones if you knew where they were, and if she crossed the water, she would be safe somehow.

'Oh, no!' Nora screamed, seeing the child's face, scrabbling to her feet as Klaus fastened his trousers, feeling such fear and shame: for her little daughter to see them like this. 'No, no. No . . . Shirley . . . Come back, love. Mummy will explain . . . Oh, no . . . no!'

Leaping up in the direction of Shirley's flight, Klaus racing ahead of her, Nora slithered through the shrubs, down the soggy slopes to the grey-white riverbank with only one thing on her mind. She must explain it was just a silly game and she was too little to understand it was just rough and tumble. Who are you fooling? Shirley had run from them . . . she understood. *Oh God forgive me. What have I done?*

As she tore through the undergrowth down the steep bank, panting with terror and shame, she saw Shirley edging her way slowly across the frozen water and it was already cracking under her tiny weight.

'Stop . . . don't move! Oh, Klaus, do something!' Nora screamed, seeing the danger, but Klaus was already edging onto the ice to rescue the child. Shirley froze at the sight of them.

'*Achtung!* Don't move . . . stay . . . wait for me!' he yelled. 'Find a big stick,' he ordered Nora. 'The ice is too thin for me.' He mimed to her frightened child with his hands how she must lie down on all fours.

'Do what he says!' Nora was edging closer to the ice, searching frantically for a broken branch. Everything was nailed down with the frost. 'Spread out flat like a rag rug,' she shouted. 'Do what Klaus says, please!'

Shirley didn't move, frozen with fear. Nora knew they had only seconds and she tore at a rotten field post with every ounce of her strength and wrapped her coat at the sleeves into a knot to give it more purchase. 'Here, Klaus . . . Save her! Oh please God, save her! Help!' she yelled, looking up and seeing a figure walking away, fading across the field like mist. 'Help us!' she screamed. There was no one there.

Klaus edged forward on his stomach, holding the stick to the child, who crouched now, wary but listening to his words. 'Come here . . . Shirley . . . take the coat and I will pull you back . . .'

'No, I can't! I'll fall in the water . . . I can't swim,' she protested, but Klaus stayed still, his eyes never shifting from her for a second.

'I can swim for both of us.'

'Do as he says, please, darling!' Nora was shouting from the riverbank, her arms reaching out to grab Shirley's coat.

Shirley hesitated for a second, seeing the look of panic on both their faces. One minute she was pretending to skate, waving to the white lady, and then she heard that funny crack on the ice and her legs were sinking into cold water. She was glad when she saw Klaus coming, but afraid too. He was going to take her mum away from her and Dad. They were doing lovey things like they did in the pictures – kissing – and she must tell Dad. If she told him would the man let her drown so no one would know?

She could hear Mum screaming at her. The water was freezing and her feet were numb. She had to move towards him but she was afraid. She turned to see if the white lady would help them but she'd vanished as she always did when grown-ups came in sight.

Now she couldn't feel her feet moving and her chest was sinking down. She stretched her arm to grab Mum's coat sleeve at the end of the post. She was going to have to trust Mr Hitler's soldier to pull her to safety but would he let her sink to the bottom?

'No, I can't!' she screamed as the ice cracked and she felt herself sinking further into the dark water as it dragged her under. She was too tired now to flail about, the ice made each effort weaker until she felt herself sinking down.

Suddenly an arm reached out, grabbing her sleeve as she floundered, her head bobbing under for a second, the ice washing over her head, but that strong arm was dragging her closer and closer. The water kept closing over her mouth in great gulpfuls, and she could hardly breathe, but the grip kept dragging her towards the bank until she felt her knees scraping on the rocks and her shins bruising, and then she was in her mum's arms and everyone was crying and shivering and she felt very sleepy and cold.

How strange that time stood still for hours in those minutes as Nora watched her lover dragging Shirley to safety. She was just a floating lump of cloth, limp and lifeless. He tore off his coat and battle jacket right up to his holey vest, still

282

dry enough to wrap around the shivering child. Everything they had that was dry they piled on her, then slowly carried her to safety. How they got back to the farm Nora would never know. It was an act of sheer will. Klaus carried Shirley all the way back until he collapsed into the yard and Tom took over.

No one spoke much after that. Shirley had been told never to go to the river without them. Ice was a tempting plaything but too thin in parts. It had happened before and it would happen again. Klaus was the hero of the day. Shirley was too shocked to remember much and was cocooned in bed with hot-water bottles.

'I'll give that girl what for . . . scaring us like that!' Tom shouted, but Nora was quick to her defence.

'You'll do no such thing! She's only a lass . . . she made a mistake. Don't make matters worse. All's well that ends well! Let's leave it at that,' Nora cried. 'We could've lost her.'

'Aye, and it's Klaus we must thank for that. He's a grand lad and no mistake.'

Nora was shaking with shame and fear. Tom hadn't a clue and she felt awful at her betrayal of his trust. If only he knew what really had happened. Would Shirley spill the beans?

It was Tom who told the *Gazette*, and it was all around the district what their POW had done. People shook his hand in church and Klaus blushed. One morning his repatriation papers came through in the post.

'You tell him the good news,' Tom laughed as if he was doing them a great favour. 'He deserves to go home after all he has done for us.'

Nora sat down, hardly daring to breathe. How could he be so blind and trusting? Was this the end of it all? How could she ever meet her lover again or ever touch his body? Should she confess everything, come clean to Tom? Could she bear the pain on his face? It was too easy to dump all her guilt and shame on him, and how could she tell him that her adultery had nearly cost Shirley her life?

Shirley knew. When she was undressed, Nora found the lace-edged hanky with the embroidered thistle tucked up Shirley's sleeve, the one she had used in Klaus's bed. For one crazy second she wanted to let the child tell Tom what she'd seen, bring it all out in the open, walk out of the farm and follow the lorry that would surely come to carry Klaus to Germany.

Then she thought of her precious child, afraid, confused, lost, and all because of her. How could she be so daft in the head? Duty before pleasure was embroidered into her heart. She had taken her pleasure and now she must pay for broken vows with sacrifice. Tom didn't deserve such a shaming. The affair must be over, the accident had thrown cold water over this crazy passion, but how could she watch Klaus walk out of her life?

A month later Shirley lay in her bed cuddling her toys, warm and toasty with a hot-water bottle and a jug of lemon barley water to sip. Sometimes she lay listening to the noises out in the yard, the cows in the dairy, the clatter of clogs on the cobbles, the horses neighing in the stable. Lately she'd heard children laughing and running over her head in the attic. They were playing tag and she wished she could join in with them. They were thumping around and calling to each other.

The doctor said she must drink but her head was sore again and she couldn't go to school. She felt sick and shivery and her tummy hurt, so Mum sometimes brought her down into the kitchen, making a bed between the two leather chairs. She could listen to the wireless music and talk to the dogs and the new farm boy who came to replace Mr Klaus.

She was glad he had gone. She had Mum to herself again and it was worth being sick just to make him go away from them. The doctor said she'd caught a bad chill from falling into the river and drinking in muddy water. She must rest until the fever broke.

She loved the kitchen smells, the tobacco smoke and the scent of the few weak lambs warming by the oven. It was a poor harvest after the bad snow and they'd lost most of their ewes in the drifts. Some were found floating like balloons in the river. Mum and Dad sat by the table counting all their losses, and then they'd look up and smile at her. 'Still, we've not lost the most important treasure in our house . . .' It made her feel important and sleepy at the same time.

For a few days the fever left her bones and she got up to play with the dogs, but now it was back again and she couldn't read or bear the bright light. The doctor came every day to see how she was doing and said he wanted to take some blood from her arm. She tried not to cry out but he hurt her and Mum held her arm out again. 'You must let him take it,' she whispered. 'So he can make you better again.'

She didn't understand why she had a yellow face, and when she was sick it came up green and she felt sore all over, but Mum sat with her until day became night and it all went fuzzy.

There was a little boy with a silver waistcoat who sat in a chair by the fireside smiling at her. She wondered if he was one of her school friends and asked Mum who he was.

'What little boy?' she smiled. 'You're imagining things. It's just the fever.'

'No, I'm not, I can hear them playing tag upstairs, calling out . . . but he sits by the fire watching me. He says his name is William.'

Mum looked at her and felt her forehead. 'I'll get you some more medicine. You're very hot. We've got to take you to the hospital to make you better. I know it's a long way away but we'll come to visit you when they allow us.'

'I don't want to go away . . . can't I stay here and play with the children?'

'There are no children, love. It's all in your head. Now get some sleep and it'll make you feel better. Good night and God bless.'

Grown-ups were funny, they couldn't hear things properly. How could Mum not hear the upstairs children calling out to her, 'Come and play with us'? Now her bedroom was filling up with playmates, smiling, children in funny dresses and caps peering down at her. It was lovely to see the room swimming with swirling figures and brightness, and suddenly it was easy to jump out of the bed to play with them . . .

It was a backward spring that year, everything late and stunted and a poor harvest of lambs. Nora didn't venture far from the farm. She wasn't fit for company and folk left her alone to get over the loss of her kiddie in her own way. They weren't being cruel, just standing back to let time help her come to. She took to riding out to watch their new stock, glad to be alone with her thoughts. One minute Shirley was the centre of her life and then she was gone, leaving a gap in her heart nothing would ever fill. Tom got on with his jobs and said nothing much. There was nothing to say, but he did insist they made an appearance at one of the local markets at Skipton Auction Mart in June for a change of scene.

It was a farmer's world but there were plenty of sideshows for the womenfolk, selling farming equipment and local produce. There was a parade of some decent horses to view.

He left her to wander around among strangers who didn't know her sorrows. She was fine until a hand touched her sleeve. She spun round to see the one face in the world she dreaded meeting again. It was Klaus.

He was dressed in a tweed jacket and old cords. His face was tanned with the sun. She turned from him but he grabbed her arm roughly. 'No, don't leave! I knew you would be here.' He paused and whipped off his cap. 'I know about Shirley. A man in the camp who works near Wintergill, he told me. I'm not going back to Germany. There's no one to go for. All I want is here now. I've got a job on a farm near Lincoln . . . no hills, no snow, with a proper cottage . . . We can start again.' He was smiling, those eyes piercing hers.

'We?'

'You and me . . . begin again, a new life. Come with me.'

Nora stared at him as if he was a stranger from Mars, stepping back. 'Why should I come with you?'

'Because we are one people,' Klaus was struggling to express his feelings, gripping his cap. 'I will work hard for us—'

'Stop! Stop right now. Have you forgotten our Shirley?'

'It was terrible what happened. There will be other Kinder—'

'She died because she saw us in the wood and ran on thin ice. We killed her, you and I, as if we had drowned her. It was our doing . . . How can I ever live with you after that?'

'But you don't love your husband.' He was pleading with her but she shook her head.

'Who are you to say that? There's love that's like fireworks in the night, a burst of flame and then nothing, and there's love like the steady slow burn of a candle – another sort of love between man and wife. I have to stay with my little girl now. I won't be leaving her alone in the church-yard.'

Klaus shook his head. 'No, no! She cannot stop our love. She is dead, nothing more we can do for her, but I am living.'

'She already has. I will never leave her.'

'I don't understand . . .'

'How can you? She's not your child but, God forbid, one day you will know what it is to have the heart ripped out of you.' There was nothing else to say as she dragged herself from the sight of him.

'Lenora!' He was calling but his words fell on deaf ears. He didn't see the tears streaming down her face as she walked away.

Nora waited until Tom had gone to church. It was the quiet end of the Sunday morning. No one else was on the farm. The roast was in the oven, the apple pie waiting in the larder and in front of her was the bottle of sherry and the aspirins. She sat staring at the bottles while the wall clock clicked away the minutes. The answer to her misery was staring back at her if she could only swallow the lot, but not here, not in the sacred place where Shirley died. She would not pollute her memory.

Shoving on her farm mac and sticking the bottles in her poacher's pocket, she made her way down to the copse, the scene of the crime, to the very place where she had betrayed all her principles. She didn't deserve to live now. Tom would find another wife once the hoo-ha died down. They would put it all down to sadness and depression. How could she go on living without her little child?

She was too ashamed of herself. Klaus had gone for good. He was part of the past now. Sitting with her dying child, pleading with the gods to bring her back from the brink, she would never forget. It was as if she'd woken up from some drunken dream into the sober chill of the morning. There was nothing to live for now but a lifetime of guilt and regret. How could she carry the heavy weight of shame and deceit from Tom? Better to end it all now and be done with it.

She sat down against the trunk of a tree, hidden from view. This was a peaceful place to end her life. It was that time of late summer when the birds were chattering, the leaves just curling from a vibrant green canopy into a silvery grey: beech, oak, rowan and ash. Life in the wood was going about its business as usual; after the rain the sun, after the snows, the spring, and then she heard Shirley singing that new hymn in the Sunday School Anniversary concert. 'Glad that live am I, That the sky is blue . . . Glad for the country lanes And the fall of dew . . .' Her voice was singing and ringing through the branches, clear and bright, and she recalled how proud she'd been to watch her daughter in her special white dress singing her heart out on the chancel steps . . .

Then in the very remembering she understood that death would be the easy way out of her pain. Her punishment must be to go on living and to make something out of the rest of her life. She must pay back Tom, the farm and Shirley for her terrible betrayal somehow.

She found herself scrabbling in the soil to bury the bottles. Their existence was an indulgence, like Klaus had been, and a part of her heart must be buried alongside them. Nothing like this must ever happen again.

Understanding

'Shirley slipped away from us before we could find out what was wrong,' Nora cried as the tears rolled down her cheeks. 'The doctor did his best. He thought it was meningitis but it wasn't. It was something you catch from muddy water.'

'Weil's disease,' Nik replied. 'Wherever rats live there's danger.'

'I killed her as surely as if I'd held a gun to her head.' Nora held her head in her hands.

'It was bad luck she fell in and drank dirty water,' Nik replied, patting her on the shoulder.

'Bad luck my foot. What I did was shameful. I can't believe it was really me. I must have been crazy but I loved that man . . . When Shirley died I nearly ended it with a bottle of aspirin.'

'I'm glad you didn't or I wouldn't be here to tell the tale . . . I wasn't by any chance . . . you know . . . me being Nikolas . . . with you and the POW making hay while the sun shone?'

Nora smiled through her tears. 'Of course not. You came years after. You were born on St Nicholas's Day and named after him. I never even thought of that connection. Tom wanted us to try again but I kept putting it off. I really didn't want another kiddie, not after what happened. I just wanted the one I'd lost. How could I deserve another chance to bring life into the world? I thought I'd got away with it but out you popped. When you were born a lad, I was that relieved and Tom was delighted. You were always his boy and I didn't interfere.'

'Did my dad ever suspect?'

'I'm not sure. He was either a saint or a fool to take such risks. It was he who insisted I give Klaus those lessons alone. He was too trusting. That's why, if I'm honest, I'm glad to see the back of that Side Barn. Too many memories. I'm not proud of what I did then but it felt so important at the time.' Nora rose stiffly, not looking at her son. 'So now you know how it was . . . I'm not making any excuses, except that I was young, full of silly dreams and bored by the sameness of all my chores. I was bowled over by a handsome face, all the sadness of war and a lost young man. There were no agony aunts to advise us about the power of physical attraction. We never talked about sex. I should have known better but I wanted him and I had him.

'Nowadays no one bats an eyelid at taking what they want. Go for it, they tell the young 'uns. Take what you want and enjoy it, but not in my day. We were brought up on the full St Augustine edict: "Take what you want but pay for it."

'I never set out to commit adultery, to be so feckless and shameless, but I was still a child at heart, a girl full of romantic notions. He was my little rebellion. It was a crazy whirlwind romance that came from nothing back to nothing, leaving devastation in its wake. Shirley died because of it and I have never forgiven myself for that.

'How many nights have I sat scratching her name into the fingers of ice on the windowpane, looking out across the snowfields in moonlight, wondering if she ever forgave me? Then I'd look down at the worn peg rugs and the washing tub and I knew that I was bolted to earth, nailed down by duty and loyalty to Wintergill farmhouse and all who slept therein for the rest of my life.

'The fire of that loving has never been entirely snuffed out. Its embers remain, stirring up memories when I sit by the firelight. I've often wondered if Klaus's still alive somewhere. Don't begrudge me that German Christmas long ago. Who was it who once said that lost loves were always the longest lived?'

'Why do you always think I'm criticising you?' Nik argued. 'This is the first time we've talked like this. It's hard sometimes to remember your parents were once as silly and young as you were. Now you've told me your story, it makes so many things clearer . . . why you never talked about my sister or took to Mandy. You saw through my wife when she fell for Danny Pighills, didn't you?'

'It takes one to know one, son. I could see their infatuation growing and I couldn't warn you what was happening under your eyes.'

'You let me down there.'

'I was trying to protect you. Dad thought I was being harsh. I've done wrong to shut you out of all this. You never asked to be born, and somewhere in my heart I was afraid of losing you too.'

'It's OK now. No point in going over what we can't change. It's what's going on now that matters. But I'm glad you've come clean on Shirley. I always felt I wasn't good enough.'

'Nik, you've been everything a son could be to your dad and me.'

'Why didn't you tell me all this before?'

'Because I'm ashamed of it and didn't want you to hate me.'

'Hate you? Why? For being human and failing to live up to your own high standards? Look at me . . . we're both in

Dicky's meadow now. Fighting about it won't solve anything but together we can give Bruce Stickley a run for his money. Don't ask me how but we'll get by.'

'I don't want to get by . . . I want to retire.'

'I know, I heard you first time. There has to be a way for both of us to make it happen.'

'Well, you'd better ask the Christmas Fairy then,' Nora muttered. ''Cos I'm clean out of ideas. If this run of luck carries on, we'll all be out on the street by New Year.'

Nik tried to busy himself making phone calls but nothing was going to happen until after Christmas. It was as if the whole world was grinding to a halt for two weeks and he was trapped here in limbo, feeling helpless. His mother's confession had shocked him more than he could admit. He was trying to stay cool about her affair but it hurt none the less. The sex lives of parents were something mysterious and uncomfortable to his generation. He'd never seen either of them naked, or showing any signs of physical affection to each other. Now he knew why. Dad must have known what was going on and let it run its course, surely?

He looked at the sepia portrait of his mother on the windowsill with fresh eyes. Why had he never noticed the sparkle in her eyes, her flawless skin and high cheekbones? She was quite a looker in her day. No wonder she attracted attention. It was this farm that had ground down those looks, sharpened her features and dulled her eyes. She'd stuck it out because that was what you did – not like Mandy, who lasted barely three years before making her escape.

He stood staring out of the window. Who would want to live here above the snow line, miles from company, with only worry and hard work as a reward? None of his past girlfriends could stomach the smells or the chores for more than a weekend or two. Now he'd got nothing to offer but the hope of restocking: just more of the same. If only he could magic some extra cash to smarten the place up a bit, but it had all gone on the barn conversion and overdrafts.

He noticed the Partridge girl in the Puffa anorak chasing the dog in the field. Poor kid, it wasn't going to be much of a Christmas for them, not after last year. He was surprised they'd stayed on.

Kay Partridge was no longer a mystery to him. Since the funny business on the lane after the quiz, when she'd seen him shaken up and he'd listened to her story, he was finding her good company. Now they were all going to be under one roof and Christmas was round the corner. Suddenly he was warming to the whole idea!

Mistress Hepzibah stirs. The season is upon us once more, she sighs. Danger is still nigh. Blanche has tried her worst and now they are all safe under the thatch, her will is thwarted but all is not well with the master. There is sadness like smoke fumes wafting through the house, choking out the chance of yuletide noise and merriment. This be a house of gloom, and the young maid will make mischief if not chastised and set to honest work. Why does she lie abed, not busy with spinning wool or at her sampler? Childer are never too young to be set to work in the dairy, the kitchen or reading their horn books. Idle hands make mischief, methinks . . .

Evie, December 2001

Nora's Christmas Biscuits

2 oz icing sugar
2 oz custard powder
6 oz margarine
6 oz plain flour

Cream them all together, shape into small balls and freeze until chilled.

Cook on a greased tray in fairly hot oven, 375°F or Gas Mark 5 or 190°C for 5 mins.

Cool on rack.

Decorate with coloured icing and silver balls.

Evie was awake, waiting for first light. She jumped out of bed and opened the curtains. 'I thought you said it was going to snow.' She reached over to the twin bed, shaking her mother out of her dreaming. 'When are we going to Granny's? I'm bored.'

'Go back to bed, it's still too early,' Kay replied, turning on her side to finish off her dreaming. Tim was in that dream somewhere and she wanted to see his face again and feel his presence. She wanted to cry but there were only fingers pinching her arm.

'Stop it, Evie! Read a book or get yourself some Weetabix,' she mumbled. Tiredness was dragging her down a spiral staircase back into sleep. The fire had drained her of all her energy. She ought to be rising soon and helping out Nora, making herself useful, not lazing in bed. She leaned over to read her watch and it wasn't yet seven o'clock.

'They don't have any Weetabix. I don't like porridge oats. Why can't we go back to Granny's?' Evie was now tugging at her pyjama sleeve.

'Then go down and watch TV or a video.'

'My videos are all burnt up . . . everything's burned. I want to go home.' Her whining was like a droning plane in Kay's ears. She pulled the blankets over her head to blank out Evie's protests. Evie pulled them back.

'Find something to play with,' Kay shouted but then remembered Evie had no toys left.

This was not how it was supposed to be – the escape to the country to find respite from all the Christmas hullabaloo. It was like living in some strange dream and the strained atmosphere downstairs didn't help.

The Snowdens must have been quarrelling. You could cut the ice between them, and it was all bound up with the fire. Perhaps they blamed her for carelessness, but it was a freak accident. Everyone assured her of that fact. She pushed back the covers. 'Come in with me, darling, just for a few minutes. The fire has made us all grumpy.'

Evie slid under the covers. Her feet were cold. The bedroom was freezing and Kay was glad of fleecy pyjamas.

'How will Daddy find us now?' Evie whispered.

Kay went cold. 'He can't find us, love. I told you before, Daddy's not coming home. He had an accident, a car crash, and he died. The doctors tried to save him but he was too sick.' She could feel her child shivering and cuddled her, but Evie sat up rigid.

'Is he with Jesus in Heaven? Mrs Nora says that's where Shirley and the Lavender Lady live but she comes down to visit here.'

'That's just make-believe, not proper visiting. Ghosts aren't real. Daddy has no body now but he still loves you.'

'He promised to bring me a real Christmas tree and he didn't come.' Evie's voice sounded puzzled. 'If he is in Heaven he can do anything. Why's there no Christmas in this house? Can Daddy bring me Christmas here?'

'It's not quite like that,' Kay groaned, knowing every word must be chosen with care. 'Daddy can't do that for you now, but we can go and find a new tree from the green-grocer's shop. There'll be some left.'

'There's plenty of trees in the fairy wood. Mr Grumpy

can cut one down.' Evie began to bounce up and down. 'I want one of them.'

'Want doesn't get. They're not our trees, but we can buy one for everyone to enjoy.'

'I want one from the wood where the White Lady plays,' Evie insisted. When she got an idea in her head she could be so stubborn. All this talk about ladies in the hall and in the wood was disturbing.

'That's enough of your nonsense. We'll ask Mr Snowden later – and don't call him Mr Grumpy. They are kind to take us in.'

'I want to go to Granny's. She says we can come. I rang her yesterday and told her about the fire,' Evie added.

'Oh, I wish you hadn't. They'll only worry . . . Perhaps we should never have come here,' Kay sighed out loud.

Evie pounced on her words. 'But you did and you packed away our house and packed us up from Granny's and now we're stuck here and Daddy won't be able to find us. I hate you!' Evie shouted, turning her head away from her mother.

'Our big house was sold when Daddy moved his job. We thought we were going to London so we were going to stay with Granny Partridge for only a few weeks. You remember Glenwood Close? I thought you liked Wintergill.' Kay could feel herself tensing up as she tried to stay calm. Evie could be such a pain and it was too early in the morning for all this serious talk and explanations. It was better to say nothing more to upset her.

'I don't like it here with no Christmas, no one to play with, nothing to do. I'm bored!' Evie added, rubbing insult into injury.

What a mess I've made of everything, thought Kay. I thought I was doing right by making this break. Nothing's going right for us and still I haven't made any decisions for the New Year. Are we going to carry on like gypsies, wandering the country? Our cash won't last for ever. If only I didn't feel so tired and such a wimp, shillyshallying, putting our lives on hold. This can't go on.

Kay felt her irritation mounting as Evie bumped up and down on the mattress. 'Don't keep doing that, it'll ruin the bed.'

'I don't care.'

'Well, I do, Geneva Partridge. It's not our bed to ruin. I've had enough of your whingeing so get up, please, and find something to do. Don't you think I would like everything to be as it was before Daddy died? But it's not . . . Christmas is never going to be the same, and especially this year. Not for any of us. I wanted to give Granny and Granddad a break, so be reasonable. I can't get us a tree right now but I will later. I can't bring Daddy back and I can't bring back what the fire burned, but I'm trying to do my best. There are children in the world far worse off than you . . . with no parents, no food or shelter.'

'I don't like you,' Evie shouted, pulling a face.

'And I don't like you very much when you're in your stroppy clogs, so just get off my case and make us a cup of tea. You can manage the little kettle, not the one on the big stove, and let Muffin out for Mr Snowden. When it's light we'll go and ask if we can find a blasted fir tree and choose a nice one. I'm sure they'll let us have it in the hall. It's Christmas Eve soon and there's lots to do. You can help me choose some proper decorations.'

The bedroom door slammed shut and Kay snuggled back down into the blankets for a few more minutes of peace. Evie could be such a little madam when she was thwarted. They had all spoiled her this last year, given in to her, and now she was fast becoming a selfish little brat. It would do her good to go without for once. Kay was tired of having to manage on her own without support. She knew it was time to start job hunting. She still had some contacts in the City, but unlike most of her old friends she'd given up work as soon as Evie was born. Now it was time to find an accountancy firm that might take her on part time. It was all too much to think about now, she thought, burying her head back onto the pillow. Why must everything rest on her shoulders? Who was there to look after her? Who would give her a Christmas present this year?

Evie padded down to the big kitchen, her feet chilled by the flag floors. She opened the door to the yard for Muffin and grabbed her new track bottoms and thick fleece, her wellies and her Puffa anorak, dressing by the stove. She was not going to make anyone a cup of tea.

It was almost light now. The outlines of the empty barns were dark and forbidding and the smell of charred timbers filled the air. No one was about, not even Mrs Nora. She would take Muffin to the fairy wood and find the perfect fir tree herself.

There was a bank of grit by the field gate and she had to climb over the gate to get into the field, rolling down onto cold grass.

There was so much to do if there was snow, but everywhere was grey-green and misty, not even Jack Frost was on the trees, so she called in the dog and ran back to the kitchen to make some toast on the wire rack on the stove. It wasn't fair if Mum was going to lie in bed all day. Nobody cared about her and she didn't want a winter with no Christmas.

She sat at the table munching toast, and then a big idea came to her all at once. She would go on her own expedition with Muff, the two of them like in *Lassie*. If she found her school bag and filled it with food from the pantry fridge: a bottle of Sunny Delight, some of the Christmas biscuits she'd made with Nora before the fire. They could stay outside all day and no one would shout at them. Perhaps if she borrowed some money from Mummy's purse or the Toby Jug on the mantelpiece, she could find a café or catch a bus to Skipton and then a train . . . Then she had the most wonderful idea.

She scribbled a note on the back of an envelope, pulling her bobble hat over her ears and stuffing her gloves in her pocket. With her school bag on her back she set off in the morning light like an explorer, a Red Indian on a trail, scouting for treasure. She'd seen *Home Alone*, and even children could have big adventures. She could be anyone she wanted in her special kingdom but first it was time to go in search of the White Lady to see if she was waiting for a secret meeting by the fairy triangle.

She waited by the wood edge but there was no one in sight, no birdsong, no sound but the crunch of twigs and dried leaves. 'I'm here,' she shouted. 'Come and play with me,' hoping the lady in the mist would come out of hiding, but it wasn't a day for hide-and-seek in the wood when there were adventures to be had. She left the shadows of the copse and turned up the high field path. She wanted to walk in a straight line all the way round the world and back, or at least to the nearest bus stop. Granny would get such a surprise when she landed on her doorstep on Christmas Eve.

Blanche stirs from fitful slumber. She can smell movement in the copse. There is always white mist when she sits vigil around Wintergill, but this morrow is clear. She feels no cold or ice, only the fire of that yearning to find her lost child warms her bones. She spots a flash of gold, little legs in the field, golden hair. Blanche starts to run. She is coming, my Nonie . . . she is mine at last . . .

* * *

302

Nik slept in after a fitful night. He had read Agnes's journal late into the night and it had troubled his dreams with strange whirling scenes. He was half expecting to wake up to a whiteout since snow was forecast sometime in the next few days and the barometer had dropped. If it were true then the sheep would be making their own way down the moor to safety. Time to get the fodder ready. And then he remembered: there was none to feed.

How would his new flock learn such survival skills? They would be strange to these hills and the dangers. It was a good job he was in no position to be buying stock yet. Agnes's scribblings had unnerved him; all that stuff about unquiet spirits needing direction back to their resting places . . . What bunkum!

Yet he could sense strange mischief in the air as he'd sat sipping last night's toddy, as if someone was in the room watching him as he read through all those recipes. He must be going soft in the head to believe a word of them but for some reason he felt compelled to finish the book. It was as if it were being spoken directly to him and it gave him the shivers. He'd tossed and turned in a sweat, uneasy, as if he needed to be on guard. What the hell had any of this to do with him?

It must be the fire and the quarrel with his mother, leading to all those revelations. Her threat to leave the farm was reasonable enough. She was past learning new ways now. He would have to set on a student to help out but there would be no shortage of farmers' lads ready to give a hand. He would manage without her.

If only he could be sure he was doing the right thing, restocking, but traditions must be continued or they would be lost for ever. This heritage was too precious to be abandoned. That's what this government wanted, no doubt – to get rid of half the upland farms – but this farmer was not so easily seduced by money or the comfort of village life. He'd cope with just his own company, he preferred the wild hills to town streets.

The thought of any weird apparition haunting this place made him uneasy. If he hadn't seen something for himself now and again, he'd dismiss it all as nonsense. Nik liked his beliefs simple. It was enough for him to be steward of these hills like generations of his forebears. He didn't like to think of some ghoul stalking round his land up to no good. Yet he had seen that face in the mist the other night on the road, and then, there was this weird barn fire. Was finding Agnes's 'Herball' a mere coincidence?

Nik sat on the windowsill, his arms stretched over the stone lintel like Samson holding up the pillars. If only walls could talk, he smiled. Sometimes he felt this house had a soul of its own and he was drawing his strength from its sunlit rooms and its friendship. He looked down through the mullioned window into the far field, with its steep slope rising towards the limestone scree. He thought he saw a flash of red climbing up the slope. Who on earth was that? Some rambler out early to catch the best of the day? Did they not realise it was almost a cliff face and the footpaths were still closed to the public? The rise was full of boulders and rocky outcrops. No one should be on his fields anyway. Still, if they wanted to fall and break their neck it was their lookout.

He turned from the window to get on with his own day. All this surmising was giving him a headache.

Evie sat on the rocky ledge, wondering how to tackle the slope. It was steeper than she'd thought but it would be more fun than the other little hills she'd scrambled up. She lay back, looking up at the grey morning sky, and had her first snack of the day. To her annoyance, Muffin kept following behind her and she couldn't shoo him back. He sat with his nose nudging her lap, touting for a biscuit. Perhaps he would show her the way to the main road.

This was not the quickest road to Granny's house, but if she followed the normal fell track, someone would soon spot her and take her home where she'd be told off and sent to her room.

It was slippery up the scree so she kept to the stone wall. She knew about north and south and following the sun, but there wasn't one in the sky, just dark clouds. Her anorak was warm and her pockets were bulging with gloves and pound coins. If she crossed the fell to Windebank village there was a bus stop and no one would know her there.

'Shoo, Muff! Go back home,' she shouted. He would be a nuisance and she couldn't afford to pay for him on the bus. The dog scampered off, then turned and followed her again. Evie turned on him in anger. 'Go away, stupid dog! Away!'

The dog hobbled off with its tail tucked between his legs, obeying her command, leaving her side to roam over the empty fields, sniffing and puzzled, limping on his gammy leg. She wanted to get out of his sight, picking out the stony track she once walked with Mummy, who told her all about the Roman soldiers with bare legs and funny helmets who made this road long ago, and the big high wall made in the olden days with squiggles in the stone.

It was mean leaving Mummy behind, but if there was no Christmas at Wintergill she was going to find one at Granny's house. She wanted decorations and twinkling lights like the Christingle in church, crackers and presents under the tree, but their stuff was all gone. There was nothing left and it wasn't fair. She turned to see the wretched dog following her again. This time she didn't shoo him away.

305

They walked for an hour until her legs were tired and she sat down and scoffed the bread bun and biscuits and drank the orange drink. The coins jangled in her pocket, and she knew it was stealing not borrowing so she couldn't turn back now.

Ahead she could see purple hills with scarves of mist swirling round them. The wide path stretched out for miles ahead and she hoped she could find the crossroads to Bankwell and Windebank soon. If Bankwell was the nearest, she knew another path by the river.

What if she missed the bus, though? It was a long walk into town then, and her wellies were rubbing her heels. This adventure was not as much fun as she'd hoped and Muff had disappeared now on his limpy leg. It was getting a bit scary on her own.

If she turned back now she could trace her path to the old wall and go home for tea, putting the coins back in the purse and the Toby Jug and no one would know she'd been stealing.

The lane was getting bumpy and steep again. It was all taking up time. There was a steep bank hugging the side of the fell, and to cross it meant walking through stiff brown cardboard grass. Her wellies were really hurting now so she stopped to take them off. There were huge red blisters on her heels where her socks slid under her feet.

She yelled for Muffin, over and over, but he'd gone so she curled up for a rest to suck her thumb and think what to do next. She'd forgotten her wristwatch and had no idea of the time, only that she was tired and fed up of tramping on her own. When she woke from her doze she couldn't see anything but cloud and mist. It had crept down from the hill, swallowing the grass up.

What was the best thing to do now? Tears of fear stung her eyes. If she couldn't see the path, she'd be lost and then it would go dark and she'd be all alone and no one knew where she was. She knew it was silly to stay out in the open air. If it snowed or rained she might catch cold and go all stiff like they did in the Lassie films when she came to the rescue just in time. How she wished she'd got Muffin for company now.

She must find the high stone wall. They all joined up somewhere so if she followed the stone wall, bit by bit, she could do like the sheep did in the picture in Mrs Nora's living room and snuggle behind it for shelter. She could make a little tent with her coat and her bag or something.

The grass was boggy so she picked her way down in the mist to a little pool of clear water, filling her bottle just in case, and found the welcome sight of a wall. She put her wellies in her bag and walked barefoot to soothe her blisters. Mummy . . . Mummy, I want you . . . she sobbed into the mist but nobody came. How could they? No one would ever find her again. Cold as she was, she kept fingering down the wall for dear life until she found a little curve with a hole built into the wall like a fairy den and she crouched down with her knees hunched up to her chin in the little shelter.

Evie was past fear, just tired and hungry as she tasted the first drops of rain. She zipped up her anorak, pulled down her fleece hat and stuffed bits of brown grass into her wellies, packing her feet in them for warmth. She found one of her gloves and stuck her wellies into the backpack. She remembered seeing that on *Blue Peter*.

Now she was going to miss the best *Blue Peter* of the year when they all gave each other presents. You have to keep warm, go to sleep and when morning came she'd find her way home or find somebody to help her.

The darkness was all around her, tickling like black wool in her face. The rain was light but she felt the wind rushing through the stones to sing her to sleep, but she was much too afraid of the night creatures to close her eyes.

Evie started to sing all the carols she'd learned at her new school. 'How far is it to Bethlehem?', 'Little donkey', 'Long time ago in Bethlehem'. No one would hear her growly voice up here and put her on the back row. Could Daddy hear her singing in Heaven? Did Granny know she was coming? How could she sing above the wind?

Only the White Lady who lived on the hills might hear her if she sang out loud enough. As the darkness thickened she knew Mummy would be out there searching for her. Perhaps she'd already gone to Granny's to find her. They would think she'd gone on the bus and been stolen.

Her eyelids were dropping now but she daren't close them, hidden as she was under the wall. The rain was turning flaky and she held out her tongue to taste the flakes but they melted in her mouth like candyfloss at the fair. It was when she leaned out of her hidy-hole that she saw the lantern swinging, flickering in the darkness like the Christingle candles, such a welcome sight. She was safe at last. Her rescuers had found her.

Fret not, sweet coz, Mama is here to seek you out. Blanche swings the lantern from side to side with bony fingers bleached by wind and rain. That which was lost is found, she smiles, and must be gathered home.

Kay was last in the bathroom. She'd fallen asleep as soon as Evie left her in peace, and woke later than planned. If she was to go into town for a tree and some gifts for the Snowdens she must get her skates on. She assumed Evie was out with Mrs Nora, getting under her feet, but when there was no sign of her there she assumed she'd taken Muffin out for a walk. Her anorak and wellies were gone from the hook. She must be out with Nora so she decided to slip into town and get on with her private shopping without a child to hamper her decisions.

It was well after lunch before she returned with all her packages, expecting Evie to bounce through Nik's kitchen with a 'Where've you been?'

She was surprised to see no anorak hanging up and went to find Nora dozing on her sofa. Evie must have tired her out. She was still weak from her flu and Kay decided not to wake her. She went in search of Nik to no avail. His van was not in the yard. The house was strangely silent with no clatter of boots on the flags. The sky glowered and the first flakes of snow fluttered past the window. Kay shivered.

She ran upstairs to see if Evie was rooting in the attic rooms but there was no sign of her and this time she burst into Nora's lounge.

'Where's Evie?'

The old woman looked up in surprise. 'Isn't she with you? Not seen sight nor sound of her all day, come to think of it.' Nora could see the anxiety on her face. 'Not to worry, she'll be out with Nik and the dogs somewhere.'

Yes, that must be it, Kay sighed. Evie would be pestering the life out of him to chop down a tree. Silly me. There'd been only one thing on her daughter's mind all morning. 'I'll make us a brew,' she smiled, and made for the kitchen when Nik strode in and kicked off his boots.

He looked under the table. 'Where's old Muff?'

'Is Evie with you?' Kay said, trying not to worry.

'Nope,' he replied. 'Should she be?'

'She was going to ask you if we could chop down a tree for the hall. I thought you'd taken her out . . . She's not in the house. I haven't seen her since first light. I've been to town, thinking she was with Nora but she hasn't seen her either. Where's she got to? It's getting dark and beginning to snow.' Her legs were turning to jelly. Something was wrong and nothing anyone could say would convince her otherwise.

'Sit down,' Nik said, pointing to the Windsor chair by the stove. 'Tell me slowly.' He poured the tea and shoved the mug into her hand. 'When did you last see her?'

'This morning at seven,' she croaked. 'It was still dark and I told her to let Muff out for you . . . Oh my God! Her anorak, the dog.' She was searching around her mind for evidence. 'They've been gone since first light!'

'We don't know that. I thought I saw someone on the scree. What colour is her jacket?' Nik leaned on the stove rail, looking serious.

'Red, pillar-box red . . . with a striped fleece hat and pink wellies. She chose those colours herself,' she whispered as if it were important. Icy splinters were stabbing her gut with panic.

'We'll search the outbuildings first, phone around the other farms to see if she's been spotted. She might have gone to play with one of their kids. They can be so thoughtless.'

Nik was trying to sound calm and businesslike but Kay could hear the worry in his voice, and Nora was standing in the doorway, looking ashen, holding a piece of paper in her hand. It was an unopened Christmas card with writing on the envelope.

'I think you should read this and call the police,' she said, her eyes glassy with concern. 'Oh God, not again!'

Kay snatched it from her, recognising Evie's attempt at joined-up writing: 'Gone to find Chrismass at grannys, luv Evie.'

'What does it mean?' said Nik as he glanced at the message.

'Just what it says,' Kay replied from a place somewhere above her head. 'We had a bit of a row this morning over

Christmas. She wants Christmas and wants to go back to Sutton Coldfield . . . How can a child get from here to there on her own with no money?' She felt her words were scrambling into syllables, fragmenting, shards of information floating through her mind.

'We'll call the police. It's been too long already.' Nik was already striding into the hall. Kay shut her eyes as waves of terror washed over her. Evie was out there alone on the tops and it was snowing, wandering about trying to find south while she was swanning around town oblivious to this danger. What would Social Services make of all that?

'I'm going out to search,' she said, jumping up for her boots and Barbour.

'You'll do no such thing. We don't want two souls lost on the moor. The Cave and Mountain Rescuers will do that better than any of us,' Nora yelled. 'They're trained for just such stuff. You'll stay here with me and give the police all the details. Happen she's tucked up somewhere in Bankwell with a friend and never got further than the main road. Even young Evie knows it's a mighty walk back to Sutton Coldfield from here. She's a stubborn head on her, that one, but she's canny with it. She'll be fine.' But Nora's eyes told a different story.

Nik couldn't believe how quick the emergency response sprang into action. They were going out in the sleet with teams of volunteers and a search dog. He rubbed his eyes with weariness as the hours spun out: screech of sirens, Land Rovers with men in orange and green jackets, the local bobbies taking statements, and questions, hundreds of questions.

The Cave Rescue guys were old school mates, and suggested his knowledge of the hills was essential to their search. Then there was the question of the old dog. Surely

Muff would have tramped back home, but he was lame and a slow old trooper, and could sit on trapped sheep for hours in his younger days, waiting on top of drifts until they were rescued.

Nik sifted through the snow to test the moisture. Wet snow came and went in twenty-four hours. Snow was better than a fierce easterly wind any time, for snow cocooned, cushioned and protected bodies from extremes. If the kid had sought shelter she'd be safe enough for a few more hours but she might not survive the night.

At least she was kitted out for weather better than when they had first arrived in flimsy clothes. Her school bag had gone, and food too. The coins from the jug were missing so the little minx had meant to run away. The forward planning was impressive for an eight-year-old. The last time he'd tried to run away he'd taken only an apple and his best Dinky tractor.

They combed all the outbuildings and barns. Weather was against them now but the tracker dog was sniffing out a scent up the scree to the high ground where Nik had spotted the red blob in the morning.

If only he'd bothered to follow up that sighting, but he assumed it was a trespasser. What bothered him most were those dreams and the image of the white hag on the road, who had stalked him for years. Was she a part of this? First the fire and now this, and both times a child was involved.

He shivered, knowing this was illogical nonsense, but that extra sense of danger was twitching and he knew that Evie was in danger not only from the weather but from that other unmentionable creature, that unquiet spirit. How could he even be thinking of such another dimension? Who would believe such nonsense, and yet . . .? He had read Agnes's book and knew the tale of her daughter's pram.

Nik fled to his room, shutting the door from the chaos

in the kitchen to grab Agnes's book of instructions. Suddenly he knew everything was connected in a jigsaw and he must discover how to put the pieces together. Agnes's knowledge was the key to him being able to thwart another disaster. If only he knew how to go about it. He must read it again for clues.

The Lord gives and the Lord takes. Blessed be the name of the Lord but 'tis not His chariot of fire that carries the prostrate child into the heavens but her cousin's mischief. Hepzibah sighs from her vantage point in the chamber window. Alack there is no joy in this snowfall. From All Hallows to yuletide, misery will come once more. Blanche is about her business and who is to stop her?

Soon the looking-glass will be covered in black cloth and the funeral wreaths hung at the door. The house will be in mourning and a new grave dug in the churchyard where rosemary garlands will be hung in honour of the little maid.

Hepzi has no heart for yuletide silliness but now it saddens her that there is no household busyness to celebrate the birthing of the Lord; dust will gather on the cupboard, the rushes afoot will not be swept this morrow, the fowls will go unfed, but out in the copse Blanche will feed on her victory and grow in strength once more.

Only the Lord in His wisdom knoweth His purposes in giving my cousin yet another consolation, she sighs as she fades into the shadows in defeat. I can give no aid in this matter. I have no strength beyond these walls but there is one mightier who can temper the wind to the shorn lamb if it is His will . . .

Fear stalked the kitchen at Wintergill, now the HQ for the search-and-rescue operation. Time was of the essence, but the weather report wasn't good and the sniffer dog had lost

313

the scent. If the child stayed put she could die of hypothermia, if she set off to come home, she could fall off rocks to her death. If she was hiding in a barn there was hope, but it was a wet chill out there. Nora kept on making tea and pulling out bag after bag of flour from the pantry to make mince pies, hundreds of them, using all her jars of mincemeat.

She no longer cared what anyone thought of her. It was her instinct to cut and kneed and roll and bake. She needed to keep her hands from shaking to blot out the panic and the memory of the accident all those years ago. It could have been yesterday.

The phone kept ringing as news of the second event at Wintergill spread like wildfire from pub to pub. Men came out with their sons, searching their own barns and ditches, prodding the falling snow with sheepdogs, scouring the fell for any sign of life. Neighbours were on the watch.

There had to be hope, and she would bake such a pile of stuff so that when Evie returned as she must . . . To lose a husband and then your possessions and a child in one season was unthinkable. It must not be so. It was against all natural justice.

Yet how small is mankind against the forces of nature. How small is a child on a savage moor top. She had feared the arrival of a child when the two of them first appeared less than two months ago but never in her wildest dreams did she imagine such a tragedy unfolding.

Poor Kay was sitting with a woman officer, rocking back and forth, clutching Evie's pyjamas in her lap, beside herself with terror, rocking like an animal in pain. How well Nora knew that feeling but was helpless to say or do anything to relieve it. There were no words, only primitive foetal movements: a mother raging against the forces, against the truth dawning in her mind that her child is lost.

If Evie survived she was going to get the best Christmas in the world for to them she would be that greatest of Christmas gifts: the gift of life itself. That was what Nora was praying for as she pounded the pastry board and scattered flour all over Nik's grubby floor, no longer caring that she was trespassing on his domain, once the family kitchen, where all the dramas of her own life had unfolded. She was here at her hearth and her stove, a woman possessed, a woman on a mission. Live, Evie, live! Don't go to sleep! Stay with us! We all want you home.

Kay couldn't sit down any more. This was all her own fault for not handling Evie's grieving with sensitivity this morning. She'd been so carried away with getting out of Sutton and the stifling atmosphere with Tim's parents that she'd put her precious child at risk in this wilderness country.

A house for winter . . . how could she have been so naïve as to suppose this flight of fancy was the answer? They should have stayed put and given Evie the usual suburban Christmas with grandparents who loved her, not brought her out to strangers, kind as they were. What a terrible costly mistake in every way, it seemed now, a calculated risk that was going so wrong. 'Oh, forgive me,' she cried.

You are a selfish coward, she sighed as she rummaged through Evie's toys, the drawer full of other children's hand-me-downs. Nothing of the old days was left. Everything was burned. It was then she stumbled upon the little drawing book Evie kept in the pocket of the back seat of the car but never showed her. It was full of strange tiny drawings and words she could hardly read, pictures of ladies in costume and Evie playing in the trees with a fairy lady. Kay fled down the stairs with it, bumping into Nik, who was supping in the kitchen with his relief team of farmers. The door

315

was open and the snow flurries had cleared to reveal a clear sky full of stars with a moon the size of a brass plate. She shoved the book into his hand.

'Look at this, Nik. I don't understand what's going on. Look at these drawings. How can a girl her age know such detail? Look at the figures and the costumes. Does she really see these people? First the fire, which no one knows how it got started. Then this. It's doing my head in thinking she's been hiding this from me. How many other poor souls have been haunting her?'

He put his arm around her, guiding her down onto one of the chairs.

He didn't look surprised, fingering the pages with care. He smiled at the picture of the witch with the feather brush and the white fairy with the hair like some ancient hippy. His words were even more puzzling.

'Kids sometimes see stuff we don't. Remember the first day she sat on my wall and talked about the white lady and you laughed and I joked and teased her. I've not exactly been honest.' He paused, looking at her with eyes wide with fear. 'I've had the odd glimpse of that presence for years around the place. I never told anyone when I was a kid. That night when I crashed the pickup . . .' he added.

Kay didn't know whether to laugh or cry. 'Now you tell me that some sort of ghost has been following my child and you've said nothing?' she snapped.

'It's only the White Lady. She's been haunting this farm for generations. She's a bit of a legend, flitting about like a faded photograph. The old biddy with the feathers by the stairs is a kind old soul, part of the furniture. Evie's drawn her just as I used to see her . . . I always think of her as an extra housekeeper.' He was trying to keep his voice casual but it wasn't fooling Kay one iota.

316

'Let me get this straight. You see ghosts?' she asked, seeing him blush.

'Keep your voice down,' he said, steering her away from earshot. 'Just now and then . . . around the house. An old house always has spirits . . . It's faded as I've got older, but recently I have seen a few things . . .'

'Why you? How? Are you psychic?' She stared at him full on, wide-eyed with suspicion.

'Dunno . . . it just happens. Why do some folks snore or scratch their heads in a certain way? I never gave it much thought until I found this old book a few days ago.' Nik pulled an old leather-bound book out of his cluttered bureau drawer.

'This belonged to my great-grandma, Agnes Snowden, the po-faced one on the stairs. It's full of old recipes and herbal concoctions. See for yourself. There's a story here you should read. It's obvious she was another who had the knack. It must run in some families and she was of gypsy stock. Mother told me you're from Norton stock so maybe it runs in your genes too.' He was trying to make all this sound normal so as not to scare her.

'For some reason this thing hasn't passed away in peace because something's holding her back, some miscarriage of justice, a sudden death. I don't know, but my guess is she's been stuck around this house for centuries and the folk tales of the white lady of the fells is probably a distillation of legends, sightings and rumour. If I'm right she needs laying to rest once and for all before she does any more mischief. Time to find if she's behind all this or whether I'm just going off my head.'

'You mean an exorcism? You think she's behind all the bad things, and now Evie . . . Oh God, what have I brought her to? This can't be true . . . it's the twenty-first century.'

'I don't think time has any meaning in these matters.

317

Agnes left this book as a sort of warning or a guidebook, I'm not sure which. Wintergill seems to be the focus of all this restless energy. Whatever happened in the past, happened here, I fear.'

Kay couldn't believe what she was hearing. 'So what can we do?'

'We've got to find Evie and bring her home, never mind the rest. Come on, let's get out of here. I can't stand by idling. There's one place that might be a good starting point . . .'

Kay was poring over the book, screwing up her eyes to read the script, shaking her head.

'I don't believe a word of any of this,' she whispered. 'Are you telling me that Evie acts as some psychic magnet, drawing this spirit back into action? It sounds such a lot of hocus-pocus to me.'

Nik steered her further into the hall with his arm. 'I know it sounds crazy but we have to go and find them and bring them home. This is Wintergill business from the past, and most of it is beyond me. I'm just a farmer, not a priest, and I don't know what the hell's going on any more than you do, but sitting here's not the answer. You mustn't despair. Sometimes things turn up for the right reason at the right time.'

She nodded, seeing he really believed what he was saying. Kay had never seen him so animated and so concerned. She felt that warmth between them again. 'I trust you, Nik.'

'Come on, let's slip away and follow our noses. I know it sounds crazy but all isn't lost yet. I just feel we've a chance if we strike now. Open your mind, Kay. Think the unthinkable. The clues are here in the book and I've been mulling over Agnes's story. The rest is up to a higher authority than my puny mind . . . whatever you call it. There has to be a way.'

318

'I'm scared,' Kay answered, grabbing the book. 'I'm too knackered to take much in but I'm coming with you. I'll do anything to make it up to Evie. This is all my fault, bringing her here on a whim.

'No time for guilt trips, Kay. This'll be more like a trek through a dicey bog moor. There's a list of stuff to gather up, warm dry clothes, kitchen bits, but first get us a flask of tea. It'll have to be a fly-by-the-seat-of-your-pants sort of effort but while there's hope we must do something.'

Kay hovered in the doorway, watching as he stood in the hall, lighting up the storm lamp, head down as if in prayer. Perhaps it was time she asked for guidance too.

The snow was swirling around Evie as she peered out of her shelter towards the speck of bright light. She felt no cold now, only a tiredness, and the drift of snow piling up before her felt like a plump cushion with comfy pillows to rest her head. Muffin had found her and lain at her feet. He was fast asleep but he kept the wind from her legs. The lemony daylight was brightening the corner of the sky but she was too scared and frozen to lift her legs. She wanted to lie down on the duvet of snow and sleep but the light coming towards her blinded like a torch in her eyes. They were coming to get her! Mummy would be waiting and worrying. How she wished she'd never left home now.

Out of the light came the face of a beautiful lady and she smiled, holding her hand out to pull her from her hidy-hole. Evie felt such relief. The White Lady of the woods had come to find her and take her home to Mummy. She felt herself floating over the grey fields, flying in the air like a Christmas angel with wings, like the Snowman in the cartoon book, and it was magic. Wait till she told them all back at school!

The Search

'I know you'll think he's crazy, Nora, but Nik thinks this house is haunted by an unquiet spirit; not within these walls, for they're protected by a kindly presence, but outside in the fields. He thinks we have a troubled presence and it's about time she was put to rest.' Kay looked up, expecting Nora to burst into peals of laughter, but she shook her head solemnly as she looked over Evie's drawing book.

'That's the old Lavender Lady Evie was always on about? My own daughter used to see her, and Mistress Hepzibah was the name my mother-in-law gave her years ago. She said she'd do no harm to anyone, for she loved this place.' Nora looked up as she was carrying on with her pastry as if it were noon, not the middle of the night.

'Nik's got some book . . . Agnes Snowden's book. Can there be anything in it or have we flipped in our panic?'

'If Nik thinks there's summat in all these funny goings-on, it's worth a try,' said Nora, as if she was talking about some aunt down the road. 'All I know is, our Shirley was taken badly and lost after snow. That fire was a funny do . . . I wasn't going to say anything to you but surely that is more than a coincidence? I'd like to get my hands on this poltergeist.'

She paused from her frenzy of activity to add, 'All these years my son's had the Snowden second sight and never said . . . Talk about see all and say nowt! Tom used to laugh when Shirley told us things. I never thought my son would be the same. I wish he'd told me. I've been so hard on him. He got the brunt of it after Shirley died. He told me so only the other day. Now he's trying to make things right for you, trying to save your little one. We must do as he says and trust that he's right.' Nora sighed, shaking her head. 'I'm baking up a storm for when Evie gets back. She'll be starving.'

She was still baking mince pies as if there was no tomorrow, sending trays out to the police team and the ambulance drivers.

'They're not having much success out there, searching blindly. If only we could find old Muff. He were always a good 'un for setting on trouble.' How quickly Nora's accent broadened when she was fired up.

'I'm going out to find her with him. I can't wait in here any longer. I have do something.' Kay made for the hall again and Nora caught hold of her, hugging her tightly.

'It'll be all right. It has to be. See this?' Nora pointed to one of the storm candles and placed it in the hall window where it flickered for a second and then blazed steadily. 'Now I'm lighting a candle in the window, an old German custom. It's the wayfarer's candle to guide the Christ child and all wanderers back from the darkness. Trust the light will bring you all home.'

Hepzibah watches the flickering candle. She sees bustle and doors banging, she scents the spices on the air and sees the comings and goings. Someone is stirring in the night, summoning all the women who have wept within these walls. There is no fire yet in the yule grate, no smoke in the chimney, only the damp chill of fear on the air. Lord have mercy on us. The time is ripe and the struggle begins in earnest now.

'I will lift up mine eyes unto the hills: from whence cometh my help . . .'

Adrenalin was pumping Kay forward now. She felt strangely calm, with a growing strength of purpose within herself. I have to do something to make amends, she resolved. My child's life depends on all our combined strengths. How curious, she thought looking up the staircase at the portraits, a line of disembodied faces, yet she sensed for one brief moment that she was not alone: that all the mothers and daughters of this strange house over so many generations were standing close at hand, praying in their own fashion, willing her good fortune in the coming crucial hours.

Nik watched the shaft of moonlight make a circle on the carpet. He could smell candle wax, the bitter taste of panic on his tongue. He looked again at those old drawings. What did they mean, the five-pointed star . . . an old witchy symbol of protection. The circle of star and light. It was all mumbo jumbo and yet the drawing of the stones was leading him out onto the moor tops and he sensed exactly the direction they must take. But what to do after that? Common sense said he should be out there with the search teams on his quad bike, scouring the fells, not striking out on his own.

Trust your instincts, he heard the voice whispering, a softer side of himself. First things first: find them and bring them home. If only it were that simple. He was out of his depth but desperate as he grabbed Kay and headed for his bike.

'Come on, Agnes Snowden, do yer stuff!'

Nora sat herself down in the hall, drunk with exhaustion and fear. She lifted the pile of unopened cards from her table and fingered all the good wishes lovingly, picturing each one in turn, feeling mean that she had not sent a card yet. She thought of all who had loved this house: Sam the builder, Joss the farmer, who prettified the house for his wife; Jacob; and all their wives; Tom, Klaus, Shirley and Nik; Kay and, most of all, Evie. She prayed for good times to come back to her home for she loved it in her own way as much as Nik did. She prayed for forgiveness for neglecting her son's feelings in the past. He was doing his best to find the child with everything stacked against him. She trusted his instincts would find true north.

Her heart was thumping like a slow drum. This was a queer do and no mistake. What would Tom make of it all? She hoped he could see the effort Nik was giving out on their behalf to protect this blessed place from any more harm. 'Come on, Tom, you know I did you a great wrong. Shirley, wherever you are, help us find the child before it's too late,' she prayed.

Hepzibah stirs from her slumbers by the embers of the yuletide log. Someone was calling her name: 'Hepzi, Hepzi . . . Guardian of the hearth.' She senses a gentle breeze wafting through the house, a breeze that wafts and cleans out the corners, that makes the linen dance along the hedgerows, rustles the rushes on the floor, sends smoke straight up the chimney and has maids scurrying to their morning chores.

It is time to step towards the open doorway and the wind that blows the cobwebs from the lintels. The household is stirring and she must go to the door and sniff the morning air. Someone is calling her over the years with words she can scarce fathom but their meaning is becoming ever clearer. It is time at last, Lord have mercy on us!

She must stand by the doorway at the furthest reaches of her domain and guide the voices back.

'Come hither, Cousin! Good tidings! Come and see. I have news of Anona. She is found at last,' she shouts into the breeze looking out across a sea of snow and mist. 'Come hither and take my hand . . . it is time you came a-calling. I can help you find her. I have waited over the years for this moment. I will not let you fail us now.' Her weary eyes strain to see if there is movement.

Nothing stirs in the copse, no sign that Blanche is heeding her, but she knows her cousin can't be far away, not in this season of frost and ice.

'Come home. We mean no harm by you. 'Tis time to patch up our quarrel and seek forgiveness, one from the other. You have caused great mischief in your anger but no matter. Our time is ending. Come home!'

'You stole what was mine,' comes a faint voice as Blanche appears out of the mist, holding her hand out to her side as if she clutches something that her cousin cannot see.

'I didn't steal your child. You were always wrong on that score, Cousin,' Hepzi pleads. 'No one here ever harmed a hair of her head. Anona was safe from harm with me. Come closer, see for yourself. You were so close and yet so far . . . 'Twas no one to blame for the storm that divided us. Hear the truth for once and harken now to one who knows where Anona abides in safety. Listen. Can you hear her laughter? Look, see, she's safe within. The Lord is merciful. He has heard your petition. He wants you back home. Listen to His words, for He speaks the truth. Come closer.

'It is time for us to leave these mortal confines in peace, time to move out of this earthly bondage, out from these shadows into a brighter light where all we love are waiting for us. Look through the open door, see the tallow candle lit to welcome you. The child is within.'

Blanche can see only her cousin through the mist, standing in the doorway of the cursed house. How old she has grown, how stooped and grey. She is a spent force and cannot harm her. Blanche pauses to hear a faint voice calling out. She clutches her bundle tightly. 'I am not a spirit. I am but a weary woman travelling far. I am tired but I cannot cease from my travail,' she sneers, turning back to her cousin with disdain. 'Am I not flesh and blood as you who stand before me are my kith and kin?'

She sees Hepzibah shaking her head and whispering, 'We've been dead for many a year, Cousin: two old crones who are stuck 'twixt heaven and earth, going round in circles like mad dogs chasing their tails, going over the same track time over again. Take pity on us!'

'You make jest. I can see your bony fingers and sunken cheeks. Granted we are old now – that is the fate of all flesh – but we are fixed to this ground. I have no grave, just as my own child's bones lie unburied,' Blanche argues into the wind, but the far-off voice keeps slipping words into her ear.

'You are misled to wander so far from your kin. Come see for yourself if you will, but hear me out. Come see, Coz. What I say is true.'

''Tis not so! You lie. You are chained to this cursed house. 'Tis all lies. My child is here safe with me,' she calls to her cousin in fear. She fears the power behind the words. How can a child be in two places? She sees the torches burning across the moor. She looks to Hepzibah for succour but there is none, only cruel words. She is afraid to let go now.

'Oh, whisht and listen. These are the chains of love that have kept me here,' Hepzibah shouts. 'Love speaks louder than hate. Look to the light and see for yourself. Step inside . . .' Hepzibah is pointing to the doorway and the flickering light beyond. 'Look through the casement if you don't believe me. You have worked enough havoc. It must end. If you will not come closer, I can do no more to help you.'

Blanche hesitates, uncertain whether to slip back from the light or move towards its source . . . caught between doubt and mistrust. 'How can that be? I do not understand . . .' she cries out.

'You're caught in a web of your own making, spinning round neither alive or dead, trapped by your pain and longing, by the rage of your grief against those you think robbed you of what was yours, but you are misguided in all these matters, I promise you. Come with me through the door and follow my words. She's here, your heart's desire. All you want is within.'

'No, you are a trick of the wind to fool me. I know you . . . I have within my grasp all I desire. Leave me be,' she screams, swirling in the snow and the mist away from the piercing light.

She hears the hound growling round her ragged skirt and strikes him with her icy hand. 'Out of my way, you cur! Nothing will bar my way.'

Nik was frantic. He was no longer sure of his bearings but he knew now where he must search: the old wall marked with the pointed star on the page, the danger point in Agnes's story. He was struggling out of dark mist up a steep hill and suddenly it was as if he were opening from a tunnel of darkness into bright light, familiar terrain: a stretch of dry-stone walls, pasture meadows, sheep pens and the far field barn towards the Celtic wall set against a rainbow of purple hills.

There was no sound or movement but he could smell fields full of grazing sheep, his Suffolks were grazing heads down, content. All was as it was before. It was a charmed stillness, but it was only a mirage. The land was bare but he could still sniff out the grazing fields. They must find Evie out there on the moor before the chill took her body

326

across that bridge from which there would be no returning. She was somewhere not far away and if they could rescue her now, it might not be too late.

Kay was clinging for dear life on the back of the quad. Against all advice they'd shot out of the farmyard onto the track across the fields, headlights blazing towards the old footpath. The snow was turning back to sleet, stinging her cheeks, but but she did not care.

Nik's face was glazed. He was silent and focused. He knew where he was going, his goggles splattered with slush. When he reached the drifts blocking his path, he dug a track like a mad man, hardly pausing for breath, and Kay dug with him with her bare hands until they raced onwards again, following the frosted stone walls that curved around the old track. She watched him stop and scour the horizon, calling out.

'She's got to be round here. This is where Agnes nearly lost her baby. There's been too many accidents round here. Evie!' he yelled into the wind.

Kay touched his arm. 'What's that . . . on the snow over there by the wall?' There was a dark object outlined in the snow. They raced across in hope but it was just a boulder jutting out from the snow, a rock, not a signpost. Kay could feel her panic rising. This was a wild-goose chase and there was nothing out there.

'It's not going to work,' she cried, making for the quad bike, her head bent in despair.

'This is close to the spot in the book.' Nik's lips were cracked and his eyes blazing. 'She must be here somewhere.'

'This thing you see, what does she look like?' Kay asked.

'Sometimes she looks like any woman in a cloak, gathering mushrooms, but lately she is old with staring eyes and looks more like a bag of bones,' he said.

'You think she may be a mother, a once-upon-a-time mother, like some deranged woman out of her mind with worry . . . searching , searching like me? Don't shout at her then. Anger never hears, Nik. Plead with her, speak to her better nature, hear her feelings. Show her compassion . . . Let me talk to her.' Where were these words coming from, she wondered. She felt only hatred towards such a monster. 'Perhaps if I leave you alone, this apparition'll come,' she cried, but he shook his head, grabbing her arm.

'I don't know, but let's scout round and shout for Evie. I'm sure this is near the place where the pram rolled down the hill into the wall.' he said.

'And the baby?'

'The baby was unharmed. Evie!' Nik screamed. 'Where the bloody hell are you hiding?' He jumped on the quad, heading out into the darkness, headlights blazing. They stopped by a high-walled sheepfold. He pulled out the torch.

They made circles with the torch. He switched on the headlights and they sat on the quad, feeling stupid and very cold. Shouting out to break the stillness of the dawn. Kay was pacing up and down the boundary. 'There's nothing here but snow and stone. Let's move on.'

'I was so sure this was the place . . . Evie!'

Blanche feels herself lifted up against her will as if floating across the snowfields, down the rough track from the heights of Wintergill towards the old farmhouse. Hepzibah is still waiting by the door waving a lantern, pointing excitedly.

'Come in, Cousin, over the threshold. What can you see? Who can you see at the fireside?'

Blanche peers and peers through the open door, catching glimpses of figures flitting across the hearth, chattering as they spin, going about their business. 'I cannot see clearly.' She is straining her eyes to make some sense of the scene.

'See for thyself who's inside, look hard, move closer . . .' whispers the silver voice, and she wants to see but she's afraid. 'Give yourself to the task . . . let go of your fear and look carefully.'

The mist in her eyes is patchy now and she can see some old familiar face sitting by the hearth – Nate and his yard boy, laughing with round faces. They look up at her. Is it a fancy or does she see Father Michael quaffing from an ale pot? But he is tall and strong again, as she first knew him.

Then her heart leaps at the sight of her husband's cloak over the oak chest. Surely, but surely it is – yes, it is Kit. She can see the lace on his cuffs and the fine jacket of blue velveteen. Is this but a devil's mirage? Blanche steps back. Surely it cannot be thus? These are but the haunting chimeras of my tired mind, she muses. The light is too bright. She is blinded by such longings. She steps back from the threshold but Hepzibah reaches out to her.

'Time for us to go forward now, Cousin, time to join our husbands by the hearth; my task is done. I have brought you home and can stay no longer. You must choose your own way now. I can do no more for you.'

'But where is my child? You promised me my child. Wait, Hepzi. I'm afraid of that bright light.'

Hepzibah was vanishing into the deep recesses of the house but her voice lingered.

'Only when you let go of that which you clutch to your side, Sister, will all be revealed. 'Tis not Nonie who you are holding . . . let go of all your greed, and envy . . . all your malice and stalkings towards innocent maids. Let go and you will see your own heart's desire. Trust in the higher wisdom and mercy. Step inside and see. Let go of what holds you fast here. It is not yours to take with you. Trust in my words. It is time for you to come home.'

Blanche is so torn now between longing and the hunger and yearning that never go away, night or day, from moon *to moon. The flagstone passageway is tempting, worn smooth by other pilgrims, a trusted path into the light, away from the dreary shadows on this cold night. If only the mist of tears would clear so that she might catch a glimpse into that room. She loosens her grip on the hand that she has grabbed for comfort and takes a halting step forward.*

Suddenly the candles flicker, and she feels a searing heat on her face, and a burning pain of anguish that she's unworthy of the company assembled by the roaring fire.

Then she sees Nonie running towards her, and Kit looks up smiling. Her beloved child with those fair locks, is laughing and she turns to Blanche waving and smiling. 'Mama! Come and dance a Christmas carol!'

Blanche is stunned and frozen for a second. How can she cross with the burden she is carrying by her side? She longs to be inside out of the cold at last.

'Come on in and get some warmth . . . All's well that ends well. You've come back to us at long last.' Hepzi steps out of the shadows. Blanche leaps forward to meet them. 'I'm here, Nonie, I'm home!'

Nik slumped forward. 'Can you see anything at all?' Kay offered him the flask. 'Why are we still hanging around here?' she snapped in frustration.

'Because I was following Agnes's warning, I'm sorry . . . Evie has to be somewhere here,' he said but his voice was heavy with doubt. 'I could do with something stronger than tea.'

'I laced it with whisky, can't you taste it?' Kay looked out over the scene. It didn't look any different, a grey-black expanse of turf and walls.

'A flask of whisky would hit the spot.' Nik stopped suddenly, screwing his eyes tightly to focus on a bundle lying on a snowdrift. 'What's that over there by the wall . . .?'

*   *   *

In her dream Evie was scared of flying, round and round, spinning into the darkness, but now the hand was clutching at her with bony fingers and she couldn't breathe. There was shouting and crying and moans like the wind under the door. She could hear another voice calling in the opposite direction, a gruff voice she recognised and she wanted to turn and go backwards to find that voice.

Evie kept tugging at the White Lady's hand and tried to call out, but her lips were not moving, frozen with ice. They were flying towards the bright light now and Evie had no strength to break free, but the familiar far-off voice was getting louder in her ear and she was afraid as the grip tightened.

'Let me go!' she yelled, but no words could stop their flight. 'Let me go home now, please!'

The light was getting so bright it hurt her eyes, a light rising in the horizon like all the colours of the rainbow in one. The White Lady was in such a hurry, rushing onwards, smiling, but she didn't hear Evie's plea. 'Please let me go home,' she whimpered one last time, and her lips were released to make the wailing howl of a creature in pain.

Suddenly the grasp loosened and the lady floated onwards without a second glance, onwards into the dawn light. Evie was left hovering and then falling, spinning down all alone but the voice was getting ever louder.

'What's that heap over there?' Nik could see a black and white rug lying on the pile of wet snow. 'Oh my God, it's Muff!' He began to dig furiously round the prostrate shape, digging through into the very wall itself. 'Kay! Kay! I've found her! Evie! Wake up! Evie! She's under here in the cripple hole. Thank God, Kay!' Nik was punching the emergency numbers on his mobile with numb fingers. Evie was asleep, frozen, deathly pale, curled up in a ball, but still alive. Every second would count from now on as he rubbed her back to life, piling on the foil and the survival bag he always carried in the pouch under his seat.

Kay was at his side. She was crying, sobbing with relief. 'Oh, muppet, we've found you! Clever girl to hide in the wall . . . Wake up. Oh why won't she wake up?' She was hugging the child with tears rolling down her face.

As dawn was rising high the air ambulance whirled over them to lift the child to safety, to the warmth of the hospital bed and the slow thawing-out procedures necessary. Kay was by her side, her cheeks flushed with concern and disbelief that it was all over.

Nik sat down exhausted. He looked down at the frozen body prostrate on the ground. He patted the iced fur feeling choked. 'You did a grand job there, Muff. You always were my best setter but I reckon you topped yerself this time . . . Good lad.' He lifted the collie onto the back of his quad. 'Time to go home.'

The camera crews arrived from Leeds when all the excitement was over, their flashlights blinding him. 'How did you know where to look?' Over and over the same haunting question, and over and over he lied. How could he explain that he had heeded a gypsy's warning? They'd think he'd gone soft in the head or lost his marbles.

'Dunno,' he smiled. 'I just did. Us Dalesbred are hefted to these fells like all those bloody sheep that were slaughtered for nowt when a jab would've seen them right, but it was the dog that did it.' That was the best way out of this inquisition.

Give credit where credit was due, he mused, recalling the frozen shape lying on the snow curled up in his last sleep. Muff had done his duty, sniffed around, stayed in contact with his charge and sat close by, old, cold and ever faithful to the end. In the quiet of his room it was another story. He turned over the pages of Agnes's 'Herball' with gratitude. He didn't understand a word of it but it worked the once and that was all he was ever going to use it for. Dabbling in mysteries is all well and good for them as knows their way about, he thought, but not this farmer. Once was enough. He was not going to tempt fate. He wrapped the book up carefully to return to the trunk in the attic. This secret must stay only within the family.

Thanks, Agnes, he smiled to himself, but no thanks. From now on I'll be saving Wintergill residents in my own fashion. He was standing in a hall splattered with snow and mud prints. Perhaps the indoor ghost would have a fit if she could see the mess. Maybe she was gone now, the shell of her spirit for so long trapped as their guardian was relieved of her duties, he hoped. The storm candle was burning in the window and he smiled with satisfaction. He was still a shepherd gathering in the flock. Their wanderers had been returned safe and sound back to Wintergill.

Then the clock struck seven and he realised it was 23 December. That childish writing on the envelope floated before his tired eyes: 'Gone to find Chrismass . . .' The poor little sod. All this because one kiddie wanted some proper Christmas cheer. Well, things would have to be a little different this year.

Aye, things must change, indeed, he nodded to Jacob who peered down at him from his vantage point on the stairs. *I could take a few lessons from you.* Was he not the very incarnation of the festive spirit in his day? He alone could brighten up any dull hearth with his magic tricks. Did he not stir up the whole district with his Christmas doings? *And am I not named after the Christmas saint?*

There'd been enough angst and gloominess to last a lifetime. It was the season to be merry said the old carol.

Perhaps Wintergill needed a stirring up, a bit of singing and dancing, a table groaning with Christmas pie like it was in the old days. There was always time to work miracles if you had a mind for it, but first he must sleep . . . sleep for England.

Christmas Eve 2001

Jacob's Yorkshire Christmas Pie

Take a turkey, a goose, a hare, chicken, a pigeon, sausage meat, some forcemeat stuffing and six hardboiled eggs.

Bone all the birds, season well and place each inside the other.

Put the goose in the turkey, the hare in the goose, the chicken in the hare, the pigeon in the chicken, and fill any spaces with sausage meat, forcemeat stuffing and quartered hardboiled eggs.

Sew up the turkey.

Meanwhile have prepared the huff paste for the raised piecrust.

Take a peck of fine flour and half a peck of good suet, boiled. Knead well until a stiff paste, set aside in cool place to stiffen.

Shape over a raised pie mould. Cut out a lid and decorate in traditional manner as befits the occasion with leaves.

Lay flesh within piecrust, cover with lid, brush with beaten egg. Bake slowly for at least 4 hours.

Prepare a savoury jelly from the boned stock, strained, cooled and fat skimmed away. Season with tarragon vinegar and salt.

Pour liquid into the pie when hot. Replace the lid and let the whole edifice cool.

Enjoy at leisure, garnished with the season's preserves but the piecrust is best left for the birds.

Nora woke late. She could hear Nik on his mobile some-where. All the terror, the exhaustion of last night's drama came flooding back and she sat up. Was Evie safe? Was that Kay ringing with bad news? She didn't think she could cope with any more bad news. Her chest was still tight and her breathing laboured, but she must find out when Evie would be discharged from Airedale Hospital.

'Any news?' she yelled over the banister rail.

Nik nodded from the stairwell and did the thumbs up sign. So far so good, she smiled, pulling on her tartan dressing gown. It was nearly eleven and not a crock washed or a floor mopped. The place looked a wreck. The whole of the local rescue force had tramped through their hall in the emergency.

Then she noticed the storm candle in its holder, just a stubble of wax left, burning on defiantly and she knew another one must be lit, especially on Christmas Eve. She wanted Evie to see it burning as they came up the drive. Hell's bells, they wouldn't keep her in over Christmas, surely? Perhaps Kay would then drive straight back to the Midlands. She wouldn't blame them if they never darkened her door again.

'Was that Kay?' she asked as Nik bounded up the stairs. 'How's the bairn?'

'Fine. In fact, amazing considering her exposure. They want to keep her under obs for a while longer but if she keeps this up she'll be back tonight. The press want to interview her but Kay is trying to keep the cameras away. They're calling her "the wunderkind who survived a snowstorm in a hole in the wall".'

'Do they want to come back here? Look at this mess. There's not a bit of Christmas trim about the place, not a card or decorations. She can't come back to this . . . not after she ran away to find her Christmas,' Nora said, looking around in dismay. Everywhere was damp, bare and depressing.

'Don't panic, Kay knows the score,' he replied. 'She's out shopping while we speak. If you need anything I can ring her, or give me a list and I'll bob down to town before the shops shut.'

'By heck! That's a first,' she laughed, and he laughed back.

'You can use the big kitchen if you like.'

Nora looked up at her son with surprise. He's changed his tune and no mistake. All those dramatics must have softened his brain. He usually spent Christmas Eve tucked in a corner of the Spread Eagle with Jim Grimoldby; and then she remembered.

There was no Jim to sup with, nothing to celebrate there. Her son had just saved a kiddie from exposure by his knowledge of his terrain. He deserved a big hug but Snowdens didn't go in for that sort of show so she nodded.

'Thanks, son. I'll get dressed. You did well. I was proud of you last night.'

Nik flushed. 'Now then, that's enough, don't go overboard. I did what I had to do. It was a team effort.' There was a twinkle in his eyes as he smiled back and she sensed something was shifting between them.

Nora drew a big breath. It would be a tall order to do

338

Christmas from top to bottom in twenty-four hours, a challenge for a woman half her age, never mind one just recovering from flu.

Something in this panic was reminding her of that first German Christmas and her reluctance to give those POWs a proper do, but their visit had turned out fine, if not without consequences for her. She smiled, thinking of Klaus. How different life would have been if she'd run away with him. Shirley might be still alive but Nik wouldn't have been born. Don't go there, she chided herself. There's no point now. Stop daydreaming. This won't butter any parsnips!

When in panic, she decided as she struggled on with her corset, it's better to make a list and delegate: jobs for her, jobs for the lad, and jobs for anyone who put their head round the door. For the moment there was just the two of them. Kay had enough on her plate getting Evie back here and settled. She would be as high as a kite, knowing that little madam.

It had been lovely having a child back in the house, especially one she could hand back at the end of the day to her mother.

Wunderkind indeed! How were they going to have a proper Yorkshire Christmas and wrap up this terrible year with a proper festive feast? They must give the Partridges some hope for the months to come so they would remember their stay with a smidgen of fondness when they returned south again.

She could still boil a hock of ham from the freezer for their supper tonight like they did in the old days when the pigs were killed on St Thomas's Day. She would glaze it with black treacle, mustard and spices and serve it with Cumberland sauce. There was redcurrant jelly in the pantry, some oranges and an old bottle of port somewhere. She had all the ingredients.

Nik could fetch a hunk of good Wensleydale to go with the Christmas cake. Tom used to love it.

What cake? There wasn't a crumb in the house and it was too late to make a traditional one. They'd have to buy one in – so what? It wasn't a crime to support the local bakery for once.

Since the foot-and-mouth circus came to town in the summer, there'd been lean pickings for local traders. Nik could do the leg work for a change and support the local economy. If he was going to live on his own, he might as well learn to shop for himself.

The next job was to find where the decorations were hidden, gathering dust in the attic roof, she mused, puffing her way up the stairs. It was years since they'd seen the light of day. If Evie was to have her Christmas, she must go rooting round herself and make it happen.

Perhaps they were still in the boxes on the top of the wardrobes. That was where she used to hide the children's gifts in old hatboxes, the little surprises that went in Santa's stockings. She would have to face the clutter in the attic for a result.

As she turned the final stairs she looked at the old sepia photos that went from the hall up to the third floor. Evie was right, their eyes did follow you everywhere. 'I bet you all know where the trimmings are?' she asked them, but none of them said a word until she heard a whispering in her ear. She spun round quickly and thought she saw Jacob winking at her.

'We're having none of that. One ghost in the house is enough. The white coats will be calling for me soon, if this carries on,' she laughed, and pulled a face at him. What had got into her? Was it the relief that Evie was safe and all was well?

The attic was as jumbled up and dusty as always, making

her cough. This was not a good idea, but now she was up there she was going to have a good root around: boxes of abandoned bric-a-brac, old vacuums, boxes of photo albums full of snapshots of the children.

Her eye caught one of Shirley on her bike smiling into the camera with such mischief in her face. Nik was right to protest, she sighed. There was no halo round her daughter. Perhaps it was wrong to make an icon of the dead but her eyes filled up just the same, and that was when she thought she heard a little voice in her head saying, 'Find the Christmas House.' It was so real and vivid she dropped the album onto her lap.

The Christmas House – she hadn't thought about that little thing for years. 'If you want me to find it you're going to have to help me. My legs are cramping up on this hard floor and I don't have X-ray eyes.' No reply was forthcoming, of course.

She picked up the album to show Kay. It was about time her family snaps were brought into the light of day before there was no one left to know who these precious ones were. It was time she put both her children in their rightful place on top of the bureau.

But where was the Christmas House? It was probably packed up with the other trimmings. If you want treasure, my girl, you'll have to search for it, she mused as she rummaged from one box to another, among suitcases full of damp curtains and old clothes, piles of tennis rackets and hockey sticks, shin pads, rugby boots but no sign of the trimmings box.

All this needed chucking out. She ferreted into drawers crammed with ancient knitting patterns and magazines that might be worth something now. The dust tickled up her nose and made her sneeze, but she was searching like a ferret down a rabbit hole and not to be thwarted. The second

341

attic room was crammed with old furniture she'd forgotten they had. As she was sifting through the junk on the windowledge, her eyes drifted down across the valley into the noonday light. The ground was etched with snow, a benign landscape, a stunning postcard view, but she shivered thinking about Evie's ordeal.

This room would make a lovely den for a girl. It should be painted bright yellow with gold stars on the midnight-blue ceiling, with room for toys in the walk-in cupboard. It would make a lovely nursery and you wouldn't hear much crying two floors down. It was here she found Nik's old farm toys, the model farm and the tractors. She bent to finger them: plastic cows and sheep and even some trees. There was a magic drawing board. If you twiddled the knobs it made lines across the screen. She'd take these back to Evie's room. She could doodle and wipe out to her heart's content.

She heard the rustle of paper and a scratching in the wall. Perhaps a mouse had come to guide her, or worse. She made a move and all fell silent but there was a telltale hole in the plaster. Nora gazed out again at the fields, imagining them once more full of stock, the tractor in the field, but there was nothing to disturb the view.

She stumbled slowly back to the top corridor with its rooms right and left. Nothing here but a load of smelly junk waiting for a car-boot sale, she sighed. It was a hopeless search, but that little voice had said, 'Find the Christmas House.' She couldn't waste any more time now.

'I've tried my best but you're not helping!' she snapped. 'You try rooting through this lot!' Nora edged down the stairs carefully with the photographs. Overhead was a skylight and, shafting down the stairwell, a beam of speckled light glittering with dust highlighted the little cupboard tucked under the turn of the stair. More in frustration rather than hope she yanked the door open into the musty darkness. Even in the gloom she could see something glinting into the light, a tinsel ribbon, some golden balls, and soon she was pulling out boxes with excitement. This must be the place.

'Thank you, Shirley,' she said, grabbing the trimmings. In a wicker basket were streamers and old paper bells, pretty glass baubles covered in tissue paper. There was a suitcase full of wrapping paper and a brass candle holder with angels dancing round with trumpets, a snowstorm – the one she had as a child – crinkled Christmas crackers and stars dancing on string. The memories of old times flooded back. She was getting warmer but there was still no sign of what she was looking for, and then she spotted a brown-paper parcel right at the back of the cupboard.

She leaned forward to pull it out, her heart racing. It was the original paper that Klaus and Hans had first brought the gift in. She'd forgotten how fine the workmanship was.

It was a Swiss chalet with sloping roof, painted with snow. The windows had shutters and window boxes painted in red and green stripes. It was a house for a cuckoo clock but the whole front opened to reveal four tiny rooms and it was about the size of a cornflake packet.

It wasn't a doll's house. It seemed smaller than she recalled, and it was undamaged. There was no furniture inside, just a painted shell but it looked so pretty and it would take pride of place on the dining table.

'Find the Christmas House, you said, and I have,' she whispered into the air. 'Thank you, my lovely. I've made you an angel all these years and forgotten you were a little girl who saw something she wasn't meant to see. I hope you forgive me and don't mind me sharing this with Evie. There's been so little joy in this house since you left it but we're going to change all that from now on.'

In her mind's eye she could see the little house on the dining table in the hall, the one pushed across the door to separate her bit of the house from Nik's quarters.

How daft can you get, living back to back, pretending the other didn't have the right to the other side of the house and all because of bad memories and jealousy. Now the table must go into the middle with a white damask cloth, with silver candlesticks if she had any silver polish left. There must be a Christmas tree too, and where would that go? Under the stairwell as of old so Mr Jacob could see it from his vantage point and know the season was being observed.

There was no stopping these fancy thoughts now, though her bony fingers were stiff and her legs aching. How on earth were they going to do all this in time?

She sat on the bottom step, feeling as excited as a child, staring at the big cold fireplace. The grate was dusty and bare but she had no energy left to clean it up. They would need a basket of dry logs chopped if they were to have a decent blaze tomorrow.

If only I was a tidy bit younger, she sighed. She looked up at old Joss's portrait but he didn't move a whisker.

You mustn't disappoint the kiddie, Lenora. Gird your loins and get cracking. Do what you can and ask for help. What was needed was a bit of co-operation, pulling together, the two of them, two horses pulling together not apart. It was Shirley's idea about the Christmas House and she was always one for keeping Christmas cheer.

They could get a fresh turkey. She still had a tin of mince pies. Nik would chop down a tree and Kay would muck in when she got back. It would take their minds off last night's drama, the fire, the search. The poor lass must be worn out with worry and this was the very day last year when her husband was killed, Nora suddenly recalled. It would take her mind off her grief to be kept busy.

They did have all the ingredients for a good Christmas right here – enough food, a tree, plenty of candles – but Christmas also needed a baby in a manger, good friends around a table and some silly games.

Nora stood up to rub her swollen knees, looking for her stick. 'You make your own Christmas,' she smiled, 'and it's the thought that counts, not the expense. That's right, Mr Christmas?' She turned to look at old Jacob. 'It begins with the right spirit and a hopeful heart. Now what more do we need? Oh, aye, a Santa. We can't have him missing Wintergill on his rounds, now can we?'

Nik returned from his shopping trip to find Wintergill in a flurry of preparations. He was commandeered to shift furniture from the side of the hall and given a list of jobs to do before dark. His mother was rooting through the larder checking for stores when Pat Bannerman called in for news bringing a huge bunch of scented lilies. She was given coffee and a mince pie, and a brush and dustpan to clean out the grate ready for a log fire, then she scooted off before she was landed with any more chores.

'I'm afraid Christmas dinner's going to be a bit of a pot luck Jacob's join this year.' Nora looked up at her son, waiting for his protest. 'A bit of a loaves-and-fishes do, but if we're going to do this properly, let's open up the upstairs drawing room like we used to. It'll need a bit of an airing. There has to be somewhere for the oldies to have a quiet snooze. Can I leave you to do that?' She smiled. 'What did you get in town? There's not enough in the larder to feed our resident mice. Oh, and I've shifted some of your smelly stuff out of the kitchen if I'm going to do a bake.'

He'd not seen his mother so animated for months – years, in fact. 'Don't you ask me to shop on Christmas Eve ever again, Mother. It was like a cattle market on auction day, a rugby scrum and a stampede all rolled into one. You'd think the shops were shut for a month, not two days,' he muttered, putting on his wellies and making for the door. 'You do what you want in here. I'm off for some fresh air and a bit of wood chopping. The forecast is ropey for tomorrow.'

'Find us a good tree, son. I want it up by the time they get back. We'll show them we can trim up as good as Sutton Coldfield any day!'

Nora was just about to find the broom and sweeper, the basket of polish and dusters and set to with gusto on the upstairs when two of her cronies from the WI turned up with presents for Evie. Before they sat down to attack her famous mince pies, she got them sweeping, vacuuming, dusting and polishing the drawing room until it sparkled like a spring clean.

The curtains were thick and lined with ancient woollen blankets to keep out the draughts, the chintzy sofa covers faded with sunlight, but it was a gracious, well-proportioned room, panelled with turquoise-painted wood. *Country Living* magazine would do a good makeover here, she smiled as she cleared out the grubby fireplace and laid down some sticks. Pat's lilies were already scenting the room with sweetness.

When Edna Danby called in for the latest update on the Partridges, she was sent out into the copse to find some greenery – holly with berries, ivy and foliage – from the front garden borders. She'd just time to fiddle with it all as only an expert of the North Craven Flower Club knew how. Then the florist's van came with a huge red poinsettia and holly wreath from her Book Circle; the plant filled the one uncracked jardinière left. Then down the track came the post van with special delivery of cards and a parcel from Sutton Coldfield for Evie.

Slowly Nora watched each room coming to life as the tins of mince pies disappeared. Everyone loved her special pastry made with ground almonds and butter. Now the house was filled with the smell of fresh baking, spices, cinnamon and cloves. There was even her spiced currant bread rising under a cloth, and outside she could hear the thud of chopped wood, kindling sticks and logs piled into the wicker baskets.

She strung up their cards on the beams and twisted holly over the mantelpiece. Edna had time to help them polish up the brasses to burnished gold. Nora had never seen her home so transformed, and it gladdened her heart no end to see it come alive again. Standing back to admire the day's hard work, she chuckled with satisfaction. *You've scrubbed up well, old girl, and now I must do the same . . .*

Nik took his spade in search of a decent Christmas tree. It took him back to the times he'd done this with his dad all those years ago and there was always one found just perfect for under the stairs in the hall.

Now he looked across the silent fields. He should be out foddering sheep, checking the ones on the tops, for the weather was drawing in with snow on the wind again; Christmas snow, just what the tourists wanted but a nuisance for farmers.

The copse was silent and for once he sensed he was alone. That tormented spirit had gone to rest and he hoped never to feel her like again. He hoped he'd bought the right gifts for everyone. He'd made his way to the jewellers on Duke Street to buy a memento for Kay and the kid: just a porcelain sheepdog, one of the Border Arts collection popular with farmers up the dale. He hadn't intended this but after what they'd all been through . . . he couldn't resist the black and tan sheepdog with the markings just like old Muff whom he must bury out in the field later on.

He nipped to Spencer's off-licence, which sold the best hand-made chocolates. He'd be giving his mother something extra too. Old Jacob would be proud of this show of Christmas spirit, he sniggered, not a 'Bah, humbug' in sight.

Since that outburst with his mother he was feeling uncomfortable and wanted to make amends. It had cheered him to see her perked up with the idea of a Jacob's join, giving her orders like a sergeant major. He could see she'd made a real effort to spruce up the place. What a disappointment it would be if the kid had to stay in Airedale for another night. He had something up his sleeve for Evie, something he hoped she'd enjoy, and he was trusting the weather to come true to form or it would all be a flop.

Much as he went on about his shopping trip, he'd rather enjoyed being in the bustle of the marketplace, meeting up with old mates out doing their last-minute shopping for their wives, moaning about the expense and the queues. It was grand to feel part of the community. Everyone was asking about the kid as if she was his own.

This must be what it feels like to be a family, he thought, and for once he wasn't shying away from this novelty. You're getting soft in the head! he laughed, and carried on his search for the perfect tree.

Evie lay back in the bed, waiting for the doctor to come on his rounds. When she'd woken it was a shock to see where she was, looking out onto a courtyard in the middle of the hospital. There were no fields or snow, no Muffin, no Lavender Lady sitting by the bedroom fireplace. She was listening to Christmas music and television, with children careering round waiting to be sent home like her. Was Christmas over? Had she missed it all? She wanted to cry, turning her face to the pillow and sucking her thumb. She wasn't sure what day it was. Had she missed the *Blue Peter* special?

There was a big Christmas tree on the ward and lots of decorations, but it was noisy and busy and she wasn't allowed out of the door. Where was Mummy? Why couldn't she go home?

Then she remembered the fire and getting lost in the snow and Mr Grumpy coming to rescue her . . . or was it Daddy? There was this funny dream of being stuck under a wall and the White Lady grabbing her wrist and flying like a snowman through the air until she fell down and woke. Mummy was crying and Mr Grumpy was rubbing her hands or something. He wasn't Mr Grumpy any more. He'd been her friend like Mrs Nora and Muff and the Lavender Lady in the big house on the hill where there was no Christmas; no decorations and no pretty lights, nothing.

If she went back there Santa would never come.

'Into the car, muppet,' smiled Kay as she threw Evie's bag into the boot. At last they were going home. Kay had waited all day for the doctor's discharge, dreading that she would be kept in over Christmas Day. Anyone could see that Evie was no worse for her terrible adventure. The thought of being stuck in hospital over Christmas miles from anyone they knew was too awful to contemplate, kind as everyone was to them both.

The press had had a field day. The papers were full of the rescue and her lucky escape. Kay was buoyed up by euphoria at first but her spirits soon flagged when she thought of what might have been. The last few days were beginning to feel like some strange dream and now she was waking up.

In a strange way Evie's rescue had taken away all the angst about Tim's anniversary, and she felt mean that she'd scarce given his parents a thought. She rang them from the hospital in case they should hear anything on the news.

349

They were all for rushing up to bring them back south but all she wanted was peace and quiet at Wintergill. They were going to come and visit for New Year instead. She rang ahead to the farm to tell them they were on their way back. Why on earth she should dare to go back there was a mystery, but nothing seemed to matter any more.

At least Christmas would be low key with no fuss, and she had bought enough presents for Evie to feel that Santa had called on his rounds.

She wanted to sleep for a week, to go for long walks and calm down. She didn't care if there was not a mince pie in sight as long as Evie was happy and in sight of her. How could she ever let her out on her own again?

She wanted to thank Nik. How could you thank a man for saving your child? She needed time to think through her future. Christmas could go hang as far as she was concerned.

Yet her spirits rose as they climbed the hill out of Wintergill village. So many people had stopped and waved and wished them well. She had to keep winding the window down to chat to wellwishers as they crawled through the main street of the village. It was like being a celebrity. Evie had fallen asleep in the back. She was still tired and the excitement was acting like a sedative. It was dusk when they bumped down the farm track and she saw the lights.

From every window there was a candle burning brightly, welcoming them in the gloom, and it felt as if her dream were coming alive before her eyes. She could see a huge holly bough bedecked with ribbons hanging from the open front door. Mrs Nora must have been watching out for their headlights for she was waiting in the hall smiling, looking frail but upright.

'Welcome back. Come in. Merry Christmas,' she said, and her eyes went anxiously to Evie, still sleeping in the back.

350

'She's fine but flat out, I'm afraid. I'll take her upstairs.'
Kay stopped, looking at the wonderful transformation in
the hall. The fire lit, the table laid. Something was different
but she couldn't decide what.

'Come and have some tea and mince pies and tell me all
about the hospital,' said Nora, guiding her into Nik's kitchen,
which was scrubbed, tidied and bustling with preparations.
'There's a ham in the stove and wine on the chill when Evie
wakes up. We'll trim the tree and then Christmas can begin
at Wintergill.'

Nora watched Evie creeping down the stairs, hearing the
laughter from the hall. Her eyes were on stalks as she
surveyed the scene: strings of holly and green leaves wrapped
around the banister rail, candles shining at the windows,
cards strung up and music playing. Kay rushed up the stairs
to bring her down.

For a second Nora fancied she was seeing Shirley grown
up with her own daughter, her family as it should have
been, but it was only an old fool's fantasy. None of that
sentimental guff, old girl, she scolded herself. Just enjoy
what you have been given. It won't last long.

They had deliberately left the tree undressed so the child
could have the thrill of putting the decorations up. How
many decorations there were in the box! It was years since
some of them had had an airing. Some were fragile and
very ancient pre-war specimens, collector's items now, no
doubt. Evie was dying to put everything on in great lumps
of tinsel.

'Slow down, little Miss Rush-it!' Nora laughed. 'First
things first. We have to test the lights to see if they are
working.' There was a large box of Pifco electric lanterns
from the 1950s, still pristine and in good order.

'Next we must find the angel for the top. She's the most

important decoration of all,' she said. 'The guardian of the tree, my mother used to say.'

Evie was not impressed with the battered celluloid doll with hand-knitted frock and feathery wings; not exactly a herald of glory. She had seen better days.

'Where does the robin go?' asked the child. 'And the corn dollies?'

'You choose', Nora smiled, fingering a white rose made out of bleached nylon stockings and stretched over wire. It was one of the post-war make-do-and-mend decorations she had made at the WI and it still did the trick.

'Everyone gets to choose a decoration in turn, put it on the tree and make a wish. It's tradition.' She was making it up as she went along, wanting to hang on to this precious moment, sharing memories with a child.

'Come on, Mummy, you choose,' yelled Evie into the kitchen, 'and Mr Grump—'

'I heard that!' shouted Nik. 'You'd better be good or Santa will miss our big chimney!'

He was standing in the doorway watching the proceedings and, much to Nora's amusement, her gruff middle-aged son began rooting in the box, searching for a faded furry flying horse: Pegasus, with bells dangling from it. 'This was always my favourite,' he said, laughing. 'Every time the wind blows in this draughty hall it will make the bells ring. I used to think it was sleigh bells,' he added, placing the horse high to catch the draught and moving back to drink his tea.

I never thought I'd see that again, Nora mused with a lump in her throat. It was strange how Christmas brought out the child in a man, just as Mischief Night and Bonfire Night brought out the naughty boy in him. Nik was full of surprises tonight. There must be magic in the air.

This was always a wintertime house as we are winter's

children, she smiled, sniffing the smell of logs burning in the grate like the old yule logs of old, which were dragged into the hearth to burn through the festive season. The shabbiness of years was disguised by swags of greenery and candlelight, but its rooms were like good bones in a face, a fine structure stands up well with the years. She would miss its face but not its draughts. So many memories within these walls to cherish, and she hoped this would be one of them.

She hoped old Jacob Snowden, that great Christmas lover, famed for his carolling and parties, could see their efforts. Sometimes she wondered just what his poor wife, Agnes, had made of the fuss. She would have to organise her servants and see that all the festivities happened.

It was women who made Christmas for their families, as they were doing now: shopping, cleaning, baking, decorating, preparing beds for guests. All over the country they would be scurrying around, trying to make their homes sparkle and welcoming fractious children and aged parents, trying to make sure everyone had a good time even if they themselves didn't, pinning the smiles on their faces that must last until the last guest had gone home.

By Christmas Eve afternoon all the little towns of England would be empty; only the noise in the pubs broke the quiet and people returned to their own hearths and began the ceremonies. On this night she thought of all the homeless, packed into refuge shelters, and the widows who wept into their lonely sherry, remembering happier days. She was glad they were opening up this big farmhouse for others to enjoy.

Wintergill must have been a rare sight in the olden days when no expense was spared and help was plentiful. Jacob was a bit of a showman. She had heard about his party tricks and conjuring shows. No doubt Agnes would be steaming over a plum pudding, cursing the season yet trying to look gracious at the same time.

Soon it would be time for carols on the radio and she wanted to be there by the warm range, sitting at the old table, not scuttling away in the old butler's pantry in tears when those majestic voices echoed down King's College Chapel. She wanted to share with Kay what the ceremony meant to her, pass on the magic, but first she must prevent the tree from being smothered under the weight of Evie's enthusiasm. Restraint was always the better part of good taste, but try telling an eight-year-old that less was more?

Evie was holding out the wooden star that Klaus had made for Shirley on that second German Christmas when he was working for them.

'Each of our decorations can tell its own story and this is a very special story,' she said. 'Did I tell you about our German Christmas visitors?'

Evie shook her head. Out it all came about the war again and their prisoners. She said nothing about Klaus, of course. Evie was far too young to understand and Klaus was not for sharing with anyone. He lived in the Christmas House in her heart.

Nik stood in the doorway holding his spade. 'Before it gets dark, there's a little job we must do, Evie. I wonder if you'd like to help me, but put your thick anorak on first.'

'What is it?' she asked, puzzled. He'd already found them a beautiful tree and it was late for gardening. Mum fussed over her, making her wear a hat and gloves 'just in case'. They all went out in the garden with a torch to a spot under a bush where there was a big hole in the ground.

Mummy put her arm round her. 'You know Muffin didn't

354

wake up from his sleep so we have to bury him now. He died, Evie. He was a very brave dog but he was old and tired.'

'Is that him?' she said, trying to swallow back her tears, seeing the shape hidden in the sack. 'Why are you putting him in the ground?' She turned to Nik.

'Because that's what we do,' he replied. 'Then we can plant bulbs over him.'

'But he won't like it!'

'He doesn't breathe any more and can't feel anything now. Muffin isn't there any more; that's what dying means. This is just a shell that's left. His spirit is free but every time you think about him, he still lives on,' Mummy said.

'Just like my daddy?' She was holding Mummy's hand very tightly.

'Yes, he lies in a church garden where Granny takes flowers, and tonight is a special night when we remember him too.' No one spoke as they laid Muff in the ground and Nik covered him over with soil.

'Would you like to put some stones around him in a pattern?'

Evie nodded and looked up. 'Can I have another dog like Muffin?'

'We'll see,' Mummy smiled. 'But not yet. When someone dies you need time to let them go and get used to being without them before you . . .' Evie wasn't listening, she was racing up to the door. It was Christmas Eve and Santa was coming soon.

Kay was sitting in the back pew of St Oswald's as the congregation shuffled in through the porch, watching families with groups of friends and relatives, muffled in pashmina shawls and chenille scarves against the biting wind outside. Why she had decided to come to the Midnight Mass was a mystery; a sudden impulse after listening to snatches of *Carols from King's*?

She wanted to be alone and yet partake in something traditional. She wanted to say thank you for Evie's rescue, to all the villagers who had kindly sent gifts and greetings after the fire and the search. She wanted to pretend she belonged somewhere, at least for this night.

The ham had been delicious and they sat down formally with napkins and crystal glasses. Evie had been well behaved, watching the clock for when it was time for bed and setting up her stocking by the hearth. In the candlelight Kay could well believe there was real magic at work. How different this was from last year's terrible trauma, and for a moment she felt guilty to be enjoying herself, but she was sure Tim wouldn't mind as long as they were safe.

Now she was sitting in a darkened church in candlelight, watching the ceremonies with a thankful heart. Kay wished she could be a true believer but she was only here to sing and pray what rang true in her heart. There was an interesting mix of worshippers, she observed: village locals she now recognised from the Christingle service, visitors swathed in Georgina von Etzdorf scarves, camel coats and southern accents, sophisticated young women with perfect hair and make-up – all of them from some big house party, no doubt.

There were others in anoraks and woolly hats and a couple of teenagers who were a little worse for drink, making their responses too late and too loud for the normal C of E custom. There were widows and a few of the school mums with their parents, local farmers and the publican's wife taking time out from the affray.

Kay felt she was joining with thousands of worshippers all over the country starting their Christmases off in traditional fashion. This felt real and natural, and she was glad to be present, if under false pretences, for she would not take the sacraments.

A country Christmas was everyone's fantasy, and she was here enjoying it now. Christmas was about giving to others and sharing, and it was Kay's wish that Evie should learn about the real spirit of Christmas, not just accumulate loads of expensive plastic or spend her time glued to the box watching canned entertainment.

She had wanted them both to know the magic of frost-frozen mittens, wind on their cheeks and snow in winter but they had experienced only danger. But there was a forgiveness in her heart too.

What do I really want for me? Kay asked herself. I want to be surprised, to see the world through the eyes of a child again and not through those of this sad, suspicious, wounded adult I have become. I want to grow a Christmas heart, a heart full of mischief and wonder, open to pos-sibilities, open to the magic of music and symbols and prayer: a heart bursting with air, a bubble-gum heart, pink, blown up like a balloon, a football, a pig's bladder. I want to lose myself in Christmas, stomp my wellies in puddles of fun and laughter, stride over the snow and skate down the slides, sing carols and blow away all the misery of this past year. I would love to hear angels sing and see candles glow in the dark, to belong somewhere rooted into the land-scape as so many of these people are tonight. I envy them.

There's a loneliness at the heart of my life now that even Evie, cherished as she is, will never satisfy, nor should she have to. I don't want to always be alone for Christmas. I loved Tim but we never made much of the season. He was always too busy to take time for celebration. 'It can wait,' he said, 'but my career can't.' Now it's too late. You're a long time dead . . .

I want to make my own celebrations, she decided, to

build up my traditions, and I want a man for Christmas one day, someone decent and honest, hardworking and kind, who'll share my vision. I want four legs in a bed, kisses drunken with desire. I want the touch of a hand on my thigh and the warmth of someone's breathing to wake me up. I want to feel that I matter to someone other than my child. Is this too much to ask? Is this greedy? she prayed, flushed with the heat of her yearnings.

Should I be thinking all this? she sighed. Where else but in a church could she confess her heart's desires? Everybody needed some meaning in life, some purpose to make it worth living.

Love was a deep reservoir, unfathomable, an inexhaustible supply at the heart of the universe. She had the right to tap into its source and sing with the rest of the congregation. The coming of light in a dark world was at the heart of Christmas too.

> Love came down at Christmas,
> Love all lovely, love divine,
> Love was born at Christmas,
> Star and angels gave the sign.

She felt such calm, peace and reassurance singing that carol. There must be a way forward if love was at the heart of her motives. She thought of the dreams that had brought her to Wintergill all those weeks ago.

The flavours of Christmas were full of spice and love and memory. And if you believed in love and light at the heart of the universe, then, she mused, she had a place somewhere – but where? When Christmas was over, what would happen?

Nik sat in the Spread Eagle amid the noisy boisterous antics of the young drinkers: long-haired girls in micro skirts and mini tops scarce covering their lardy white bodies, plastered in make-up, high as kites on booze and goodness knows what else. He had brought Kay down for the service and he was getting his own spiritual nourishment at the bar. He had earned every free pint, fêted as a hero, thumped on the back, made a fuss of by the barmaids, but somehow it wasn't as good as he expected. If truth were told his heart wasn't in it tonight.

He'd had such a good meal, watched a bit of television. Tomorrow would take care of itself. He was restless inside, churning over his decision to stay put and restock in the light of all good sense.

'You must be cracked in thy 'ead!' said one retired farmer. 'Get yerself a nice bungalow and spend yer brass, not flush it away down the beck!'

That was fine for Mother but not for him. He was still young and fit enough to make a go of it. He wanted to see what was on offer. He wanted to stay on at Wintergill, but rebuilding the holiday barn would have to take a back seat for a while.

He looked around at all the young students back for the holidays. None of them would ever return to Wintergill. The farmers' sons might marry out of the dale, the old codgers fall off the bar stools. Where would he be in twenty years' time? Not sitting here, he hoped, with his pension and his bungalow, a lonely old geezer playing dominoes and making his pint last the night. There's got to be more to life than this.

You have to take a risk, he thought, change with the times. Go with the flow. It was times like this that he missed Jim's company. It was not much fun on your own. He needed someone to share his life and his vision.

A Jacob's Join Christmas

Kay's Kishmish

4 oz each of dried figs, prunes, currants, apricots, dried apples and sultanas

Soak overnight in 1½ pints of water.

Drain and use water and a tablespoon of dark sugar, a thick twist of lemon peel, a few cloves and a dessertspoon each of allspice and nutmeg.

Bring to the boil and simmer for 10 mins.

Add the soaked fruit and simmer slowly for an hour until fruit is soft.

Serve warm or chilled with cream, crème fraiche or yoghurt.

'He's been! He's been!' yelled Evie at full blast from the bottom of the stairs, dragging her stocking up the stairs to show everybody. It was seven o'clock on Christmas morning. Kay turned over, desperate for another few minutes after her late night, but Evie jumped on the bed, tearing open the parcels in her stocking.

'Don't wake up the rest of the household,' Kay whispered, peering into the stocking herself as if she didn't know what was in every little package. Stockings should be fun, full of surprises, silly joke books and whoopee cushions, power crystal bracelets and transfers to stick on your arm, a stocking needed pencils and sharpeners shaped like the pop stars, face paints and colouring books, chocolate coins and tangerines, pretty hair clips and comics, a bumper pack of sweets, a *Blue Peter* annual and things that glowed in the dark, fake spiders and swap cards, a dancing puppet or a mobile, and tin whistles to drive everyone crazy on Christmas morning.

At the bottom was a sugar mouse with a string tale; all very predictable but magic for a young child to play with on the bed. At the top was a storybook: Alison Uttley's *Little Grey Rabbit's Christmas*, which Kay had always loved herself as a child. They snuggled up together to read it out aloud.

Evie brought out her own wrapped present. 'It's something I know you wanted for ages. I hid it safely and it didn't get burned in the fire,' she said proudly. 'Go on, open it!'

Evie was breathing down Kay's neck with excitement and she had to pretend her biggest surprise. The journal was carefully wrapped in fancy hand-made paper.

'We made the paper at school and I saved mine,' Evie said with pride. 'It's for you to remember the winter house so we won't forget our holiday.' Evie pointed to the writing and detailed small drawings. 'You know when we went to the Brontë house, I saw all their tiny writing and thought I could do it too. It'll take you ages to read it going round and round in a spiral. I put as much down as I could, and there's some stories too.'

'How lovely, just what I wanted,' Kay beamed. 'I thought you'd given up on that idea long ago and all this time you've been recording our visit.' There was so much detail, so painstakingly executed. It must have taken Evie hours of work.

'Look, here's the fire and there's Mr Grumpy with his ladder, and there's the White Lady waving at us over there,' she gabbled all in one breath. 'Do you like it?'

'I think it's brilliant, and I'm so proud of you for sticking at it,' Kay replied. How could she tell the child that it had probably saved her life? In showing the hidden diary to Nik she had prompted his unexpected response and set them off on that strange quad bike ride into the hills.

'I didn't want to do it at first but I like writing the stories,' Evie added. 'I can't smell the Lavender Lady any more. I've looked for her on the stairs but she must be busy with her own Christmas.'

'That's right, and we must get up and get our own Christmas surprise ready for breakfast.'

She had insisted that the two of them do something for the feast. If this was a Jacob's join, then they must offer something too. Her mother had often told her of the wonderful feasts that a village could create when every household provided a dish or two. Now it was time to start the day with her part of the Jacob's join Christmas.

This breakfast feast was planned down to the last slice of Galia melon and Bucks Fizz. She had shopped frantically in Skipton while Evie was asleep in hospital. It had given her something to do.

Wintergill would never have seen such a festive breakfast before. It was more of a brunch than a breakfast, which should last them until their evening dinner in the hall. There were slices of melon and mango arranged around prosciutto, Parma ham slices, a grapefruit salad and a kishmish of prunes and figs and dried fruit in a compote with creamy yoghurt, a cheese board of continental cheeses, grapes and passion fruit, lychees and strawberries. It was decadent but fresh to the palate on a day notorious for unloosing zips and belts. She bought muffins and croissants and flat oatcakes, a local speciality, to be warmed with butter and home-made jam and honey. There would be a pot of the finest Arabica coffee she could find, and guava juice.

It was going to be a serve yourself, come again breakfast, and she hoped the Snowdens would not miss the traditional bacon and eggs.

Evie kept hovering over the large parcel under the tree. 'Can I open this one before we go for our walk?' she pleaded, fingering it carefully.

'Go on then, just one more.' Kay hoped she would not be disappointed with the substitute paint box. She watched Evie tearing into the paper, pulling out the box. 'Wow! Brill! I can paint the tree. Can I open another from Santa? This one's not from Santa, it's from Mr Snowden.'

'No, you must wait until he's there to see it,' she ordered. 'We've got the table to set first and then we'll go out for a walk.' She did not know what the ritual of present opening was in this family.

Leaving all the breakfast laid out in the kitchen, and putting on anoraks and boots, they made for the open fields. Rising on the morning air, they could hear the church bells ringing down in the village. There was no time to walk down to join the villagers who had braved the cold to sing carols around the village in some age-old custom. It would have been good to take Evie down for the singing but the breakfast had taken up the time somehow.

'I like it here. Do you think Daddy would like it here too? Can we stay and then I can take flowers to Muff?' She skipped on and then stopped. 'It's easy to fall asleep in the snow, isn't it?'

'These hills are dangerous and you must never ever go out alone without telling me again. I'm sure Daddy would have loved to have a holiday here, but not to stay. It would be too far from his work, but you know now Daddy can't come,' she said, hoping Evie was coming to terms with his death at last.

'I know, he didn't bring the tree so Mr Snowden did it for him. He's my friend now but he's not my daddy, is he?'

'No one will ever be your special daddy, love. He worked so hard. He made it possible for us to come here and rest.' Kay found herself gulping the words, hoping they were the right ones. 'But it's not been very restful, has it?'

'Santa found us. He must be magic to know everyone's address in the world. He can go anywhere,' said Evie, trying to skip with her new skipping rope.

'Well, you can't ... so no more wandering off without telling me, ever again,' Kay insisted. If only she could have the resilience of her child. If only life were that simple. The thought of packing up and leaving these hills was unsettling. She kept shoving it to the back of her mind. How could they stay on? What would she do?

Looking out onto the grey-green hills and the patchwork of stonewalls running in all directions, she felt an aching to make her own mark, build something for herself, but her skills were limited for permanent country living.

The sap was rising, her energy was flooding back somehow, but all she had to offer were town skills: accountancy, computing, marketing.

Tim had cushioned them from reality by his generosity. She had lived a pampered suburban life until his death, and now she felt useless. Yet a voice in her head was nagging her.

'You're not useless,' it whispered seductively. 'You can learn, you can do anything if you put your mind to it. It's not too late to retrain, to grasp the nettle and go for what you want in life. Think big, keep it simple and do it for yourself.'

This was not what she wanted to hear on this fine Christmas morning, but her mind became alive with possibilities none the less. 'Come on, young lady,' she shouted to Evie as they turned for home.

Together they took Mrs Snowden her breakfast and presents on a tray as a special treat, and Mrs Nora said she had never had such a posh breakfast in all her life. She gave Kay a pair of hand-knitted fingerless gloves and a book. There was also a hand-knitted replica doll in Stuart costume, which looked suspiciously like Evie's mysterious Lavender Lady.

'I thought you'd like this as a memento of our resident ghost. I've never met her but I know she's supposed to be here,' said Nora, winking at her. 'I like to think there's still someone watching over us here.'

'I'm not so sure,' Kay found herself replying. She had heard enough about ghostly spectres to last a lifetime.

'Thank you for this book of walks,' she changed the subject. 'I've heard of Mr Wainwright but never seen his maps and drawings before. I hope you haven't read my gift. Nik said you enjoyed a good read.'

'You shouldn't have given me anything. This breakfast is fit for the Queen. It'll set me up for the day.' The old lady was looking around the room with a smile. 'This has turned out a topsy-turvy Christmas and no mistake. Just like the old days. I'm so glad you're staying on. I never did thank you for all you did when I was ill. There needs to be young legs around the place now.' Nora Snowden shook her head with a smile. 'I'm too old for bothering with a big house but we've all made it shine. It's had its own Jacob's join polish and makeover too. I've had my day here. Soon it'll be someone else's nightmare to upkeep, I hope, if things go on as they are.' She sighed back into her pillow.

'Are you really going to sell Wintergill?' Kay whispered. 'I thought Nik said—' She stopped, thinking she had better not say anything more.

'Never mind what Nik says. His head is full of romantic nonsense about keeping it on for the next generation. What generation?' Nora chuckled. 'Unless he's got some bairn stashed away that I don't know about. It'll have to go. We can't keep putting off the day.'

'Oh, such a pity,' Kay replied, sad that this might be the Snowdens' last Christmas here. 'It's such a characterful old house . . . Is there anything else for me to do?' she offered.

Mrs Snowden was struggling to her feet. 'You two, get along and enjoy yourselves. I shall crack on at my own pace. Wintergill is going to have a grand blowout tonight.' She looked around her room, smiling. 'What time shall we eat? After the Queen, by candlelight, I was thinking.'

'Wonderful,' Kay replied, knowing she would miss this place. She could get used to living here but she'd want to do something with the paintwork and the curtains, and that patch of damp.

'You will come back and see me in my new place?' Nora winked, her sharp grey-blue eyes sparking like flints.

'Nik will be glad to see the back of us both,' Kay said, thinking out loud, but Nora sprang to his defence for once.

'Don't you believe all that bluff and gruff. A mother knows, and he's taken to you both. He's even let me back in his kitchen,' she said with a twinkle in her eye. 'And you'd better watch yourself under the mistletoe tonight!' There was a chuckle of mischief in the air.

Fortunately there is no mistletoe in the house, Kay thought, but Nora laboured her point. 'They say Christmas sparks many a fire . . .'

'Please don't . . . I would hate to spoil the Jacob's join.' Kay felt herself blushing at the thought of being observed, and Nora was giving her another long hard look.

'Only teasing . . . don't look so serious. It's Christmas and strange things can happen, believe me, I know.'

Evie kept looking through the windows to see if it was snowing, but there was not one feathery flake to be seen. Her mouth was covered in chocolate and she felt sick so she flicked through all her new books and watched cartoons on the television until it was time to dress up the Christmas table with crackers and paper napkins. Mrs Nora brought out bottles of wine and a big trifle in a glass bowl with hundreds and thousands on the top. They gathered together, all dressed up, to open the presents under the tree. There were so many gifts from people she didn't even know: a set of wind chimes made from bamboo to hang in the breeze, a jigsaw and Fuzzy Felt. So many thank you letters to write tomorrow. Mummy always insisted they were written straightaway.

There were smelly bottles for Mummy and Mrs Nora, and a lovely statue of Muffin from Mr Snowden. Evie didn't understand why grown-ups got all excited about tiny bottles of oil to put in their bath – she liked masses of bubbles – but the best present came last from Mr Snowden.

'Mummy! Look, a real sledge . . . Thank you, it's brill. A red sledge with handles and reins. Is it snowing yet?' She raced out of the front door to examine the sky but it was grey and dark.

'Don't worry,' smiled Mr Snowden, who looked cool in his sweater and cords. 'If they're plucking geese in Scotland, the feathers will soon fall our way.' She didn't understand his words but she smiled and pretended to slide the sledge over the lawn.

'Do you like Mummy's book? I made it,' she said, shoving it under his nose, and he peered at it with interest.

'Is that the Lavender Lady sitting in the wooden chair with a baby all wrapped up in a towel?' he asked. 'She used to sit by my bed when I was little too.'

At last someone believed her. She looked up to his face with fresh eyes. He did have a creased smile and a crinkled face, but if he had seen the Lavender Lady he must be OK.

'I thought you were afraid of the dark?' Mummy, wearing some new velvet jeans and a glittery sweater, looked down at her.

'I knew you wouldn't believe me but Mr Snowden does . . . I've seen her loads of times when Mummy is asleep in the next bed.' She pointed at her drawings. 'Look there, in the picture, see . . . She keeps all the bad men away.'

Mrs Nora smiled. 'So how does she speak to you?'

'I don't know . . . I just know. She tells me stories sometimes about the olden days.' She was glad that someone was interested but she was puzzled by all these questions.

'What are you two plotting about? You look very serious.'

Mummy, looking hot and flustered, was carrying a tray of glasses from the kitchen. 'You can help me finish the table now.'

It was then that Mrs Nora brought out the little Christmas House to place it right in the middle of the table. It was like the gingerbread house in Hansel and Gretel, and Evie wished it was made of sweets.

'What's that?' she asked, pointing to the ribbons poking out of each window.

'Wait and see. We can have some fun with this little house,' came the reply.

'I don't think I could eat another crumb,' sighed Nora as she crushed her linen napkin with satisfaction. 'I'm fair brussen, as they say in these parts, stuffed to bursting, and it was a grand effort by all! The goose was cooked to perfection, the gooseberry chutney the perfect complement . . . I hope you all had enough plum pudding and trifle, young Evie?' Her gaze was directed at the pink cheeks of the girl in the velour tracksuit, a line of glittery butterfly clips in her blonde hair.

'I found a silver sixpence in my pudding.' Evie was looking pleased.

'And look what I found in mine,' laughed Nik, pretending to choke as he pulled a five-pound note out of his mouth.

Evie's eyes were on stalks. 'You didn't?'

The years rolled away and Nora could see Tom performing that very old trick. Like father like son. He had not forgotten the old Christmases after all.

'Anyone for seconds?' she said, but there were groans of appreciation and satisfaction.

'Time for coffee and liqueurs,' Nik replied, rising from the table to do his bit for the meal.

'Time for a game first, to let our meal settle,' Nora whispered, seizing the moment. 'Something I've cooked up for you all. Just a bit of fun to say thank you for all my presents. It's been a lovely occasion and I feel such good vibes around us tonight. It must be Mr Christmas up the stairs, egging us on to play silly games,' she laughed. 'This is a special house. It was built not only with pride but with love.' She lifted her glass in a toast. 'I think each generation adds something to its magic. I wish it well. To Wintergill . . . may it stand for ever!' she toasted.

'To Wintergill,' smiled Kay, her eyes bright with wine and contentment. 'To the Snowdens, who've made our Christmas so special. We were strangers and you took us in, gave us shelter and made us welcome. Thank you.'

'Cheers,' laughed Evie, her hair slides glittering in the dark as she copied her mother with her cranberry fizz.

'To the old house,' Nik joined in, his expression so warm that Nora felt the tears of pride welling. *This is my son and he's a good lad.*

'Right then, this little Christmas House got me thinking about a game we played around the table when I was young. We used to do it with a home-made Christmas cracker. There's a note attached to each piece of ribbon in all the open windows and door. All you have to do is pull the string and see what it says on the paper and, of course, do what it says!' Nora pointed to the ribbons. 'No cheating. All just a bit of fun but we'll see what we see.'

Evie was dying to start the game off. 'You must go first . . . Mrs Nora,' she said.

She stretched over the debris of party poppers and cracker remains, her party hat cocked to one side. She pulled the string, opened the note and burst out laughing.

'What does it say?' Evie jumped up and down. 'Tell us!'

'I was hoping I wouldn't get this one,' she laughed. 'It says, "Tell us about your most embarrassing Christmas."

Well, that's easy enough. It was when Tom's parents came for their first Sunday dinner on Boxing Day and I wanted to show off,' she smiled, relating the tale of the pheasant she'd left so long hanging that it stunk to high heaven and they'd had to have bread and cheese instead. Everyone was laughing at her story.

'Will that do?' She took a deep breath as everyone was clapping. 'I can still see that carcass full of maggots. The stink lasted for a week! Can I have my brandy now? I think I've earned it!'

'Who's going to go next?' shouted Evie, looking at Kay, who was half asleep.

'Go on then,' she smiled, pulling her string and opening the instructions. 'It says, "If I won the lottery, what would be my Christmas wish?"' Here, in the candlelight, she was feeling at peace with the world just as she had felt in the little church the night before.

'I think my wish would be that other people could share what we've shared today, mucking in together. Until a few months ago none of us knew each other. We came from different worlds. So if money was no object I'd love to build a house like this, full of bedrooms so that tired, sad, washed-out people could come and seek a week or two's respite from their daily grind, and Christmas would be our speciality.

'I would install a swimming pool in the old slurry pit – heated of course – with hot tubs under the stars too. I would make a studio so people could paint or quilt, do salsa dancing or yoga. It would be like a glorified health farm without the hassle. My clients could go for long walks and breathe fresh air in their lungs. It would be a community together, preparing good food, supporting local produce, a base where townies could be introduced to country life.'

Where's all this coming from? she thought even as she was speaking.

'There would be lots of nooks and crannies for tired people to sit and dream and do nothing. I'd want a big table like this so we could gather in the evening and talk. I would like them all to help on the farm, feel the soil, repair walls, feed the stock, make themselves useful too, and tire themselves out with activity. This would be a place for pampering and peace and contemplation but most of all a growing place where ideas could be generated and energy restored . . .'

She stopped abruptly, aware that all the eyes were on her. 'Is that OK?' She wondered if she had gone too far.

'That sounds wonderful,' Nora answered. 'When can I sign up? They say there's always an element in our dreams that is not only a wish but a possibility. Where there's a will there's a way.'

The attention was making Kay blush.

'Where there's a will there's usually relatives!' Nik quipped, wanting to get this game over with so that he could relax with his new malt whisky to sample. He pulled out his string and laughed. 'I think you've spiked these forfeits, Mother! So I'll get mine over with. It says: "Tell us your best Christmas joke."'

'*Moi?* Surely not!' Nora replied, and he was glad that she seemed to have thawed out about the barn fiasco.

'I'm no good at jokes. I can never remember the punch lines, but practical jokes, now that's a different matter. Just let me fill my glass and I will bore you all to tears.' He looked up at their faces. 'Only joking! Here's one against myself. This goes back to my Young Farmers days, before the ark, when our Christmas parties were a blur of alcohol and vomit, I'm afraid. We decided to hold a fancy dress ball near Skipton so on Christmas Eve we went to collect our costumes. I drew the short straw and had to go as Father Christmas, white beard, cloak, the full Monty, complete with Ho Ho Hos. It got very hot inside there and we got very silly and very drunk.'

'That's my boy!' shouted his mother.

'We danced a bit but there was no one we fancied so a gang of us decided to go diving in a duck pond in the middle of winter, as you do,' he continued, waving his glass in the air expansively.

'I stripped off and jumped in and then realised I was on my own! The gang had beetled off with a cheer, leaving me almost starkers, jumping in a Land Rover to dump my costume down the road. They didn't leave me to freeze to death but a cloak and a beard and a pair of wellies was all I had left to get back home in. It was well after midnight. I was twenty miles from home, stuck in that flaming costume, trying to look as if I wasn't. There was no transport in sight so I had to leg it back as best I could, cursing them all to high heaven. A driver took pity on me and drove me back to Hellifield. It was a nine-mile hike after that. I didn't half get some funny looks. You'd be surprised how many people are out and about on Christmas Eve.'

'Did you see the real Santa?' said Evie, suddenly alert.

'No, love, not a peep, I expect he was too busy to notice me,' Nik replied. 'So there. My worst joke.'

'I never knew about that, son,' Nora smiled.

'There's a lot you don't know, Mother, about those days, and least said the better.'

'It's me, it's me now,' cried Evie. 'It's my turn,' she said, pulling the string through the window. 'It says I have to light another candle in the window, sing a carol and make a wish.' She lit one of the fancy candles in the brass candlestick and placed it by the window. 'I know why we're doing this. It's called the Wayfarer's candle, to guide people to the light. It's for the Christ child to enter the house. Candles clear the air of bad things.'

She peered through the open curtains, singing two verses of 'Away in a manger'. Suddenly she paused.

'Are those really the stars in the bright sky?' She pointed up. No one answered but Mummy was smiling.

'Don't forget your wish,' Mrs Nora reminded her.

'I've been wishing very hard for snow all day so that doesn't count,' Evie replied. 'I wish, I wish that my mummy buys the Side House and we can mend it and stay here for ever.'

There was a funny silence after that.

No one wanted to spoil the moment, but Evie's words had stunned her audience.

'Thank you, Evie,' said Nora. 'It was just a bit of fun. *In vino veritas*, and all that . . . Chocolates, anyone?'

'No, I'm full to the brim. Washing up for me and then bed for you, Geneva,' Kay yawned. 'It's been a lovely day. I want to sample the lovely room upstairs.'

'I'll help you,' Nora offered, rising from the table but her eyes were tired.

'No, I'm doing the washing up, you've done enough,' Kay said. 'Evie will get herself ready for bed and I'll give her a story. It's been a lovely day. Thank you.'

Everyone fled to their respective rooms, busying themselves, sad that all the fun was over. Tomorrow there were invitations for drinks at Pat Bannerman's house down in the village, and a party in the evening. The guests of Wintergill House were going to be a nine-day wonder.

It was when Nik went to the back door to bring in some more logs that he shouted up to Evie with a grin.

'Evie! Come and see! Look out there!'

Evie was dashing down in her tartan pyjamas to the front

door, jumping up and down. 'It's snowing goose feathers, real snow, just like you said.' Kay came clambering after her so fast she took a rough turn on the stairs, nudging one of the pictures off the wall with a clatter of broken glass.

'Oh, no! I'm so sorry!'

'Don't move!' Nik ran up towards the shards of broken glass and lifted the sepia print from the floor. 'It's only the portrait of Jacob and Agnes, the one I never liked. Don't touch the glass or you'll get cut. Evie'll find the dustpan and brush.'

'I'm so clumsy,' Kay apologised, but Nik was not listening. He was too busy collecting shards and then examining the old wooden frame as it collapsed apart in his hands.

'Wait a sec, there's something else behind this photograph . . . You be careful and step over the mess, I'll take it to the light.'

They all crowded round the portrait as Nik lifted from the back another piece of stiff paper wedged between the backing and the print. It was a black and white sketch of a waterfall with some hand-tinted tones and notes at the side with a date on it. '*16th July*'. The watermark on the paper held up to the light was dated 1816.

Nora stared down at it and then at the two of them. 'You know what this is, don't you? I don't believe it, after all these years. Look! It's the sketch . . . the lost Turner. It must be. But why is it hidden behind this picture? Kay, you've struck gold!'

Nik sat down on the step, winded. 'I thought that was lost years ago. What a find. Thank you . . . I think I need another brandy . . . What a turn-up. Do you realise if this is genuine it might just be the answer to all our problems?'

Kay left the two of them to their discovery, standing with Evie on the front steps, trying to catch the snowflakes in their mouth. 'Will it stick?' She turned to Nik and he nodded.

'It'll stick and still be here in the morning. You'll be sledging tomorrow, promise.'

'Magic!' Evie cried. 'I made one wish and it came true! I hope the other does.'

The house was quiet. Evie was flaked out upstairs, surrounded by her stocking and her sledge. Nora had retired with the sketch and Kay was finishing tidying up in Nik's kitchen. The wall clock ticked gently. She could hear the cat purring under the table as she put the remains of their dinner safely into the fridge. It was so peaceful and she thought over their wonderful day.

Nik's unexpected and thoughtful present, a reminder of Muffin the collie dog, Evie's disturbing little journal, a splendid dinner and revealing party game, and then the discovery as well as snow falling. It was like living in a Christmas card, she mused.

Then Nik came through the kitchen door, looking like a snowman. 'It's sticking fast now. Evie will have her wish,' he smiled, kicking off his boots and shaking himself like a dog.

'How could you tell it would snow?' Kay asked, busying herself around his sink.

'You can sniff it in the wind if it's in the right quarter, and my barometer never lies. It won't last long, but long enough for Evie to have some fun. We usually get a white Christmas up here, enough to make a frost topping but not like the old winters, of course. I reckon those are gone for ever with global warming.'

He paused, watching her polishing the sink as if it had never been done before. 'We used to have to put snow fences all around us but I've not done that for years. Wintergill will look a picture in the morning. Fancy a hot toddy?'

'Lovely,' she murmured.

'Let's take it up into the old drawing room, seeing as we

lit the fire and Mother made it festive,' he suggested, gathering his ingredients on a tray. 'I'd like to examine that picture more closely. I owe you a big drink. Just let me make the toddy first. I was taught this by a Highlander who I once met at an auction mart. It's the only bit of cooking I can do,' he confessed, carrying his tray carefully up the stairs and into the fire-lit room that smelled of woodsmoke and lilies and pine.

She watched as he put two sugar lumps in a glass with a silver spoon and poured enough boiling water to cover the bowl to dissolve the sugar. He slanted the glass at an angle over the spoon and drizzled the whisky slowly over the surface of the liquid. Steam was rising as he waited for the whisky to heat through to flavour the whole glass with its peaty aroma . . .

'Slowly slowly for the best effect.' He was looking at her with a twinkle, and somehow she knew he was not talking about the toddy, or was he?

She appraised his long fingers caressing the glass, stroking the curve of the crystal, and she could feel herself steaming up. Lips and hands, hands and lips to the glass, sipping, savouring, warming her growing Christmas heart. *I could get used to this but I've had far too much to drink already.* Though she sipped his offering nonetheless. It was awfully hot in the room.

He brought down an old box to the fire for her to examine. The contents were covered in brown tissue paper and Nik brought out the most exquisite Christmas cards she had ever seen. Some were hand-made, padded with silk, watercolour scenes of figures skating on a river.

'I like an excuse to bring these out for an airing. They're part of old Jacob's collection; some are hand-painted, others are printed. What do you think?' He handed each one to her slowly and she fingered them in turn with a gasp.

'Nik, they're amazing. Are they originals?' She looked up and he was bending down so close, she could smell his aftershave and tobacco-drenched jacket. She liked his scent.

'My great-grandfather, the one on the hall stairs, was what you might call a Nativitist. He was obsessed with all things Christmas. They used to call him Mr Christmas in the district. He kept every card he was given, and all his invitations. Anything to do with Christmas was stuck in his boxes,' he said. 'Sadly, most of them have disappeared. He was a glutton for ephemera. Thank goodness he also kept envelopes and their postage stamps. They are worth a fortune to the right collector.'

'You're not selling these?' Kay gasped.

'No, but they were my insurance until now. If that is a genuine Turner sketch how did it end up hidden behind the portrait?' Nik turned from her gaze and stared out of the window, watching the snow falling down in streamers. 'You don't think it was put there deliberately for someone in the family to find one day or was just slipped in there and forgotten? This has been such a strange time, I could believe anything tonight.' He smiled across at her. 'And once again it's you we have to thank.'

'It's about time you had a lucky break,' she smiled back. 'Doesn't everything look beautiful under snow?'

'It's a rare sight, is snow, when it first comes, but after a few hours it's a nuisance. In normal times I should be up at the crack of dawn to check the feed, but these aren't normal times, are they?' There was such a look of sadness on his face.

'It's been so hard for you both this year,' Kay said, still holding the decorated cards with reverence. 'I never realised just how unpredictable a hill farmer's life could be. You have to see the devastation, the emptiness and the sadness to understand. There are no guarantees, are there?'

'You can say that again, especially when you forget to pay your insurance bills,' said Nik grimly. 'My cover for the contents of the barn is fine but not for the building.' Nik was sitting opposite her, looking into his glass.

'What will you do now?' Kay leaned across concerned.

'I'll get help and start small, build up slowly, but I'm going to restock. I have to. I'm not giving up now. As for the other, I'll have to put it down to experience. The Side House is more or less a write-off. I've no mind to do it all again. Were you serious about all that stuff about doing up a place into a retreat or a studio?' he said, staring at her intently.

'Tonight,' she laughed, 'I was just talking off the top of my head, but I'd like to build something up in my life. Do you think there'd be a market for it?' Suddenly the idea was growing before her eyes. What if she bought the Side House off the Snowdens? 'I think you're very brave,' she added.

'Stupid, more like, and out o' my head. There has to be a way forward out of this mess and happen I'll have to sell the barn, but if I flog off this bit of treasure, my accountant will be relieved.'

'Give me first offer when you decide to sell the barn,' she heard herself say. 'We've both grown to like it here, fire and storm, bad weather or no. I can be just as stubborn too. I must get that from my mother's side, from the Norton gene pool.'

'Doing up a place is a tall order. It'll cost you. The National Park are sticklers for getting it just so. Labour is expensive too,' he said, gazing into the firelight with tired face, weathered cheeks, the flecks of grey at his temples spreading fast.

He's a comfortable man to talk to by firelight, she thought. I like this man. I like his no-nonsense gruffness, his sense of his own rootedness in this place. I envy him his tenacity in fighting for his livelihood and what belongs to his family, she thought. I should miss him if we went.

He looked up at her and smiled as if reading her thoughts.

'I've got used to you two being around,' he confessed, cocking his head to one side and grinning. 'I never expected to hear myself saying that to a holiday let. I don't mix much with offcomers, but you're a bit different, especially Evie.'

'I hope there's only one Evie Partridge in the world; one of her is quite enough, believe me. She'll keep getting into more scrapes than a puppy in a pie shop,' Kay smiled, surprised by such a back-handed compliment from him. 'What will your mother say to you staying on?'

'She can have her cottage now,' he said, waving the picture in the air. 'I'll see to that. She deserves a change, but not me. I'm not ready for my pipe and slippers just yet awhile. I've got plans. If you bought the barn how would you manage?' He leaned forward and she knew he cared what became of them.

'I don't know. If I can rebuild my life after all that's happened to us recently then I can learn to put a roof on. Perhaps I'll go to college and learn to build a house from scratch. I like taking things to pieces so why shouldn't I learn to put something back together again like you rebuild stonewalls? We shall have to rent somewhere in the village so Evie can continue at school. It'll take some time before I get some skills. I could see if I can get a job doing farm accounts for a while, or doing business plans for clients. I'd want to redesign the whole thing my way. What am I dreaming of? I must be drunk,' she laughed, carried away by her ideas.

'We owe you for your rental up front until the spring, and then you could rent some rooms off me, if you like. Once Mother goes, I'll be rattling around here. It's much too big for one.' Nik raised his eyebrow, searching out her response.

'Evie would love that but I'll have to give it some thought,' Kay smiled, wondering what people would make of his mother leaving and them taking up residence.

As if reading her mind, he suddenly jumped up. 'You can do me a business plan – I'm going to need one – or you can be the housekeeper and Evie can be the guardian of the hearth, like old Hepzibah. It'll be a New Year and a new start for all of us.'

She nudged him and he nudged her back, and then they both locked eyes. 'Merry Christmas, Nik,' she whispered, raising her glass.

In the firelight of this farmhouse, with the snow falling, she knew now why Christmas night was so magical. With new friendships, new possibilities, new dreams racing through her mind, she stood up and kissed him on the cheek; just a Christmas kiss with no mistletoe.

There was a tobacco and whisky tang to Nik's breath and a strength in his embrace, a gentle tentativeness to his response as he kissed her back.

'Think on, there's a place for you here, if you want it Merry Christmas and welcome to Wintergill.'

The candles flicker as Nik glides up the stairs to check his kingdom. He stops to wind the grandfather clock, to tap the barometer, all part of his nightly routine. All is well, and so it should be this Christmas night. Everyone is sleeping and the child is tucked up for the night with her sledge, waiting for morning light.

There are twelve days of Christmas to come, with parties, rugby matches and farm visits to establish their newcomers around the district. Time off to party for a change.

Now the darkness of the season is broken. The days will soon be pulling out. This old house needs new life to be born again, new ventures to protect against the anxious times ahead. Where men and maids meet oft comes mischief, he winks to his ancestors on the stairs.

What this house needs is a pram in the hall and a tiny occupant in the rocking crib, if Wintergill is to stand firm in years to come. There must be a succession. He pauses, savouring those whisky kisses on his lips. Who knows after tonight?

Is the present not child of yesterday and father of tomorrow? There's still time yet for seedtime and harvest if he gets his act together.

Kay slipped downstairs and opened the front door. She wanted to walk down the driveway to the far bench and sit in the snow, looking up at the house with awe. From Nora's window there came the softness of a bedside light; from Evie's room the glow of her toadstool lamp burning through the night; from the upstairs drawing room, the flicker of candlelight, and in the dining hall the candelabra shone. Over the stone porch the storm lantern waved in the snowy light and at the hall window the Christ candle blazed out its welcome to all wanderers.

Her house of dreams had become a home. Wintergill was truly a Christmas house.

'Thanks, to all of you, wherever you are. Thanks for bringing us home,' she whispered as she walked towards the lights, and closed the door.

Read on for Exclusive Reading Group Questions

Reading Group Questions

Compare and contrast the different male figures within *Winter's Children*. What are their values, concerns and priorities? Does Nik differ from his forbears in his motivations?

Hepzibah and Blanche can't see things the same way. Why do their respective viewpoints differ so much? Could either of them have done things differently?

How have the women through the centuries shared their burdens? Nora keeps everything bottled up but Kay is more open. Do they share any similarities?

The role of motherhood is shown as having the greatest importance in *Winter's Children*. How have their different parenting styles been shaped over the centuries?

Discuss the relationship between Evie and Nora. What role does Nora provide for her?

In which ways is the theme of death explored in the book?

Mother's Ruin
Kitty Neale

You Can't Choose Your Family . . .

CRUEL When her beloved Gran has a stroke, Sally and her family move back home in order to look after her. But Sadie's illness has made the wise women they once knew bigoted and bad-tempered. Sadie is testing everyone's patience, including Sally's mum Ruth, and her husband Arthur.

CALLOUS Their problems are nothing compared with Tommy, the little ruffian next door. With an absentee father and an alcoholic mother, Tommy has a hard life. However, Ruth sees the good in him and takes him under her wing, but his unpredictable and violent mother has other ideas.

CRISIS Meanwhile, the stress of living cheek-by-jowl with Sally's family is starting to push Arthur away. As cracks in their marriage begin to appear, both Sally and Arthur must work out where their priorities lie before it's too late . . .

Another compelling family drama from the Sunday Times best-selling author of *Lost Angel* and *Nobody's Girl*.

Praise for Kitty Neale:

'Full of drama and heartache.' Closer Magazine

'Heartbreakingly poignant and joltingly realistic.' Annie Groves, author of *Some Sunny Day*

'This pageturner is a gritty tale of survival.' Tesco Magazine

What's next?

Tell us the name of an author you love

Leah Fleming   Go ▶

and we'll find your next great book.